THE
WIN...
G...

Kay Brellend, the third of six children, was born in North London but now lives in a Victorian farmhouse in Suffolk. Under a pseudonym she has written sixteen historical novels published in England and North America. This is her sixth novel set in the twentieth century.

Also by Kay Brellend

The Street
The Family
Coronation Day
The Campbell Road Girls
East End Angel

Kay Brellend
THE
WINDMILL
Girls

HARPER

This novel is entirely a work of fiction.
The names, characters and incidents portrayed in it are
the work of the author's imagination. Any resemblance to
actual persons, living or dead, events or localities is
entirely coincidental.

Harper
An imprint of HarperCollins*Publishers*
1 London Bridge Street,
London SE1 9GF

www.harpercollins.co.uk

Copyright © Kay Brellend 2015

Kay Brellend asserts the moral right to
be identified as the author of this work

Windmill Theatre photographs © Getty Images;
three girls in their dressing room © Hulton-Deutsch Collection/Corbis

A catalogue record for this book
is available from the British Library

ISBN: 978-0-00-757528-2

Set in Meridien by Palimpsest Book Production Ltd, Falkirk, Stirlingshire

Printed and bound in Great Britain by
Clays Ltd, St Ives plc

MIX
Paper from
responsible sources
FSC www.fsc.org **FSC™ C007454**

ACKNOWLEDGEMENTS

Donald Thomas, for his fascinating book,
An Underworld at War. And thanks to Juliet Burton,
Susan Opie, Kate Bradley and the HarperCollins
editorial team.

For Mum, who worked as a telephonist at Holborn Exchange during the height of the Blitz and went fire-fighting after shifts.

For Dad, who served in the RAF as a Leading Aircraftman, keeping the planes flying.

For all those people who didn't see active service, but helped to win the war, working behind the scenes.

CHAPTER ONE

'You shouldn't risk going out on a night like this!'

'I must . . . I want to see how my mum is.'

Gertie Grimes blew a cautionary hiss through her teeth. 'Take it from me, there's going to be a bad raid tonight, I can feel it in me bones. And if that weren't enough I'm getting a fright from that moon out there. It's like a peeled melon.' Gertie shook her head. 'You know how Fritz likes to come over on a full moon. You should stay here, love, tucked up safe and sound.'

That remark earned Gertie a dubious frown.

'I'll look after you, Dawn. Don't you worry about that,' Gertie chuckled slyly. 'I can see off a randy sod for you with one hand tied behind me back.'

Dawn Nightingale didn't doubt the older woman's promise to protect her virtue. Her wry expression was due to her understanding the reason behind Gertie's mirth: the staff at the Windmill Theatre, where Dawn had just finished her shift as a showgirl, had been allowed to bed down on the premises since the start of the London Blitz. Some stagehands welcomed the arrangement as it provided opportunities for sexual shenanigans. The management insisted on segregated quarters and lights out after the theatre closed at eleven but a few men had been discovered creeping about to try their luck.

But Dawn wasn't interested in any nocturnal visits from fumbling Romeos. She had a boyfriend in the RAF and though she hadn't seen Bill for months, she would never be mean enough to casually two-time him.

'Best get off now; don't want to miss my bus home.' Dawn whipped her coat from the peg and slipped it on.

'You take care of yourself.' Gertie watched her colleague doing up her buttons. 'Get yourself down the underground sharpish if the sirens go off.'

'Will do . . .' Dawn gave a wave as she set off along Great Windmill Street.

She kept her head lowered as she walked, protecting her cheeks from the bitter late January night air, her mind preoccupied with thoughts of her mother. She hoped Eliza was feeling better, yet doubted she would be. If anything, her mother seemed to be getting worse. And Eliza could only blame herself for that.

Eliza Nightingale liked a little nip, as she called it, and had done so for very many years. By anybody's standards, the woman had had a run of bad luck that might send her to the bottle. She'd lost her husband to pneumonia when her daughter was just five, then her intended second husband had scarpered, leaving her pregnant with her son. But according to Eliza she felt unwell not because she drank too much but because of the weather. It was too hot or too cold, too dry or too damp, for a body to be healthy, she'd mumble while stacking up the empties under the sink.

Dawn and her brother knew why their mother vomited and looked like death warmed up on some days. Dawn tried to be tolerant but often lost her temper and shouted at her mother to leave the booze alone. But Eliza continued to empty a few bottles of gin or port a week, saying she needed a drop of medicine to steady her nerves.

Dawn was startled from her worries by the whine of an air-raid siren. She came to an abrupt halt, cussing beneath her breath. She'd just passed Piccadilly tube station and pivoted on the spot, wondering whether to hare back and shelter there. If the planes passed overhead she'd be safe enough in the open till the all clear sounded and she could get on her way home. Her mother and brother, of course, might not be so fortunate in Bethnal Green as the East End had been taking a dreadful hammering. But they had an Anderson shelter in their back garden that had done its job so far during the Blitz.

A hum of engines grew louder, making Dawn instinctively shrink back against a brick wall. Her eyes scoured the inky heavens and she was relieved to see that the moon's milky surface was patterned with stringy cloud, hampering the Luftwaffe's mission to obliterate London. Dawn attempted to count the swarm of aeroplanes but found it impossible to separate them, there were so many. She jumped in fright as an early explosion rocked the pavement beneath her feet. She skittered sideways into a shop doorway and crouched down, arms instinctively coming up over her head to protect it from any shrapnel.

The sound of a person sobbing nearby reached Dawn's ears, as did the crash of falling masonry and shattering glass. She jerked upright, peering into the flame-daubed darkness. Finally she located a young woman hobbling along on the opposite pavement. At first Dawn thought the stranger might have been injured but then noticed that her uneven gait was due to her having one shoe on and one in her hand.

'Here! Over here!' Dawn called out, feeling sorry for the girl and hoping to comfort her.

The young woman swivelled about. Removing her shoe she pelted over the road in stockinged feet, breathlessly collapsing onto her posterior in the doorway.

'It'll all be over soon.' Dawn crouched beside her.

An abrupt blast made them huddle together, heads so close they were in danger of cracking foreheads.

'I thought I'd have time to get to the underground shelter.' The newcomer swiped her wet eyes with the back of a hand.

'Me too . . .' Dawn returned in a soothing whisper. 'Passed it by only moments ago. Unlucky, eh?'

'Them planes came out of nowhere . . .' the girl complained. 'Warning came too late. Don't think those damned Jerries will swoop down and strafe us, do you? Gonna get killed, ain't we?' she rattled off, peering up fearfully at the sky.

Suddenly a pane of glass on the opposite side of the street fell in smithereens from its frame to the pavement.

'Told me dad I didn't want to go out tonight, but he made me do some deliveries.'

'Hush . . . we'll be alright . . . the bombardment's over there . . .' Dawn hoped she sounded convincing because she wasn't at all sure they were safely out of harm's way.

'We'll get cut to bits if we stay here! I'd sooner have

4

a bomb land on me head than get me face all scarred up.' The girl agitatedly eyed the glass doorway of the shop in which they were sheltering, pressing her flat palms to her cheeks to protect them from any imminent flying shards.

'The planes usually head towards the East End; perhaps just a couple of stray bombs have landed over this way.' Dawn prayed that was so and that her mother and brother were safely inside their Anderson shelter. A burst of flames illuminated the street and Dawn got a better look at her companion. The girl was fair and pretty and about eighteen, three years Dawn's junior.

'What's your name?' Dawn hoped to calm the girl down by chatting to her. 'What were you delivering for your dad at this time of the night?'

'I'm Rosie Gardiner and it's none of your business if I was running an errand or not . . .' she snapped then broke off, listening.

Rosie started to rise but Dawn pulled her back into the shadows, sensing something was amiss.

She realised now why the window opposite had shattered despite no other premises having been affected by tremors: a brick had been thrown through it. Another missile hit the outfitter's shop, demolishing what remained of the pane.

A trio of men, now in full view, immediately began crunching forward over the debris to ease clothes through the jagged hole. They appeared careful not to damage the merchandise as they began bundling goods onto a handcart. The smallest fellow then leapt agilely through the aperture and disappeared. Soon he was back to start lobbing his haul onto the cart.

Dawn squinted at him through the darkness; his

stature was remarkably short and slim, putting her in mind of somebody, but she couldn't recall who it was.

'They're stealing that stuff on purpose!' Rosie gasped, turning to face Dawn. '*They* put in that window!' Her astonishment transformed to glee. 'Let's go and help ourselves too. Me dad could do with a new overcoat.'

'Fancy a spell in prison, do you?' Dawn whispered, dragging on her companion's arm to make her again sit down. ''Cos that's what you'll get if you end up mixed up in that lot.'

The courts were treating more and more harshly the 'bomb-chasers' who turned up undercover of raids to rob premises. While the police were otherwise occupied with saving lives, seasoned criminals exploited the mayhem, seizing the opportunity to go unhindered about their business. But there were grave repercussions facing the thieves if caught: prison terms and even a death sentence had been handed down. Dawn was shrewd enough to realise that she and Rosie could be in peril if these men felt they had nothing to lose by adding battery – perhaps murder – to their charge sheets.

The looters seemed well-organised; the barrow was already stacked high. Seething with rage though Dawn was at their vile behaviour, she'd no intention of interfering, or of advertising her presence. She hoped they'd soon be on their way so she and Rosie could also get going. They'd trouble enough negotiating the rubble and infernos, and finding some transport running to get them home, without these men adding to their problems. The gang would not want witnesses to their night's work. Dawn realised she'd come to feel responsible for Rosie Gardiner's safety yet she knew nothing about the girl other than her name. And Rosie had been quite rude to her when Dawn had tried to make conversation about what she'd been out delivering for her father.

The laden cart had been pushed about fifty yards along the street when Rosie's impatience got the better of her. Shaking off Dawn's hand she ran to the damaged shop front and scrabbled amongst discarded coat hangers and broken glass for something to take.

'Greedy sods have taken the whole lot,' she complained loudly. 'Not even a bleedin' scarf left for me dad.'

The slightly built man had heard her and swung about. He had hung back to light a cigarette while his cohorts – one tall and one stout – pushed the cart. At any other time Dawn would have thought them a comical-looking bunch: short, fat and thin. As it was she simply broke cover and yanked on Rosie's arm to drag her away. Finally Rosie seemed to understand the peril in the situation. Hand in hand they hared in the opposite direction with the sound of flying footsteps behind them.

Dawn darted into an alley tugging Rosie after her. She kept going, her lungs burning with exertion, making sure to dodge around overflowing dustbins that smelled of cooking fat and rancid food, yanking Rosie clear of the obstacles too. Having tried a few back doors she finally found one unlocked. She shoved Rosie inside and quickly followed her.

Dawn raised a finger to her lips, miming that Rosie should keep quiet in case their pursuer was sniffing around close by.

They settled back against opposite walls, their chests heaving with every painful breath, straining to listen for a sign that they'd been followed.

Five minutes passed in the dim corridor without a sound other than their suppressed pants, but the young women's eyes remained wide open and locked together. Suddenly Dawn took a tentative step towards the door and eased it open an inch. There was a sound of frantic industry in the area as the rescue crews raced from place to place. But there had been no more blasts close by. Further afield could be heard the rattling retorts of anti-aircraft guns and the crump of exploding bombs. Immediately Dawn was thinking of her mother and brother in the East End that was surely now bearing the brunt of an attack.

'Cor . . . the smell of that Chinese grub's making me feel hungry.' Rosie sniffed the stale aromatic air in the building, her voice high and cheery as though she'd never been snivelling earlier. 'I bet the kitchen's through there. If they've all gone off down the shelter we could see if they've left any noodles in the pot and help ourselves.'

Dawn shook her head. 'Time to go,' she said quietly, realising the young woman might be on the verge of having hysterics, she was talking such rot.

'I suppose I'll have to settle for a bit of toast and dripping for me supper.' Rosie pushed past Dawn into the street. 'Hope a bloody bus is running my way. I've got blisters all over me feet from me new shoes . . .' She swung the leather courts she'd been carrying in her hand.

'Well . . . if yer a good gel, maybe I'll give you a ride home on me cart and save yer tootsies.'

A man plunged out of the shadows, clamping his fingers over Rosie's mouth, stifling her shriek of fright.

''Course, if you upset me I'll feed you a bunch of fives and you won't get home tonight . . . nor any night . . .' he threatened close to her ear.

Dawn had been on the point of defending her companion when she felt as though her arms might be ripped from their sockets. Another one of the looters had sneaked from the gloom to drag her backwards.

Dawn stamped her heel down hard on her captor's foot making him howl and loosen his grip. She spun to confront him. 'Brave lot, aren't you?' She glared at the short fellow who'd had hold of her, then turned her attention to his stocky accomplice. 'So where's your lanky pal? Hiding the stuff you nicked?' She guessed the third man had scooted with the night's haul.

'You've got a big mouth for a little gel,' the big man snarled. 'Now . . . you two are gonna keep your gobs shut if you know what's good for you. You ain't seen us do nuthin' . . . ain't that right?'

Rosie quivered her head in agreement, blinking in fright.

'That's good . . . very sensible, 'cos pretty gels like you two wouldn't want yer faces rearranged, would yer?' He pinched Rosie's chin in hard fingers.

'You leave her alone!' Dawn shouted, pleased to see that Rosie had elbowed her tormentor in the ribs. 'As you're not off fighting the Germans the least you two brave souls can do is go and give a hand clearing up the mess they've made.' She pointed at the orange glow in the sky, visible above the rooftops. The smell of charred timber was heavy in the air. Suddenly she was bubbling with fury. Her mother and brother might be digging themselves out of rubble . . . if they were lucky. She might not have a home or a family to return to, yet these vile men were out to make a profit from the raid.

Without a clue as to what had jarred her memory Dawn realised why the small fellow seemed familiar.

Yet, according to his sister, Michael Williams had shipped out and was on his way to Malta with his crewmates. Gertie's brother shouldn't be in London at all.

'What you staring at?' Michael snapped. He'd got a brief glimpse of Dawn by the outfitters and thought he recognised her. Stupidly he'd mentioned that to his associates and they'd been furious at the idea they might be arrested before the goods were concealed in the warehouse. 'What you staring at, I said?' he snarled.

Dawn's intuition was telling her to play dumb as though she didn't know him. Inwardly she prayed that the horrible little man was for the high jump – from his sister and the authorities when they found out he'd deserted.

'Never seen such a short-arse before, has she?' the stout fellow taunted his cohort. He'd taken Dawn's blank response at face value and was reassured that she didn't recognise Midge, as Michael was nicknamed by those who knew him.

'Shut yer mouth, Roof.' Midge Williams was sensitive to such comments, especially when women were around.

'That's fuckin' clever, ain't it, blabbermouth?' Roof roared. 'Want to tell 'em me address 'n' all, do you?' He loosened his grip on Rosie to swing a fist at his sidekick.

While Michael nimbly ducked away from the punch Dawn saw her chance. She grabbed Rosie's elbow and they bolted to the end of the turning, out into an empty lane then kept going. Finally Rosie's whimpering penetrated the deafening thud of blood in Dawn's ears. She let go of the hand that was straining in hers.

Rosie folded over at the waist gasping in breath, hugging her shoes to her waist. 'Me feet are cut to ribbons!' She hopped from foot to foot. She was in pain and still scared. 'We lost 'em, d'you reckon?' she moaned.

Dawn shrugged and grasping Rosie's hand again she began tugging her towards the crossroads ahead.

'This is me only pair of nylons,' Rosie wailed. 'They only had one ladder 'n' all – now they're like lace!' She lifted a torn and bloodied foot for inspection. 'Look at the state of me!'

'You'll live . . .' Dawn returned shortly, aware of mingling shouts up ahead. Turning the corner she was relieved to see that people were milling about a few yards away. Mounds of debris had fallen to block the road and flames were dancing from a gaping hole that once had been a window of a house. She and Rosie merged into the crowd. There were cries from people desperate for help for an injured companion, while others could be seen wandering dazedly to and fro.

Despite the chaotic scene Dawn was still conscious of pursuit, and glanced over her shoulder to see if there was any sign of the men. They had followed! And they hadn't been far behind even if they had taken a different route, no doubt in the hope of intercepting them.

Roof and Michael were standing at the mouth of a junction, watching them. Roof slowly raised a finger and jabbed it in their direction. Dawn swung her face away, understanding the threat in the looter's gesture. But she knew they'd not hound them further with so many witnesses about.

CHAPTER TWO

'Mum says she's gone up to bed with a headache and to tell you to get me supper ready.'

Dawn had barely put a foot over the threshold when she received that greeting from her brother. Weary she might be, following her run-in with the crooks, but she was relieved to have arrived back and found that her family was safe. A house on the corner of their street had lost its side, showing how close to home the bombardment had been. Curbing her exasperation with her surly brother she managed to give him a smile.

'You're old enough to get your own supper ready, y'know.' Dawn hung her coat over the back of a chair then rolled up her sleeves and went to the pantry to see what it contained. She didn't hold out much hope of an appetising selection: if her mother were under the influence again the grocery shopping would have borne the brunt of the cost of her 'medicine'.

'Don't want no tea anyhow,' George muttered. 'Lost me appetite cramped up in that Anderson shelter for hours. 'Nuf to make you want to puke, it is.'

'Stop whining and thank your lucky stars you got out of it in one piece. I've only had a shop doorway for protection on my way home from work.'

Some neighbours had helped dig out their shelter and fractured a sewage pipe while doing so. Now the garden, and especially the Anderson, stank to high heaven because the repair hadn't been done well.

'Ain't eating anything so you're wasting yer time poking around in that cupboard.' George slumped into a chair.

'That'll be the day, you turn down a plate of grub.' Dawn didn't want to fall out with her brother. He could be selfish and lazy when it came to lending a hand about the house but then a lot of teenage boys were like that.

It seemed daft to get tetchy over something trivial when she lived with a constant fear of rounding the corner of their street to find her home blown to smithereens. 'There's half a loaf and some plum jam left . . . d'you want a jam sandwich?' Dawn moved a packet of custard powder and pounced. 'Or . . .' She turned with a large potato rotating in her fingers. 'D'you fancy waiting while this bakes in the oven? There's no cheese but you could put a bit of marge in it . . .'

'Ain't waiting that long!' George whined. 'I'm hungry now.'

'Thought you said you didn't want anything,' Dawn reminded him wryly.

With a scowl, George slunk out of the kitchen, leaving his sister to spread jam on chunks of bread.

A few minutes later Dawn gave George his tea plate. She left him in the parlour with it balanced on his lap, listening to the wireless and tucking into his jam sandwich, and went upstairs to her mother's room.

'Want a cup of tea, Mum?' Dawn whispered into the gloom. The stale air hit her, making her wrinkle her nose. But she didn't retreat; she approached the bed and looked down at her mother's drawn profile. 'It's – not yet ten o'clock, why don't you come downstairs and I'll make you a snack? We can listen to the news on the wireless.'

'No appetite, dear,' Eliza mumbled. 'Don't want to listen to the wireless. Just bad news all the time, ain't it.'

'There's a big old moon out tonight, have you seen it? Shall I open the curtains a bit?'

'No . . . the light makes my headache worse . . .'

'The gin gives you a headache, Mum,' Dawn snapped. The fug in the room was overpowering her, making her tetchy. Suddenly she reached beneath her mother's pillow, feeling for glass. With a mutter she pulled out the half-empty bottle and tossed it onto the coverlet.

Eliza burrowed further into the bed. 'It's alright for you. You ain't been stuck out in that shelter with the bombs banging down all around,' she moaned. 'Bitter cold it was; enough to give a body pneumonia let alone a migraine. Anyhow . . . what have you been up to today?'

'I did a couple of matinees and finished early. I told you about it yesterday.' Dawn knew it was pointless trying to reason with Eliza, so gave up. 'Have the Gladwins got their national assistance sorted out?'

A family in the next street had been made homeless last week following a direct hit on their house. Thankfully they'd all been in a shelter so only the property had been lost.

'Those Gladwin kids should have been evacuated long ago, in my opinion.'

'George should have been evacuated as well.' Dawn's blunt comment drew a snort from her mother.

'George is old enough to stay where he is. He's nearly thirteen and getting a job soon.'

'Yeah . . . but he wasn't when war broke out, was he, Mum?' Dawn reminded dryly.

'I will have a cup of tea, dear.' Eliza meekly changed the subject as she invariably did when stuck for an answer. She liked having George's company and was determined to keep it.

On the point of leaving the room, Dawn returned to her mother's bedside. By the time she got back with a cup of tea Eliza would have emptied the bottle if she left it where it was.

'I'll put this in the kitchen cupboard.' Dawn ignored Eliza's peevish mumble and went downstairs feeling tempted to empty what remained of the booze down the sink. But she didn't because it would make matters worse. Her mother would only buy more with their housekeeping money.

'Can't get a bit of extra sugar for love nor money up at Royce's.' Eliza's complaint about the corner shop preceded her shuffling into the kitchen.

Dawn had hoped that her mother might drag herself out of bed and come downstairs for her tea. Although Eliza's wispy hair looked matted and in need of a brush the simple act of putting on her dressing gown and slippers seemed to have bucked the woman up. Dawn set a steaming brew in front of her mother as she settled down at the kitchen table. Planting her elbows on its wooden top Eliza sunk her chin into her dry palms.

'Don't like me tea without two sugars in it. It looks weak as well. Have you used fresh leaves, Dawn?'

'There isn't any tea . . . only the grouts in the pot.'

'I'm fed up with this rationing lark; the war should've been over by now. It started off like a damp squib . . .'

'But it's gone off like a rocket now,' Dawn returned bluntly, setting two pieces of bread on the grill ready to be toasted. She shoved the pan into position beneath the gas flame. She found her mind returning to the looters and whether she'd been right in thinking her colleague Gertie was related to one of them.

Gertie Grimes was mum to a brood of young kids as well as being a cleaner. The woman worked very hard, not only at the Windmill Theatre but doing odd charring jobs in the evening. Dawn hadn't known Gertie long as the woman had only recently started at the Windmill. But Dawn liked Gertie and wondered how the woman would feel knowing that her own brother was looting while she was working her fingers to the bone. Of course, Dawn couldn't be sure it *had* been Michael . . .

'There was a letter for you today. Reckon it's from Bill.' George had appeared in the kitchen to give his sister that news and to slide his empty plate onto the table. 'Wouldn't mind a bit of toast if there's any going.' He patted his belly.

'Don't be so greedy, George!' his mother scolded. 'Me and your sister's not had a bite of supper yet.'

Dawn got up and felt on the shelf where the post was put every day. She usually checked it morning and night but George's demand to be fed as soon as she walked in the door had broken her routine. The kettle started to steam but she ignored it for a moment and smiled at the envelope she'd found, recognising her boyfriend's handwriting.

'Go on then; open it,' Eliza nodded at the letter. 'And

take the toast out of the grill or it'll be charcoal. And that kettle's hissing fit to put me teeth on edge.'

Dawn pulled out the grill pan and turned off the gas under the kettle. She was ready to pop Bill's letter in her pocket to savour reading it in private but knew it would be mean to deprive her family of a bit of interesting news. She inserted a thumbnail under the envelope flap.

'Oh no! Not again!' An air-raid siren had made all three of them stand stock still, grimacing up at the ceiling.

'Turn off the lights!' Dawn ordered her brother and he obediently hurried round turning off the gas lamps on the walls.

'Blackout curtains are all in place; I checked earlier,' Eliza said. She'd suddenly bucked herself up no end.

'Get that bit of toast spread,' George called to Dawn, still thinking of his belly despite the imminent danger. He was hovering close to the last lamp still alight, before plunging them all into darkness.

'I'd better get something warm to put on,' Eliza wailed. 'I'll catch me death in that ice box in just me dressing gown.'

Dawn whipped her coat off the chair back. 'Here, you can put this on. Now hurry up . . .' She settled the warm tweed about her mother's shoulders then opened the back door and looked up, straining her ears and eyes. In the distance she could see anti-aircraft ammunition tracing fiery lines in the sky.

Together, Dawn and George helped their mother down the back step into the garden then they hurried arm in arm towards the bottom end where the corrugated roof of the Anderson shelter was just visible.

17

CHAPTER THREE

'Had a letter from my Fred.'

'Ooh, ain't you the lucky one . . .' Gertie Grimes's acid muttering was intentionally audible.

Olive Roberts turned to give her colleague a withering stare. 'My Fred always keeps in touch. Doesn't matter how busy he is with all his duties, he's always found time for his wife.'

'Way you go on about him you'd think he was a brigadier general instead of a bleedin' corporal.'

'He's got the responsibility of having men under him . . .'

'That wouldn't surprise me,' Gertie snickered.

'What you implying, you dirty-minded cow?'

Olive was a skinny, big-boned woman of above average height but she didn't frighten Gertie who was tubby, a good six inches shorter and, at twenty-six, nearly ten years younger. Gertie stuck her hands on her hips, staring defiantly at Olive.

'We all know you're like a bitch on heat but there's no need to think we're all at it,' Olive spat. 'Four kids and only in your mid-twenties?' she scoffed. 'You need to get that husband of yours down the recruiting office. A bit of active service'll take the lead out of his pencil.'

'My husband knows his duty to his family comes first, so you can piss off trying to tell us what to do. Just 'cos you ain't got five minutes for those boys of yours, don't think we're the same. My kids are my life.' Gertie began poking her broom beneath a chair to drag fluff and hair out from beneath it. 'You're just jealous of us because we're a happy family.' If Gertie was annoyed that her colleague had hinted she was a scrubber she didn't let on. Gertie preferred talking dirty to actually doing the deed. *The other*, as she called it, robbed her of sleep and always seemed to bring her another mouth to feed.

'Jealous of you, Gertie Grimes? You're jealous of me, more like, 'cos your husband might get you up the spout regular as clockwork but he ain't man enough to join up, is he.'

'You leave my husband out of this!' Gertie threw down her broom in temper. 'Don't you dare say nothing bad about him. He's a father with little 'uns to consider before he considers himself.'

'Reckon he *is* considering himself . . . that's why he's sweeping roads instead of carrying a rifle,' Olive scoffed, turning away to bring the row to an end.

'You'd better apologise for that.' Gertie poked Olive in the shoulder. ''Cos if you don't . . .'

'Oh, shut up, you two!' Dawn exploded. She'd just entered the dressing room to find the theatre's cleaner and kiosk attendant at each other's throats as usual. Her feet were aching and she had a thumping head because she'd been on the side of the stage close to the trumpet player. Her temples were still throbbing from the ear-splitting toots.

'Customers won't like hanging around in the foyer waiting for you to sell 'em tickets. If Phyllis finds out you ain't where you're supposed to be you'll be for the high jump.' Gertie stared pointedly at Olive until the woman stormed towards the door.

'All her airs 'n' graces yet she ain't got a minute of time for those two boys of hers.' Gertie's lip curled in disgust. 'Kids should come first in my book, not shoved to one side soon as the opportunity turns up.' She glanced at Dawn for a comment but her colleague flopped down onto a seat at the dressing table.

Dawn averted her sore eyes from the glaring bulbs edging the mirror in front of her. She eased off the feathered headdress and once released from confinement her honey-blonde hair cascaded to her shoulders in untidy waves. She dropped her face forward and gave her tender scalp a massage with her fingers. 'If Phyllis finds out you two are still at it you'll be for the high jump too.' Dawn's caution emerged from behind a screen of glossy hair.

'Well, Pocahontas.' Gertie tweaked the feathers that Dawn had discarded on the dressing table littered with brushes and cosmetics. 'I don't care if I do get the sack from here for telling Olive what I think of her; she deserved it. How did the performance go? Was it a full house?'

'Almost, and the comedian got a lot of applause, even though he forgot his punchline a couple of times . . .' The rest of Dawn's report was drowned out as more showgirls came into the room, chattering like starlings. The troupe was dressed in beaded Red Indian costume, with colourful feathers embellishing their hair.

'What's up with Olive Roberts? She's got a face on her fit to curdle milk.' Sal Fiske was stepping out of her short, fringed skirt while speaking.

'No change there then . . .' Gertie muttered. 'The woman's ugly as sin, don't know what her husband sees in her.'

'Have you been upsetting Olive again, Gertie, you naughty thing?' Lorna Danvers had entered the dressing room to boom that out in her cut-glass accent. She began unhooking fancy suspenders and rolling down her fishnet stockings. 'I dearly hope we don't have to wear these costumes again; this leather's made me itch dreadfully up here.' She started to scratch close to her groin. 'I'll wriggle about in a mermaid tail for my wages but I really don't fancy getting eczema on my Minnie for a thousand pounds.'

'I reckon you would!' came a chorus of voices.

'Gordon'll scratch it for you,' Sal called out.

It was well-known that the senior stagehand had a thing for La-di-da Lorna, as she was fondly called due to her upper-class roots. Gordon was starting to get on Lorna's nerves because he wouldn't take no for an answer.

'You need a bit of Endocil cream on that.' Gertie examined the angry rash Lorna was picking at. 'My brother suffers with eczema something chronic on his knees 'n' elbows. Told him to always dab a bit of Endocil on to soothe it.'

Dawn carried on hanging up her squaw's costume, strolling to and fro in just her brassiere and camiknickers, as were the other girls as they moved between the various dressing cupboards. But her ears had pricked up on hearing Gertie mention her brother. She'd tried to forget about the robbery last week and hadn't mentioned

21

anything to Gertie about suspecting Michael might be a looter.

Dawn had never been introduced to Michael but Gertie had once brought her brother to Dawn's notice by telling her that he'd bagged a prime spot in the front row of the theatre. Dawn had promised to look out for him and when she went on stage had squinted through the lights in the direction of a boyish-looking able seaman. Dawn's boyfriend had spoken about Midge Williams too, not because he liked Gertie's brother, but quite the reverse. In Bill Sweetman's opinion Midge was a troublemaker with a chip on his shoulder and he was glad their paths crossed only rarely when they both had leave. But before saying she suspected Michael was a deserter and a thief, Dawn knew she'd have to be sure of her facts. Gertie was short like her brother but could be aggressive, especially when defending her relatives. Gertie's animosity towards Olive stemmed from her disgust because the older woman didn't fawn over her children in the same way as Gertie did. Dawn had to agree that Olive seemed a remote mother, but different people had different ideas about bringing up kids.

'Don't suppose it's easy for your brother to get Endocil cream on a frigate.' As Gertie had brought up her brother's name a few minutes ago Dawn took the opportunity to carry on the conversation. In that way she might discover if Midge was in Malta and put her suspicions to rest.

'You'd be surprised what the NAAFI can get hold of.' Gertie laughed.

'I wouldn't!' Sal chipped in. 'I'm beginning to wish I'd joined the NAAFI instead of taking this job. Could've made myself a packet selling hooky stuff on Loot Alley. Not that I've ever been there . . .' She dropped a sly wink following her mention of the haunt in Houndsditch where merchandise changed hands.

'Had a letter from your brother Michael yet?' Dawn tried again to pump Gertie for information while putting on her outdoor clothes.

'Ain't one for letter writing, is Michael. I expect he drops Mum a few lines in Clacton.'

'Michael's in Malta then?' Dawn continued doggedly, making Gertie glance sharply at her in surprise.

'Reckon he might have docked. But he don't give us his timetable,' she said rather sourly.

Dawn supposed that reply would have to do; she must have been mistaken in thinking Michael a villain. Having dragged a brush through her hair she gave the others a cheery wave as she'd finished her shift. Gertie followed her towards the cloakroom.

'Off home then, are you?'

'Yeah . . .'

'Mum better, is she?'

Dawn gave Gertie a speaking look; Gertie was aware of her mother's drinking because Dawn had once mentioned it to some fellow dancers. Afterwards, she'd wished she'd kept schtum because women working together forgot nothing and gossiped about everything.

'Don't you worry, she'll pull herself round once this war's over with. It's taking it out of all of us.' Gertie nipped at her lower lip with her teeth, looking thoughtful.

'What's wrong?' Dawn prompted.

'Were you asking about Michael for a reason?'

Dawn blushed guiltily.

'Now you tell me what's wrong,' Gertie demanded.

23

'Come on out with it. I knew there was more to it than eczema and Endocil cream.'

'It's nothing really . . .' Dawn blurted. 'It's just . . . I thought I saw him recently; but you've said he's abroad, so I must be mistaken.'

'Yeah . . . you must.' Gertie gave a slow emphatic nod. 'If people got to hear he was still round these parts, they'd think he was a deserter now, wouldn't they?'

'I've said I'm probably mistaken.' Dawn sounded cross too. 'It's an easy mistake to make as he is quite . . . remarkable, isn't he.'

'What d'you mean by that?' Gertie snapped.

'Well . . . there aren't many men about as small as him; that's why I thought it might be him.'

'I suppose you could say he's wiry . . . Anyhow, I'd be obliged if you'd keep your ideas to yourself.'

'Right . . . sorry I mentioned it,' Dawn muttered to Gertie's retreating back.

Gertie got her coat out of the cloakroom, obviously ready to leave work herself. Dawn loitered for a moment wondering whether to offer to walk a short way with the other woman, as they sometimes did. At Piccadilly Circus Gertie would then head off towards her home in Holborn while Dawn travelled east to Bethnal Green. Gertie barged past and hurried out into the street. Dawn shrugged to herself and slowly followed her colleague into the dark early evening, hoping that she'd get home without the need to bomb-dodge.

No such luck! Dawn inwardly groaned a few moments later as the sirens started. With a cursory scouring of the sombre heavens she joined those dashing towards the underground station. Her heart was pumping and her misty breath bathed her cold face as she ran down the steps, jostled and bumped by others seeking shelter. As she stepped onto the busy platform, the smell of urine and dirt immediately struck her, making her wrinkle her nose. Picking her way through bodies and bedding she found a small space close to a tiled wall and squatted down. After a moment fidgeting to find a comfortable position she shrugged out of her coat and folded it, lining outward to protect the tweed, planning to use it as a cushion to sit on.

'You'll ruin your lovely coat, love. Here you are, you can borrow this.'

Dawn gratefully accepted a worn blanket being held out to her. Before handing it over the woman helpfully folded the wool into a pad.

'Thanks very much . . .' Shivering, Dawn quickly donned her coat, buttoning it up to the throat. Despite the press of humanity she felt chilled from the draught whistling down the steps that led to the street. A moment later she spied Gertie also sheltering from the raid, sitting some yards away, and decided she might as well try and make up with her colleague. Some of the Windmill girls liked nothing better than a bit of a ding dong at work, but Dawn lived by the rule: don't go looking for trouble 'cos it'll find you soon enough. Handing back her make-shift cushion with a smile and thanks, Dawn picked a path over bodies to Gertie's side.

'Crikey . . . where did you get him?'

Gertie was attending to a baby in a makeshift wicker crib. She tucked the covers in about the mewling infant, making hushing noises. 'Met me husband down here with the kids; he was bringing 'em to meet me from work. He does that sometimes . . . so he can get shot of them and bugger off to the pub.' Gertie's mouth turned down in a rueful smile. 'Anyway the raid's put paid to that idea for him. So he's gone off with the older ones to keep them occupied.' She gave Dawn a conciliatory smile. 'Sorry about . . . you know . . . earlier . . .'

'Yeah . . . me too,' Dawn said, peering in at the baby. She knew that Gertie had four boys but because Gertie was a fairly new recruit at the theatre, Dawn had never before met any of the woman's family. In fact, if Midge Williams hadn't turned up to watch a show at a time coinciding with Gertie's evening shift at the theatre, Dawn would never have had him pointed out to her.

Even when Dawn was a bit dishevelled, as now, she still looked pretty in Gertie's opinion. Self-consciously she pushed some lank brown hair behind her ears. 'Don't get a lot of time for me looks any more.' She glanced at the sniffling baby. 'Got Harold here and then the other three all playing me up.'

'Where have they gone off to?' Dawn took a look about.

'Oh, they're around somewhere, with their dad. Me husband gets bored stuck here all night so goes looking for somebody to have a game of cards with. He takes the boys to watch him play. Teaches him his tricks, so he says . . .' Gertie started unbuttoning her blouse as Harold let out a wail. 'Feeding time at the zoo,' she muttered, looking around, her face a study of distaste. Picking up the infant, she concealed him, as best she could, inside her coat. 'Like a bleedin' farmyard it is down here, stinks to high heaven.' She mimed gagging, then turned her attention to the baby's feed. 'I'd sooner not come here but we've not got a shelter dug out the back, you see. Rufus keeps saying he'll do it but never gets round to it.' Gertie raised her eyebrows, displaying fond exasperation for her lazy husband.

'Pretty unpleasant down here, isn't it.' Dawn politely averted her eyes from Gertie's exposed flesh, staring instead at the exit and straining her ears for a sound of the all clear. She'd not heard a bomb drop so was praying the planes had gone straight over, or it was a false alarm.

'Wish we could go back to the phoney war we had at the beginning. At least we all got to sleep in our own beds,' Gertie mumbled, stroking her baby's cheek. 'Worried all the time about my boys, I am.'

'Are your older sons being evacuated?' Dawn asked conversationally. She gazed at the contented baby, his fine auburn hair verging on flaxen and nothing like Gertie's dark brown locks.

'Oh, no! Nobody would look after them properly for me.' Gertie sounded adamant. 'I know them best. They'd never settle with anybody else.'

'Bet our troops overseas miss their own beds . . .' Dawn had reverted to their previous topic of conversation. Gertie had sounded defensive in the way her own mother did when talking about children being sent away into another woman's care. Dawn thought of Bill, far away, perhaps soaring high in the heavens in his Spitfire, under the moon and stars. But there was no romantic side to any of it. Wherever Bill was, he was probably cold and scared, especially if he had a Messerschmitt on his tail. 'I wish the bloody war was over with . . .' Dawn said on a heartfelt sigh.

''Course, we all wish that.' Gertie rubbed slowly at her baby's back as he suckled. 'War to end all wars, that last one was meant to be. Now look at us. Bloody Hun!' she muttered. 'Your boyfriend's a pilot, ain't he, Dawn?'

Dawn nodded. 'I think about him, and pray for his safety, day and night . . . but I'm so proud of him too . . .'

'My Rufus wanted to do his bit, of course,' Gertie piped up, as though fearing Dawn might think him a coward for not enlisting. 'But I need a bit of help with the four boys,' she added flatly, as though she'd forgotten saying a moment ago how happy her husband was to avoid looking after his sons in favour of a trip to the pub.

'They mustn't half be a handful,' Dawn said. It was the most Gertie had ever spoken about her family.

'You're not kidding! Run me ragged, they do. Oi . . . what's your game? Never seen a hungry baby before?'

A young fellow had been lounging on his coat next to them. He'd been reading a book, in between slyly trying to get a glimpse of Gertie's bare breast. He blushed scarlet and rolled over onto his other elbow, bringing the novel right up in front of his face.

'Bleedin' saucy git!' Gertie muttered, giving Dawn a wink.

'Oh . . . here he is . . .' Gertie put the quietened baby back in his basket and whipped the edges of her coat together, surreptitiously buttoning her blouse underneath. 'He don't like me flashing me tits in public, as he calls it,' she whispered. 'So don't let on I've given little 'un a drink or that the young bloke there was having a gander or Rufus'll cause a scene.'

Gertie suddenly waved to attract her husband's attention. 'He don't look happy; probably lost a packet at cards,' she grumbled beneath her breath.

Dawn turned to look at some people making their way through the crowd. She froze for a few seconds before shrinking back against the tiled wall. Her shoulders were hunched up towards her ears in an attempt to conceal her face while she darted glances to and fro. But there was no chance of a quick getaway without drawing attention to herself; she was hemmed in on all sides. From under her lashes she flicked another look at the stout, red-headed fellow approaching, accompanied by three boys of varying sizes.

It might have been dark that evening, and she might only have seen the brute for a matter of minutes, but she was certain Gertie's husband was the same man who'd threatened her and Rosie Gardiner to keep their gobs shut about the robbery at the outfitters. It occurred to Dawn then that she'd heard the man she'd thought was Gertie's brother call his mate 'Roof'. With sudden clarity she realised it was Rufus's nickname. She was now wondering if she'd been right in thinking that she short bloke had been Midge Williams . . . Rufus's brother-in-law. It'd be an odd coincidence indeed if it weren't the case . . .

'I'm going to make my way to the exit so I can escape as soon as the all clear sounds.' Dawn whispered the remark, trying to remain inconspicuous while sliding upwards against the tiles.

'Don't think you have to shove off, Dawn, 'cos me old man's turned up. He won't mind you sitting with us.'

Dawn gave a fleeting smile, watching the little group getting closer. She realised that, with the press of bodies all around, she'd not manage to get clean away before Rufus joined them so crouched down again with her face lowered into her collar as though she felt very cold.

Rufus swung his smallest son over the seated people, then stepped over too. The other two boys made their own way to their mother's side. On squatting down by Gertie, Rufus immediately began bickering with his wife because one of the boys had been misbehaving, making him lose concentration while playing Rummy.

Dawn turned further away from the couple, as though to give them privacy, glad Rufus Grimes was too pre-occupied to have glanced her way. Now she'd heard his coarse voice there was no doubt he was one of the thieves. But he hadn't recognised her, and at the first opportunity she'd slip away.

A little stack of novels, belonging to the fellow who'd ogled Gertie, drew Dawn's lowered eyes. She was tempted to pilfer one, and pretend to read it. She knew, without conceit, that she was pretty and men tended to eye her up. She feared that once Grimes stopped chastising his son he might take more notice of his surroundings, and her . . .

'Sit yer arse down, Joey, and stop fidgeting,' Dawn heard Rufus snap at the eldest boy. Dawn slid a glance at the child, realising he was like his father with his chunky limbs and reddish hair.

Dawn's heart began pounding beneath her ribs as Gertie's husband turned his head in her direction. She adjusted her collar, pulling it to her cheeks as though for warmth. Remembering that she had Bill's letter in her bag, she delved inside for it. Angling it carefully to shield her face she stared sightlessly at it.

'So you ain't won any money at cards then?' Gertie sounded upset.

'Shut up,' Grimes rumbled beneath his breath while clumping Joey, who'd continued irritating him. 'Might as well get going,' he said testily. 'Ain't heard one bomb drop . . .'

A moment later a short whistle preceded a loud explosion that rocked the ground and sent a cloud of choking dust into the underground.

'That'll learn you to keep *your* mouth shut,' Gertie chortled, making her eldest son erupt in laughter at his father's expense.

Grimes shoved Joey in the shoulder for mocking him and in doing so started another row with his wife.

Dawn realised she wouldn't get a better moment to flee. She stuffed Bill's letter back in her handbag and keeping her face covered with a hand, as though to sift the filth floating in the air, she got carefully to her feet. She gave Gertie a small smile and a farewell wave.

The peeping Tom rolled over, attempting to get a look up Dawn's skirt as she stepped over him, making her lose balance.

Grimes put out a hand to steady Dawn and prevent her trampling his kids. ''Ere, mind your step, yer clumsy cow . . .'

'Oi, she's me workmate!' Gertie protested. 'Watch your language.'

'Oh . . . friend of yours, is she now . . .' Grimes was peering at Dawn's face. He drew his head back on his thick neck, cocking it to one side. 'Is she indeed?' he muttered softly. 'Wondered why she looked familiar. Gonna introduce me then, are yer, Gert?'

'No, I ain't! And there's no need to stare at her 'cos she's pretty,' his wife hissed resentfully.

'Going over there by the steps,' Dawn whispered, twisting her arm free of Grimes's fingers when he seemed reluctant to let her go. There was a horrible leering mockery in his expression that let her know he remembered where he'd seen her before.

'So . . . what's yer friend's name then?' Grimes repeated his question as Dawn negotiated the lounging bodies.

''Bye, Dawn . . .' Gertie called out. 'She's Dawn Nightingale and she's a dancer at the Windmill Theatre. You shouldn't have stared at her like that. She'll think you're a dirty old man.'

Dawn let out a sigh as she carefully put distance between herself and the Grimes family. Rufus Grimes now knew not only her name, but also where she worked. Dawn rarely swore, but she cussed repeatedly beneath her breath as she made her way towards the exit. She hunkered down close to the steps, ready to make a dash up them the moment the all clear sounded.

CHAPTER FOUR

'Would you show the new girls the ropes, Dawn? I'm in a bit of a rush. The accountant's turned up and is waiting for me in my office.'

Dawn had been comfortably lounging in a chair, aching feet up on the dressing table, having a crafty smoke. Quickly she stubbed out the cigarette and stood up, tightening the belt on her dressing gown as Phyllis, the manager's secretary, ushered in two young women then hurried out again.

Dawn had a couple of matinees to do before home time. A short while ago she'd been rehearsing for a new tap routine in shorts and top with her fellow dancers. Her colleagues in the chorus line had sped across the road to the café to snatch a bite to eat before the first show started at half past two.

'This is a bit poky, ain't it?'

'I've seen worse in other places.'

'Suppose it won't matter in any case; ain't gonna need a dressing room much if I'm in me birthday suit all the time.'

Dawn thought she recognised that chirpy voice and she tilted her head to see the young blonde standing behind an older brunette.

Rosie Gardiner noticed Dawn then. Her mouth dropped open in surprise before she grinned. 'Well I never. It's you, ain't it! Didn't know *you* was a Windmill girl. You got home alright that night after the commotion then?'

'So did you, I see.' Dawn looked Rosie up and down. She'd only seen her before in half-light. In the glare of the dressing-room bulbs Rosie's hair looked artificially blonde. But she had pretty dimpled cheeks and a snub nose dusted with freckles that made her look impish rather than vampish. 'Didn't know you were in theatre work too,' Dawn remarked.

'Didn't get much time for chitchat, last time we met, did we?' Rosie widened her eyes in emphasis. 'Anyhow, I ain't in showbiz . . . I was a shop girl but I need better pay, so thought I'd give this a go.'

'So, *you've* been a showgirl at other theatres, have you?' Dawn turned her attention to the brunette, holding out her hand. 'I'm Dawn Nightingale, by the way.'

'I've worked at a few other places in my time. My name's Marlene . . . Marlene Brown.' Marlene shook Dawn's hand. 'So you two already know one another then?'

Rosie nodded. 'Lucky, weren't we, that night?' she said to Dawn.

Dawn hoped Rosie wouldn't mention the incident. She reckoned the fewer people who knew about *that* the better. 'We sheltered together from a raid in a shop doorway,' she briefly explained to Marlene.

It had been several days since Dawn came face to face

with Grimes in the underground shelter. She'd convinced herself that he'd want to forget they'd bumped into one another as much as she did. Gertie hadn't done a shift since and in her absence Dawn had been brooding on whether Rufus had told Gertie what had gone on. Of course, there was a good chance that Grimes kept his looting sprees from his missus. But meeting Rosie unexpectedly like this had brought back a feeling of foreboding. From Rosie's attitude Dawn guessed the younger woman hadn't been able to fully dismiss the episode from her mind either.

'Right then, I'll show you where things are kept,' Dawn said briskly, hoping to buck herself up.

'Are you one of the nudes?' Rosie asked, as Dawn opened a cupboard to reveal racks of colourful costumes.

'No fear! I didn't fancy going on stage starkers; anyhow my mum would have a fit . . . or a few gins.' Dawn muttered the last bit to herself. 'I'm a chorus dancer and can sing a bit.'

'I wanted to be a showgirl,' Rosie sighed dejectedly. 'But I made a mess of me audition . . .'

'Probably 'cos you can't dance,' Marlene piped up. 'Thought *I* had two left feet but, bleedin' hell, you was all over the place, Rosie.'

'Thanks! Anyhow, the manager and his secretary said I'd got a great figure and shouldn't cover it up.' Rosie flounced about, turning her back on Marlene.

'Been here long?' Marlene asked, poking through some gilt headdresses in another cupboard.

'About a year,' Dawn replied. 'I used to work in a hotel as a cabaret singer and dancer but I got put off when the war started and the hotel closed.'

'Bloody war!' Rosie announced with feeling. 'I've had

enough of it. Can't even get meself a new pair of stockings.'

'I know where you can . . .' Marlene said slyly.

'Where?'

'Loot Alley.' Marlene smiled. 'Can get anything you like down there.'

'If you can pay for it,' Dawn chipped in dryly.

'Don't always need cash to pay for it,' Marlene said. She drew out a pack of cigarettes and handed it round. 'A girl can get what she wants if she's prepared to do a bit of sucking up . . .' She giggled and struck a match.

Dawn shook her head at the offer of a cigarette but Rosie took one. 'Don't let Phyllis hear you talk like that.' It was a light warning from Dawn. 'The management likes to think us Windmill girls draw the punters in with our nice personalities, and big smiles . . .'

Marlene hooted a laugh. 'It ain't my big smile those randy sods will come to see.' She thrust forward her full bosom. 'Let's face it, if I didn't have them, I wouldn't have got the job, would I?' She took a drag on her cigarette. 'It's right, is it, we've got to stand there as still as a statue 'cos if you move it's rude?'

'If you move we'll get closed down!' Dawn stressed.

The Windmill Theatre's management were sticking to the rules laid down regarding the *tableaux vivants*. The Lord Chamberlain had threatened to use obscenity laws against any theatre that allowed a nude 'statue' to so much as fidget on stage.

'Why's that then?' Rosie asked. 'We're still gonna be in the altogether whether we stand still or prance about.'

'You don't see statues in museums moving about, do you? You're supposed to be works of art, not flesh and blood,' Dawn explained.

'Good Gawd.' Marlene took another pull on her cigarette, then held it at arm's length so she didn't catch the flimsy gauze alight while she riffled through garments.

'Did those men catch up with you that night?' Rosie hissed the question at Dawn the moment the other woman wandered off to sort through some cosmetics discarded on the dressing table. Marlene opened a Yardley lipstick and striped her wrist with it to examine its colour.

'No. I've not told a soul about it, have you?' Dawn returned in a low voice.

Rosie shook her head, looking sheepish. 'I *was* after taking something for me dad from the shop they robbed, after all. Don't know what come over me . . . I feel ashamed about that now.'

'You were probably in shock,' Dawn said kindly. 'Those bombs came down pretty close.'

'I reckon I *was* in shock, too. I've never got caught out like that in a raid. We've got a cellar at home, you see, so me and Dad go down there.' She glanced at Dawn. 'Hope I never run into any of those men again. Thing is . . . I thought one of them seemed familiar to me.'

'Oh?' Dawn demanded. 'Which one?' She was wondering if Rosie also thought she recognised Gertie's husband, or perhaps her brother, if Midge *had* been involved. And the more Dawn thought about it, the more she reckoned she'd been right first time about Midge.

'The tall one who went off pushing the cart. I never got a look at his face though so wouldn't recognise him again. It was just something about him . . .' Rosie shrugged.

Dawn bit her lip, wondering whether to own up that

she'd already had the misfortune to run into one of them, and she'd recognised him straight away. And what's more he was a colleague's husband!

'You've seen one of 'em!' Rosie had guessed what was making Dawn look so preoccupied. 'Who was it . . . the short-arse? You stamped on his foot, didn't you?' Rosie pulled a comical face. 'The big bloke who had hold of me . . . what was his name now? The little bloke got a punch for saying it, remember?'

'Roof . . . he's the one I bumped into. I was chatting to his wife in a shelter.' Dawn felt she might as well admit to the awful meeting. 'Of course, I didn't know she was married to him until he turned up. Just my luck, eh?'

Rosie's eyes had grown round in disbelief. 'What did Roof say?' she squealed.

'He recognised me, just as I did him. But that was it. Neither of us said anything. That's the way I want it to stay.' Dawn settled on leaving it at that. She wasn't going to stir the pot by adding that Roof's wife worked at the Windmill too. If Gertie were kept in blissful ignorance over it all by her husband, then Dawn was happy to play along.

'Seen him since, have you?' Rosie gasped.

Dawn shook her head in a reassuring way. 'He won't want to see me any more than I want to see him. I expect he's keeping his head down.' She barely knew Rosie so couldn't recount the full story and trust her to keep her mouth shut. Gertie could be abrasive, as Dawn had already found out, and if challenged over her husband's thieving, all hell might break loose. As far as Dawn was concerned the less said the better! Her life was complicated enough as it was.

''Ere! What you playing at?' Sal Fiske had entered the dressing room to find Marlene testing her lipsticks. She snatched one from Marlene's hand. 'Give it back. That's mine.'

'Sorry . . . only taking a look. Got me own stuff anyhow.' Marlene threw another tube back on the dressing table and stalked off.

'Look at these beauties!' Lorna came in carrying a posy of early spring flowers. 'Phyllis just handed them over. A fellow called Peter sent them for me,' she said, reading a small card resting in the foliage. 'He thinks I'm beautiful and he'd like to take me out.'

'Ah . . . sweet . . .' Marlene mocked, having listened to Lorna's cut-glass accent with some amusement. 'He'll be out the back waiting for you later then,' she added knowledgably. 'So be prepared to show him how grateful you are for his daffs.'

A lively banter continued between Marlene and the chorus girls wearing dressing gowns who'd trooped in from the café. Dawn took the opportunity to draw Rosie to one side as the younger woman appeared rather downcast about Roof's reappearance.

'Buck up!' Dawn said, smiling. 'We can't let you out on stage at the Windmill with a face like a wet weekend. You'll scare away the customers.'

That raised a smile from Rosie and Dawn linked arms with her. 'Come on . . . I'll give you a guided tour of our lovely Windmill Theatre before we open up.'

'Me mum brought me here to see a variety show when I was a kid; I remember it as being a lot bigger.' Rosie grimaced. 'Reckon she must be spinning in her grave to think of me prancing about starkers on stage.'

'No prancing!' Dawn wagged a finger in mock reproof.

'When I was doing me audition I was too nervous to have a good look beyond the footlights.' Rosie was standing in an aisle close to the stage. Pivoting on one heel she gazed at the rows of seats fanning out in front of her.

'All good things come in small packages,' Dawn said proudly, tweaking the heavy tasselled curtain pooling on the stage.

'Blimey! Didn't see that when I was up there earlier!' Rosie was pointing down into the small orchestra pit. 'Better watch me step or I might end up crashing down the hole,' she giggled, taking another careful peep. 'That ain't very big either, is it?'

'The building used to be a cinema, till it closed and Mrs Henderson bought it and turned it into a theatre.'

'Good for her . . .' Rosie said.

'Anyway it might only have about three hundred and twenty seats but we could fill twice that amount. Most nights we've got queues of servicemen stretching round the corner. Our revues are the original and best, you see.'

'The Piccadilly and Pavilion are catching up fast with their nude shows.' Marlene was sashaying into the auditorium, newly lit cigarette glowing between her fingers.

'They're imitating us; we're the original and best,' Dawn repeated immediately. She felt a good deal of loyalty to the Windmill. 'Have you worked as a nude at either of those places, Marlene?'

Marlene gave a lazy nod. She'd told Phyllis at the audition that she was experienced in working in the nude . . . which was true, but not in the way Phyllis might have hoped. In fact Marlene had only ever been a cigarette girl at the Piccadilly although she'd had jobs at several other nightspots. But lies and exaggeration came easy to Marlene.

'I've never taken me clothes off for strangers before.' Rosie gave a shy grimace.

'Always best to get to know him first, Rosie . . .' Marlene mocked.

'It ain't funny!' Rosie exclaimed. 'If the pay weren't so good, I wouldn't do it.'

Marlene cocked her head, blowing smoke, and giving Rosie the once over. Suddenly she pointed her cigarette at Rosie. 'You're a good looker . . . and young. How old are you?'

'Eighteen . . .' Rosie mumbled.

'Girl like you should wise up, and make all that work for her.'

'You sound as though you've been a few places,' Rosie said, half in awe of her fellow new recruit.

'Me?' Marlene tilted her head and took a long lazy drag on her Sobranie. 'I've done it all and regretted none of it . . .' she drawled, ending her boast on a dirty chuckle.

Dawn stepped forward; she'd heard enough from Marlene. There was something hard and brash about the woman that was already putting her back up. And she'd only known her about an hour! 'Come on,' she urged Rosie. 'I'll show you the roof terrace. We go up there to cool off . . . or sunbathe, depending how we feel, when we've got some spare time. There's an outside staircase too goes down the building. We have fire drills . . .'

By the time the trio had finished looking around and had got back to the dressing room it was time for the showgirls to start getting into costume.

'Reckon I'll need a nip of gin to get me out there first time,' Rosie said while watching the dancers applying their make-up.

'You'll be fine,' Dawn said, using a sponge to put on grease paint.

'Well, look what I've got . . . handy, eh?' Marlene gave Rosie a nudge in the ribs as she took a small flask from her bag. She gave her pretty young colleague a wink, dropping the gin back whence it came.

Dawn had seen that in the mirror while outlining her large green eyes with kohl; again she sensed she wasn't going to get on with Marlene Brown . . .

CHAPTER FIVE

'I ain't going to cause problems, so stop bleedin' nagging.' Rufus Grimes turned his attention back to the sports section of the *News of the World*.

Gertie began bouncing the pram up and down to hush Harry who'd started to whimper at the sound of raised voices. 'Well don't expect me to ask Dawn to keep her gob shut, 'cos I won't do it.'

'I ain't expecting you to do nuthin'!' Rufus exploded. 'Ain't your business, anyhow.' Exasperated, he picked up the newspaper and hurled it at the wall with a loud oath, making little Harry cry louder. 'Just play dumb and she'll do the same. Dawn Nightingale don't want no trouble . . . guarantee it.'

Gertie whipped the baby from his pram and began rocking him to and fro against her shoulder while glowering at Rufus's stubbly profile.

'Is my business now though, ain't it?' Gertie snapped. 'You should've told me that Midge was still about. Why d'you let me think he'd sailed when you knew all along he hadn't?'

"Cos he asked me not to tell you!' Rufus roared. 'He knew you'd go on about it, like this, and didn't want earache off you. Can sympathise with the bloke. You're driving me nuts. Now fer Gawd's sake shut up.'

'You won't say that when the coppers turn up looking for him, will you?' Gertie stormed. 'You'll scarper and leave me to do the talking.'

Rufus approached his wife, fist raised and shaking. 'I said shut up about your bleedin' brother. He's a pain in the arse at the best of times. Now if you got a gripe with Midge, take it up with him, the bleeder.'

Rufus stalked off and flung himself down in a chair at the table.

Far from not knowing about her husband's criminal activities, as Dawn had suspected, Gertie Grimes encouraged Rufus to supplement his municipal earnings as a road sweeper with 'overtime' worked during bombing raids. So far she'd done quite nicely out of his thieving. She'd received a few bits of quality clothing for herself and the kids, and some household stuff. But he didn't like to upset Pop, who controlled the gang Rufus was in with. Most of the stolen merchandise went straight to the fences, or to Loot Alley, to be sold and the proceeds were then split between the gang members. Gertie had moaned at Rufus that she deserved a little dip in before the stuff was spirited away, but her husband was charier of Pop than he was of her. That annoyed Gertie because she'd got used to being the person pulling her husband's strings.

When Rufus had his cut of the proceeds in his pocket, that's where it stayed. His 'bunce', as he called it, was his alone. And Gertie knew where his money went: booze, gambling and prostitutes. There might be a war on, but there was still a thriving market in every sort of vice in London, if you knew where to look.

'No point sulking over it, Gertie,' Rufus lilted in a conciliatory way. He never fell out with his wife for too long; she was too useful to him to upset. 'Tell you what, gel, we've got our sights on a tobacconist next 'cos Pop wants a nice briar pipe. See if I can get you a few packs of Players, shall I?'

'Reckon you can do that, do you?' Gertie muttered sourly.

Rufus came up behind her, nudging her buttocks with his groin. 'Do anything for you, gel, you know that . . .'

Gertie gave a smile, unseen by Rufus. He always came round when he was feeling horny . . . which was most of the time. She let him open her blouse and slide a hand inside to squeeze her warm breasts.

'Nip upstairs, shall we?' Rufus breathed against her cheek. 'The boys ain't due in from school for a while. Stick Harry back in his pram; only be five minutes, won't we . . .'

'No fear!' Gertie pushed him away. 'I reckon it's the wrong time of the month for me and I don't want another kid filling that there . . .' she pointed at the pram '. . . before I've even turfed Harold out of it and onto his feet.' She turned to confront Rufus, hands planted on her hips. 'I've got enough kids running round me ankles, Rufus, and I don't want no more.'

He looked sullen, avoiding her eye. They'd had this conversation before and he always got moody when she mentioned visiting the Marie Stopes clinic. Like most men he thought women who used birth control were sordid, yet he wasn't prepared to spoil his own pleasure by using a Johnny instead so they could limit the number of mouths they had to feed.

'Please yourself,' Rufus muttered, shrugging himself away from her. He began gathering pages of the newspaper scattered on the floor. 'Probably won't be able to get you no fags on the sly anyhow when we do the tobacconist.'

Gertie knew his game; it was always the same one – she was nice to him and he was nice to her. She put little Harry back in his pram and sat next to her husband at the table. He had his elbows planted on the open newspaper and his chin cupped in his palms, continuing to ignore her.

Gertie's fingers crept to undo the buttons of his fly. He was hot and hard . . . as usual. It didn't matter what time of the day or night it was, Rufus was ready for action. In a way, Gertie felt quite sorry for him and his affliction.

'Could do with a lighter as well as some fags,' she murmured as her fingers started to pump beneath the table. 'Silver's nice . . . if you spot one like that . . .'

Dawn bobbed to and fro on the station platform looking for a tall figure dressed in smart blue uniform. Suddenly she spotted him, and dodging around a couple strolling in front of her, she broke into a trot.

Bill Sweetman dropped his kit bag, ready to grab Dawn as soon as she was within reach.

'You look well,' Dawn said breathlessly, hanging onto her hat as he spun them around. She touched his freshly shaven cheeks.

'Plenty of bracing air where I've been,' Bill said, swooping to kiss her on the lips.

Picking up his bag they strolled arm in arm towards the station exit.

'How have you been keeping?'

'Not bad . . .' Dawn smiled.

'How about your family?' Bill had picked up on a slight hesitation in Dawn's reply.

'Mum's driving George and me bonkers. She won't let up on the gin.'

Bill grimaced in sympathy. 'Everything alright at the Windmill?'

'We've got opening night for a variety show next week. We've got to dress up as ghostly wraiths. A couple of new girls have been taken on as living statues.'

'I'll come and take a look,' Bill said wolfishly.

Dawn gave his arm a playful thump. 'If you come and have a look at anybody, it'd better be me.'

'I wish you'd get another job, Dawn,' Bill said, growing serious. 'I don't like you working there with loads of blokes leering at you all the time.'

'They don't leer . . . well, some of them do, but mainly at the nudes.' Dawn knew that wasn't strictly true. All the showgirls, whether in the chorus line or in the artistic tableaux, received attention from fellows in the audience. Naturally, naked female flesh was fascinating to the opposite sex – especially those youths who'd never before clapped eyes on an unclothed woman. 'A lot of the servicemen who come along seem quite young and sweet.'

'Fancy going to the pictures later?' Bill changed the subject quite abruptly.

'I don't finish till eight o'clock. We could try and fit in a late show somewhere,' Dawn suggested. Bill had frowned on hearing she had to work, so she added quickly, 'Are you planning on seeing your folks?' Bill's parents were quite well to do and lived in Surrey.

'I'll drive over to them this afternoon then meet up with you later on this evening.'

Dawn went onto tiptoes and kissed his cheek. 'How is it all going in Suffolk?'

'The main news – and very bad it is too – is that our local brewer has been sent to prison. Shame about that, 'cos he produced a decent whisky.' Bill, tongue-in-cheek, recounted a tale about the fellow in Ipswich who'd had his illegal still, and his liberty, taken by the authorities. 'Oh, and there's a rumour that Midge Williams has gone AWOL. Top brass in the Navy know our top brass and the news filtered down that there's a bit of a to-do about it. A rating called Jack Chivers was found stabbed in a lifeboat, and Williams has gone missing . . . odd.' Bill hadn't noticed that his girlfriend had turned pale at his news. 'Midge didn't return to his ship. But to give him his due, there were some heavy raids on London during his last shore leave.' Bill paused. 'He might be under rubble or perhaps he's still recovering from the effects of too much rotgut.' Bill glanced at Dawn for a comment, realising she'd remained quiet. 'Oh, God, I forgot . . .' He grimaced in apology. 'Midge's sister does cleaning at the Windmill, doesn't she?' He drew Dawn close with an arm about her shoulders. 'Is the poor girl in a state? Has Midge come a cropper somehow or other?'

'I haven't seen Gertie for a few days . . . different shifts,' Dawn explained.

She'd been mulling over whether to voice her suspicions that Gertie's brother was alive and a member of a gang of bomb-chasers. Bill had never liked Midge since the seaman and some of his Navy pals had taunted Bill and his RAF colleagues in a pub, calling the airmen nancy boys and starting a fight. Dawn certainly didn't want Bill feeling he ought to jump to her defence and confront Midge, especially now she knew that Gertie's brother was wanted for questioning about a murder. But there was no proof of anything, she reminded herself. Nevertheless she decided to keep quiet about the horrible night she and Rosie had witnessed the gang out looting.

'Is that you, Rosie?'

'Yeah, it's me home, Dad.' Rosie slipped out of her jacket and hung it on a peg on the wall before closing the door. The hallway of the Victorian terraced house was dog-legged and painted in a sepia colour that deepened the gloomy interior. But dark or not, she'd glimpsed her father, in his tan cotton coat, scurrying out of the cellar a moment ago. He'd obviously been alerted to her presence by the sound of her key grating in the lock. 'You've been down there again then?' she accused. 'You said you were going to pack it in.'

'Well I've changed me mind.' John Gardiner sounded obstinate. He shoved his hands into his overall pockets. 'How else are we going to get by if I don't tinker around and make us a few bob?'

'I got a job posing with no clothes on so you wouldn't need to *tinker around*,' Rosie shouted, rapidly approaching him.

John Gardiner pulled off the rubber gloves he'd been wearing and stuffed them in his overall pocket. He turned his back on his angry daughter and disappeared into the kitchenette, throwing over a shoulder, 'I've told you what I think about that! Daughter of mine, acting like a little tart! Disgusting!' A moment later Rosie could hear the squeaky tap being turned on.

'And I think it's disgusting what *you're* getting up to . . . and dangerous too.' Rosie sighed, thinking it was pointless arguing with the stubborn old git. 'You'd better pack it up, Dad,' she warned with a hint of despair in her tone. 'We can manage now I'm working at the Windmill Theatre and getting good pay.'

John started setting cups as though he'd not heard her pleading with him. 'Brought me in any empties, have you?'

'No! And I'm not going to! And I'm not doing any more deliveries for you neither. Nearly got me head blown off in a raid last time.' Rosie kept quiet about the fact that she'd also almost got set about by looters. Her father exasperated her, but she didn't want to worry him unnecessarily. Besides, Dawn had reassured her that nothing more would come of it. And Rosie put a lot of store in what Dawn Nightingale said. She wasn't sure why that was, being as they hardly knew one another.

'I'll pay you for them . . . a shilling a pop . . . that's a good amount for an empty bottle of whisky.' John carried on as though he'd not heard his daughter's complaint. He glanced slyly at her. 'Must be loads of places round in Soho where they're putting out empties. Can't you just have a poke around the dustbins, dear, and fetch me some in?'

'Somebody died of rotgut poisoning the other day, you know . . .'

'Nothing to do with me.' John banged the filled kettle on the gas stove and put a match under it. 'I know what I'm doing; I worked as a chemist's assistant for a long time.' He tapped his nose in emphasis.

Rosie's father had always been one to do a bit of home brewing, just for the family, but since the war started he'd seen the profit to be had operating an illegal still, as had many other people who'd turned to peddling hooch.

'Mum would hate what you're doing, you know,' Rosie said in desperation, hoping to talk sense into her father.

'Oh, yes, I know that. Prudence never liked me enjoying myself or having cash in my pocket.' John's lips thinned as he recalled his dead wife. She'd been gone seven years, having succumbed to pleurisy, leaving him to raise their daughter.

A bang on the door made Rosie start to attention and stare wide-eyed at her father. She was on tenterhooks all the time fearing that either the police or the Revenue men would get a tip-off and turn up to search the house. Rosie knew if her father's still in the basement were uncovered he'd get a long prison sentence. If he were implicated – even wrongly – in supplying lethal moonshine that had poisoned somebody, he might hang.

Unconcerned by the rata-tat John finished filling the teapot with boiling water. 'Calm down,' he told his agitated daughter. 'That'll be Lenny fetching me round some labels. I've been expecting him.' John held out a cup of tea towards Rosie.

'Don't want no fuckin' tea!' Rosie was incensed by her father's attitude. From the moment she'd heard the knocker crash against the door her heart had been crazily racing. 'I'm sick of being scared half to death all the time,' she hissed. 'If you don't pack it in, I'm moving out.' She stormed out of the kitchen and ran up the stairs. About to enter her bedroom, she hesitated, smearing angry tears from her lashes. Crouching down by the banisters, she watched through the sticks as her father opened the door and ushered inside a young man.

They started to talk in low voices and Rosie strained to hear what her dad said to Lenny Purves. Lenny and his father had a legitimate printing business on the High Street and did some under-the-counter stuff on the side. Rosie watched her father hand over some money in exchange for a brown paper package that the young man took out of his pocket. Then her father was ambling away, leaving Lenny to see himself out.

But he didn't; he glanced up and saw Rosie watching him.

'Ain't sure you should be up there earwigging, should you?'

'Ain't sure you should be wearing civvies. Too scared to fight?' Rosie taunted.

'Got poor eyesight. Can't see nuthin', me,' Lenny said slyly. He'd swung the lead at his medical. His father had dodgy eyes so Lenny had pretended he was afflicted too and couldn't see past the end of his nose. He'd been discharged from the army on medical grounds almost before he'd been enlisted.

Lenny liked to think he wasn't a coward, he was just protecting his inheritance. His father was a crafty git who'd stashed away a tidy sum, and Lenny was an only child because his mother had died having him. Lenny didn't want to risk taking a bullet and losing out on enjoying a pot of money coming his way.

'Can't see nothing . . . that right?' Rosie said sarcastically. 'Just saw me well enough, didn't you.'

'Yeah . . . well, you're a sight for sore eyes, ain't yer, Rosie,' he purred.

'Piss off,' Rosie said defiantly, standing up. She knew Lenny fancied her; he'd tried to touch her up before on one occasion when he'd come round to bring her father's order. But she'd nothing but contempt for him. He was a gangly, spotty youth with unkempt greasy hair.

Lenny swaggered to the bottom of the stairs and gazed up at her, head cocked to one side. 'Gonna give us a show then?' he asked coarsely. He pulled out the money her father had just handed over. 'Want paying to flash yer tits, I suppose, do you?' He peeled off a ten-shilling note. 'There . . . how about that for a start?' He began climbing the stairs, leering at her and waving the cash in his fingers to and fro. 'If I like what I see I'll pay up for the works . . .'

Rosie felt her face burning in anger and embarrassment. She hadn't told many people that she'd started working as a nude in the Revudeville shows at the Windmill Theatre, but obviously word had got around.

Lenny lived just a few streets away and was about twenty-one. He'd been at the same school but in a different class. Rosie had never liked him; he'd always been a show-off with a fast mouth.

'I told you to piss off, so get going before I call me dad and tell him what you just said to me.'

Lenny was just below her on the stairs now. He poked his face forward giving Rosie a close up of a yellow-headed spot on his chin. She recoiled from his sour breath but refused to back away.

'What's yer old man gonna do to help you?' Lenny drawled. 'I'll knock him down with a punch. He's probably disgusted by you anyhow now you're stripping off. Come on . . . how much to go all the way?' He looked Rosie up and down, suddenly grabbing at her breast.

Rosie shoved her palm into Lenny's face making him stumble down a few stairs and clutch at the banister.

'Rosie? Want any tea this evening or are you still sulking up there?' John Gardiner had come out of the kitchen and ambled along the hallway. He stopped when he saw his daughter and his business associate face to face on the stairs. 'What's going on?' he demanded.

'Nothing, mate, just thought I'd say hello to Rosie being as we used to be school pals.' Lenny descended the stairs in a cocky, rolling gait, grinning. 'Let us know when you need a few more of them labels run off. Nice doing business with you. Me dad says hello . . .'

As the front door slammed shut after Lenny's departing figure John stared suspiciously at his daughter. 'Was you misbehaving with him just then?'

Rosie choked a laugh. 'I can't stand the creep and I wish you'd tell him not to come here. Anyhow, it ain't me misbehaving, Dad, is it? It's you; and if you keep doing business with people like him . . .' Rosie jabbed her forehead at the front door. 'Then *you're* gonna be in big trouble.'

CHAPTER SIX

'Are you driving to Surrey to stay at your mum and dad's tonight?'

'Is that an invitation to come home with you instead?'

Dawn smiled wryly, moving her cheek against Bill's pleasantly scratchy jaw as they waltzed to the jazz trio. 'I don't think my mum would appreciate seeing you on the couch in your vest first thing in the morning.'

'If you top the old girl up with gin she'll be too sozzled to see me at all, arriving or leaving. Then I could bed down upstairs with you,' he whispered in her ear. 'I'll happily stump up for a bottle of Gordon's for your mum and a few beers for that brother of yours, if you agree to me staying over.'

Dawn drew back, frowning at Bill. Sometimes his sense of humour was too black for her to appreciate; that was, of course, assuming he *was* joking. If he weren't then she'd be worried . . .

'Don't take it so seriously, darling.' Bill drew her close again, nuzzling her neck. His hands, stroking at the centre of her back, began massaging closer to her buttocks. 'Let's get a room in a hotel, then, if you don't want to upset your family. I don't intend driving to Surrey, and I'm damned sure you could do with a break from your set-up in the East End.'

Dawn *was* fed up with things at home: her mother drove her mad and her brother George's moodiness was a pain, but she didn't want Bill rubbing it in simply to get her into bed. Dawn knew he was getting impatient with her because she hadn't yet agreed to sleep with him. She wasn't holding out because they'd only known each other for a short while, or because he would be her first real lover. She'd been kissed and caressed by boyfriends but the thought of an unwanted pregnancy was always at the back of her mind, terrifying her when she was aroused and tempted to capitulate. But the main barrier to her throwing caution to the wind with Bill . . . and he was by far the boyfriend she fancied the most . . . was Bill himself.

His callous joke about her mother's alcoholism had added to her niggling doubts that he might not be the right man for her. When they'd first met she'd been sure she'd fallen head over heels for him after the first few dates, but then the giddy pleasure of the newness of it all had faded, removing the blinkers from her eyes.

On the first occasion she'd seen Bill he'd been in the audience at the Windmill Theatre, giving her his undivided attention. He'd sent her a lazy wink, blown her a kiss that had almost put her off her step, and then disappeared at the end of the show, or so Dawn had thought.

She'd been disappointed not to find him amongst the crowd of eager fellows hanging around the stage door, hopeful of chatting up a showgirl. Then she'd spied a man dressed in RAF uniform lounging against a lamp-post further along the street, smoking.

As she'd walked towards him Bill had blocked her path, telling her he'd not let her pass till she agreed to go out with him. She'd thought him wonderfully handsome close to and his persistence had excited her. His eyes were startlingly blue and his hair as fair as her own. So she had agreed to meet him the following evening; that had been five months ago, yet although they wrote regularly Dawn realised she'd only been in Bill's company a handful of times. The war kept them separated, as it did most young couples.

Dawn felt warm fingers fondling her behind and gave her boyfriend a ghost of a smile. Taking his hand she started leading him back to their table before the saxophonist had finished playing. As they weaved through swaying bodies, in half-light, the atmosphere was thick with cigarette smoke and the sultry scent of brandy cocktails. They sat down opposite Bill's pal. Glenn Rafferty was stationed with Bill and was a squadron leader. Dawn got the impression that it riled Bill that his friend was about the same age but held a higher rank than he did.

Bill had said Glenn had plenty of girls to choose from when he came to London on leave. But this evening he had with him the same girl who'd accompanied him last time, called Tina.

Dawn had been surprised by how different in looks the men were; her boyfriend had the quintessentially fair and dashing looks of a middle-class Englishman, whereas Glenn was dark-haired and tanned and in Dawn's fanciful opinion might have Romany blood. A gold earring would have completed his startlingly handsome, rather villainous presence.

They'd not planned on meeting up for another double-date this evening; Glenn and Tina had been leaving a bottle party club when Dawn and Bill had bumped into them on Regent Street. They'd entered the Kitkat Club as a foursome.

The last time they'd all been together Tina had acted sullen; she didn't seem any friendlier this evening although she slid flirtatious glances at Glenn . . . Bill too, Dawn noticed with a pang of annoyance.

Determined to be friendly, Dawn attempted to draw the young brunette into conversation. 'Do you live locally, Tina?'

'Yeah . . .'

Following her terse reply Tina lifted her port and lemon and took a sip, leaving Dawn thinking she'd had no more luck in having a chat with Glenn's girl-friend than the last time she'd attempted to make conversation.

'Gonna dance then, are we?' Tina nudged Glenn's arm and pouted him a kiss.

'Just let me finish this. I'm parched.' Glenn lifted his glass of beer.

For a man who was thirsty he drank little, Dawn observed with a slight smile, watching Glenn take a single mouthful then replace the tankard. He hadn't even looked at Tina when she'd spoken to him.

No need to get upset, Dawn told herself as she again noticed Tina's dark eyes slide Bill's way. The brunette looked quite young – about nineteen – and was probably testing her powers of attraction on every good-looking fellow she met.

'I'll dance with you.' Bill had taken the hint when Tina continued staring at him and swirling her port and

58

lemon to attract his attention. Discreetly Bill raised his eyebrows at Dawn by way of apology then led Tina towards the thrumming music being belted out by the band.

'She's not standoffish . . . just shy . . .'

Dawn shot a look at Glenn; it was the first time the two of them had been left alone together to talk. 'Shy?' Dawn queried with a snort. She might have toned down her sarcasm had she not noticed, in the light of the flickering candle on the table, a gleam of amusement at the backs of his eyes. Glenn knew as well as she did that Tina was downright rude. And that begged the question: what did Squadron Leader Rafferty see in her? Dawn got her answer quickly enough: young or not, Tina had a very vampish manner. The brunette was dancing cheek to cheek with Bill and a moment later Dawn felt her temper rise as a pair of shapely arms slid about Bill's neck. Tina's palms suggestively cupped the back of his head as though she might urge his face down and kiss him. Dawn's insides writhed in anger. Tina was deliberately making a play for Bill, no doubt to punish Glenn because he wouldn't dance with her.

'Shall we give them a run for their money?'

Dawn snapped her eyes back to Glenn who was draining his glass. He pushed to his feet, held out a hand. 'Come on. Bill's not stupid . . . well, not all the time,' Glenn said very dryly. 'He didn't have a lot of choice in it. I'm sure he'd sooner have kept on dancing with you . . .'

From that Dawn deduced that Glenn was letting her know he'd seen Bill's hands roving her body a few minutes ago. Well, if Glenn Rafferty thought he could try it on too . . . he'd find out he was mistaken. He wasn't going to make Tina jealous by touching her up! Slowly Dawn stood up. Once his long fingers had closed on hers he tugged her behind him onto the small dance floor.

His touch was light and cool and he kept his hands to himself. He moved very well . . . as well as Bill; but he was a bit taller than her boyfriend, Dawn realised. With Bill she'd no need to stretch her arm so far to rest it on a broad shoulder. Dawn darted glances Bill's way, trying to get a glimpse of the swaying couple through the crowd.

'Aren't you bothered about your girl flirting?'

'Nope . . .'

'Why not?'

'She's not my girl,' Glenn said and suddenly whipped Dawn around so fast in time with the beat that her next words were lost in a gasp.

It was his way of telling her to shut up and mind her own business, she realised. So she did, stiffening in his arms. As though he found her pique a challenge he urged her closer, dropping his head towards hers. As soon as the music faded Dawn pulled away, trying not to make it too obvious that Glenn had succeeded in aggravating her . . . and more. The pleasant scent of his sandalwood cologne clung to her cheek where their skin had scuffed together. She was the first to sit down; moments later Bill joined her.

'She's an odd sort of girl.' Bill was glancing at the dance floor. Tina had intercepted Glenn before he could leave and they were now waltzing.

'That's an understatement,' Dawn said sourly, taking a long swallow of her drink. 'She's rude and arrogant and the most outrageous flirt.'

'You're not jealous, are you?' Bill sounded genuinely

surprised. 'Forget about her, sweetheart; I've only got one girl on my mind this evening.' He leaned forward and slowly tickled her chin. 'Want another brandy and soda?'

'I think I've had enough, thanks all the same.' Dawn could feel a warm glow on her cheeks and a cold top lip . . . sure signs that she'd had too many cocktails! Besides, she suddenly wanted to leave. She knew she had no reason to be jealous but, even so, resented another woman rubbing her nose in it while she flung herself at Bill.

Pulling out a packet of Players, Bill offered one to Dawn then took one himself.

'She doesn't have much to say for herself, either,' Dawn said, dipping her head to the lighted match cupped in Bill's palm.

'She seems to have enough to talk about to Glenn.' Bill drew hard on his cigarette. He sat back in his chair, watching the couple. 'Probably discussing her price,' he added caustically.

Dawn shot him a glance. 'You think she's a working girl?'

''Course she is . . . those bottle party hostesses are all the same. They'll charge you a week's pay for a watered-down beer and a fruit juice for themselves, then they'll try and get you to stump up again for having the pleasure of their company all night.' He tapped ash into an empty glass.

'How do you know?' Dawn asked waspishly. It sounded as though her boyfriend was admitting to using prostitutes.

'The lads in the barracks are always moaning about that sort of girl emptying their wallets.' Bill stuck the cigarette back between his lips.

Dawn squinted through the half-light at Tina's profile. She was undeniably pretty: petite and with shoulder-length dark brown hair, but done up to the nines with cosmetics. Her lips were a ruby red bow and her complexion chalky with powder; but done up or not it couldn't conceal the fact that Tina was young, perhaps not even Rosie Gardiner's age.

'Your friend should watch himself; she could be underage . . .' Dawn frowned, thinking she didn't like Glenn Rafferty very much.

'It's up to him what he does.' Bill ground out his cigarette and shook another from the pack. 'He's not the sort of bloke who'll worry if her father, or her husband for that matter, comes after him. Glenn's an East End boy and can look after himself.'

'You make him sound a callous so and so . . .'

'Oh, he'll go for the jugular. He's shot down twenty enemy aircraft – that's why he's a squadron leader and I'm a lowly flying officer.'

Dawn took Bill's hands in hers and gave them a fond squeeze. 'You stay safe . . . all the time, stay safe and don't take stupid risks. I don't want to be left with just a photo-graph to kiss because you tried to rival your pal's kills.' Dawn glanced at Glenn and saw that he was watching them. For a moment their eyes locked, as though he knew she was talking about him. 'He does seem callous,' Dawn said, tearing her eyes away from a mocking gaze.

'Unlike me, who would lay down his life for a fair maiden,' Bill teased and leaned forward to kiss Dawn. 'I blame him for our moonshine drying up too,' Bill added, still nuzzling at Dawn's lips.

Dawn drew back an inch, smiling uncertainly. 'What did he do?'

'Glenn's in with the top brass and on their say so's on the lookout for illegal stills.' Bill sat back with an easy shrug when Dawn seemed more interested in talking than smooching.

Bill's comment about his friend made Glenn seem a bit of a nark, yet Rafferty appeared anything but. Dawn wouldn't have been surprised to learn he was a barrow boy who did a bit of ducking and diving himself! They'd only exchanged a few words but she'd noticed Glenn had a pronounced London accent, as did she. Bill on the other hand sounded as though he might have recently come down from Harrow. Dawn let Bill light her a cigarette, although she didn't really want it, having just put one out.

'Shall we make tracks and find a hotel?' Bill stared at Dawn through the smoky mist he'd exhaled.

'I'm ready to go . . . but straight home. I'm all in.' Dawn gave him a winning smile, but it did little to erase the annoyance pinching his features.

'Right . . . I'll fetch your coat,' Bill said distantly.

As he strode away, Dawn watched him, biting her lip. She squashed the unsmoked cigarette in the ashtray, sorry they'd bumped into Glenn and Tina. Bill had been in a better mood when they'd been on their own. She wished they'd gone to the pictures as they'd planned, then for a bite to eat in a cosy café, rather than heading towards a sophisticated nightclub. She knew Bill had only a forty-eight hour pass and needed to relax and forget just for a short while that he was a Spitfire pilot. But she wasn't sure yet whether infatuation or true love was drawing her to Bill. Before taking that leap into the unknown and spending the night with a man she wanted to be certain of the depth of her feelings.

Bill had not offered to use a rubber, and Dawn had not wanted to vulgarly bring the subject up because it would seem teasing if she then again said no. The idea of having a baby and perhaps raising it alone was terrifying. Her mother had had George out of wedlock and the upset surrounding the dreadful episode had started Eliza's alcoholism and brought about the end of Dawn's childhood.

'Another drink somewhere else?' Bill suggested as they exited the Kitkat Club. Despite there being a war on the West End was thriving. As they started strolling along Regent Street they were jostled and bumped by boisterous people – civilians and servicemen and women – intent on having a good time.

They stepped around some fresh-faced sailors squatting close to a wall playing dice, roll-ups dangling between their lips. They were just boys, Dawn realised, possibly no more than five years older than her own brother.

A tout approached Bill and shoved a flyer for an illegal bottle party at him before sidling away to a group of soldiers chatting up girls. The lads eagerly took the invitations promising them a good time.

Bill stuffed the paper in a pocket and tightened his arm about Dawn. 'Do you fancy another drink?' he repeated.

'Sorry . . . daydreaming . . . no thanks, not tonight, but I'd love it if you took me to the Café de Paris when you're next on leave.'

'It's pricey,' Bill said. 'Have you been there before?'

'No . . .' Dawn murmured. 'I've heard the girls at work talking about it though. Lorna thinks she might meet a toff there who'll carry her off and give her a life of leisure.'

An army corporal, showing off to his friends while pretending to use a machine gun, bumped into Dawn, making Bill scowl and shove him in the shoulder.

Dawn dragged him on. 'He's had a few too many, that's all,' she said, smoothing over the situation. She didn't fancy Bill getting involved in a fight with a bunch of soldiers over something so trivial.

'So you like a shindig with the girls when I'm not around, do you?' Bill resumed their conversation and slung a possessive arm about Dawn's shoulders again.

'Sal and me sometimes go the pictures then have supper in a corner house, but since we met I only go to dances with you.' Dawn snuggled up to him.

She looked up at the stars. She was glad that the war hadn't frightened people into huddling indoors behind blackout curtains. 'Two fingers up to Hitler,' she murmured tipsily to herself with a smile. 'Up there it's been a quiet night; please God it stays that way.'

'I'll drink to that . . .' Bill drew her arm through his and they strolled on. 'Sure you don't fancy another bevy? The night's still young.'

Dawn kissed his cheek in thanks. 'No . . . sleepy . . .' She hugged into him again.

Suddenly Bill backed Dawn against a wall and kissed her tenderly. 'I really want you to wait for me, you know. When this bloody war's over I've got important things to say to you, sweetheart. But I don't want to promise you anything now when I don't know if I'll be around next week, let alone next year.'

'Don't say that!' Dawn whispered, touching a finger to his lips. 'I pray for your safe return every day . . . and the war might soon fizzle out . . .' She gave a wry smile. 'Not much chance of that happening, eh?'

Bill caressed her cheek with a finger. 'Let's go and find a hotel . . . please. I need you so much . . .'

'I can't, Bill!' Dawn said softly. 'It's not that I don't want to . . .' She put a hand to her forehead. 'Oh, I don't know what I want . . .'

'Well let me show you,' he urged huskily. 'I swear I won't ever hurt you; I know I've fallen for you, Dawn, in a big way . . .' He kissed her again with passionate pressure.

'I feel the same about you but . . .' Dawn frowned, feeling warm and cosy from his closeness and the brandy cocktails she'd had in the Kitkat Club. She was swayed to agree to go with him just so she could revel a while longer in the lovely muzzy sensation in her head. The word yes froze on her lips and Dawn almost jumped out of her skin. Usually she was primed for that eerie sound but tonight, submerged in a sensual daze, it had come as a complete surprise. She heard Bill curse beneath his breath as they gazed at the skies, listening. Bill grabbed her hand and tugged her into a run towards Oxford Circus underground station as the drone of aeroplane engines became louder.

About to descend the steps Bill pulled Dawn around to face him. 'Saved by the siren?' he asked, his vivid eyes demanding an honest answer from her.

Dawn smiled and went ahead of him, merging into the throng of people.

'Got a mo, Dawn?'

'Yes . . . of course . . . how are you, Gertie?'

'So-so,' Gertie said evasively.

Dawn had just arrived at the Windmill Theatre and had been stopped by the cleaner at the top of the stairs leading to the basement dressing rooms. Dawn hadn't seen Gertie for a while, and she realised that the older woman didn't seem her usual cheerful self. Gertie had been off work nursing a sick child who'd gone down with bronchitis, so she'd heard. Dawn had her own ideas on what else might have been keeping Gertie occupied at home: the woman had found out her brother was a deserter and a suspected murderer. To cap it all, Rufus might have owned up to his wife that he'd been going looting with his brother-in-law, and an almighty row had probably erupted.

Poor Gertie! Dawn realised the men in Gertie's family must be a constant burden on her. Then she had the four little boys to deal with too!

Dawn drew aside to let a couple of dancers wearing exercise shorts and shirts pass by and clatter down the stairs towards the dressing room. She sensed that Gertie wouldn't want their conversation overheard.

'Last time I saw you, you said you'd seen my brother Michael,' Gertie began as soon as the chorus girls had disappeared.

'I couldn't be absolutely sure it was him 'cos I don't really know him,' Dawn said neutrally.

'I think you know now you *did* see him,' Gertie replied. 'And so do I, 'cos I asked Rufus about it and he owned up to Midge being around. I've not seen me brother in months,' she added quickly. 'But you have. You saw 'em at work, didn't you.' Gertie slid a look at Dawn from beneath her lashes. 'Yeah . . . I do know what me husband gets up to – but I ain't his keeper,' she added defensively. 'Not saying it's right to go bomb-chasing . . . but it's wartime, ain't it, and people don't always act normal. They just get by.' Gertie suddenly clammed up on that front.

'But . . . what about your brother deserting?' Dawn asked; she understood some of Gertie's blunt philosophy, but not all of it.

'Don't know nothing about it, as I said, ain't seen Midge in ages. But yesterday we had some Navy bigwigs come round looking for him, so he's gone AWOL alright.' Gertie's head dropped close to her chest. 'Really bad thing about it is, seems a sailor by the name of Jack Chivers was found dead about the same time Michael disappeared.' Gertie wiped her moist eyes with the back of her hand. ''Course me and Rufus had to lie and tell them we thought he'd sailed 'cos it wouldn't be right if he was arrested on a murder charge. He might be a deserter but he's no killer! Stake me life on it!' Gertie shook her head. 'Wouldn't hurt a fly . . .' She knew that was stretching the truth so shut up.

'Sorry, Gertie, to have to tell you this, but Michael was aggressive with us. When we ran off he and Rufus chased us 'cos we'd seen them breaking the shop window and stealing the stuff from the outfitters.'

'We?' Gertie croaked, pulling out a handkerchief to dab her eyes.

'A girl was with me. It's an odd coincidence, but Rosie now works at the Windmill too.'

'I've not met her.' Gertie shoved her hanky back up her sleeve. 'Does this Rosie know all about the looters being my family?'

'No . . . and I'm not going to tell her 'cos we just want to forget all about it. I'm not saying I wasn't angry to see those selfish buggers stealing . . .' Dawn pressed together her lips, feeling enough had been said on it all. She didn't want to end up having an argument with Gertie. 'Look, I've more important things on my mind, Gertie, and Rosie feels the same way. I expect you do too . . .'

'You're a good sort, Dawn,' Gertie mumbled. 'Sorry for snapping your head off that time, but I didn't know then what I know now. I really thought me brother was on his way overseas.'

Dawn shrugged. 'My mum often sticks up for me or George when we don't deserve it.'

Gertie suddenly burst into tears, using a sleeve to shield her eyes. 'You'll keep it all to yourself, won't you, Dawn?' she snuffled.

''Course . . . said so, didn't I?' She put an arm round Gertie's shoulders. 'Come on, let's go and make a pot of tea before we get cracking on the new routines.'

'What costumes you wearing today?' Gertie asked with a bright sniff.

'We're pixies, for a couple of matinees.'

'Kids'll love that,' Gertie said. 'Shame that sour-faced Olive don't bring her boys home and treat them to a show once in a while.'

'You managing to keep yer head down then?' Rufus Grimes flicked down the queen of hearts. Midge trumped it with a king and, grinning, pocketed his winnings.

Rufus scowled as he saw his cash disappearing into his brother-in-law's pocket.

'Yeah . . . not had no trouble so far.' Midge sat back, stretching out his short legs. He yanked down the brim of the cap he wore as though to conceal his features.

Rufus could have laughed: in his opinion if Midge wanted to disguise himself he'd be better off wearing a pair of stilts.

'So, you and Gertie come up with a good story, did you, when the Navy boys turned up looking for me?'

Rufus could feel his brother-in-law's steady stare on him, but he carried on shuffling cards. 'Yeah, said we was under the impression you was sailing the high seas.' Rufus raised a pair of lazy eyes to Midge's face. 'Did it, did yer?'

'Did what?' Midge drawled.

'They've got you down for a murder.'

'Don't know nuthin' about that,' Midge lied and took a nonchalant swig of whisky from the bottle balanced on his knee.

Midge wished he'd hopped it to a remote spot rather than getting himself enlisted when war broke out. But when a group of bombastic pals had gone along to the Navy recruitment centre, Midge had tagged along, caught up in the moment. Following the Battle of the River Plate Midge had had enough of fighting for king and country. He'd no intention of ending up with his legs blown off, as his fellow stoker had when their frigate got torpedoed.

'Should've left Hitler to it out in Europe,' Midge muttered. 'Weren't nothing to do with us what he was getting up to.'

'Fuckin' is now though.' Rufus was used to Midge sounding off to try and conceal his cowardice. But as Rufus had so far managed to avoid joining up, he knew not to have too much to say on the subject. Besides, he wished he'd kept quiet about the sailor who'd been found knifed in the back and dumped in a lifeboat about the same time as Midge jumped ship. Rufus reckoned the man opposite was a vicious git as well as being crafty, and he wouldn't put anything past him.

'Way I see it, I could've been blown to smithereens in the East End on the weekend I went missing.' Midge crossed his arms over his chest, looking quite smug. 'Bad raids fer days as I recall . . .'

'So how you gonna square it when you eventually turn up bright as a lark?' Having rolled himself a smoke Grimes generously held out his tin.

Midge started separating strands of tobacco, watching his stained fingers. 'War ain't over yet . . . I still could come a cropper,' he replied philosophically. 'Anyhow, cross them bridges when I come to 'em, won't I.'

Sticking the limp cigarette in a corner of his mouth he glanced about at their murky surroundings. They were huddled in a corner of an air-raid shelter, each man seated on an upturned box with another positioned between them and employed as a rough table. On its wonky top were scattered a pack of dog-eared playing cards, a depleted bottle of whisky and Rufus's tin of Old Holborn.

During the daytime, when bombing raids weren't expected, and ordinary folk went about their business, the shelters were mostly empty, but for rolls of bedding and makeshift bunks lining the walls. Midge saw the opportunity to be had, as did others. Tramps and deserters, looking for a hidey-hole, thought the vacant shelters a godsend. Petty thieves also passed through hoping to find abandoned possessions they could make a bob out of before the owners returned at night to find their stuff missing.

Midge wrinkled his nose against the odour of latrines pervading the air. Idly he began playing solitaire. "Course there's those two women who got a look at us when we did the outfitter's,' he said, the roll-up

71

wagging in his mouth. 'But I ain't too concerned over that 'cos doubt we'll run into them again.' He chuckled gruffly. 'Nice-looking pair of girls . . . wouldn't have minded getting down to business with either of 'em under different circumstances.' Midge carried on laying down cards on the box top. 'Funny thing is, Roof, I thought the older gel seemed familiar; ain't sure why though . . .'

Grimes shifted on his seat. He'd not owned up to any of the other members of the gang that he'd bumped into Dawn Nightingale, and worse than that she was his wife's friend and workmate. And he knew, even if Midge didn't, why the little man thought he knew Dawn: Midge had been to the shows at the theatre and had probably clocked her on stage.

Rufus had no interest in sophisticated entertainment, or classy women, so had never seen a revue himself. He'd no time for striptease; a good drink, a rough shag then home to bed was all he was after, when his wife made herself unavailable. In his own way he loved Gertie very much. It was just the constant itch in his balls that made him unfaithful.

Midge held out the bottle of whisky, swaying it by its neck. 'Want a swig?'

'Nah . . . better get back, me shift ain't finished yet.' Grimes got to his feet. Half an hour ago he'd been road sweeping and had taken an unofficial break, thinking he might find Midge sneaking about in the shelter. He'd fancied a game of cards, feeling his luck was in, but he'd lost five bob and that wouldn't go down well with Gertie if she found out.

He'd fancied a tot too, but he knew if his boss smelled booze on his breath he'd be for the high jump. Not that he liked shovelling up shit for a living . . . but Gertie would kill him if he lost his regular pay packet. Tonight he was too skint for a prossie, so he hurried up towards the exit, hoping to keep in his wife's good books at least till bedtime.

CHAPTER SEVEN

'Come on, you'll enjoy an outing, Mum.'

'Oh, I don't know, Dawn . . . the sky's overcast. It's bound to rain and the damp affects me knees.' Eliza Nightingale continued sitting obstinately at the parlour table, frowning at her clasped hands.

'We'll take an umbrella then, just in case,' Dawn persisted.

Dawn had a free afternoon and had got complimentary tickets for the variety matinee at the Windmill Theatre as they'd not sold out. Her mother had got herself ready, dressing in her best frock, but as usual Eliza was attempting to cry off at the last moment so she could stay at home close to the gin bottle.

'I'm not wasting these tickets!' Dawn forced her mother to her feet and into her coat. 'Come on, let's go. We don't want to miss the start of the show when the clown and juggler do a double act.'

Dawn began ushering her mother and brother towards the front door before one of them tried to duck out of the trip. Walking towards the bus stop she wondered why she went to the trouble of trying to arrange outings for her family when they acted as though they were doing her a favour in accepting a treat.

'Can't we go to the pictures instead?' George moaned as they joined the back of the bus queue. '*Captain Blood*'s back on at the Gaumont. Errol Flynn's me favourite.'

'No, we can't,' Dawn said on a sigh. 'You'll like the show; it's rather comical . . . and the mermaid costumes are nice . . .'

'Any nude girls in it?' George asked cheekily.

Eliza glanced, horrified, at her son. 'That's quite enough of that talk, young man,' she whispered, glancing about to see if anybody in the queue had heard his cheeky remark.

'Do you stand about with no clothes on?' George deliberately taunted his sister, and got an immediate clip round the ear from his pursed-lipped mother.

Eliza dragged her son to one side as a woman turned around to glare at them. 'Now you listen to me, young man. Any more of that and you'll go straight home.'

'Good,' George mumbled, although he knew he'd overstepped the mark. He'd been bored all morning and had been looking forward to getting out of the house on a Saturday afternoon. But he was reluctant to let on to his mother and sister how excited he was to be going to the theatre with them.

'No, I don't stand about with no clothes on. I'm a chorus dancer, as you know,' Dawn finally answered her brother in a steely tone.

'How do you know about nudes and so on at the Windmill Theatre?' Eliza muttered, glaring at Dawn as though it was all her fault George was talking dirty.

'One of the boys at school told me about it. He had a picture of the girls doing their gas-mask practice. They only had on their vests and drawers.'

'Well they weren't in the nude then,' Dawn retorted. 'And everybody does gas-mask training, even you kids at school.' She dragged her brother forward by an elbow as a bus wheezed to a halt at the kerb. 'Now behave yourself, George, or you'll ruin our trip out.' Dawn cast her eyes heavenwards. It wasn't an auspicious start to what she'd hoped would be a relaxing afternoon.

'Stop fidgeting, George.'

'Seats are itchy . . .' George shifted again on the brown velour seat but he soon forgot about his discomfort. He howled with laughter as the clown's red nose fell off for the second time and the juggler trod on it, causing him to lose concentration and drop his skittles. 'Need some glue for that conk?' George called, and earned himself a slap on the arm from his mother.

But Eliza was laughing too, and dabbed her streaming eyes with a hanky. The clown and juggler had reappeared to bring the show to a close with apparently farcical consequences. Probably nobody in the audience, apart from Dawn, knew that the performers' calamity was a well-rehearsed trick that always had the customers rolling in the aisles.

'Did you enjoy the show?' Dawn asked as the heavy curtain descended, although she already knew the answer to that. She had been gladdened to see her mother and brother hooting and clapping as the cast took a bow. The light-heartedness between them reminded her of days long ago, when George had been small and their mother drank in moderation. Standing up, Dawn waited patiently for the crowd of people in front of her to file towards the exit. She was pleased to see that Olive had sold more tickets during the afternoon. It was by no means a packed house but more than half-full. It was a good sign that many opening nights were still to come for Dawn and her colleagues at the Windmill, despite the opposition from rivals.

The Windmill might have been the trailblazer where nudes on stage were concerned, but many other venues had since jumped on the bandwagon, taking custom away from the original show. The management insisted the Windmill remain better than its imitators; all the cast and crew knew they must do their best to keep the queue of punters snaking along Great Windmill Street.

Once out in the foyer, Dawn told her mum she was just off to say a quick hello to the girls in the dressing room. Eliza, seeing Olive Roberts in the kiosk, diverted to speak to her.

'You're Olive, I remember you from last time I came over to a matinee with Dawn.' Eliza struck up a conversation while George read the colourful billboards advertising current and future shows.

'How are you keeping, Mrs Nightingale?'

'Oh, I'm bearing up, thanks, love. How're your kids doing?' she asked. 'You've got two boys, haven't you?'

'They're nice and settled down in Brighton . . . sea air and veg straight from the farm; so they're doing alright.'

''Spect they miss you though.' Eliza gave the woman a sympathetic smile. 'You off on a visit soon, are you?'

Olive gave a customer his change. 'I'm busy with my WVS duties so can't fit in too many trips away. But I do the journey from time to time to check up on things.'

'I went to a WVS meeting once,' Eliza said. 'A girl younger than me daughter was trying to tell us how to make jam. I said, listen here, love, I've been making jam since before you was a glint in yer father's eye.'

'I drive the mobile tea wagon and know first aid so turn up to help the poor souls after a raid. The servicemen are always grateful to have someone to talk to.' Olive pulled from her pocket a WVS badge. 'This goes on all the time after I've finished work here.'

'I've been fire-fighting with me neighbour,' Eliza said, feeling a bit left out.

'Victory's not far off, I know it,' Olive said serenely. 'My work then will be done and I can go home and put my feet up.'

'Home? Thought you were a Londoner, Olive.'

'I was born in Crouch End, but I've attachments elsewhere.'

'Where's that then?'

'Your lad back on a visit, is he?' It was a sly enquiry; Olive knew very well that Dawn's brother had never been evacuated and regularly sought shelter from the Blitz with his mother out the back of their house, in an Anderson shelter.

'George is home with me 'cos he's out to work soon.'

'How old is he?'

'Twelve . . . going on thirteen . . .' Eliza added defensively.

'He's not old enough yet to get a job. I could help you get him placed somewhere safe, you know, Eliza. I wouldn't like to see him hurt. The WVS has played a big part in the evacuation programme . . .'

'Very good of them. But no thanks,' Eliza abruptly interrupted.

'It's a shame England involved itself in this war.'

'It's a shame I can't get a thing I need from the shops,' Eliza countered.

'We need to have peace.'

'We'll have to win the bloody war first to get peace.' Eliza grimaced.

'The Nazis are a powerful force to reckon with. Perhaps too powerful for this small nation.'

'Not sure I agree with you on that,' Eliza retorted.

Olive sniffed and slammed shut the till drawer as Eliza stalked off to stand with her son and wait for Dawn to return.

'She might be young but she's got a dirty mouth on her.' Lorna Danvers smeared rouge off her cheek then lobbed the dirty cotton wool onto the dressing table. Picking up the cigarette that had been smouldering on a tea-stained saucer, she took a long drag. 'If she won't stop flirting with every man she claps eyes on she'll be getting herself and the Windmill a very bad reputation.'

'She's a mite too friendly with Gordon as well, if you ask me.' Sal Fiske added her two penn'orth to La-di-da Lorna's criticism. '*And* he's old enough to be her father.'

'Nobody did ask you, so button it.' Dawn had come into the dressing room on the tail end of the bitching, but she knew who they were talking about. She'd only popped in to say hello on her day off; now she wished she'd not bothered. She'd grown tired of listening to her colleagues ripping Rosie Gardiner to bits; it had been going on all week.

'What's up with you?' Lorna demanded, stubbing out her cigarette. 'Are you bosom pals with Rosie?'

'Just don't see that there's a need to talk behind her

back.' Dawn shrugged. 'If you think she's doing what she shouldn't, tell her to her face.'

'Ain't saying a word to her!' Sal stated bluntly. 'Not my task, is it, to teach her her manners. That's her mother's job.'

'Me mum's dead.' Rosie had just turned up to get ready for the evening show but had stopped outside the door, listening, before bursting in. She gave Dawn an exaggerated smile as thanks for championing her, but Rosie's bravado didn't disguise the fact that the gossip had upset her.

After an awkward silence Lorna took up the cudgels again. 'Well, sorry to hear about your mother, Rosie. But perhaps it explains a lot about the way you behave if you've not had her to guide you. The trouble is,' she warned with a finger wag, 'if you keep on acting like a trollop you'll get us all tarred with the same brush, and I for one am not having that.' Lorna surged out of her chair at the dressing table. 'We chorus girls might wear skimpy costumes but we go on stage with our modesty covered. You go out flashing your tits . . . and more.' Lorna's posh accent seemed more pronounced the angrier she got. 'I know it's your job to stand about starkers, but there's a right and a wrong way, just as there's a right and a wrong way for a girl to behave.'

'I'll wait for Phyllis to tell me I'm getting it all wrong, thanks all the same,' Rosie spat sarcastically. 'But I don't reckon she ever will, seeing as I'm the one all the fellows come to see.'

'You conceited little madam!' Sal spluttered indignantly.

'Now you listen to me, Rosie Gardiner,' Lorna said bossily. 'This is a theatre, not a knocking shop.' Having said her piece Lorna sashayed regally out of the dressing room, slamming the door behind her.

Dawn rolled her eyes. She'd worked in the theatre for over a year now and colleagues had come and gone; she'd been on stage with cockney girls, northern lasses and performers from overseas. But wherever the women hailed from there'd always been tension and rivalry between the nudes and the chorus. As far as Dawn was concerned she didn't give a monkey's if a girl removed her clothes to earn a living. What was the point in being jealous or spiteful when every day corpses of men, women and children were being dug out of their wrecked homes?

Dawn couldn't deny though that Rosie was overstepping the mark, and if the girl thought the management would overlook serious indiscretions, she had a rude awakening in front of her. The senior stagehand was a widower and though Gordon had an unrequited yen for Lorna he seemed flattered by Rosie's winks and pouts. And of course Rosie wasn't really interested in him; she was being a silly little tease, and that was unkind. Apart from that Dawn knew that Rosie would run a mile from a fellow who demanded more than a kiss and cuddle.

'Lorna's right, you know.' Sal tapped a Sobranie from its packet and lit it, then eyed Rosie over tobacco smoke. 'I saw you outside the stage door last night with half a dozen army fellows. You was flirting with all of them and it looked like things might turn nasty 'cos you were playing 'em off one against the other.'

Rosie's cheeks flooded with guilty colour at that reminder. In fact a scuffle *had* broken out between a private and a sergeant when she'd said she'd meet the senior of the two for a drink later in the week. She

81

pursed her lips, sitting in the chair vacated by Lorna. 'You're all just jealous because I get more attention from the men than the rest of you put together.'

'That's what you reckon, is it?' Sal had had enough of the younger woman's boasting. She shot to her feet, sticking her hands on her hips. Her loose silk wrap fell open, displaying her naked belly beneath.

'Yeah, it is what I think.' Rosie jumped up too, barging to confront her. 'I'm young and pretty and I've got a gorgeous figure, that's why I got taken on as a nude. You're getting fat and couldn't get a job with no clothes on even if you wanted to. Who'd want to look at your saggy tits?' she scoffed. 'And you're the wrong side of thirty, if you're a day . . .'

Sal leapt forward to slap Rosie's cheek. 'Wrong side of thirty?' she yelled, outraged. 'I'm twenty-six, you cheeky bitch. And I get more flowers sent in than you do.'

'*Flowers?* Who wants fuckin' flowers?' Rosie had stumbled from the unexpected blow but quickly got her balance. Swinging a fist in retaliation she caught Dawn on the side of the head as she moved to separate her warring colleagues.

'Sorry . . . sorry, Dawn . . . didn't mean to hit you.' Rosie wailed, mortified.

'For God's sake shut up, both of you,' Dawn thundered, rubbing her scalp. She'd thought her mother and brother might get on her nerves this afternoon; she'd not counted on her workmates being the problem instead.

'What's all the shouting about?' Marlene Brown had just arrived for the evening shows to find the three women glaring at one another. The atmosphere was icy despite the electric heater being fully on.

'You watch out!' Sal pointed a threatening finger at Rosie. 'Or I'm gonna rat on you to Phyllis, you trouble-making cow.' Grabbing her clothes off the chair Sal stormed towards the door.

'Didn't mean to get you, Dawn, it was an accident.' Rosie put an arm around Dawn in an attempt to apologise for whacking her. 'You're much prettier than me . . . it's just those two are always bitching, so I had to say something to shut them up.'

Dawn impatiently shrugged the younger woman off. She hadn't liked to hear her fellow dancers running Rosie down, but the truth was that Rosie *was* flirting too much and if she carried on she was likely to cause aggravation all round. Brawls in the theatre didn't happen that often, but when they did the management went mad, especially if one of their girls had sparked it.

'Anyone going to tell me what the commotion was all about?' Marlene shook the teapot that was on the table, grimacing in disappointment on finding it almost empty.

'Those two old hags are jealous of me.' Rosie scrubbed at her face. 'They was saying I act like a tart but Dawn stuck up for me, didn't you, Dawn?'

'I told them to stop talking about you behind your back. I didn't say they were telling lies,' Dawn retorted. Her blunt answer brought a forlorn look to Rosie's face. 'You know, don't you, what they mean?' she said with a significant nod. 'So think what you're doing, Rosie.' Rather than rub it in Dawn knew that it would be best to leave the younger woman to stew in her own juice. She said a brief goodbye, glad to be going back to her mum and brother.

Marlene shrugged off her dressing gown and watched

Rosie thoughtfully as the girl preened in front of the mirror. Rosie reminded Marlene of herself at eighteen: eager for compliments and excited to discover that her youth and beauty wielded such power over men. Marlene was now twenty-five but because she had an enviably youthful appearance, she easily got away with giving her age as twenty-one. The younger you claimed to be in the business, the better you got on, Marlene had come to learn. Lying about her age was just one of the tricks in her repertoire, and with her boyfriend's help, she'd certainly perfected a few.

'You gave Lorna and Sal what for, I take it?' Marlene said admiringly.

'Not going to take any notice of two over-the-hill hoofers, am I?' Rosie replied, teasing her platinum waves with a hairbrush.

'That's the spirit,' Marlene said approvingly. 'Us nudes have got to stick together.' She gave Rosie a lewd wink. 'Not your fault you've got fellows fighting over you, is it?'

'I never asked that sergeant to start on the other bloke for me.' Rosie was as eager to convince herself of her innocence as she was Marlene.

'Sergeant?' Marlene scoffed at the low rank. 'You could have a major with your looks, Rosie.'

That compliment prompted Rosie to smile and resume styling her hair. She'd already noticed that a few older officers were regularly coming in to give her the eye. But she didn't fancy getting involved with somebody's husband. She didn't want to cause that sort of trouble when she could enjoy herself with single men of her own age.

Young as she'd been at the time, she remembered her parents' shouting matches. Her dad had caught her mum with another man and thrown her out. Her mum had been allowed back after what seemed an age but had probably only been a matter of months. In a way Rosie had wished her mother hadn't returned. The arguments had stopped by then but the long cold silences had been even worse to bear; Rosie sometimes wondered if her mother had been glad she'd got ill and died rather than having to endure the awful atmosphere any longer.

'So what d'you reckon, then, Rosie? Shall we find you a rich handsome man who'll take you to posh hotels instead of treating you to a night at the flicks before he jumps on you?'

Rosie frowned at the hint that she slept with her admirers. 'I've not let any of them . . . you know . . .' she said falteringly. 'I'm not that sort of girl.'

Marlene eyed her mockingly. 'Honestly? You're really still pure as the driven?'

''Course,' Rosie said rather bashfully. 'Aren't you?' she asked curiously.

''Fraid not . . . but you are sweet . . .' Marlene murmured with a private smile. 'And all the more reason to get you the man you deserve . . .'

She turned to the wardrobe cupboard, her expression very thoughtful. She earned decent money working at the Windmill but her real employer was her boyfriend, a Maltese fellow by the name of Nikola. Marlene, in common with others, called him Malt.

Malt was a heavy-set, swarthy fellow who liked to think people respected him because he'd fostered for himself a hard reputation. In fact the men he classed as his rivals saw themselves as his superiors and despised him for trying to muscle in on their territory when he'd neither the brains nor the financial clout to do so. Malt was under his uncle's thumb and just a hireling.

But Marlene seemed enthralled by her pimp, and when he told her that he needed to run more girls if he was to be a success and earn enough for them to settle down, she'd eagerly offered to do what she could to help. She'd got a job at the Windmill Theatre at Malt's suggestion because he'd told her he didn't want any old slags but classy birds: young, shapely and preferably blonde had been the shopping list of requirements he'd given to his girlfriend.

Marlene turned about, holding up a hanger on which was a wispy Grecian toga. When on stage it was artfully draped about the nudes' hips. She looked past her costume at Rosie; the younger woman had put down her hairbrush and was now outlining her mouth in different colours; first one shade then another was put on and wiped off with tissue. Marlene felt satisfied that Rosie fitted Malt's bill. All she had to do was get Rosie away from home because the blonde seemed ripe for the picking. She'd already mentioned to Rosie that she had a spare bedroom going begging and wanted very little rent for it. Marlene had seen Rosie's eyes light up at the thought of her own little place, away from her father's watchful eye. Rosie was pretty and popular with the servicemen and sooner or later she'd fall for one and want to take him back for the night. So Marlene reckoned she'd need to do very little to lure Rosie into her nest.

CHAPTER EIGHT

'Be reasonable, love,' Rufus appealed with an elaborate gesture. 'I can't take kids with me on a job. Midge will go nuts fer a start, and Pop won't like it.'

'I don't care about them! I'm sick of carting our four boys about with me.' Gertie pulled on her gloves and wheeled the pram containing baby Harold into the hallway. Adam, who was six, grasped the handle in readiness for the off while Simon, who was just two years older than baby Harold, was swung up by Gertie and settled atop the pram's coverlet. With a hand on his shoulder she propelled the eldest boy in her husband's direction. 'Joey ain't staying here on his own in case the house gets hit while we're out. Can't risk it. If the Grimeses' luck's out, and please God it ain't, then we all go together as a family.'

The idea of one of the boys dying alone in the house was enough to make Gertie feel faint. She was determined that at all times the kids would either be protected by her, or her husband. 'You take Joey with you, Rufus. I've me job to do and old Pickering won't like having

Joey turn up after he caught him dipping in his coat pocket.' Her eldest son got a reproving glare.

'Best take Joey with you then; our kitty could do with a boost,' Rufus joked, giving his son a wink.

'Think it's a lark, do you?' Gertie snapped. 'You'll be laughing on the other side of your face if me boss turns nasty. Just as well Joey didn't take nothing that day . . .'

'I did.' Joey was anticipating Rufus's approval and he soon got it. He'd not owned up sooner about the theft because he'd thought he'd get a clump, but his father had delighted him a moment ago by praising him for stealing.

'What d'you find then, son?' Rufus asked eagerly.

'You did *what*?' Gertie squeaked, swinging a horrified look between her husband and eldest son. 'Give it here!' she demanded. 'I'll take it with me and give it back. You little sod!' She snatched the folded pound note that Joey had withdrawn from the top of his sock where he'd had it stashed. No sooner had she appropriated the cash than her husband prised open her fingers.

'You can't do that, you silly cow!' Rufus spluttered. 'Pickering can't be sure Joey's had it or he'd have cut up rough at the time. 'Sides, I could do with that quid.' He gave Joey a grin and a rewarding pat on the shoulder. 'But I'll give it you back, son, don't you worry about that. You deserve to keep it for being shrewd.'

'Deserves to keep it?' Gertie bawled, making the baby start to cry. 'What he deserves is a hiding!' When her gormless husband continued smiling soppily at the miscreant Gertie gave Joey a hefty whack on the backside that shot him forward a pace. 'That's for lying as well as thieving.' She felt her heart thudding. If Pickering had made Joey turn out his pockets that evening, he'd have called the police there and then, and got her arrested. She forcefully recounted her theory to her husband.

'But he got away with it, didn't he?' Rufus came back at her, chuckling.

'You wouldn't have been so jolly if the coppers had started snooping around here, asking lots of questions about your thieving son. They might just have found out where Joey gets his ideas from. Fancy a spell in gaol, do you?' Gertie taunted. She stuck out a hand for Rufus to put the stolen money on her palm.

Rufus closed his fist on the pound note, remaining silent, then he grabbed Joey by the hand and yanked him towards the front door. 'I'll take him with me then . . . just this once . . .'

Gertie sent a silent curse after him while buttoning up her children's coats. A few evenings a week she cleaned Wilfred Pickering's office. He was the accountant who did the Windmill's books. She'd readily agreed to take on extra shifts when she'd heard him talking to Phyllis about contacting an agency for domestic help. The extra cash always came in handy. Gertie had only been doing Pickering's job two months so had been mortified when the man had recently caught Joey in the office cloakroom, delving into his overcoat pockets. Gertie had managed to persuade the fellow that the similar-looking gabardine coats hanging on the pegs had confused Joey. She'd said her son thought he'd been looking in her coat pocket for a handkerchief. Gertie would have liked to believe her own tale, but in her heart she knew that Joey was out of the same mould as his father, and getting more like Rufus every day. If the accountant caught Joey at it again he'd not listen to excuses.

* * *

'What the hell d'you think yer doing bringing a kid along?' Midge snarled.

Rufus positioned himself in front of his son when his associate lunged forward as though angry enough at the sight of his nephew to clip Joey's ear.

'Ain't nuthin' to do with you whether I bring along one of me sons or not.'

'Got enough on our plates getting the stuff away without having bleedin' kids getting under our feet.' Midge pointed a finger at Joey. 'Keep him out of me way or I'll land the tyke one.'

'Try it and I'll knock you on your back,' Rufus spat, eyeing the small man up and down. In common with his wife, Rufus adored his children even if sometimes he had a funny way of showing it. With no more ado Rufus hoisted Joey to sit on the handcart and the little party started off at quite a pace along the dark streets.

As soon as the air-raid sirens had sounded earlier in the evening the same trio of men who'd robbed the outfitters had met at their prearranged spot by the recreation ground for a bit of bomb-chasing.

Midge had turned up with the cart that was stored in Pop's lock-up. It was already loaded with some tatty household paraphernalia, as was usual on a job. If spotted, while out in a blackout, they appeared to be a bunch of fellows with goods salvaged from their bombed-out home.

Hearing an explosion off to the left they started hurtling in that direction. Joey, grinning in excitement with his auburn hair fluttering about his small face, clung to the handles, as the men charged along deserted black back streets.

Suddenly Rufus pulled back on the cart, hissing a

warning. He'd spotted an ARP warden on the opposite side of the road.

'Alright over there?' The warden raised a hand in greeting.

The trio immediately mumbled back a chorus of agreement while Joey dipped his head and silently stared wide-eyed from beneath his brows.

'Get yourselves under cover, quick as you can. No lights,' the warden called out.

'Will do,' Rufus answered, nodding solemnly, while the other two men shuffled aimlessly.

'Like fuck I'll get under cover,' Midge chortled beneath his breath as the warden carried on about his business. 'In a minute I'm gonna earn meself enough to keep me in pussy every night for a week.'

Rufus shoved Midge in the shoulder. 'Watch yer mouth; kids about . . .'

'Ain't my fault you brought him along on a job,' Midge snarled belligerently. He looked Rufus up and down. Considering the man was a prolific skirt-chaser and would put a leg over anything under seventy Midge thought Rufus had a cheek coming out with that one.

Lenny Purves had barely spoken so far; he was sick of his two cohorts constantly sniping at one another when they were on a job. He was out to get the stuff and get home and had been too busy scouring the streets for a likely premises to rob to bother telling Rufus he also thought the man had a nerve bringing along a brat to slow them down. But Lenny had just spotted a good prospect up ahead.

''Ere . . . look . . . that'll do . . .'

Lenny spurted ahead, the other two trotted behind

and within minutes the group was outside a large haber-dashery store. It was situated on a corner, away from the main street, but close enough to the explosions to have been damaged.

'You clumsy git! Look what you made me do!' Midge Williams clenched his fist and shook it to ease its throbbing.

Purves had just bumped into him while frantically loading up the cart with merchandise. To steady himself Midge had grabbed at the nearest wall and sliced his palm on a shard of glass and some rusty nails sticking out of the broken window frame.

'Get that bandaged up at the hospital, can't you?' the culprit blustered, dodging out of the way of a kick aimed at him by the injured man.

'Yeah, and get asked all sorts of questions . . . like me name,' Midge hissed, swiping out again with a foot.

Lenny Purves drew out his handkerchief and threw it at Midge by way of apology. 'Here, use that to bind it. I'll get me dad to take a look at it, if you like. He's a dab hand with a needle and cotton and a bit of paraffin gauze.'

'Fuck off . . .' Midge muttered, using his teeth to hold one end of the snotty linen while winding the length about his bloodied palm.

'You two done gossiping and gonna lend a hand?' Rufus growled. He'd whipped his son off the top of the cart to make room for the boxes he was loading up. The cartons of blankets had been heavy and he was puffing with exertion. ''Course we could just piss about for a bit longer till the coppers turn up,' he said sarcastically, dumping some sheets and tablecloths on top of the blankets and closing the box lids.

Rufus had been under instructions from Gertie to get hold of a decent sheet and blanket if he could. Tonight it looked like he might be able to get his wife her wish. The haberdashery had been the perfect target for them in Rufus's estimation, being a double-fronted shop. Tremors had taken out one pane, saving them the trouble of bricking it.

Rufus glanced at the crisp folded sheets, gleaming white, then at Midge. The little sneak was never more likely to be otherwise occupied than he was now, dancing around with a damaged hand. Rufus reckoned he could filch something without his brother-in-law noticing and telling Pop. Midge was effing and blinding while trying to staunch the flow of blood from his wound. Rufus reckoned, from the amount of claret down Midge's front, that he needed a few stitches, and he told him so.

'Gonna swing fer you.' Midge pointed a finger at Lenny. 'You're a fuckin' liability, you are.'

Lenny again dodged Midge's vicious boot.

'Let's get going,' Rufus muttered. 'There's a crowd gathering up there.' He cocked his head at the High Street about fifty yards away. 'I'll take the cart back this time as Joey's with me, to save his legs; you two make yerselves scarce. I'll meet you in Houndsditch in about an hour's time.'

'Yeah . . . make sure you come and meet us right away, 'n' all. And come alone this time.' Midge stared suspiciously at Rufus. His brother-in-law always wanted something extra before the stuff got divvied up to keep quiet that greedy missus of his. If Midge's hand hadn't been giving him gyp he'd have made sure he was the one pushing away the haul and Rufus could walk home with Joey.

Midge and Gertie had never been close as kids. In fact Midge had been closer to Rufus, even though his brother-in-law was a few years his senior, being as they'd played in the same neighbourhood football team. In Midge's opinion Gertie was a whiner, always wanting this and that. Instead of being outraged that Rufus was always cheating on his sister, Midge could see his brother-in-law's point. It was obvious Gertie thought a lot more of her four kids than she did of her husband. He was just there to keep the cash rolling in. And Rufus knew it.

Midge felt blood dripping from the sodden cotton wound about his palm and stuffed the hand into his pocket. He realised he'd have to take Lenny up on his offer to let his old man stitch the wound because he couldn't go to the hospital and be interrogated.

At the corner of the street the men split up: Midge melted away into a side alley and Purves carried on straight ahead.

Rufus puffed and grunted, pushing the cart towards the warehouse in Houndsditch where Pop stored the stolen stuff. On top of the newly plundered linen, he'd tossed the jumble of tatty decoy pots, pans and eiderdowns, helpfully concealing the haul from any prying eyes. Adding to the load now on the cart was his son's weight.

'Jump off, Joey, and give us a hand pushing it,' Rufus grumbled. He might look to be a brawny type but he was flabby and averse to exerting himself.

Joey quickly did as his father asked, enjoying the adventure. 'We got some stuff for mum?' he piped up. 'Put her in a good mood if you bring something in, won't it?'

'You mind yer nose,' Rufus barked. 'Ain't nuthin' to

do with you so don't go getting cocky just 'cos you was allowed to come with me this one time.'

Joey sunk his chin towards his chest. He'd like a chance to have another outing with the men doing a job. He might be only nine but he wasn't daft. He'd listened to conversations and knew his father and uncle were involved in bad stuff. He knew too that his mum did alright out of it, although she pretended to be against it all when it suited her.

'What was that?' Rufus halted, squinting into blackness.

'Torch . . . up there . . .' Joey pointed helpfully at a pinprick of dancing light.

Rufus and his cronies knew that the authorities were getting wise to the organised looting going on under cover of the air raids. Police patrols were often out scouring the streets for bomb-chasers.

'Shit!' Rufus ground out between his teeth. He started rearranging the stuff on the cart to try and conceal the stolen boxes. Quickly he grabbed Joey and sat him down on a pile of towels.

'Hey . . . you over there . . . alright, are you, sir?'

Rufus averted his face and blinked, blinded as he was by the beam of a torch, but he glimpsed the silhouettes of a pair of helmeted men and his heart leapt to his throat. The constables were heading towards him on the opposite pavement. He raised a hand but kept going with a mumbled greeting.

The two policemen crossed the road, swinging an arc of torchlight in front of their boots.

'You've taken a hit, have you?' the older policeman asked sympathetically, casting an eye over Joey and the cart's jumbled contents.

'Yeah . . .' Rufus croaked. 'Gotta get going; the wife's waiting on me to bring this lot.'

'Any injured? We can get you some help,' the younger constable offered. 'Whereabouts d'you live, sir?'

'No need, honest; we're managing as we are, ain't we, Joey?' Rufus tried to walk quickly on but the constables tagged alongside him.

'Where you heading now, then? Got family to put you up, have you?'

'Yeah . . . that's it.' Rufus licked his dry lips.

'Where do they live, then?'

'Them people we come past need some help,' Joey said, rubbing his eyes then sprawling over the cart as though tired. Only Rufus knew that his son was concealing some pilfered pillowcases wrapped in cellophane.

'Who's that then, son?' the older policeman asked, cocking an ear Joey's way.

'Man back there got his hand cut by glass . . . there was blood everywhere . . . felt sick . . .'

The wail of the all clear made Rufus jump in alarm. He knew lights would be coming on and the stuff on the cart would then be much easier to identify as stolen.

'That man fainted . . .' Joey said. 'Blood all down him . . .'

'All the best to you and your family.' The senior officer clapped Rufus on the back, then he and his colleague set off back up the road in the direction Joey had indicated.

'Get off the bleedin' barrow,' Rufus hissed to his son as soon as he judged the coppers to be at a safe distance.

Joey hopped down and put his weight behind his father's in pushing the cart. He looked cheekily up at Rufus. 'Can I come out with you again, Dad?' he asked.

Rufus gave him a grin. 'We'll see.' He chucked his son under the chin by way of reward before the two of them started downhill at a run, hooting and pulling back on the handles to prevent the loot getting away from them.

CHAPTER NINE

Following a robbery Midge would usually dive under cover to lie low then at dead of night make his way to Houndsditch to join his pals in examining their plunder. This evening though he had diverted immediately to the Purves house and arrived there before Lenny strolled into view some five minutes later.

Initially, Midge had considered getting Gertie to bind up his cut hand, but she wouldn't be pleased to see him, the miserable cow. Gertie knew he'd deserted and was living rough, but she'd not even sent a couple of bob with Rufus to help him out. And Rufus hadn't given him a penny either; he was as tight-fisted as they came. So Midge needed his looting money just to survive.

Midge cursed his bad luck; his hand was throbbing and he knew that his wound needed more than a bit of wet lint dabbed on it. The gaping flesh on his palm was sticky, caked with fluff from his pocket and hardened snot from Lenny's dirty handkerchief. Midge had started to feel light-headed; he knew he'd lost a lot of blood and the pain was spreading up his arm.

As Lenny unlatched the gate Midge darted from his hiding place in the hedge opposite.

'Fuck's sake! You nearly gave me a bleedin' heart attack!' Lenny gulped, having turned white with shock.

'I'll give you a bleedin' heart attack, alright,' Midge snarled. 'Take a fucking gander at yer handiwork!'

Despite the darkness Lenny could see that the upturned palm his associate had thrust beneath his nose was a mess.

'Your old man up to this?' Midge poked his rigid fingers against Lenny's chest.

'Yeah . . . yeah . . . said so, didn't I . . .' Lenny muttered. In fact, as far as he was aware, his father had only ever once stitched up a wound, and Lenny had been the recipient of Popeye Purves's handiwork. Lenny would never forget the pain of it; he had been thirteen at the time and still at school when he'd almost sliced off the end of his thumb using his father's paper guillotine. Even at that tender age, Lenny had been on the lookout for a sly chance to make some money at his old man's expense. He'd appropriated his father's factory key and attempted to print off some posters for a butcher's shop opening up. The proprietor had promised him a pound for two gross of flyers done under the counter. His father had quoted double that figure and when Popeye had found out his son's game he'd been incensed. To teach Lenny a lesson he said he'd see to the damage rather than let a doctor charge him an arm and a leg for stitching up the devious tyke.

'Get the door open, then.' Midge gave Lenny a shove in the back with his good hand. He turned his head, scouring the dark pavements. Midge was always conscious that, once it got round he'd deserted, a nosy parker might report a sighting of him to the authorities.

When inside the house Lenny called out for his father . . . and got no reply. 'He's probably pissed in the back room,' Lenny said jovially.

'Go and find the squint-eyed old sod,' Midge muttered. 'Me hand's aching fit to drop off.'

Lenny understood the seriousness in the situation when Midge swayed and stuck a buttock on the wall for support. He knew Williams wasn't putting it on and he'd obviously lost a lot of blood. 'Go and sit in there.' Lenny opened the door to the front parlour. 'I'll fetch me dad.' He hurried off but was conscious that his father might tell him to fuck off, and Midge too, if he'd got too comfortable with his brown ales.

'Didn't hear you come in . . . been listening to the wireless. What you done to yerself then, mate?'

'Ain't what I've done, is it?' Midge swung about as Lenny's father shuffled in. 'It's what that dozy sod of a son of yours did to me.'

Popeye Purves was a tall, thin man like Lenny. But, now sixty-three, the years had given him a stoop that made him appear a head shorter than his son. But he was no slouch where money was concerned; he had an agile brain and had, almost from day one, seen the profit to be had from the Blitz. The blackouts and bomb-damaged premises all provided Popeye with opportunities to fill his warehouse in Houndsditch with stock. His little gang didn't target just retail premises; in the past people had returned to their damaged houses following a bombing raid to find they'd had a visit from Pop's men. Of course they'd no idea who'd removed their furniture and valuables while they were crouching in a shelter, they just knew that decency and community spirit was missing in some folk.

Frank Purves's nickname made it seem he had bulging eyes but in fact they were badly crossed, making it unclear where his attention was. Midge was pleased to see the fellow seemed steady on his feet, even if he had been drinking, so should be capable of stitching him up.

Midge held out his palm, moving it to and fro beneath the older man's grizzled features in the hope Popeye would get a good enough look at the damage. When Frank continued frowning, hands in pockets, Midge cussed, about to take himself off round to his sister's after all. He'd barely moved an inch when he felt his fingers caught in a surprisingly firm grasp.

'That don't look too good, son.' Having stated the bleeding obvious, Popeye sucked his teeth. He increased pressure on the hot swelling on Midge's flesh until Midge yelped and snatched back his hand.

'Charge you a couple o' nicker to sort that out and throw in a half-bottle of Scotch so you get a good night's sleep. Be right as rain in the morning, you will.' In fact Popeye knew that it wasn't Scotch; it wasn't even proper whisky. He'd got a few bottles of rotgut off John Gardiner as a deposit for some labels he'd ordered for a forth-coming batch of gin.

'You're gonna charge me?' Midge exploded in outrage. 'Give him the bill!' He pointed at Lenny, shuffling sheep-ishly to and fro.

'I'll stump up for it,' Lenny agreed in a mumble. He felt guilty about Midge getting injured, but was happy to shift some of the blame. 'Weren't all my fault, y'know. If Rufus hadn't brought his bleedin' kid along we'd have had our minds properly on the job. I got distracted . . .'

'Brought a kid along on a job, did he?' All of a sudden Popeye was a different man. He began blinking rapidly, lips drawing flat against stumpy brown teeth. Any chance his profits might suffer and Frank sprang to attention. 'That ain't on, and I'll make sure and fucking tell him so!' Popeye had never been out robbing with his gang; he thought he was the brains of the outfit and should put some distance between himself and his minions. Besides, he was too unfit to walk any distance, let alone sprint to safety if it became necessary.

Midge could see that his boss was het up but, given his circumstances, he snarled, 'Never mind about the kid; I'm feeling right rough.' Uninvited he sank down into a chair and held out his hand. 'Get on with it, will you, Pop? I'll have to shove off soon.'

'I'll get the sewing box,' Popeye said grumpily. 'See if I can find something to clean it with too, shall I?'

'Yeah,' Midge mumbled, glancing at the debris stuck on his palm. The sight of it was making him feel queasy. 'Go and get us the Scotch then,' he grunted at Lenny, as soon as Pop was out of earshot.

Within a short while Frank Purves was back with an old biscuit tin filled with needles and cottons and other sewing paraphernalia. To Midge's amazement Popeye managed to thread up quickly. The proof that the fellow could see straight should have calmed Midge; in fact it had the reverse effect and he sensed his stomach lurch.

'Right-oh, give us yer hand,' Popeye said rather jovially.

'Thought you was gonna clean it,' Midge reminded his boss, snapping closed his fingers to protect his throbbing flesh.

'Oh, yeah . . .' Popeye snatched the bottle of Scotch

from Lenny who'd just reappeared. Roughly prising open Midge's fingers he tipped some onto his quivering hand. 'Here . . . take a swig,' Popeye said solicitously as Midge screeched in agony.

Midge needed no second telling. He took a gulp, threw up down his front, then as the needle touched his skin he passed out cold.

Dawn had picked the post off the doormat that morning; both letters had been for her. The demand to pay the electricity account had been stuffed in a drawer. Her mother always left the bills untouched for her to deal with when payday came around. The other envelope bore Bill's writing and she'd opened it straight away.

'When's Bill getting his next leave?'

'He hasn't said.' Dawn folded the letter, half-read. She wouldn't need to finish the few paragraphs to know that there'd be no mention of Bill visiting her in London.

'Has he proposed yet? I know you're missing him.' Eliza pushed the iron to and fro on the shirt on the kitchen table while speaking. Picking it up by the collar she gave the garment a cursory inspection then hung it over the back of a chair.

Dawn simply shook her head in response to the likelihood of an engagement.

'George! Come on, hurry up and get downstairs! Time you was off to school!' Having poked her head into the hallway to bawl those instructions to her son Eliza turned about to stare thoughtfully at her daughter. 'Penny for 'em,' she persevered. All she got in answer was a shrug and smile from Dawn.

Dawn felt unable to say what was on her mind. Perhaps she was being daft in suspecting that Bill might soon throw her over, so didn't want to voice her suspicions. Not so long ago the idea of them breaking up would have left her heartbroken but now she wasn't sure how she'd react.

In the three short letters she'd received since she'd last seen Bill, he'd signed off casually rather than romantically. His letters still contained amusing information about the antics he and his colleagues got up to – in between them patrolling the skies for enemy planes to shoot down – but Dawn had noticed there had been fewer endearments. And her letters back to him had been similarly cooler in tone.

They had parted on good terms at the railway station on the morning he'd journeyed back to East Anglia, but Dawn couldn't forget how withdrawn, almost sulky, he'd been on their last evening together. They'd not stayed in a hotel because of the air raid and had been stuck down the underground dozing on each other's shoulders for the best part of the night. They hadn't emerged from the shelter, crumpled and tired, till after first light.

'Here you are . . . eat that up before it goes cold.' Eliza pushed a plate of jammy toast towards her son as he entered the kitchen in his vest. 'And keep that shirt clean. Can't go washing and ironing midweek 'cos you've got into a scrap with a pal and got mud all down your front.'

'He ain't a pal or I wouldn't have had a scrap with him.' George grinned.

'That's enough lip from you.'

'Buy me a spare shirt, then you won't have to do no extra washing, will you?' George took a greedy bite of toast.

'Buy you another, indeed!' Eliza clipped George round the ear. 'Made of money, am I?' She raised her eyebrows. 'Hear that, Dawn?' She jerked a nod at George. 'He thinks we're flush enough to be buying new school shirts.'

'This is still damp round the collar.' George moaned, unbuttoning the shirt at his throat.

Dawn had unfolded Bill's letter again, but instead of reading to the end she shoved it into her bag. Exasperated, she turned to her brother. 'You've got too much to say for yourself lately, you ungrateful sod.'

Taken aback by his sister's reprimand George grabbed his jacket off the peg and slammed out of the house.

'Going to the privy . . .' Eliza muttered, frowning at Dawn. She'd known George was just larking about rather than giving serious backchat.

'You look better since you've stopped drinking so much gin,' Dawn blurted when her mother came in from the garden. She regretted being snappy because things at home had improved lately and she didn't want to upset the applecart. She had resolved to get the three of them out as a family more often as the theatre trip had seemed so beneficial to her mother.

Eliza rinsed her hands under the tap and flicked them into the butler sink. 'Yeah . . . well . . . cup of tea don't taste so bad when you've got a bit of sugar to put in it,' she retorted. 'Used up me rations though. Going up to make the beds now.'

She went out without looking at Dawn, something that made her daughter grimace wryly. Eliza would never talk for too long on the topic of her drinking. But Dawn was optimistic things would keep getting better for them as a family.

'Off to the shops,' she called out to her mother, slipping into her coat.

Dawn walked briskly along the street hoping to catch up with her brother as he was walking to school.

'How d'you think Mum seems?' Dawn asked, falling in step with George.

'What d'you mean?' George blew into his cold hands then stuck them in his pockets. It was a bitterly cold February day.

'You must have noticed there aren't so many empties lying around these days. Not long ago she wouldn't have washed and ironed your shirt for you during the week. If I'd been staying over at the theatre, and not around to rinse it through, you'd've had to wear it dirty.'

Dawn glanced at George, waiting for a comment, but he simply looked bored. ''Course you could always try putting a bit of washing in the sink and dunking it up and down yourself,' she added dryly. Still her brother trudged silently at her side. 'Mum seems more cheerful, don't you think?' She made another attempt at conversation.

'She's got a boyfriend, that's why.'

Dawn stopped dead. Catching hold of George's elbow she pulled him round to face her. 'Got a boyfriend?' she parroted. 'Mum has? How d'you know that?'

'Saw 'em together.' George liberated his arm and ambled on.

'But . . . how d'you know this fellow's not a friend, or a neighbour? What does he look like? Where did you see them?' Dawn charged after George, rattling off her questions, wondering how he could seem so casual about it all.

'He came round one day just after I got in from school.

106

Didn't recognise him from round here.' George pulled a face. 'Mum weren't pleased to see him anyway. She sent me upstairs but I could hear her giving him what for even though she kept her voice down so I wouldn't hear what they said. The bloke went off . . . then a few minutes later she went out to meet him.'

'Did you follow them?' Dawn asked, intrigued. She wasn't sure how she felt about the news other than being shocked that Eliza had kept something so important to herself.

'I craned out of the window and could see them up the top of the road together. They was standing really close; thought they were going to have a clinch.'

'You should have said something before,' Dawn burst out.

'Why?' George shrugged. 'Ain't as if she'll stop seeing him for us.'

The bitterness in her brother's voice surprised Dawn. 'It could be a good thing that Mum's got a boyfriend,' she gently pointed out. 'Whoever he is, he might be very nice and be good for her. Perhaps she might introduce us to him soon,' she added brightly.

'Don't care what she does.'

'Don't be like that, George.' Dawn smiled wryly. 'Mum's not going to up sticks and abandon you; besides you've always got me to fetch and carry for you,' she teased.

'Ha, ha,' George snorted sourly.

'Perhaps Mum's sobering up because this bloke's told her to. That's not a bad thing, is it?'

'Suppose . . .' George mumbled. 'Meeting me friend over there,' he said and suddenly crossed the road.

Dawn watched her brother lope towards the opposite

pavement where a boy was lounging against a wall. She felt confused; she had imagined that her mother was finally making an effort to curb her drinking for her own sake, or her children's sake, but perhaps Eliza was on her best behaviour for a new man in her life.

Dawn's thoughts circled back to the man in *her* life . . . but for how much longer Bill would be in her life, she'd not a clue. She knew he had cooled towards her because she hadn't slept with him on their final evening together. She had been tempted to and had the sirens not sent them hurtling into the shelter . . . who knows? She might have been a different girl . . . woman . . . today. Dawn wasn't a prude: she joined in with some very salty talk at the Windmill Theatre. But she bucked against any form of bullying – even the subtle persuasiveness that randy men used to get a girl into bed with them.

Dawn was honest enough to admit that she'd like to salvage her pride by being the one to end things between them; but first she had to make sure that's what she really wanted because there was a way to breathe new life into their romance. And if she decided to go along with it, all she had to do was write and tell Bill to book them a room in a hotel next time he was in town.

CHAPTER TEN

'Mrs Grimes . . .'

Gertie muttered beneath her breath on hearing her boss's crisp accent, but she looked over her shoulder with a fixed, pleasant expression.

'Mrs Grimes . . . the box room needs cleaning again. There's still a cobweb hanging from the ceiling. I pointed it out earlier in the week, if you remember.'

'So you did, sir . . . my mistake.' Gertie was already returning little Harry to his pram. She deftly buttoned up her blouse, hoping that Pickering hadn't noticed what she'd been doing. She'd only stopped sweeping up to feed the little 'un because he'd been whimpering. The other kids she'd managed to leave at home with Rufus. Her husband had moaned, as he always did, about having the boys foisted on him, but he'd backed down, as he always did, when she reminded him he welcomed the extra pay packet she brought in on a Friday night. Gertie had warned Rufus that she'd need to toe the line or lose her job; Pickering's eyes had been on her ever since that occasion Joey had been nabbed dipping. Gertie knew the fewer kids she had with her the less chance there was of one of them acting up and getting her the sack.

Briskly, Gertie pulled the broom from where she'd propped it in the corner and marched determinedly over the threshold of the box room. In her opinion it was only a store for mouldy old files so what did a few cobwebs matter, but she kept her lips tightly buttoned. She wouldn't grumble because very few employers would tolerate a char bringing her kids in to work. In the past Pickering had rarely been about. By the time Gertie turned up to do her shift, he'd gone home, and the elderly caretaker would beetle out of his cabin round the back and let her in to the office building. Only occasionally had Gertie found the accountant still working at his desk. But that had changed since Joey got caught out with his hand in the man's coat pocket.

Wielding the broom at the ceiling Gertie zealously swung it to and fro, catching the sooty web on its bristles. She sensed her boss had come up behind her so said cheerfully, 'There you are, sir . . . all spick and span now.'

Before Gertie could lower her arms she felt two hands clamp on her breasts then a burst of hot breath made the hair at her nape stand on end. She squealed, dropping the broom in shock, and tried to swing about. But despite his scrawny appearance Pickering had firm hold of her.

'There, there . . . no need for alarm, my dear,' Pickering murmured. 'I think you know I like you. And I know an invitation when I see one. Open your blouse again and let me feast my eyes on that splendid bosom of yours.' He began kneading Gertie's swollen breasts beneath her cotton blouse, making a nipple leak milk.

Gertie struggled free, and whipping around, she gagged in revulsion when she saw him licking his wet fingers. 'What d'you think yer doing?' she squeaked.

'Come . . . show me them both . . . let me at least have a look and a stroke.'

Gertie gawked at him, wondering if he'd gone mad, or whether she'd always been mistaken in thinking him a little mouse of a man. Her boss's complexion was flushed with excitement but when he raised his eyes from her bust to her face Gertie noticed they had a ruthless glint. He advanced on her, roughly undoing a few of her buttons.

'Get off! I'm a married woman!' Gertie shrilled, and her hands began frantically batting at his fingers to keep him at bay.

'I should hope so too with that brood of yours,' Pickering chortled. 'How is that eldest boy? You know the one I mean. I haven't seen him since he stole from me. Perhaps I was too lenient that day and should have pursued the matter . . .'

Gertie's battling hands became still then dropped to her sides as her mind raced ahead. So that was his game, was it? He was hinting at reporting the incident if she didn't play ball with him. Gertie was on the point of telling him to go to hell and stick his job, but the words refused to roll off her tongue. Stunned as she was by Pickering's bizarre behaviour her mind had swiftly dived on the consequences for Joey and for Rufus if the accountant made good on his insinuation to cause trouble for them. If her boss went to the police, and Joey was interviewed, Gertie reckoned her boy would crack under pressure. God only knew what Joey might come out with now he'd been on jobs with Rufus's gang. Gertie was feeling a blasted idiot now for having insisted her husband take the boy out looting with him. Then, there were consequences for her too: Wilfred Pickering didn't turn up very often at the theatre to have meetings with the management, but if a stray word reached Phyllis's ears that Gertie Grimes's son was a thief, Gertie would be mortified. She liked to keep her business private and gossip went round that place like greased lightning . . .

Pickering had read her fears; he had his head cocked to one side, his pale, crafty eyes fixed on her.

'I lost two pound notes from my coat pocket, you know.'

'Wasn't *two* quid . . .' Gertie protested before biting her lip.

'Was it not? How much was it then, Gertie? You know, don't you, because you set him to it.'

'I did not! I'd never do such a thing! I ain't a thief.'

'But your boy is, Gertie, isn't he.' Pickering was again reaching for her buttons, very confidently. 'You don't mind if I call you Gertie, do you?'

This time Gertie made only a token resistance when he slid his hand inside her blouse to pull and squeeze at her warm flesh. A moment later his sparsely covered pate dropped below her eyeline and he started to lick her nipple. Gertie stumbled backwards a few steps, trying to escape him, grimacing in disgust. But he hung on, and when he had her backed against the cold filing cabinet and she'd nowhere to retreat to, Gertie kneed him and nipped past.

'Not here, sir . . . can't do it now,' she muttered

desperately. 'My little 'un's stirring . . . I heard him.'
She hurried towards the pram, yanking at her clothes
and fastening buttons with shaking fingers.

'Where, then? When?' Pickering demanded urgently,
grabbing her wrist before she could push the pram out
into the corridor. He greedily eyed her big milky bosom
through its patterned cotton covering, his fingers itching
to touch her naked skin again.

'Next time I'm here . . . got to go . . . me husband's
expecting me back soon.' Gertie charged past with the
pram towards the exit.

'I don't think I need to say that this is our little secret,
just as your son's theft is our little secret . . . for now.'
Pickering raised his eyebrows enquiringly.

'Won't tell a soul . . . promise . . .' Gertie mumbled.
And she wouldn't. Rufus would go berserk on finding
out what her boss had done, thinking he, rather than
his wife, had been insulted. Gertie knew Rufus would
batter Pickering and open up a can of worms to protect
his own pride.

Wilfred Pickering watched his cleaner's wide swaying
hips as she fled from him, his wet tongue moving on
his lips. He had fancied Gertie from the moment he'd
interviewed her for the char's job. He'd felt frustrated
when she'd started bringing her brats into work with
her because he knew a seduction was out of the question
with the older ones about to witness, if not understand,
what was going on. Then there was Gertie herself to
conquer; although she was common, she seemed decent.
The object of Wilfred's lust had proved to be a reasonable worker, so he'd let her stay on. Now he was very
glad he had. As soon as he'd caught the biggest boy
stealing from him he'd known he had the means to

manipulate Gertie and get what he wanted – if only he could catch her on her own. When she'd turned up earlier with just the baby, Pickering had known it was his lucky day.

Compared to Wilfred's immaculately groomed wife, Gertie Grimes was a slattern. But Pickering liked buxom women with a certain musky smell and a harassed, dishevelled appearance. They reminded him of his mother. His wife's body on the other hand was fashionably thin and gave off a sickly sweet scent that reminded him of the perfume counter at Gamages. Caroline was an excellent hostess and a perfect consort in every way for an ambitious fellow. In fact Wilfred had been obliged to her for marrying him in the first place, considering she came from money and gentry and he'd striven to escape being known as the youngest child of an impoverished bookkeeper. But the downside to their unlikely pairing was that Caroline was too fastidious to want to go through the dirty business of conceiving or bearing children. And now she was nearly forty-five, nature had made the likelihood of Wilfred becoming a father very remote.

When Gertie Grimes had turned up at the office to clean that first time Pickering had been appalled and delighted at the same time. Gertie was plainly saddled with brats, and young enough to be his daughter, but the brood congregated about her had indicated she was woman enough to like keeping a man satisfied.

Gertie had got halfway home, pushing the pram and crying tears of rage and frustration at how she'd been treated by Pickering, when she realised she'd left her wages behind. She came to an abrupt halt and swore, doubly furious that the old lecher hadn't called her back to pick up her pay as he'd caused her to bolt for the exit. Scrubbing at her wet eyes with her knuckles she let out a sigh. Her brown envelope containing five and six would be lying in the cupboard in Pickering's office, as it always was on a Friday evening. While she considered what to do she began agitatedly rocking the pram although little Harry was fast asleep under the covers. The idea of going home without her money was almost as infuriating as the idea of going back to get it. But Gertie knew if she had to choose between tackling her husband or her boss, Rufus was the one she needed to keep sweet. She didn't want him getting suspicious as to why, for the first time, she'd come home without her pay. Besides she'd done her shifts, and got touched up into the bargain. In Gertie's opinion she more than deserved her money.

Turning about, Gertie marched back the way she'd come, breaking into a trot with the pram bouncing in front of her, when she realised the accountant might already have left the building.

Wilfred Pickering was just emerging from the cloakroom with an arm jammed in a sleeve of his overcoat when Gertie, breathless from exertion, burst in the front door.

'Ah . . . I imagine you have returned for your wages.'

'I have, sir,' Gertie gasped stoutly.

'Your husband will be cross, of course, if you return empty-handed.'

'They're *my* wages,' Gertie snapped, riled that he'd guessed correctly that Rufus would immediately appropriate her earnings.

Wilfred removed his arm from the sleeve and threw the coat on a nearby chair. 'And you're entitled to them, my dear.' A smirk undulated across his thin lips. 'You're the one expected to come here and be at my beck and call after all . . .'

Gertie gave a crisp nod, avoiding his eyes. She'd never bothered studying him before but she did now in sliding glances that lingered no more than a second. He was at least fifty, she guessed, and nothing like Rufus in appearance. Her husband was a big bear of a man with a shock of reddish hair; this fellow was going bald and looked like a stiff breeze might blow him over. Yet she reckoned this quiet little chap could be as dangerous in his way. 'I'll just get me money then.' Gertie gave a little cough. 'Envelope in the same place as usual, is it?'

'Come into my office – leave the pram there,' Pickering ordered softly, glancing inside at the sleeping baby. 'He's dead to the world and it's probably time we negotiated a pay rise for you. We can do that now . . .'

It was bad enough having her husband continually trying to get inside her knickers, Gertie thought as she once again trudged towards home, pushing the pram. She was walking gingerly because of a burning throb at the apex of her thighs. Pickering had coaxed her into letting him sprawl her on his desk then rammed into her as though his life depended on it, panting and growling as he did so. Gertie allowed herself a tiny giggle. He might look a weedy fellow but he had the equipment where it counted, she realised wryly, discreetly adjusting her knicker elastic to prevent it chafing her sore spot. Other than giving her a punishing seeing to, her boss had not treated her too badly; he'd not mentioned the theft again. She'd told him she'd not risk getting pregnant for any amount of pay rise and true to his word

Pickering had pulled out and come on top of his desk to protect her. Gertie wouldn't mind her husband being as considerate. Afterwards her boss had pulled up his trousers and gone off with a polite goodbye leaving Gertie to quickly clean up the desk, and herself. After she'd handed the key in to the caretaker she'd set off home, hoping Rufus wouldn't get a whiff of another man on her.

Pickering had been true to his word about giving her a rise too. In fact Gertie had doubled her wages this evening. She refused to focus on why her boss had been so generous, or what he thought he was paying for. She concentrated on the fact that, after she'd given five and six to Rufus, she still had the same amount for herself. Letting the accountant do what he wanted to her hadn't been that hard to bear. In fact in an odd way she'd found it exhilarating being manhandled and slobbered over by a man praising her body and saying how desperate he was to have her. Rufus never complimented her and was always on and off in a flash, leaving Gertie wondering what all the fuss was about. If she got a few more goes at it with Pickering she reckoned she might find out . . .

In the meantime she was going to buy herself a Yardley lipstick and tell Rufus she'd come by it by lucky chance when at work, which was true in a way – even if she'd not got it from one of the Windmill girls . . .

CHAPTER ELEVEN

'What's up?'

Dawn had arrived at the theatre to find Sal in the dressing room with her head in her hands and Lorna fussing over her.

Lorna's expressive grimace made Dawn jump to the conclusion that a calamity had befallen Sal's boyfriend. Dawn knew that Peter was serving in the Fusiliers.

'What's happened?' she asked gently, crouching by Sal's side at the dressing table. 'Is everything alright with Peter?' She didn't notice the letter by her friend's hand until Sal pushed it her way.

'No, it's not bloody alright!' Sal raised her head from her cupped palms, turning teary eyes on Dawn. 'The bastard's got another girl. He doesn't want to marry me.' Her shoulders began shaking with sobs.

'He's a damned fool then,' Dawn said, having taken a moment to digest that surprise.

'I'll have to write to Mum and let her know,' Sal gurgled. 'She's been making bookings for July; Dad'll go mad if he can't get his deposits back.'

'Shh . . .' Dawn put a comforting arm around Sal's shoulders.

'British soldiers . . . no self-discipline . . .' Olive muttered, shaking her head.

Dawn turned a frown on the older woman and Olive shrugged and started tidying the blankets strewn on the floor. She regularly bunked at the theatre rather than brave the blackout back home. In the morning it was Olive's job to make sure the bedding in the dressing rooms was neatly stacked away.

'Has she got the sack?' Rosie had come into the dressing room, assessed the commotion and delivered her verdict on its likely cause.

'No.' Dawn gave Rosie a meaningful frown, hoping to shut her up.

'Her fiancé's jilted her, the rat!' Lorna said and went off to find the teapot.

'You've been jilted?' After a moment's reflection Rosie said, 'Well, only one thing to do about that . . . have a brandy and soda and go out on the town.'

'That's two things,' Lorna pointed out.

'So it is.' Rosie took the mild criticism in good part. 'But you can do 'em at the same time.' She approached Sal and took hold of her chin to turn up her face. 'Right, I'll buy you a brandy but we'll have to clean you up a bit before we can take you out on the town. You do look a bloody state.'

Sal managed a watery chuckle, smearing away her tears. 'She works in the NAAFI.'

'NAAFI?' Lorna echoed, looking as though she'd sucked a lemon. 'He could have had a Windmill girl yet he goes off with a tea lady?'

Dawn caught Rosie's eye and gave her a wink in

thanks. The atmosphere had been a bit icy in the dressing room since Rosie caught Lorna and Sal gossiping about her. But it had lifted since they'd all rallied round Sal to buck her up.

Sal sat back in the chair, studying her blotchy face in the mirror. With a sigh she picked up her comb and tidied her tangled dark hair. 'My dad never liked Peter anyhow; said he was neither use nor ornament.'

'And so say all of us . . .' Rosie said then started singing. 'And so say all of us, for he's a jolly *bad* fellow, for he's a jolly bad fellow . . .'

Within a second the other girls joined in with her, Olive too, and Sally belted the words out the loudest.

'What on earth!'

Midge stuck his inflamed hand into a pocket, out of sight of his sister's eagle eyes. 'Don't fuss. I'll keep on bathing it in salt water. That'll do the trick.'

'Ain't no use trying to hide it!' Gertie began yanking on her brother's sleeve to no avail. 'You'll have to see a doctor, Michael.'

Gertie hadn't been happy when he crept in the back way, startling the life out of her. There was only one reason her brother would come and see her: money, and she hadn't been about to give him any till she saw the state of his injury. Rufus had told her Midge had got hurt on a job and she'd thought little more of it . . . till now. Her brother needed medical attention, and that cost.

'Where's Rufus?' Midge sidled into the hallway and angled his head to see up the stairs as though he thought his brother-in-law might bound down them at any minute and throw him out.

120

'He's at work, and Joey and Adam's at school.'

Midge cast a glance at the toddler and baby squashed top to tail in the pram. Both seemed to be dozing although it looked an uncomfortable fit.

'Did you do it?' Gertie burst out. She had to know whether her brother was a murderer.

'What, jump ship?' Midge said, playing dumb. ''Course I did . . . that's why I'm here . . .'

'You know what I mean.' Gertie wagged a finger, scowling.

'Ain't done nothing other than stay home 'stead of going back and risk getting me legs blown off like me mate.'

Gertie wasn't convinced. Her brother had always been a liar, and a coward, even when he was a kid. There was a dull pulse in Midge's hidden palm that was keeping time with the pounding in his head. He imagined he had a fever from blood poisoning. 'I'm gonna swing for Purves, the fucker,' he snarled.

'Language!' Gertie hissed, glancing at the pram. But she could understand his frustration. Purves deserved a belt for causing her brother to get wounded. Midge might have stayed away if in good health but now Gertie knew the blighter would make a damned nuisance of himself, and keep coming round on the scrounge. Rufus had told her her brother wasn't welcome back looting with them because he'd slow them all down till his hand healed.

'Got anything for headache?'

'Beechams powders, that's all . . .' Gertie took a small box from a wall cupboard.

'I'll go back and see Lenny's old man.' Midge didn't bother mixing the medicine with water, he just emptied the powder into his mouth, grimacing as though he were chewing a wasp. 'P'raps Pop'll know why it's swole up and gone yeller.' Midge's tongue roved his lips as though he were trying to remove the taste in his mouth. 'Them stitches he put in's full o' pus.'

'You'll have to turn yerself in and get seen to,' Gertie said bluntly.

'Got anything for me to eat? I'm starving.' Midge cocked a deaf 'un to his sister's advice.

'You'd better let me clean that up first.' Gertie jerked her head at the hand her brother had stuffed in his pocket.

'Don't fuss . . . get us a bit of bread and marge, will you?'

With a mutter beneath her breath Gertie disappeared inside the pantry to see what she could rustle up. She just wanted him gone; he was her flesh and blood but Gertie knew he was a wrong 'un. Besides, she didn't want any of her neighbours seeing him. The police would be round in a shot if they found out Midge Williams had been visiting his sister.

'Spam sandwich?' Gertie had emerged from the pantry carrying a small can of Spam balanced on half a loaf of brown bread.

'Got no white?' Midge demanded grumpily and earned himself a look from his sister.

While Gertie cut bread Midge paced restlessly. He reckoned his bad luck hadn't just been all down to Lenny; Rufus had played his part by turning up with a kid in tow and putting everybody off their stride. So he thought just in case his sister felt like telling him never again to sneak in and ask her for anything, he'd bring that subject up.

'Wouldn't have happened that night if Joey hadn't

122

come along. I was more interested in making sure me nephew was alright than concentrating on what we was doing.'

Gertie had been waiting for that one. Her brother was a weasel, Rufus was right on that score. Her husband had told her that Midge had cut up rough as soon as he saw Joey that night, threatening to clump the boy. So she ignored the comment, spreading marge. If her brother ever so much as touched one of her sons she'd rip his face off.

'Don't know what you was thinking of letting a kid out on the rob at that time of the night.' Midge had another go at getting his point across.

'I was thinking of getting to work and feeding me kids with me earnings,' Gertie snapped. There was no way she was telling her brother about Joey being a right little pain and thieving off her boss, making her leave him behind. And look where that had led to now! Getting her knickers pulled down, and the rest, was something else she wouldn't tell her brother about . . . or her husband!

'I'll take it with me. I'd better get off, just in case that nosy cow across the road's snooping behind her curtain.' Midge picked the sandwich off the plate his sister was holding out to him.

'You'd best not come back either. Don't want the police turning up asking questions; anyhow Rufus'll go nuts if he knows you've been here. He don't want the kids getting dragged into investigations; can't expect them to tell lies about seeing their uncle.'

'I'm gonna head off to Chislehurst anyhow,' Midge said through a mouthful of Spam sandwich.

Midge had heard about the caves in Kent that were

used by hundreds of people sheltering from the bombing raids. The warren of interlinking tunnels was also known in underworld circles as useful for people who wanted to disappear from sight for a while. Midge reckoned he'd be able to see a doctor in an area where he wasn't known. Then he could lie low in the caves recuperating, and come back to London all merry and bright and ready to start bomb-chasing again. He just hoped Fritz didn't call a halt to the Blitz in the meantime and cut off his cash flow.

'Could do with a sub, Gert . . .'

'Ain't got no spare cash.' Gertie refused immediately.

'Fiver, if you've got it.' Midge carried on as though he'd not heard her. 'I'll see a doctor in Kent; he'll want paying. Plus I've got a train to catch and fares ain't cheap.'

'A fiver!' Gertie gave a contemptuous snort. 'Like I've got a fiver!' Furiously she opened her purse; she knew she'd never get rid of him if she didn't. 'That's all I've got!' she fumed. 'Now piss off and don't come back!'

Midge took the ten-shilling note with a look of distaste. 'Ain't gonna get far on that . . .'

'End of the street'll do for me,' Gertie snapped, pointing at the back door.

Dawn was sitting at the parlour table idly flicking over the pages of a magazine. In the background she could hear her mother washing up while singing along to the music playing on the wireless. When Dawn heard the staccato rhythm of soles and heels hitting the stone floor in the kitchenette her smile transformed to a chuckle. Her mother had been a good tap dancer in her time. Eliza had met Dawn's father at Betty's Stage School in

Hackney when in her early teens. Dawn's parents had been keen for her to learn to dance as a child, and the training had stood their daughter in good stead as an adult, providing her with a job she loved. Her mother's gaiety was infectious and, closing the magazine, Dawn got up from the table, ran to the kitchen and joined in. Mother and daughter jigged in the small space between sink and cooker, bumping hips and laughing till the tune came to an end.

Eliza pulled a hanky from her pinny pocket and mopped her brow. 'This old girl's still got it,' she said breathlessly.

'I'll get you a job with me, Mum,' Dawn teased. 'Phyllis is always on the lookout for good hoofers.'

'Cor, that's given me a thirst . . .' Eliza thumped her ample chest with a fist to ease her racing heart.

As her mother turned towards the sink to get herself a glass of water Dawn looked more thoughtfully at her. She'd not yet found a suitable time to bring up the subject of the man George had seen with Eliza. But this afternoon, with her brother out of the way and Eliza in such a light-hearted mood, Dawn thought it was too good an opportunity to miss. Her mother was turning off the tap, raising the glass to her mouth to take a sip.

'Have you got a boyfriend, Mum?' Dawn blurted out.

For a moment Eliza stood stock still then she lowered her face and put down the glass on the wooden draining board. 'What makes you say that?' she demanded.

'Well . . . it's just that George said a fellow came here to see you recently.' Dawn knew that there *was* something to it because her mother had immediately become defensive.

'That's right . . . a man came here to see *me*.' Eliza's

125

mouth had thinned into a stubborn line. 'And if I'd wanted George to know more about it all, I'd've said something to him at the time.'

'Who is he?' Dawn asked doggedly.

'None of your business, and nobody you need to know about.' Eliza grabbed her glass of water and took a swig. 'Now, I've got chores to get on with, 'cos they ain't gonna do themselves.'

'George wasn't causing trouble, Mum,' Dawn said, not wanting her brother to get an ear-bashing. 'He just mentioned it in passing. I was the one showed an interest in finding out more about this fellow.' She put a hand on her mother's arm. 'We wouldn't mind if you did have a boyfriend, you know.'

'Well thank you very much,' Eliza said tersely. 'I'll remember it for the future.'

Dawn rolled her eyes at the ceiling, growing impatient with her mother's attitude. 'Well, as you've turned narky over a simple question about a fellow who came calling, I imagine that he is a boyfriend. What's wrong with him? Perhaps he's not very nice, and that's why you don't want us to know anything about him, is that it?'

'Oh, he ain't very nice, you take it from me,' Eliza said bitterly. 'If he'd been nice, he'd've stuck around and married me, instead of pissing off as soon as he found out I was in the family way.'

Dawn felt her jaw dropping. 'He's George's father?' she whispered.

Eliza gave a single nod. 'You keep it to yourself, hear? I've told him never to show his face here again.'

Dawn moistened her mouth and murmured, 'I won't tell George, promise.'

126

Eliza barged past towards the garden door. 'Washing needs to be put through the mangle.'

Dawn had heard the huskiness in her mother's voice and knew she'd been close to tears. Her mind raced back through the years to when she'd been about seven or eight. She could vaguely remember the man who'd arrive in a car to take her and her mother for a drive. They'd go to the park on a Sunday and have a picnic on mild afternoons. She also remembered that sometimes she'd see him in the morning at breakfast time, and that her mother called him Rod. To her he'd been Uncle Rod but she'd been in his company only rarely, and even at that tender age had realised that she was often left at her late nan's house for tea because her mother and Uncle Rod were off out somewhere together, and didn't want her around.

Then Uncle Rod had stopped coming on Sundays, and her mother started getting fat. They'd moved from Bermondsey to a house in Bethnal Green and Dawn could recall moaning at her mother about having to leave behind her friends and start at a different school.

George had been born a few months later.

The new neighbours had been told, truthfully, that Eliza was a widow . . . only she'd not been widowed as recently as she'd have them all believe. And some suspicious souls had their own ideas about it. Young as she'd been, Dawn had become adept at avoiding probing questions from inquisitive women in the street when her mother wasn't about to see them off.

As she'd grown older and wiser, Dawn had put two and two together and worked out for herself that Uncle Rod had fathered her brother and then either couldn't, or wouldn't, marry Eliza so they'd be a proper family.

But they'd muddled through, just the three of them, and Dawn had forgotten all about Uncle Rod. The only uneasiness she'd ever felt was that her brother George knew nothing about any of it. But at some time he must . . .

Of course, George had asked about his father, but when Eliza had explained he'd died before George was born, her brother had accepted it. He and Dawn had the same surname, and as far as George was concerned they had the same father too, and just cruel fate had prevented him knowing the man in the photo on the sideboard. Dawn had wondered if a blank space had been left on George's birth certificate where his father's name should be. But she'd never asked her mother about it. George would ask for the document himself in time, but not yet.

When her mother came in from the back garden Dawn was still standing, gripping the china sink, mulling things over in her mind.

'It's too late to tell George the truth, you know that, don't you.'

Dawn's nod was barely there. She could tell her mother had been outside crying; her eyes were bloodshot and her complexion pallid. Dawn gave Eliza a spontaneous hug.

'Don't worry, Mum, if he comes back here to pester you, I'll see him off.' She planted a kiss on her mother's cool forehead. 'We've done alright, just the three of us; so we'll carry on as we are and he can sling his hook. He had his chance and he blew it.'

Eliza nodded and sniffed.

'What made him come back after all this time?'

Eliza elbowed free of her daughter's embrace. She shrugged.

'Tell me, Mum,' Dawn coaxed softly, guessing there was more to it.

'His wife died recently, so he came back to tell me that and ask me to marry him now he's free.'

Her mother's response had been almost devoid of emotion; Dawn on the other hand felt momentarily struck dumb, then angry enough to spit feathers, having digested the news. 'He was married!' she breathed in disbelief. 'But . . . but he was supposed to marry you . . . I remember you were engaged.'

Eliza delved into her apron pocket for a handkerchief, used it to wipe her nose. 'Stupid fool, wasn't I, eh? Never once occurred to me at the time that I was being courted by a married man. He fooled my mum too, and she was cute as they come, God rest her. Your nan liked Rod, you know. Finished her off knowing what he was really like . . . what he did to me.'

'You never knew then . . . about his wife?' Dawn's relief was apparent in her tone, making her mother's lips twitch in a wry smile.

'Wouldn't do that to another woman, 'cos I wouldn't like it done to me. In the end I suppose he did the right thing going back to her. Just grateful in a way that he didn't end up a bigamist.'

'Don't fucking care about him!' Dawn exploded.

'No . . . me neither,' Eliza said quietly. 'But we would have got dragged into it. Your nan as well, 'cos something as bad as that was sure to have got reported in the papers.'

Dawn swallowed a painful lump in her throat, feeling utterly sorry for what her mother had suffered.

'Nip of gin helped,' Eliza said self-mockingly, as though reading her daughter's mind.

Dawn choked a reluctant laugh. 'Yeah . . . well, you don't need that any more, and you certainly don't need him . . .' She broke off on hearing the sound of the front door opening.

Eliza sprang to attention, brushing down her pinny and sniffing as she heard her son arriving home.

'I'll put on the kettle,' Dawn said brightly although she was still feeling angry enough at the man she'd known as Uncle Rod to want to go straight out and find him so she could throttle him.

CHAPTER TWELVE

'Hello . . . you're Tina, aren't you?'

Dawn had just entered the crowded powder room of the Café de Paris when she saw a familiar face reflected in the mirror.

The brunette in the scarlet dress had been using her compact but swung about on hearing her name. Her darting eyes skidded back to Dawn with a gleam of recognition, but she gave no reciprocating smile.

'Oh, hello.' It was an abrupt greeting before the young woman snapped shut the compact and dropped it into her bag.

'Are you here with Glenn?' Dawn persevered, attempting to avoid treading on toes as she edged closer to talk to Tina. A group of glamorous women, chatting in posh voices, obligingly shifted aside to make way for her.

'Who?' Tina asked distantly. Her head was lowered towards her handbag, and she delved repeatedly into it as though to avoid facing Dawn, now at her side in front of the mirror.

'Glenn . . . the fellow you were with when we all

went out together. We went to the Kitkat Club. Glenn Rafferty's my boyfriend's pal . . . they're both pilots in the RAF . . .'

'Sorry, can't hang around chatting, someone's waiting for me . . . g'bye . . .'

Frowning, Dawn watched the young woman hurrying towards the exit. She recalled that Tina had been down-right rude last time she'd seen her; her behaviour hadn't improved one iota.

'Let's borrow your lipstick, Dawn.'

Automatically Dawn pulled a gilt tube from her bag and handed it over.

'Ta,' Rosie said. She'd been a short distance away, primping her hair, so had heard the brief exchange between Tina and Dawn. 'Who was that?' she asked casually.

'Oh . . . just somebody I saw last time Bill was on leave. We all went to the Kitkat Club. Her name's Tina and she was with Bill's pal but she danced with Bill as well.'

'Like that, was it?' Rosie had guessed from Dawn's tone of voice that Dawn hadn't got on with the brunette.

'She never stopped flirting, and wasn't half rude to me.'

'Bit like just now, you mean.' Rosie's voice sounded peculiar because she was speaking and applying coral lipstick at the same time. 'Don't think it suits me.' She cocked her head, rubbing together her lips to blend the colour.

Returning the lipstick to her handbag, Dawn reflected that meeting Tina unexpectedly had left her feeling oddly deflated.

'When's Bill next got leave?' Rosie asked. 'You can introduce me to him.'

'I won't do that, Miss Tease,' Dawn ribbed her friend. 'But I'll show you a photo.' She pulled from her bag a small head and shoulders shot that she carried in a wallet.

'Quite a dreamboat,' Rosie said, handing it back. She joined the queue for a lavatory.

'I'll see you back in the ballroom.' Normally Dawn would have waited and walked back with Rosie, but she was curious to see if Tina was outside with Glenn; if so she might be able to ask Bill's friend how her boyfriend was as she'd not had a letter from him in over a week.

Dawn was humming along to the music as the band started up after the intermission. She was close to the entrance to the ballroom when she again came face to face with Tina. This time though Dawn ignored the young woman and instead stared at the person at her side, feeling as though she'd been doused in icy water.

'Hello, Dawn . . . I've just found out you were here so was coming to find you . . .'

'Were you?' Dawn eventually forced a bitter response from her dry mouth.

Bill was attempting to conceal his guilt behind affected earnestness whereas Tina seemed happy to brazen it out with a smug stare. Dawn swung an enlightened glance between them. Bill hadn't been coming to find her; he'd been heading towards the exit because Tina had warned him trouble was brewing.

'Everything alright, Dawn?' Rosie had come up behind and quickly taken in the scene. She stared at Bill. 'Not been introduced but I think I know you.' She turned to Tina. 'As for you, why don't you sling yer hook?' She poked Tina on the arm. 'Could tell you was up to no good.'

133

'It's alright . . .' Dawn gave her friend a shaky smile; she didn't want a catfight starting on her account. Tina had squared up immediately at Rosie's provocation. 'You go and join the others, Rosie . . . go on . . .' Dawn urged.

Rosie moved away, throwing a dirty look over her shoulder at Bill and Tina.

'Wait for me outside.' Bill snapped his order at Tina.

The brunette's expression turned petulant but Dawn halted Tina before she could flounce off. 'There's no need for you to leave; I'm going, 'cos I've nothing more to say to either of you.'

'I need to talk to you, Dawn. This isn't how it looks!' Bill hissed a protest, grabbing her elbow.

'Of course it is,' Dawn said quietly. 'It's exactly how it looks so don't bother with stupid lies.'

Bill tightened his grip, forcing Dawn with him into a nearby alcove and positioning himself in front of her so she'd no escape. 'Look . . . I told Glenn I'd take Tina out for him when I was back in town. He'd promised to treat her to a night at the Café de Paris but couldn't get a pass this weekend so . . . that's all there is to it.'

'So you thought you'd come to London and take Tina out instead of me.' Dawn's lips felt icy yet inside she was burning with hurt and humiliation. 'I asked you to bring me here,' she reminded him quietly. 'But you never did, did you.'

'We can come another time,' Bill purred, stroking her naked forearm. 'I was coming to see you tomorrow at the Windmill. I wanted to make it a surprise,' he said, sounding quite affronted. 'I knew you'd get the wrong end of the stick about this so wasn't going to mention to you about taking Tina out.'

'I bet you weren't!' Dawn forced the words through

gritting teeth. Her anger was starting to overtake her shock and she clenched her fists, overcome with an urge to lash out at him.

'What are you doing here anyway?' Bill suddenly demanded. His gaze wandered over her curvaceous body and sophisticated black cocktail dress, then returned to her wavy blonde hair and artful make-up. 'You look lovely tonight. Are you with somebody?' He scoured the room behind as though to spot a lurking fellow.

Dawn could have laughed. He'd been caught out red-handed with another woman yet had the cheek to suspect *she* might be two-timing *him*.

'What are you doing here?' Bill repeated. 'You told me you never went out dancing without me.'

'Is that why you brought *her* here?' Dawn jerked a nod at Tina. 'You thought you were safe, didn't you, 'cos this was the last place you were likely to run into me.' She wrenched her elbow from his grip. 'Well, sorry to disappoint you. I came here because it's Sal Fiske's birthday. A few of us from the Windmill came for a night out to celebrate as she's had a rough time of it lately.' Dawn tilted up her chin. 'And I'm damned glad I did, 'cos I've just seen you in your true colours at last.' She drew in a shaky breath. 'I never want to see you again, Bill, so carry on and enjoy the rest of your evening with your pal's girl.'

Bill tugged Dawn back as she would have walked away. 'So you've caught me out with a good-time girl. What did you expect?' He took her pointed chin in hard fingers, his narrowed eyes blazing at her. 'If you weren't frigid I wouldn't have needed to look elsewhere, would I.' Bill plunged his head down to kiss Dawn and she noticed a reek of alcohol on his breath.

'You're drunk.' She squirmed free of him. 'I hope Tina's boyfriend comes to hear about you two messing around. You deserve a clump off him . . .'

'Glenn?' Bill threw back his head and barked a laugh. 'He won't care. He's had a dozen more like her since that night in the Kitkat Club. He finished with Tina a while back. No more use to him, he said. And I'll finish with her now . . . for you.' Bill glanced over a shoulder at Tina, watching them sulkily. 'I've not slept with her yet, I swear.' He hauled Dawn against him, nuzzling her neck. 'She's nothing compared to you, darling. Can't you see that I need some *real* loving? I might be killed tomorrow, shot down in flames . . .' His hands roved her buttocks, forced her against the bulge in his trousers. 'I need you, Dawn . . . all of you . . . before it's too late . . .'

'Let go of me.' Dawn shoved a fist between them, then when that didn't work and his hands became more cruel and rapacious, her fist lurched upwards to his face and she punched him under the chin.

Bill grunted before snarling, 'You little cow . . .'

'Let go of me or I'll create a scene,' Dawn enunciated between gritted teeth. She could see that it wasn't only Tina watching them now. A couple of the posh women from the powder room were frowning in their direction.

Bill continued imprisoning her rigid body for a moment longer then flung himself aside with a muttered oath.

Dawn dragged her feet along the street. She'd not even told her friends she was leaving; she'd not been able to face their pity. She knew Rosie would put Sal in the picture about how she'd caught Bill out with another woman. The thudding of blood in Dawn's ears and her hiccupping sobs had drowned out her own senses as the German bombers approached. She vaguely heard the sirens but didn't react and continued walking with her head down to conceal her tears from passers by. For weeks she'd been wondering if Bill were about to throw her over, and if he did, whether she would be heartbroken. Now she knew she wasn't heartbroken but she was feeling utterly distraught at his betrayal. How she wished he had just written ending it between them! To treat her so despicably was beyond bearing. Her world seemed to have disintegrated and she didn't care if she lived or died. A woman charged past her holding her velvet hat firmly on her head as she sought cover from the raid. She turned to look at Dawn, seemingly strolling, unperturbed by the idea of being blown to bits.

'Alright, dear?'

Dawn nodded. The woman's yelled concern finally galvanised her into action. She joined the people hurrying towards Leicester Square to shelter in the underground station then was knocked sideways into a brick wall as a bomb exploded.

Dawn picked herself up, tottering on her feet, her ears ringing painfully. Feeling her head spinning she crouched down again using a wall as support while the sound of shattering glass made her instinctively protect her head beneath her cradling arms. When she felt steady enough she straightened up and stared in horror, then began racing back the way she'd come along Coventry Street.

CHAPTER THIRTEEN

Shouts and moans mingled with a clamour of bells as ambulances and fire engines raced towards the bodies and buildings that had been shattered by the blasts.

Dawn had come to a breathless stop, clutching at the stitch in her side, while surveying the awful scene outside the Café de Paris. She darted towards the entrance, desperate to find Sal and Rosie, but was bumped aside by an army officer who was emerging with an unconscious girl in his arms. Dawn stumbled away to make room for him but wasn't quick enough to prevent the woman's limp body brushing a sticky trail on her beautiful dress.

The young captain placed his precious burden on the pavement then squatted by the girl with tears streaming down his face. Dawn stifled a small anguished noise with her fingers as she watched his raw misery. The wet patch on her skirt had stained her palm and it took her a moment to realise that her hand was smeared with blood. Briskly she wiped it away and made a renewed effort to enter the building, but again her way was blocked with people fleeing into the street. Some staggered haphazardly onto the pavement; others, unable to escape unaided, were being propped up or carried out in clouds of choking dust.

Dawn began hopping to and fro, frantically scouring dirt-smudged features to find a familiar face. Finally, through the dusk, she glimpsed a shock of pale hair. Dawn squeezed a path through the crowd to get a better look. When certain that the small woman in a pastel dress was Rosie, she rushed up to enclose her friend in an immediate embrace and in doing so she worsened Rosie's hacking cough. That apart, Dawn was relieved to see that the young woman seemed relatively unscathed; however the poor soul was trembling violently and she had a gash on her forehead that had trickled blood down one cheek and onto her bodice. Rosie's hair, usually so immaculately crimped, was a matted mess of dirt and tangles.

With a shaking hand Dawn pulled a hanky from her handbag. With gentle wipes she began cleaning her friend up while Rosie brought her breathing under control and blinked her dust-encrusted eyes.

'Where's Sal?' Dawn croaked.

'Don't know if Sal's still in there . . .' Rosie shook her head, repeatedly swallowing and heaving as though about to throw up. 'Sal was dancing with a fellow then . . . then . . .' Suddenly she clung to Dawn, wailing, 'It was horrible . . . the ballroom exploded . . . there was bits of bodies everywhere . . .'

Dawn cuddled Rosie for comfort, closing her eyes tight against the gruesome image tormenting her mind. 'Did you see Bill?' she whispered.

Rosie cleared the wet from her face with her knuckles. 'He was waltzing with that girl Tina just after you left . . . but don't know if he's alright . . . didn't see him again . . .' Rosie suddenly howled in despair. 'Where's Sal? I couldn't see her. D'you think that she's copped it?'

'Come on . . . let's look for her; I expect she's looking for you.' Dawn sounded encouraging, buoyant even, but inwardly a knot of dread had curdled the pit of her stomach. She was worried not only for Sal's safety but for Bill's too. Arm in arm the two young women set off, picking a path through the groaning, sobbing crowd. They had made a thorough search of dirty, haggard features but there was nobody they knew. Although people were still emerging from the wreckage, Dawn began to lose hope and so did Rosie.

'She's still in there . . . Sal's dead . . .' Rosie wailed. 'I'm gonna go back inside and look for her. I know where she was . . .'

'They won't let you in there, Rosie,' Dawn said, restraining her as she tried to break free to hurtle towards the entrance. Oddly Dawn was reminded of another time when, frightened stiff, they had clung together for comfort during a raid. But it had been nothing like this.

'How are you, my dear? Do you need any help?' A kindly woman wearing a WVS lapel badge had heard Rosie's hysterics and approached them.

'Our friend's still in there,' Rosie wailed.

'You need a nice cup of sweet tea. We'll have some on the go shortly when the mobile canteen turns up.' The woman patted at Rosie's arm; having guessed that Dawn was providing the immediate comfort Rosie needed she moved on.

A fellow hopping on one leg struggled from the building giving a defiant wave then a two-fingered salute. 'Bugger Hitler!' he boomed in a cultured voice and gained a ripple of laughter from those still capable of having a sense of humour.

'Would you be able to give a hand?' The woman from the WVS had returned and found Dawn. 'The canteen has turned up . . . would you mind serving, dear, while I carry on patching people up?' A group of walking wounded, sitting on the pavement in dazed silence, drew her weary eyes. 'I've had first aid training and there are so many who need attention.'

'Of course I'll help . . . *we'll* help.' Dawn forced herself to focus on the job in hand but was so anxious about those still missing that she could feel her legs wobbling, and a trickle of sweat trailing down her spine. But she knew that she had to pull herself together for Rosie's sake as well as her own.

'Come on, Rosie,' Dawn urged gruffly, propelling her friend by the elbow. 'You're right as ninepence, and so am I. Let's thank our lucky stars we're able to make ourselves useful and get that tea poured . . .'

'I thought it was you!' Olive Roberts had hurried up behind Dawn and Rosie as they reached the canteen. She clapped a hand over her mouth as she saw the state of the younger woman, smeared in grime and blood. 'You weren't in there?' she said, jerking her head at the wrecked building. She assessed the glamorous attire of her Windmill Theatre colleagues. 'Thank God you both got out alive.'

'Sal's still in there,' Rosie whispered, swaying on her feet, her cheeks ballooning.

'We're helping make the tea, Olive; show us where all the things are, will you.' Dawn grabbed Rosie by the arm, giving her a rousing shake. 'Buck up; don't you dare be sick. You won't be of use to anybody if you keel over. Sal might be out in a mo and gasping for a cuppa, so look lively.'

'I'll go off and help the wounded if you can manage the teas,' Olive said, gazing about. 'So many servicemen . . . I'll just get my first aid case and do what I can to help them. Sometimes a chat's all that's needed.'

Dawn nodded. 'Get those cups set, Rosie,' she said calmly. 'We've got a queue forming.'

As Dawn put her key in the lock at just after six o'clock in the morning she realised that her mother would have been frantic with worry over her. She'd promised to be back before midnight.

She'd barely got a foot over the threshold when Eliza and George appeared in the parlour doorway. They both wore dressing gowns and strained expressions.

George was first to speak. ''Bout time too,' he snuffled. 'We thought . . .' He broke off and stomped towards the stairs.

While her son sought his bed, Eliza leaned against the doorframe for support, her eyes vivid with relief as she gazed at her daughter. 'You were caught out in a bad raid, weren't you?'

Dawn nodded, unable to speak from exhaustion and grief. But she closed the door, leaning back against it. The comprehension that she could relax now because she was home and safe was suddenly too much to bear and she began weeping silently.

Eliza approached unsteadily and although Dawn could smell the alcohol she said nothing; at that moment she didn't care that her mother had been drinking. Eliza was alive – they all were – and that was all that mattered.

Dawn had experienced, first-hand and for the first

142

time, the carnage of war. Of course, she'd heard reports on the wireless and seen pictures in the papers, but it had always been others who'd suffered terrible loss. Now she understood that unbearable sadness and that death didn't discriminate between wealth or class. She'd seen dead waitresses laid on the pavement beside the corpses of women decked with diamond jewellery.

Eliza comforted her daughter with back rubs until Dawn controlled her sobbing.

'Any gin left, Mum?' She finally quietened enough to hiccup her question.

Eliza led her daughter by the hand into the kitchen.

'I meant it, Mum . . . I want a proper drink.' Dawn had slumped into a chair and watched her mother putting the kettle to boil. 'Bill and Sal were there . . . they didn't come out . . . we think they got killed . . . it was horrible . . . I need a drink . . .'

Eliza swung about, stunned into speechlessness at what she'd heard. Then questions cluttered her mind but her intuition was warning her to keep quiet for a while to let her daughter calm down.

'No, you don't need a drink,' she said gently. 'You're still in shock. But you're strong, you'll cope. You're not like me.' Eliza spooned tea into the pot with a shaking hand.

Just hours ago she had watched proudly as her lovely daughter got herself dressed and made up to go out with her friends. The black silk cocktail dress had been Eliza's; the most expensive gown she'd ever owned, bought for a party to mark her fifth wedding anniversary. She'd put it away in tissue paper shortly afterwards, when her husband's chill turned to pneumonia and he died. On Dawn's seventeenth birthday she'd got it down from the loft, given it an airing, then wrapped it up for her as a present. Eliza had joked she'd have liked such a neat bust when Dawn took it in to fit her slender figure. Now Eliza could see that her treasured gown was crumpled and stained beyond repair. But she didn't care. Her daughter would recover and be fine.

'You're handing in your notice?'

'No! Not yet, sir. But I will have to, eventually. My husband's getting fed up having the kids while I'm here, and as he's got a pay rise he expects me to be at home now.' Gertie told a convincing lie. Rufus had no pay rise and no idea she intended jacking in her evening job at the accountant's office. In time she'd have to tell Phyllis too that she couldn't carry on cleaning the Windmill Theatre. Gertie would miss the girls, Dawn especially. But she'd yet to deal with how to explain the loss of her wages to her husband.

'I see . . .' Wilfred Pickering again glanced up from the ledger that he'd been writing in. He wasn't unduly bothered about losing Gertie's services – any of them. Cleaners were ten a penny and as for the other business . . . the pleasure was dwindling because for him the excitement had been in the beginning when their sessions had bordered on rape. Now the business of her son's theft was in the past and she was climbing eagerly onto his desk instead of him forcing her down onto it. Besides, when his hands roved her figure Gertie now seemed more fat than curvaceous, and her air of troubled exhaustion sometimes irritated rather than aroused him.

'I can carry on for a good while yet, sir,' Gertie said hastily. 'I was just giving you plenty of warning so you can get a new char lined up.'

144

'Most considerate,' Wilfred murmured.

Gertie took off her pinafore and opened some buttons on her blouse while edging a hip onto his desk. She left the rest because she knew he liked to do it.

'I'm off home early tonight.' Wilfred locked away his books in his desk and stood up. 'Don't forget the lights, Gertie, on your way out.'

Gertie's jaw dropped, then her disappointment transformed to a frown. She wondered if her boss had guessed the truth and that's why he'd not immediately tugged her knickers down and spread her legs. Well, it was a bit bloody late now to pull out on her!

Later, when she got home, and before she'd even got her coat off, Rufus had unhooked his from the peg and gone off out with a grunt. Gertie put her pinafore back on and started on the washing up, glancing at intervals at her three boys sitting on the floor playing cards. Their small auburn heads were close together as Joey taught Adam and Simon a card trick. Harry was fast asleep in his pram. Gertie acknowledged the harmonious little scene with a wry smile.

But it wouldn't last. She prodded angrily at her abdomen beneath her pinafore and closed her eyes in despair. She couldn't believe it had happened when she'd thought she and Pickering had made sure to be careful.

She knew the baby wasn't Rufus's. Since she started having an affair she'd been feeling so sore from her boss's poundings that she'd rarely let her husband near her. She'd thought herself lucky that Rufus hadn't made a song and dance about it.

But she wasn't feeling so lucky now. Only last week she'd been convincing herself she was just late; then this morning she'd thrown up in the back yard when pegging out washing. She couldn't kid herself any more: she'd been pregnant enough times to know the early signs. She was having Pickering's baby and there was nothing for it but to make Rufus think it was his.

There was no reason why her husband would be suspicious, so long as she cosied up to him in bed for a few weeks. But for now Gertie knew she'd have to keep quiet then pick the right time to announce the news. Rufus was no fool and she dreaded to think what he might do if he suspected the truth.

Gertie sighed, and went upstairs carrying some clothes she'd ironed.

She pulled open a drawer and placed some frayed bloomers on top of a faded petticoat. She hesitated, then pulled up her skirt and took off a pair of fancy nylon knickers that she'd bought herself with Wilfred's money. She never let Rufus see them because he'd start wondering. She pushed them underneath the old cotton, knowing she wouldn't be wearing those for much longer. She'd pack in her evening job first and with a pang Gertie realised she'd miss it.

Over the weeks she'd come to like more and more what Wilfred did to her and to feel quite fond of him. Of course she knew there was no future in it.

They were both married. And despite his shortcomings she loved her husband and knew he loved her. She'd have to make sure that Rufus loved the new baby too, and never found out that there was a cuckoo in the nest.

'Will you go to the funeral?' Eliza asked.

Having read the brief note from Bill's parents giving details of the arrangements they'd made to bury their son she handed the letter back to her daughter.

146

When she'd found out the whole tragic story of what had gone on at the Café de Paris, Eliza had been shocked. She'd been angry too on learning of Bill's reason for being there when they'd all believed him to be on duty in East Anglia. Eliza knew she'd been fooled too by Bill Sweetman. He had been invited to dinner with them on a few occasions and Eliza had come to think of him as her future son-in-law. George had liked him, and had listened avidly to Bill's reports of life in the RAF. Eliza would never have thought Bill a deceitful man. But then she knew she was a poor judge of character where handsome charmers were concerned. She'd been flummoxed completely by Rod when he'd promised to marry her and look after her and her daughter.

'No, I won't go to the funeral . . .' Dawn finally gave an answer, having mulled things over in her mind. Although more than a week had passed she still felt quite raw over it all. 'I'd better get dressed.' She left the letter on the parlour table and went up to her bedroom. A moment later Eliza poked her head around the door and found her daughter still in her dressing gown. Dawn was seated at the dressing table, gazing into the large green eyes reflected back at her and slowly drawing a brush through her thick honey-gold hair.

Dawn gave her mother a smile to welcome her in then got up and started plumping up the pillows and straightening the covers on her crumpled bed.

'You're going to write back to the Sweetmans though, aren't you?' Eliza gently resumed their conversation as she helped her daughter tuck in the bed sheets.

'Of course I will. I only met Mr and Mrs Sweetman that once, but they were very welcoming.' A small smile tipped up one corner of Dawn's mouth as she recalled

Bill taking her to Surrey with him to meet his parents a few days before Christmas. She had taken a present of chocolates for them and they'd laughed and given her a gift, saying she'd laugh too when she opened it. When she unwrapped it on Christmas morning she realised the boxes of chocolates were identical. Dawn recalled that her brother George had polished most of those off before Boxing Day.

Then she'd opened Bill's gift of L'Aimant perfume. She still had some of it left in the bottle. She knew she'd never use it.

'You're doing the right thing, Dawn,' Eliza assured her gently. 'I know you want to shout and scream at the world . . . but it'll get better.' She put her arm around her daughter's shoulders and planted a kiss on her forehead. 'Now get yourself dressed and you can give me a hand digging up some earlies out the back.' Eliza wiped her hands on her pinafore. 'I swapped some of our sugar and butter with Glad up the road for a bit of mutton so we can have a stew for tea with some nice home-grown veg.'

'Thought you didn't like your tea without sugar in it,' Dawn reminded her mother with a smile, making Eliza chuckle as she went out.

Dawn stared out of the window into a fine March morning. In the garden border a few daffodils were opening their sunny heads amidst withering snowdrops. And she could see the feathery tops of the vegetables her mother wanted her to dig up. It was a lovely scene, but she felt her eyes smarting with tears.

She yearned to go and see Bill's parents and offer her comfort, but she couldn't. She couldn't act the hypocrite and be the grieving girlfriend. They'd written previously, on first learning of Bill's death at the Café de Paris, and asked Dawn if she'd been there that night. Quite naturally they had wanted all possible information about their son's last few hours.

Dawn had picked out innocuous truths to tell them: she'd been outside at the time of the blast . . . Bill had looked very handsome that night . . .

She wanted it left at that: no cross-examination by heartbroken people, no half-truths, then perhaps at some time in the future she might journey to Surrey and quietly visit his grave.

CHAPTER FOURTEEN

'I wasn't sure if you'd remember me.'

Dawn dug her hands further into her coat pockets, feeling flustered by this man's unexpected appearance. 'Of course I do,' she blurted rather breathily. She couldn't pretend otherwise; the moment she'd noticed him standing there, his gypsy dark countenance illuminated by a gas lamp, she'd come to an abrupt halt.

But she understood why he'd made his remark; they'd only met a few times before, in dimly lit nightclubs with their partners, and hadn't exchanged more than a couple of short conversations.

Glenn Rafferty moved away from the car he'd been propped against. 'I'm sorry about what happened to Bill.'

'Thanks . . .' Dawn managed a weak smile and wondered whether to return condolences. But Bill had told her in their final conversation – if you could call their vicious argument such – that Glenn hadn't considered Tina to be his girlfriend. And now she came to think of it, the man himself had told her the same thing at the Kitkat Club.

She might not be able to recall all of what she and Glenn Rafferty had talked about, but every word of her confrontation with Bill was fresh in her mind, because she'd gone over it a thousand times since that awful night. Aware of a pair of hooded watchful eyes on her she gazed into the distance, wondering if Glenn knew that Bill and Tina had been a couple on the night they'd perished in the Café de Paris.

Dawn made a small movement as though ready to say goodbye. But instead of hurrying off home she delved into her handbag and pulled out her cigarettes. Clumsily she offered the pack, dropping it in the process and scattering its contents. 'I'm sorry as well about you losing Bill as a friend. And about Tina,' Dawn burst out while they were knee to knee, retrieving the cigarettes. 'Bill said it was . . . nothing special between you and Tina but even so it's a dreadful business.' Inwardly she told herself to shut up before she said something that sounded stupid.

'Tina wasn't killed that night.' Glenn straightened, slotting the cigarettes back in the pack then handing it back to her.

Dawn had immediately placed a cigarette between her lips but she withdrew it and her hand dropped back to her side. 'But . . . I thought . . . they were seen dancing together before the bomb exploded . . .' she stammered.

'She was luckier than he was. Perhaps Bill shielded her with his body. Tina was dug out with concussion and cuts and bruises.'

Dawn jerked the cigarette back between her lips and began searching for matches in her handbag.

Glenn flicked a lighter at her cigarette and the one

he'd helped himself to. Again he returned the pack to her, smiling wryly.

'I've something else to tell you . . . but not here . . . somewhere private.' Glenn glanced at the stage door where some showgirls and servicemen were chattering and laughing. 'Were you off home?'

Dawn nodded.

'Like a lift?'

'Thanks,' Dawn said after a brief hesitation. She saw no reason to refuse his offer and besides was very curious to know what else he had to say.

'Bethnal Green, isn't it?'

'Yes . . .'

'Bill told me you lived there,' Glenn said in response to an unspoken query in her tone.

'What part of London are you from?'

'Walthamstow,' he responded.

He slowed down at the traffic lights and gave her a searching look.

'You know that I was at the Café de Paris that night, don't you?' Dawn blurted, sensing his stare.

'Tina told me.'

'Bill told me you'd finished with her.'

'I went to see her. I wanted to ask her about Bill.'

'I see . . . is she recovering well?'

'Seems to be.'

Dawn sucked smoke deep into her lungs, exhaling it slowly. So he'd had a report from Tina and knew that she and Bill had had a fight because she'd caught Bill cheating on her. Dawn remembered that when in the Kitkat Club Bill's description of his friend had made Glenn seem a callous so and so. Glenn certainly hadn't shown any emotion when mentioning Tina a moment ago, yet Dawn's boyfriend – the man she had believed was falling in love with her – had wanted Tina.

Dawn had stormed out of the Café de Paris that night certain that Bill would follow her and apologise for being a fool. As she'd walked along, sobbing, Dawn had agonised over whether to give him a second chance. But Bill had wanted Glenn's cast-off more than his own girlfriend . . . and had died because of it.

A wave of indignation came over Dawn that Glenn knew all about her humiliation and rejection, without understanding why it should upset her. 'You said you had something to say to me,' she reminded coolly, blowing smoke.

'Bill was having an affair,' Glenn said.

'I don't think dancing with Tina at the Café de Paris proves he was having an affair,' she returned sharply.

'I wasn't talking about Tina,' Glenn explained quietly. 'Look . . . I wouldn't have told you about this, but I thought it might be better coming from me.' He steered with one hand and gestured with the other. 'If you want me to shut up I will – just say so.'

Dawn felt as though her heart was being squeezed into a tiny space. She'd battled her jealousy about Bill and Tina, convincing herself that her boyfriend hadn't lied when he'd said they'd not slept together. 'Bill was seeing someone else?' she murmured.

'Yeah . . . a woman in Ipswich.'

'You knew . . . when we went to the Kitkat Club that night, you knew about her then.' It was an accusation yet Dawn realised Glenn wasn't obliged to her in any way. Why would Bill's pal – a man who barely knew her, and was a womaniser himself – rat on his friend for being a two-timer?

'Yeah, I knew. Anyway, she's pregnant and has written to Bill's parents for their support.' It was a terse statement but suddenly Glenn pulled up at the kerb and turned off the engine. 'I'm sorry to be the one to tell you . . . but I thought you'd sooner have it from me.' He frowned through the window into the dusk. 'I didn't make the funeral in Surrey but I'd met Bill's folks on a couple of occasions and thought them nice people. I went to see them to pay my condolences when I next had leave. They were cut up about Bill, as you can imagine, being as he was the only child.' He paused. 'The Sweetmans told me they'd received a letter from a woman they didn't know about Bill fathering a child. They asked me if I knew if it was true, or whether the girl was lying to get a payout.' Glenn glanced at Dawn. 'I told them honestly what I knew. They were pleased about it. They see the kid as a gift . . . as Bill living on.' He dug in a pocket for his Weights, offered Dawn one and lit both their cigarettes. Glenn remained quiet for a few moments, allowing Dawn to recover from that blow before delivering the next. 'When I was there they mentioned you. The Sweetmans feel it's only fair they write to you to tell you about their future grandchild and explain why they don't want to keep in touch in the circumstances.' He blew smoke in a savage hiss. 'I just wanted to warn you about it, that's all . . .'

A tear slunk from a corner of Dawn's eye and she angrily brushed it away. 'When's the baby due?' she whispered.

Glenn shrugged. 'She's quite big . . . soon, I imagine.'

'What's her name?'

'It doesn't matter,' Glenn said kindly.

'It does matter!' Dawn spat through her gritted teeth, sucking repeatedly on her cigarette then grinding the stub underfoot on the floor of the car.

'Valerie.' Glenn flicked the stub of his cigarette through the open car window.

Dawn turned away from him, crouching back in the seat, arms wrapped around herself. The streetlights splintered into starry fragments as brine burned her vision. 'Well.' She choked a bitter laugh, smearing away the drizzle on her cheeks. 'You know something funny? I really thought I knew him . . .'

'I'm sorry . . .'

'Don't keep bloody well saying that!' Dawn screeched and slapped away his comforting hand on her arm.

Snatching at her handbag on the floor in front of her she grabbed another cigarette from her pack, striking blindly at a match to try and get it alight.

Glenn flicked the lighter at it for her then sat back quietly while she took deep agitated drags.

'He made out he was Mr Nice Guy and you were the creep who walked all over the girls.' Dawn wiped her face with a hand, coming close to burning it in the process. She angrily flicked the sagging ash onto the floor of the car. When Glenn remained silent she turned to glare at him. 'Was he right about you?'

Glenn shrugged, looked out of the window.

'I reckon he was right about you.' She let out a shrill giggle, unable to control her rising hysteria. She felt desperate to provoke him into reacting to her taunts. She wanted to hit someone . . . him . . .

'All bloody pilots are the same. Conceited bastards. Squadron leaders like you must think they're God's gift to women. I bet you can't even kiss nicely.'

'Any other time I'd take you up on it . . . but you're overwrought . . .'

'Don't bloody patronise me,' Dawn shouted.

With a gruff, mirthless laugh Glenn turned the ignition.

'Well, show me then!' Infuriated by his placid attitude, Dawn launched herself at him, plunging her mouth towards his, but missing and grazing her lips on his cheek.

He caught her chin in five dark fingers, forced her back an inch or so before touching together their lips then shoving her back into her seat.

Dawn sank slowly into the upholstery, her eyes closing as she fought back tears.

'Royston Street?'

She nodded.

'Number?'

She told him in a gasp.

The rest of the journey passed in silence, apart from Dawn's snuffling as she smothered her sobs. A few minutes later he pulled up and got out to open her door.

Dawn knocked away the hand that offered her help when she seemed unable to move. She stood up, feeling unsteady as though she was drunk, yet she'd had nothing but tea all day.

'Thanks for the lift . . . sorry about that . . .' she murmured, avoiding his eye by fumbling for her key as she walked away. Within a second of her getting inside the front door she heard the car pull off. She collapsed back against the panels in the way she had on the night Bill died. But this time she cried not for him, but for herself.

CHAPTER FIFTEEN

Dawn and Gertie Grimes spotted one another at about the same time. Dawn came to a halt but she could tell that Gertie would have preferred to hurry on by.

'Hello, Gertie,' Dawn offered pleasantly as they drew closer. 'Not seen you in a while. Heard you'd been off sick. Kids alright, are they?'

Gertie's husband might be a toerag but Dawn liked Gertie. The woman seemed a caring mother and she'd readily owned up to Midge and her husband being thieves rather than lie her way through the embarrassment of it.

'Been well as can be expected, thanks for asking. Had a bout of food poisoning and one of me sons had bad earache. Phyllis let me change me shifts around as well 'cos I'm doing a little evening job and need to fit that in.'

'I heard that Wilfred Pickering had given you a charring job.' Dawn had seen the accountant a couple of times and thought him a bit creepy. She knew he had his own office and didn't need to come to the theatre to do the books. She reckoned he turned up at odd times in the hope of eyeing up the showgirls in their underwear.

'Yeah . . . I'm working for Pickering.' Gertie cleared her throat, bouncing the pram by the handle, avoiding Dawn's eye. She knew she'd had quite a bit of time off work at the Windmill but most of her shifts there were earlies and she'd been throwing up every morning. Sometimes she felt too rough to get out of bed and get the kids to school. But she did because otherwise Rufus would start asking questions. So far she'd got away with blaming her queasiness on germs. Gertie had a far more pressing problem on her mind than missing shifts at the Windmill, and it was growing every day. 'How have you been, Dawn?' she burst out, putting the focus on the younger woman. 'I heard on the grapevine the terrible news about Sal Fiske. Didn't know the poor girl well . . .' Gertie sorrowfully shook her head, feeling rather ashamed that she'd been too preoccupied with her own problems to ask sooner about the dancer who'd perished at the Café de Paris.

'Oh, I'm . . .' Dawn's answer faded away. She'd been about to say, as she invariably did when asked, that she was fine, thanks. But she wasn't and she needn't pretend to Gertie that she was.

With her mother and brother, and with her other colleagues, Dawn made out she was coping stoically with Bill's loss and his betrayal. At times she was sure she even seemed a bit callous about it. With Gertie she could be honest because she'd inflict no lasting worry on a woman who already had more than enough problems of her own to contend with. 'I've not been so good actually,' she admitted with a sigh.

'I'm very sorry to hear that.' Gertie stopped rocking the pram and cocked her head at Dawn.

Dawn felt a prickle of spontaneous tears at Gertie's gruff, genuine sympathy. 'D'you remember that evening in the shelter when we moaned about the war and said that we'd had enough of it?' Dawn shook her head. 'I've come to realise that I didn't know I was born then, Gertie. I'd turn the clock back to that day if I could . . .'

'I'm guessing that you've recently lost someone dear to talk like that.' Gertie gave Dawn's arm a little squeeze.

'My boyfriend was killed as well as Sal when the Café de Paris was bombed.' Dawn felt immense relief at unburdening herself. The hateful memory would be back to torment her but sharing it gave some respite.

'Oh, that's dreadful bad luck!' Gertie exclaimed softly. 'I read in the newspaper that Snakehips Johnson and some of his band members were killed, weren't they?' She gave Dawn a searching look. 'If your boyfriend was there . . . I'm guessing that you were there too that night?' She clapped a hand to her mouth. 'Oh, Dawn, I didn't realise . . .'

Dawn nodded. 'We had a bad argument and I walked out on him . . . just before . . .' The rest she left unsaid, knowing Gertie could work it out for herself.

'Now you're feeling guilty about that 'cos you came out of it in one piece and he didn't.'

Dawn answered with a brief nod, her eyes glistening.

After a quiet moment Gertie said, 'I've heard it all from Rufus . . . according to him, he'll move heaven and earth for me, yet all he does is let me down one way or the other.' She touched Dawn's arm in comfort.

'Thing is, they mean it when they say it, and I'm guessing that during the good times your boyfriend told you he'd lay down his life for you . . .'

Gertie's words rang true; although Dawn had found out that Bill was a cheat and a liar she believed he'd been sincere when telling her he'd fallen for her and would propose when the time was right. The time never had been right for them, but Dawn cherished the memory of their tangling of hope and affection.

To stop the tears flowing she blinked into the pram, glimpsing a small face framed with auburn hair. 'Harold's grown . . .'

Gertie gave her youngest a fond look. 'He's almost eleven months and a good little lad . . .'

'He'll be toddling soon, won't he?' Dawn gave the baby's soft pink cheek a stroke with a fingertip.

'Yeah, he'll be up on his feet before too long.' Gertie's voice sounded hoarse. It made her insides squirm to think that in a matter of months she'd have a new baby to take Harry's place in the pram. And then she felt guilty for resenting a new life when death was everywhere.

Well . . . best get on,' Dawn said, bucking herself up. 'I just nipped into Gamages for a lipstick but I'm due on stage at seven o'clock. We're done up to the nines in Cleopatra costumes tonight.'

'Ooh, sounds lovely,' Gertie chuckled. 'Nothing so glamorous for me; I'm just off to do me evening job. Rufus is minding the others.' She let the brake off the pram. 'You take care of yourself.'

'And you too, Gertie. Be back working at the theatre soon, will you?'

'Oh yeah . . . anyhow the stagehands know how to use a broom. And Mabel doesn't mind doing an extra few hours.' Gertie mentioned the mother of one of the young lads who painted scenery.

Dawn gave a little wave, feeling oddly glad to have bumped into Gertie Grimes.

The women went their separate ways, unaware that their meeting had been observed.

Rufus wasn't pleased to see his wife in jolly conversation with the young woman who'd spied on him looting. Dawn Nightingale wasn't the person Rufus had been expecting to catch Gertie with; she was the wrong sex for a start. As Gertie walked on, Rufus continued brooding and following her at a safe distance.

Rufus knew he'd taken his wife for granted over the years, but he knew men who treated their womenfolk much worse. He knew fellows who would regularly give the missus a clump along with their housekeeping money, for no more reason than they didn't like parting with it.

They'd been married when they were both seventeen and Gertie had been pregnant with Joey. Over almost ten years of marriage he'd only laid into Gertie a handful of times. In Rufus's opinion Gertie was lucky to have him.

His wife wasn't ugly or fat, but she wasn't a shapely looker either like Dawn Nightingale. She was just plain Gertie . . . his wife, mother of his sons.

His wife. Yet Rufus's suspicions that she was playing around behind his back had grown to such a proportion that he sensed something was ready to explode in his head. He'd had an inkling for a while but done nothing, because he thought he must be dreaming. Who'd want Gertie when she lay like a sack of spuds under a fellow. Or perhaps with *him* – whoever he was – she didn't . . .

At first Rufus had swallowed her lies at face value: a lipstick given away by a girl at work. A cut and set done for nixes because a hairdresser she knew had wanted her shop windows cleaned on the quick, making Gertie late home. The money she brought in was handy so he'd accepted he'd have to look after the older kids when his wife did her shifts. Rufus didn't want Pickering turning nasty and sacking Gertie. He'd gone, uninvited, into the accountant's office once to fetch Gertie home because Joey had the toothache and wouldn't stop bawling. It had been shortly after Gertie started cleaning for Pickering. The accountant had looked up from his desk, scowling, then slammed his door shut on them. Rufus could remember saying to Gertie that he pitied her working for the miserable old sod.

His wife had tidied up her appearance but Rufus hadn't taken a lot of notice . . . till now. He'd taken a sly look in Gertie's chest of drawers in a hunt for clues as to what his wife was up to and found new underwear and lily of the valley talcum powder. Rufus knew lily of the valley talcum powder and fancy knickers weren't for his benefit and he'd wondered too where Gertie had got the cash to buy luxuries. He hadn't given her any extra and she still handed over her wages to him.

So something wasn't adding up.

Since Harry had been born Rufus had grown used to Gertie turning her back on him in bed because she didn't want another nipper round her ankles. They both knew that when he'd done well from his looting he'd not bother her and head for the red-light district. Gertie had only ever bawled him out over his other women once, when he'd given her a dose of the clap. That was another reason he sometimes held back on insisting on his full conjugal rights: he didn't want to risk infecting his wife again.

But last night had been the third night in a row that Gertie had turned to him in bed and stuck a hand down the front of his pyjamas before easing herself on top of him. The first time Rufus had been pleased as punch; the second night he'd got suspicious.

This morning Rufus had taken a look at Gertie while she was washing up, and noticed her belly looked a bit bigger. And that had *really* got him thinking . . .

When she'd set off for work earlier that evening, pushing Harry in his pram, Rufus had left the house too, just a few minutes later. He was hoping to catch her diverting to see her lover so he could knock the bloke's teeth down his throat. After that he would teach Gertie a lesson she wouldn't forget.

Rufus was stamping his feet to warm them when his wife bumped the pram down the steps of Pickering's office an hour and a half later. He'd hung about outside in the shadows, waiting for Gertie to finish her shift in case she was meeting her fancy man then. As soon as he realised that she was heading straight home he took a short cut through some back gardens. He knew he had to somehow beat his wife back to the house because she'd go mad if she found out he'd left their three older children alone indoors. There'd been no air-raid warning but darkness hadn't yet fully descended and the bombers could suddenly appear. He arrived five minutes before her, warning the boys to keep schtum about being left on their own.

'See anyone on yer travels, did you?' Rufus asked as his wife plunged her hands into the sink and began dunking socks in suds.

Gertie gave her husband a surprised look. He never usually asked her anything about what she'd done; in fact he usually collected his coat as she walked in the door. But he hadn't this evening. Rufus was still in the same place: sitting in the armchair with an open newspaper on his lap.

For a moment Gertie considered telling him that she'd bumped into Dawn Nightingale and they'd had a chat. But she reckoned that any mention of that young woman might cause her husband to fly off the handle. And Gertie knew she needed to keep Rufus sweet.

'Seen nobody apart from me boss.' The memory of that encounter made Gertie inwardly wince. The accountant had wanted his money's worth this evening and been quite a tiger with her, too . . . She turned to the sink, eyes lowered, and resumed dunking.

Rufus saw his wife's private smile and felt his gut writhe. So she was lying even about meeting Dawn Nightingale. But he was prepared to bide his time and catch her out with her lover rather than put her on her guard too early. Then he'd make them both pay . . .

'Who was that gorgeous man I saw you talking to earlier in the week?' Lorna sighed when her question went unanswered. 'Are you going to tell me, Dawn? I'm desperate to know whether he'll be back with his chums. I'd like an introduction.'

Dawn had been poking around in the props cupboard, looking for nothing in particular, and had had no idea that the question had been directed at her till hearing her name.

'Gorgeous man?' Marlene echoed with a tobacco-gruff chuckle. 'I wish I'd seen him. Come on, spill the beans.'

'Tall, dark, handsome, RAF type, smart car.' Lorna listed out the fellow's qualities, ticking them off on her elegant white fingers.

Dawn knew who Lorna was referring to and her stomach lurched, proving that she had not conquered her embarrassment over that encounter with Glenn Rafferty.

'Leave off, you two,' Rosie said, giving the two older women a fierce speaking look. 'It was just Bill's pal, come to see how Dawn's doing, that's all.'

Rosie had been at the stage door chatting with some servicemen on the evening Dawn had gone off with a stranger. She'd already asked Dawn about him. Her innocent query had brought an immediate blush to her friend's cheeks, and a brief explanation that he was Bill's pal. Rosie had judged the fellow must be of some importance to Dawn. Just a few weeks ago Rosie would have made a jokey comment similar to Lorna's about the good-looking pilot, but not now.

Rosie had witnessed most of the fight between Dawn and her boyfriend on the night Bill died. She reckoned that Dawn must be racked with heartache and guilt following such a bitter final parting.

Ever since they'd sheltered from the bombs together, watching the gang of thieves at work, Rosie had appreciated Dawn acting as her friend and guardian even if she'd never said so. Rosie knew Dawn now needed some support in return, and she was determined to give it.

Well-meaning people had told them they understood what they'd been through, and knew how they felt, but in Rosie's opinion they didn't have a clue. She and Dawn were the ones haunted by images of casualties and corpses. Olive Roberts had been there too but she seemed able to shut out the horror, probably because as a member of the WVS she'd turned up to similar scenes to dish out tea and sympathy. Olive had barely mentioned the incident since.

Rosie knew she'd never get used to such havoc. She had woken at night in a sweat with her skin burning and her ears ringing with screams. She'd realised what she'd heard were her own screams when her father had burst into her bedroom to cradle her in his arms. Rosie feared that sickening sounds and smells from that night in the obliterated ballroom would remain with her forever, robbing her of her peace of mind.

Dawn closed the cupboard door and sat down at the dressing table. She began touching up her make-up; the troupe was due back on stage soon. She gave Rosie a smile in the mirror as thanks for watching her back for her. Dawn always returned the favour, giving short shrift to anybody who probed her young colleague for gory details of her escape from the wreckage.

'His name's Glenn Rafferty and he's stationed in East Anglia, the same place Bill was.' Dawn had suddenly felt able to satisfy Lorna and Marlene's inquisitiveness. She squinted past the small brush sweeping her lashes. 'He came to tell me . . .' She hesitated, moistened the block of mascara with a small spit then scrubbed the brush to and fro to blacken it. 'He came to tell me . . .' Dawn resumed her report and her make-up '. . . that he'd seen Bill's parents recently and they'd rather not keep in touch with me. It was good of him to warn me I'd get a letter soon telling me so.'

'Well, that's a bit rich considering their son did the

166

dirty on you!' Rosie exclaimed. She sat down abruptly on a pile of pillows Olive had stacked up that morning.

'How terribly mean of them!' Lorna took up the argument. 'It's not your fault you caught him out cheating on you with another woman so walked out on him that night.'

'They don't want to punish me.' Dawn put away her mascara. 'It's just . . . the Sweetmans want to look to the future, not to the past and the bad memories. I feel the same way.' Once said, she realised that it was true.

'Good for you,' Rosie said and gave her friend an encouraging smile.

'I think we need to get over that awful night out by having another night out,' Dawn declared. 'We mustn't let Hitler cow us. We shan't hide away scared, but carry on regardless till the Hun are defeated.' Dawn stood to attention, chin tilted, with an exaggerated air of defiance that made her colleagues give a rousing cheer. 'How about we go to the 400 Club and dance till we drop?' she suggested with a grin.

'Well, I'm game.' Rosie sat down in Dawn's chair at the dressing table. Leaning forward she gently pressed a small healing scab close to her temple.

'Don't pick it.' Dawn tapped aside Rosie's fidgeting fingers. 'It's almost gone and you don't want a scar to remind you every time you look in the mirror.'

'It's itchy . . .'

'Endocil cream'll sort that out.' Gertie had just entered the dressing room carrying her cleaning paraphernalia in a tin pail.

'Hello, Gertie. Better now?' Rosie asked.

'I was till I saw her,' Gertie muttered beneath her

breath as Olive followed her in and shook the full teapot on the table. 'Anybody else fancy a cuppa?' she offered brightly and counted the hands that shot up.

More enquiries about Gertie's health followed, making the woman smile bashfully. Apart from her arch-enemy, they were a nice bunch of girls and she'd miss their company when she quit . . . as she must. Surreptitiously she eyed her belly beneath her pinny, loosening the strings, although she realised it was unlikely anybody else had noticed the tiny bump.

'Fit as a fiddle,' Gertie confirmed, dumping down her bucket. A moment later Gordon entered the dressing room, giving Lorna a soppy smile as he got out his screwdriver and set about tightening some loose fixings on a wall shelf.

Gertie suddenly went over to Rosie and gave her a hug. 'Glad to see you looking so good. So sorry about . . . everything . . .' She left the rest unsaid, sensing Rosie would prefer it that way.

'We got a thank-you note from Sal's parents for the flowers I took to the funeral. It came in the post this morning. Phyllis showed it to me.' After Lorna's announcement the little assembled company fell silent; they were all aware of a ghost occupying the empty chair in front of the mirrors.

'I wish I'd gone to the funeral,' Dawn said.

'We couldn't all go,' Lorna said kindly. 'The show must go on. We'll never close no matter what the damned Hun throw at us, and all that . . .'

'Rousing talk, that's the spirit,' Olive suddenly piped up, punching up a militant fist before distributing the tea.

Lorna had been working with Marlene and other showgirls in the theatre on the evening Dawn, Rosie and Sal went to the Café de Paris. At the time Lorna had grumbled because she'd wanted to go too; now she considered herself the luckiest girl alive. Between themselves they'd agreed that Lorna – who had worked the longest with Sal – would go to the funeral and represent them all.

'Phyllis told me that interviews are lined up for Sal's replacement,' Gertie chipped in, polishing a mirror.

'Well, it must be done. We are short now,' Lorna reminded her prosaically.

'We'll go out at the end of the week and toast Sal, that's what we'll do.' Dawn raised her teacup in salute and the others joined her. In unison they downed tea as eagerly as if it had been finest champagne.

'Sal'll be teaching the angels to tap dance, that's for sure,' Rosie said, clattering down her cup onto its saucer. 'Go on, Sal! Break a leg!' She jumped up and twirled herself around, jigging her feet. She lacked rhythm but she carried on energetically, holding up her silk wrap to prevent it tangling between her slender legs.

'Has somebody put a nip of gin in her tea?' Lorna laughed, watching Rosie cavorting.

'She doesn't need gin,' Dawn said softly. 'She needs to let off steam.' She'd noticed that Rosie, always a free spirit, had a more pronounced devil-may-care attitude since she'd escaped with her life from the ruins of the Café de Paris.

'Let's eat, drink and be merry, for tomorrow we may die . . .' Rosie cried, striking a theatrical pose, fingers at forehead, before her feet resumed flying.

Dawn got up and danced with her, because she couldn't deny that Rosie had a point.

A moment later Marlene and Lorna joined in and

having watched, grinning, for a moment, Gertie threw down her duster and did a version of 'Knees Up Mother Brown', with her pinny held out in front of her. Not wanting to be left out Gordon downed tools and linked arms with Olive and round and round they went.

CHAPTER SIXTEEN

'We got a letter from Sal's mum today, thanking us for the funeral flowers.'

Dawn had called that news out to her mother on getting home. She walked through into the kitchenette. Eliza was reaching up to the shelf where the post was kept.

'Talking of letters . . . this came for you today. It's postmarked Surrey.' Eliza gave her daughter a sympathetic smile. She knew Dawn had been expecting a letter because a fellow called Glenn Rafferty had told her Mr and Mrs Sweetman would be writing to her.

'Don't you want to open it?' Eliza asked when her daughter seemed reluctant to take the envelope.

'I will later.' Dawn pocketed it.

She'd not told her mother much about her meeting with Glenn. Eliza had twitched the curtain when she'd heard a car outside her house so had known her daughter had been given a lift home. Glenn Rafferty, Dawn had briefly explained, was Bill's friend and had come to pay condolences and warn her that Bill's parents wanted to cut ties with her. But Dawn hadn't given Mr and Mrs Sweetman's reasons for shunning her. Dawn had expected her mother to be up in arms on her behalf but she'd been surprised on that score. Eliza's theory was that the couple were embarrassed to admit that their late son was a wrong 'un so would sooner ignore the problem Dawn presented. Grief made people unpredictable, Eliza had said with a shrug, and left it at that.

There was another reason Dawn hadn't wanted to discuss in detail all that had gone on during her meeting with Glenn: she couldn't explain – even to herself – why she'd behaved so badly with a man who'd wanted to do her a favour. And Glenn had wanted to help; there had been no malice in him when telling her that Bill had fathered a child with another woman.

Dawn had told nobody about Bill's Suffolk mistress; it was her secret to keep. Bill was already diminished in the eyes of her family and colleagues because he'd cheated on her with Tina. If they really knew what he'd done they'd be horrified, and Dawn didn't want to further blacken Bill's memory.

'Reckon we might have a few late snow flurries on the way; it's nearly Easter too. George lit the fire earlier. Go and have a warm in the parlour, dear,' Eliza urged her daughter. 'I'll start on tea. It's Welsh rarebit; not a lot of cheese to go on it, I'm afraid, but we've got a nice pot of windfall chutney to liven it up.'

Through a crack between kitchen door and frame Eliza watched her daughter enter the parlour and stand by the glowing fire. A moment later Dawn drew the letter from her pocket, barely glancing at it before feeding it to the flames, unread.

Eliza smiled with a mixture of pride and sadness then turned about to cut bread to toast.

'Rosie's showing us all up. Do make her sit down, for goodness' sake.' Lorna crossed her legs in a slither of nylon. Tilting her head up to display her white throat she drew on her cigarette, blowing smoke from the corner of her perfectly rouged mouth.

'Leave her alone,' Dawn replied mildly. 'After what she's been through she deserves some recreation.' Every so often Dawn would catch a glimpse of Rosie's platinum hair. Her young colleague was on the fringes of the dancers, swaying to the band music and surrounded by a group of dashing gentlemen who at intervals were replenishing her brandy glass. 'Give Rosie a little while longer and she'll be back to her old self, you'll see.'

Lorna gave a tipsy chuckle. 'Maybe she will, but I'm not sure that's an improvement.' Ash fell from her cigarette onto her velvet cocktail dress as Lorna thumped her elbow on the table then supported her chin in a cupped palm. 'I wouldn't be at all surprised if the manager ejects us into the street in a moment.'

A whoop of laughter from Rosie's most ardent admirer came right on cue; sardonically Lorna raised her pencilled brows.

Rosie wasn't the only one who'd had a few too many drinks. Lorna hadn't noticed her skirt smouldering so Dawn brushed the ash away for her, making her companion jerk upright in surprise.

'I say . . . he's rather nice,' Lorna purred, stubbing out her cigarette in the ashtray. She gave a distinguished-looking fellow approaching their table a come-hither glance, but he walked on with a smile.

'Probably a queer,' Lorna mumbled disappointedly, dropping her chin back on its rest. 'We're supposed to be remembering Sal tonight.' She jerked her head in Rosie's direction. 'Sal would tell you the same about Rosie's behaviour.'

'What d'you reckon she'd say?' Dawn asked, taking a cigarette then sliding her pack across the table towards Lorna.

'She'd say, Rosie's acting like a trollop.' Lorna sighed in regret at having to be brutally honest, and helped herself to a Sobranie. She pointed the unlit cigarette at the fellows with Rosie. 'Hooray Henrys every one; I know the sort . . . no use to any girl. They'll scatter if Rosie goes arse over tit and probably won't even help her up first.'

Dawn smiled, liking the way her colleague's cut-glass accent mangled the vulgarity. 'Why did you start working at the theatre?' It wasn't the first time she had asked the question. Previously, Lorna had brushed it aside but this evening Dawn's fellow hoofer seemed obligingly talkative. Dawn was curious as to why a girl with Lorna's pedigree and connections would take to the stage. Dawn didn't know a lot about debutantes but reckoned they could do better for themselves than dancing their socks off at the Windmill Theatre.

'Daddy lost all his money because he liked to gamble . . . and womanise . . . and sodomise . . .'

Dawn choked on a mouthful of brandy and soda.

'Sorry . . . I really must stop repeating Mummy's sayings.' Lorna's bony shoulders undulated in a languid shrug. 'Once upon a time we lived in a country pile but we were always in debt up to our eyeballs. So Mummy sent me to dance school. Thick as two short planks, you see. I'd never have got a job as a secretary.'

Dawn gave her a smile and sipped her drink, thinking that Lorna might be a bit bossy and stuck-up but on the whole she was an alright sort. And perhaps she had a point. It was probably time to leave before Rosie keeled over.

They'd arrived at the 400 Club in Leicester Square at just before nine o'clock. It was a place renowned for having an exclusive clientele, so Lorna, with her crisp tones and superior air, had swept in first. But it would be best to drink up and go before somebody complained that they were lowering the tone.

Dawn finished her brandy and stood up, shaking her head at a young naval officer, resplendent in navy blue brocaded uniform. He'd started to approach her, hand outstretched in wordless invitation to waltz. Dawn had been aware of him watching her, trying to catch her eye, but she didn't feel ready for a dalliance – or even a dance – with any man. Her friends' company was sufficient for her for now. But she gave him an apologetic smile.

Rosie noticed Dawn approaching and side-stepped her gallants to catch her in her arms.

'Are you going to tell me off?' she asked. 'I know I'm a bad girl. Marlene reckons I could be a *very* bad girl without too much trouble at all.'

'I reckon you're a very sozzled girl,' Dawn said ruefully, steering Rosie back towards their table. She was about to sit down when she belatedly realised she'd skimmed her vision over a familiar figure. Dawn turned back, her heart thumping as she stared at a young brunette wearing a red dress. It wasn't the same red dress . . . but it was near enough for Dawn to momentarily feel she'd been dizzyingly transported back to the last time she'd seen Bill alive. Without giving a thought to what she was doing she marched across the room. The sound of the band playing 'Oh Jonny, Oh Jonny, Oh!' was drowned out by the pulsating thump of blood in her ears. Before she'd come to a complete stop Dawn announced, 'Well . . . I see you're already back on your feet and enjoying life.'

Tina swung about, her smile collapsing when she saw who'd spoken. 'Oh . . . hello . . .' Uneasily she glanced about. 'Sorry about everything that happened.' With a shrug she turned back to the fellow with her. He languidly dug into a pocket of his dinner jacket and produced a silver case and lighter. He lit the cigarette Tina had placed between her crimson lips while cocking his sleek head to give Dawn a top-to-toe look.

Dawn ignored his leer and concentrated on Tina. She felt incensed by the brunette's attitude. She wasn't about to let this woman dismiss Bill, or her, so carelessly. Catching Tina's arm, she jerked her around.

'Bill died that night.' Dawn's reminder was quiet and cold. She saw that Tina's face bore a scar, close to her cheekbone, that had been inexpertly concealed with thick face powder.

'I know he didn't make it.' Tina's red mouth pursed in resentment. 'And *I* was lucky to survive, you know.'

'Did Bill protect you from the worst of it?' Dawn asked.

Tina nodded, looking arrogant rather than humbled by her admission that Bill had probably saved her life and in doing so lost his own.

'Look, what do you expect me to do about any of it?' Tina rolled her eyes. 'He was *your* boyfriend, not mine. I only went out with him a couple of times. I know I shouldn't have stolen him . . .' She simpered at her suave companion. 'But it was easy enough to do. Anyhow, you had nothing to worry about; I was going to give him back. Bill was never special to me.'

Hearing Tina speak so about Bill made Dawn feel as though she'd been winded by a punch. 'You callous cow!' she breathed. 'Because of you I had a huge argument with Bill the night he died and I can never tell him how sorry I am for that. Yet all you've got to say is he was never special to you.'

'You'd no need to be jealous. I was only with him to get to Glenn.' Tina kept her voice low so her escort couldn't hear what she was saying. 'I wanted *Glenn*, not your boyfriend, and if you'd stuck around I would have told you so.'

'I thought I recognised her . . .' Rosie had ambled up behind Dawn and was wagging a finger at Tina. In her other hand she swayed her brandy and ginger ale. 'She's the one who was throwing herself at your boyfriend in the Café de Paris.'

'Perhaps he dreamt I did . . .'

Tina's sarcasm was the last straw. Dawn spontaneously slapped the brunette's face, making her howl.

'I'd've hit her harder,' Rosie said with a grin that widened as she saw an elegant woman close by was gawping at the commotion.

Tina soothed her smarting cheek with red-tipped fingers. In a show of bravado she tossed her brunette waves over a shoulder before turning back to her companion. 'A pair of drunks. Shame they don't know when they've had enough.' She gave a contemptuous laugh.

Rosie tugged Tina round by her hair. 'There . . . you have that then, if you reckon I've had enough.' She threw the brandy and ginger ale in Tina's face then followed it up with a thump that sent the brunette flying. 'Laugh that one off, if you can.'

Tina sprawled onto the floor, her dress askew and her knickers on display.

'Surprised she's wearing any,' Rosie said, eyeing the lacy frillies.

Tina scrambled to her feet, lunging at Rosie, claws at the ready, but her embarrassed escort sprang between the girls, holding them apart.

'I'll swing for that bitch,' Rosie spat through her teeth, trying to get a hand to Tina's face so she could deliver a scratch.

'I never wanted your fucking darling Bill anyhow,' Tina snarled at Dawn. 'He wasn't a patch on Glenn, in bed or out . . .'

'But Glenn doesn't want you, does he?' Dawn got a small amount of satisfaction in seeing Tina wince from her cutting remark about Glenn's indifference. A moment later she was blinking back tears; Bill had lied to her more than she'd imagined. Tina had seen him more than once, and had slept with him. Yet Bill had vowed the opposite was true.

'Who told you that Glenn doesn't want me?'

Dawn turned to go without answering, dragging Rosie with her. But Tina darted to intercept them.

'Have you spoken to Glenn?' she demanded.

'He came to the Windmill Theatre to see me.'

'Oh, yes, you're one of *those* girls, aren't you?' Tina jeered. 'Bill told me he didn't like what you did for a living . . .'

'He didn't like what you did either, or so he said,' Dawn retaliated. She suddenly stopped attempting to get past the small brunette and slumped into her shoes. She felt sickened to know that Bill had discussed her with a woman he'd once described as a prostitute. 'You talked about me?'

'Not for long.' Tina began dabbing with a handkerchief at her damp face and stained dress. 'Bill had more important things on his mind that night . . . *me* . . .'

Dawn recognised the calculated malice behind Tina's words but she'd no more capacity to be provoked into a fight or a slanging match. She felt ashamed of herself for having been the first to lash out. She was also hurt and humiliated by Tina's taunting comments. But mostly she felt raw with sadness and anger that Bill had so wholly betrayed her trust in him.

Dawn was lucky to get home before midnight; she'd seen Rosie safely home to Shoreditch before making tracks towards Bethnal Green.

As she turned the corner she was vaguely aware, from the corner of a lowered eye, of a car parked close to her door. Preoccupied as she was with poring over the disastrous evening spent at the 400 Club, she took little notice of it.

When a man got out of the vehicle and started to approach Dawn, her face jerked up and her steps faltered.

'Hope you didn't mind me waiting for you. Your mother said you were due home soon.'

'You've spoken to my mum?' Dawn eventually croaked, having stared silently at Glenn Rafferty's dark features. She glanced past him to her front door.

'Yeah . . . do you mind?'

Dawn simply moistened her lips, thinking about that one.

'She invited me in to wait for you,' Glenn explained. 'I stopped for a while and had a cup of tea with her, then left. Didn't seem right making her wait up with me if she was ready for bed.'

'What do you want?' Dawn's mind had leapt ahead and she was already wondering whether he'd come to give her yet more bad news about Bill's sins.

Glenn shrugged. 'It was nothing really. I just wanted to see how you were, and apologise for last time.'

Dawn felt a blush steal into her cheeks. *She* was the one who should say sorry; but she'd already done so, at the time, and had no intention of reminding him of her temper tantrum or that clumsy kiss.

'It was a stupid thing to do, turning up out of the blue like that and upsetting you. I could have been a bit more diplomatic about it.'

He stubbed the toe of his shoe repeatedly into the ground in a way that seemed to Dawn quite boyish. Yet he was no boy; he might be about Bill's age, twenty-eight, but Glenn Rafferty had a jaded air that made him seem older and more dangerous to know.

'I . . . I'm glad you did tell me,' Dawn blurted. 'The letter turned up from Bill's parents.'

'Right,' Glenn said. He glanced at her as though waiting for her to elaborate.

'I didn't bother reading it before I burned it. I knew what it would say after all.'

'You trusted me that much?'

Dawn felt taken aback by his astute comment. 'Yes . . . I suppose I did . . .'

'Do you trust me enough to go out with me one evening?'

Dawn looked at him as he drew out a packet of

180

cigarettes from a trouser pocket. His face was lowered to his moving hands; she couldn't see his eyes and she wanted to. But she remembered that Tina liked Glenn Rafferty very much . . . and Dawn hated everything about her.

'No, I won't go out with you . . . but thanks for asking.' Dawn stepped past him on her way to her door.

Glenn seemed unruffled by her rejection. He fell into step beside her, casually offering her a cigarette. She shook her head so he took one himself then put away the pack. 'Your mum said you were out socialising. Where have you been this evening?'

'Out dancing with some girls from work. We went to the 400 Club because we wanted to cheer ourselves up. One of our colleagues was killed; Sal Fiske was with us at the Café de Paris,' Dawn briefly explained.

'Sorry to hear it. Did it work?'

Dawn glanced quizzically at him as he bent his head to a light cupped in his hand.

'Did you cheer yourself up?' He flicked out the burning match.

'No, not really,' Dawn murmured. Again she was aware of his eyes searching her profile. 'We got into a fight.'

'At the 400 Club?' She could discern the mockery in his voice. It was proof enough that he'd frequented the classy venue . . . perhaps with Tina.

'Yes, the 400 Club. And I bet your ears have been burning this evening.' Dawn turned to face him, one hand on her garden gate.

'You've been talking about me?'

'I didn't have as much to say about you as Tina . . .' Dawn felt an odd sense of satisfaction. He hadn't concealed his expression quickly enough this time and

181

she saw a glimmer of anger in his eyes before his long black lashes fell.

'Tina was there and you had a fight with her?'

'Yes she was and yes I did.'

'Who won?'

'Well, it wasn't a fair contest; one of my friends got involved, so I'll be generous and call it a draw.'

Glenn dropped his half-smoked cigarette and ground it beneath his toe. 'Bill wasn't worth fighting over, you know that, don't you.' He gazed straight at her. 'I knew him better than you.'

Dawn felt her hackles rise. She knew he was right but she didn't want any lectures on morality from a man like him. The tussle between Tina and herself had been over Bill at the start, but had ended up in a clash over Glenn Rafferty. And she was confused and exasperated to acknowledge the fact.

Dawn stared into a dense dark night. There had been no air raid yet this evening but the windows in the houses lining the street leaked only slivers of light through their blackout curtains. Most people were constantly on tenterhooks and prepared for an attack.

Throughout their conversation Glenn had kept his tone soft, as if conscious of disturbing her family and neighbours. Dawn was grateful for his consideration. But nothing else about him pleased her.

'Perhaps you did know Bill better than I did; but he'd have been better off without a friend like you. You introduced Bill to Tina.' Her voice was as mild as his had been but the accusation in her eyes was lethal.

'I didn't introduce him to Valerie. He found her all by himself.'

'He found me all by himself too,' Dawn returned.

'So he did . . . lucky bastard, eh?'

Dawn was astonished by that comment, and unsure whether the edge to his tone was sarcasm or envy.

By the time she was ready with an answer it was too late, as Glenn had got in his car and was soon pulling away from the kerb.

CHAPTER SEVENTEEN

'I'd love to know what's he done with his big mouth.' Marlene chuckled lewdly. 'Are you going to tell us?'

Dawn snatched the small card that Marlene was tapping against a fingernail. She threw it into the waste bin under the dressing table where it landed amidst rouge-smeared tissues and a crust of bread from a sandwich.

'Well, if you don't want them, I'll have them.' Rosie picked up the beautiful bouquet that Glenn Rafferty had had delivered to the theatre. Accompanying it had been a card, hidden in the foliage, on which he'd apologised for having a big mouth.

A moment ago Phyllis had brought the flowers along to the dressing room for Dawn. On first receiving them she had felt rather flattered. A sweet little old army officer had been sitting in the front row of the stalls all week winking at her and she'd thought he must have sent them.

'I'm popping over to the caff for a bun,' Rosie said, laying down the bouquet on the dressing table. 'I'm hungry as a horse.'

184

'I'll come with you,' Marlene said, stepping over blankets strewn on the floor. 'I've not had a bite since breakfast.'

'Ooh, what lovely flowers . . . my Fred buys me nice flowers.' Olive had come into the dressing room to start tidying away bedding before the ticket office opened. She sniffed the scent given off by waxy petals.

'Have you seen Fred lately?' Dawn asked. She wished Olive would go away so she could mull over why Glenn was being so nice to her when she seemed to constantly blame him for everything. Besides, there was something about Olive and her perfect husband and obedient children and her good works that grated on Dawn's nerves. She knew that the whole business surrounding losing Bill had given her a short fuse so tried to be tolerant with the woman.

'Oh, my Fred's a busy man, what with his cadet training duties and so on. He never gets time to come home. I don't mind; he's doing it all for the greater good.'

'How about your boys . . . are they coming to visit you?' Dawn interrupted, hoping to piss Olive off enough to make her go away of her own accord. The woman invariably found something urgent to do when questioned about her neglected sons.

'Who sent you these in? One of those nice airmen?' Olive changed the subject rather than leaving the room. 'Your boyfriend was stationed in East Anglia, wasn't he?'

Dawn nodded.

'Bad business at the Café de Paris, wasn't it? Did you ever visit him at his base?'

'I was planning to go, but never did get around to it . . .'

Olive squeezed Dawn's shoulder. 'Never mind; is this chap a pilot?' She again fondled the bouquet on the dressing table.

'A squadron leader . . .' Dawn murmured.

'Oh my. One of our best aces, I'll bet.'

'No work to do?' Gertie had entered the dressing room and given Olive a sour look while emptying a waste bin into a sack. She might be feeling anxious about the way things were going in her life but Gertie still found time to snipe at the woman.

Olive mumbled beneath her breath and began folding blankets.

Gertie picked up the bin by Dawn's legs. 'Bloody woman,' she said. 'With all her airs and graces you'd think she'd be working in Whitehall, not manning a theatre kiosk . . .' Gertie broke off, startled by Dawn suddenly whipping something out of the bin she was about to upend.

'Fell in by accident,' Dawn explained as she grabbed the card Glenn had sent.

A moment later Gertie had dragged out the rubbish sack and Olive had gone too, leaving Dawn in peace. She picked up the flowers and breathed in their delicate perfume. Turning over the parchment she'd retrieved she read a line of sloping black script.

Sorry about my big mouth. I really don't want to hurt you.

Having reread the message Dawn closed her eyes for a moment then crumpled the note in her fist.

Having got a vase from a cupboard she filled it with water then carefully arranged the hothouse lilies. She stood the flowers by the mirror that Rosie usually used before stepping back and cocking her head in consideration. The display was gorgeous, far more lavish a gift than the few posies that Bill had bought her. But those she had been glad to have. This bouquet was like the man who'd sent it: flash and overpowering. She didn't want Glenn Rafferty's flowers or his apologies because she suspected that they weren't sincerely given; she knew too that he could hurt her whether he wanted to or not.

'Fucking hell, what's that stink? Did something die in here?'

Popeye Purves had just got home from work at his printing shop. He'd entered the back parlour to find a nauseating smell and his son and Midge slouching opposite one another at the table with a bottle of John Gardiner's 'Scotch' between them.

'What've I told you about starting on that too early in the day?' Frank Purves pointed at the rotgut. His son had been getting a bit above himself lately, and Popeye knew why that was. Lenny thought he was taking over both the legal and illegal enterprises before Popeye was ready to hand over the reins to them. His son had been pushing his weight around, and when he was in drink, Lenny could get vicious. Frank knew he could come across as a bit soft but if his son thought he'd get one over on him, he was heading for trouble. And so was anybody else who thought they could rip him off. He was still in charge and that was the way it was staying.

'Giving Midge a snifter, ain't I?' Lenny sullenly told his father. 'He needs it; he's in a right state.'

Popeye approached Midge, wrinkling his nose in disgust on realising that the stench was coming off the little man. He looked at Midge's bloated fingers, wrapped in a dirty bandage, and felt himself gagging.

'Need your help, Pop,' Midge coughed. 'Can you do something for me?' Limply he lifted his poisoned hand.

'You should've kept it clean, you idiot,' Popeye snarled. 'What you expecting me to do to put that right? I ain't a doctor.'

Midge was simmering with rage despite his shivering fever and thumping headache making him feel weak as a kitten. In Midge's opinion it was everybody's fault but his own that he was in the mess he was in. Lenny, Rufus and his brat, Popeye . . . all of them had had a part in it. 'The stitches are infected.' Midge wafted his bandaged fingers in front of Popeye's face.

'They wasn't fuckin' infected when they went in, was they?' Popeye snapped defensively, rearing back from the stench. 'Ain't my fault you're living rough. You need to get to the hospital and get it sorted out.'

'Yeah . . . I'll get sorted out alright; I'll be behind bars.'

'Go and see yer sister, then. She'll do what she can for you.'

Midge grabbed the bottle of whisky and upended it into his empty glass. He took an immediate swig.

He'd been to his sister's. He'd felt so ill that he'd not waited till it was dark but crept in the back way. Gertie had gone spare because the kids were just having their teas and had gawped at him as though he were a stranger. Midge knew he looked a mess and didn't need Gertie rubbing it in. But she'd given him a couple of bob to get rid of him before Rufus finished work and went berserk.

Midge knew he had a decision to make; he could carry on as he was and die of blood poisoning or he could hand himself in and risk facing a noose. Either way he'd end up in the same place: the cemetery.

'I thought you said you was going off down Kent way to get yourself seen to where you wasn't known?' Lenny was pacing the room. He was worried. He knew that Midge was bitter over how things had turned out with his injury. Midge was the sort of snide character who'd make sure everybody suffered along with him when things turned bad.

'Didn't get no help down in Kent. The Chislehurst caves were a lark though . . . before I started feeling too rough to make the most of me time there.' Midge's mouth drooped in disappointment.

When Midge had arrived at the caves he'd been feeling quite chipper in himself. His hand seemed no worse and he thought it might get better on its own. The moment he met Eunice plying her trade in the dimly lit tunnels his health was no longer top priority. He'd used nearly all his cash on having a good time with her. Midge's theory was that he could be gone tomorrow so he was going to make sure he enjoyed himself today. Then one night he'd woken up in a sweat and knew his hand was playing up again.

'Why didn't you get a doctor to look at it for you?' Popeye knew the little git was trying to pin the blame on him for his septic hand.

'Went to the local hospital. Nurse in there wanted to phone London for me records, suspicious bitch.' Midge thumped down his glass and he began to chortle at some amusing memory. 'She said I looked like a vagrant and they couldn't be too careful 'cos in the past an injured German had bailed out over Kent and tried to pass himself off as a Polish shepherd to get his mangled leg looked at.' Midge bashed the table in mirth with his good hand. 'I said to her, you silly cow, I'm a dirty so and so 'cos I'm a chimney sweep and me accent's cockney not Kraut.'

Midge threw back his head and roared with laughter so infectious that Popeye and Lenny joined in.

Despite his disgust, Popeye had a horrified fascination to see what lay beneath the filthy cloth covering Midge's hand. Gingerly he unwrapped the bandage and grimaced in revulsion at the mound of red and yellow flesh. 'Could try lancing it I suppose.' Popeye rubbed his chin thoughtfully.

'Do that then. Anything,' Midge said, reaching for the liquor bottle and slumping back in his chair.

'Lenny, go and put the kettle on,' Popeye ordered. 'We'll need hot water. Bring us in the washing-up bowl and some old towels . . . clean, from the airing cupboard. Get us a needle too.' He looked at the monstrous carbuncle. 'Second thoughts, perhaps a meat skewer might be best,' he said. 'Get one out of the kitchen drawer.'

When Midge came round – he'd passed out on seeing the assembled instruments of Popeye's amateur surgery – he was feeling quite a bit better.

Lenny on the other hand had thrown up into the washing-up bowl the moment the pus started spurting from Midge's rotting palm. He was sitting in the corner with his head in his hands.

'Be good as new,' Popeye said, winding terry towelling about Midge's tattered flesh. 'I've given it a good bathing. Now you'd best get yourself off, mate. I'm expecting John Gardiner to come by with a few more of those.'

Popeye nodded at the empty whisky bottle. 'Don't want no strangers getting a look at you now, do you?'

'Got any work coming up? I could do with some cash.'

'Yeah . . . yeah . . . be in touch about that. Lenny or Rufus'll know where to find you. Give you a shout, they will . . .'

Once Midge had gone, father and son looked at one another. Popeye shook his head. Lenny knew what he meant by that. Next time they saw Midge – if they saw him alive – he'd only have one hand and wouldn't be much use on a job at all.

John Gardiner had been frightened witless when his daughter had been caught in the blast at the Café de Paris. For weeks afterwards he'd fussed around his only child although Rosie had escaped with minor physical injuries. Her cut face had healed well but John knew his daughter still bore the mental scars of what she'd witnessed that night. Rosie had always been outspoken but since suffering the trauma she'd become belligerent with it. John had made allowances at first – he'd even packed in brewing in the cellar for a while to please her – but he had had enough of Rosie's moods. Earlier when she'd gone out to the market to meet her friend he'd breathed a sigh of relief to have the house to himself once again.

When John heard his daughter's key go in the lock he raced up the cellar steps as fast as his arthritis would allow, and met her in the hallway.

'Is it alright, Dad, if Marlene has a cup of tea before she heads off home?'

''Course it is; we're a hospitable bunch, us Gardiners.' John gave the pretty young woman with his daughter a smile. He held out his hand. 'John Gardiner and pleased to meet you, Marlene.'

'Likewise.' Marlene gave him a crafty look. To her it didn't matter who a fellow was, or what age he was, he was a potential punter.

But as far as John Gardiner was concerned, she was on her best behaviour, so she adopted a demure expression. Marlene's idea was to worm her way into this old fellow's good books. She'd pestered Rosie that afternoon to take her to meet her father as they were in the area. Rosie had warned Marlene that he could be a grumpy old so and so. But Marlene knew if she were ever going to persuade Rosie to move into her spare room, she'd need to win over John Gardiner and gain his trust. Rosie might act tough and brash but underneath it all she was just a little girl who listened to her daddy.

If Mr Gardiner believed Marlene Brown was a nice, decent sort he was less likely to make a fuss when Rosie told him she was moving out to be Marlene's flatmate. Malt was getting impatient with her hooking the blonde and Marlene knew the sooner her boyfriend started pimping more girls – especially cute virgins like Rosie – the more he'd earn and the sooner they'd be able to get married.

'I'll put the kettle on, and I reckon I might find some custard creams too,' John said, feeling quite chuffed that Rosie's pretty friend had given him the eye. Oh, yes, he'd seen her doing it, then pretending not to.

He might be in his fifties but he'd kept himself in trim. He'd noticed the woman in the bakery giving him a look too when he'd told her she'd given him the wrong change, handing back a threepenny bit. When the war was over John reckoned he might find himself a lady friend. His wife had been gone a while and Rosie was of an age to be settling down herself. John was sure that once they'd all got back to normal his daughter would want a family of her own. With her lovely looks and smashing personality Rosie would soon meet a nice young fellow who'd make her happy and give her a brood of kids to keep her occupied . . .

CHAPTER EIGHTEEN

'I don't want you to keep coming here to pick me up. I don't need anything else from you. I don't want your pity or your apologies or your flowers.'

'Yeah, I know.'

The day after he'd sent her a bouquet Glenn had been parked outside the theatre waiting for Dawn when she finished work. Butterflies had circled her stomach at the sight of him but she'd continued walking as she turned down his offer of a lift home.

His curt response now brought her to a halt. She pivoted about to find he hadn't followed her and still had both elbows resting on the roof of his car.

'So why have you wasted your time coming here?'

'I'm hoping I've not wasted my time coming here,' he returned.

'I'm not interested in hearing any more tales of Bill's infidelity either,' Dawn said flatly.

'It's not about Bill. It's not about you either. It's about me. I want you to help me . . . that's why I'm here.'

That took the wind out of Dawn's sails. 'I don't under-stand . . .' She approached him hesitantly.

'Have you wondered why I've not returned to base?'

'No . . .' Dawn realised then that he certainly had been on leave for a long while. 'I don't think about you. Why would I?' she lied. She'd thought of him more than she cared to admit to him or herself.

Glenn smiled sardonically at his entwined fingers on the top of the car. 'That's put me in my place. And I reckon it's answered my question about whether you'd want to help me.'

He opened the car door, about to get in.

'Well, don't go off in a huff,' Dawn exclaimed. 'You might as well tell me the rest, now you've started it.'

'Get in the car then.'

'You can tell me here,' Dawn said suspiciously. Perhaps the sort of 'help' he wanted was the sort that Tina provided for him.

'Get in,' Glenn said dryly, reading her mind. 'It's confidential.'

His hard-eyed stare travelled to a group of sailors clustered about the back door, eagerly awaiting more showgirls to emerge so they could chat them up. Dawn had been approached, but had good-naturedly rebuffed the cocky ringleader who'd tried to win her over by jokily dancing the hornpipe, egged on by his friends. She wondered now how much of it Glenn Rafferty had seen.

'You can say what you have to while taking me straight home.' Dawn didn't want him to think she was succumbing to anything other than curiosity.

'I'm not just doing my bit for king and country as a Spitfire pilot.' Glenn's announcement came shortly after he'd pulled away from the kerb.

Dawn shifted on the seat so she could better read his expression. 'Oh . . .?' She was already interested enough to want to hear more.

'I'm making a few undercover investigations, for the nobs in Whitehall I imagine; my immediate superiors don't give me the full picture. I wouldn't expect them to.'

Dawn mulled over that information, in between sliding him glances. 'Espionage?' She sounded as though she was torn between finding the idea horrifying and amusing.

'Sort of,' he smiled. 'Don't worry, I'm not getting dropped behind enemy lines in civvies. You've no need to fret over my safety on that score. 'Course I might crash and burn at any time.'

Dawn felt that there was a barb aimed at her somewhere in that comment.

'I'm after the enemy behind our lines, if you like.'

'If you're telling the truth . . . shouldn't you be keeping quiet about it?' Dawn moistened her dry lips, suddenly feeling ill at ease.

'I'm not making it up and I do want your help. I'm trusting you not to repeat what I say . . .'

'I don't know if I want you to say any more,' Dawn interrupted. She worked as a dancer in a theatre, entertaining the troops, and ran the gauntlet of German bombers on the way home from work, the same as every other Londoner. She wasn't sure she wanted to get more involved in the war effort than that.

Glenn pulled over and turned off the engine. 'Look, I've taken a chance on you and I want you to come through for me. I did you a favour . . .'

'*Did* you?' Dawn had a burst of enlightenment. 'I

reckon you did yourself more of a favour. You didn't tell me about Bill cheating, or his parents' letter, out of the goodness of your heart! You wanted to make me feel beholden to you, didn't you? That's why you came to see me in the first place.'

'Partly,' he admitted, seemingly unrepentant. 'But I reckoned you'd want to help the fight against the Nazis, in any case. The Germans killed your boyfriend and your colleague; but for a stroke of luck that night, they might have killed you too at the Café de Paris.'

Dawn couldn't deny the truth in any of that, and of course she wanted the Nazis defeated as much as anybody; but she sensed danger ahead and her duty as far as she was concerned was first and foremost to her family. And she'd be no use to them at all if she ended up arrested . . . or dead.

'I'm not getting dragged into any of this. I don't want me or my family snooped on by blokes in false moustaches. I've got enough problems with my mum as it is . . .' Dawn broke off. She'd no intention on elaborating about that. 'You shouldn't have told me any of this!' she cried angrily.

'You stopped me driving off a moment ago, and asked me to finish what I'd started to say,' he reminded her mildly.

'Well, I didn't realise what you'd say,' she argued. 'You shouldn't have told me!'

'But I have, and now you know all about me.'

There was an odd inflection in his voice that put an icy shiver on Dawn's spine. 'Are you threatening me?'

'Of course not.' He smiled at his fingers tapping the steering wheel. 'I'm the good guy.' He turned fully towards her in the seat, studying her with confident directness. 'You're not in any danger and you won't get snooped on.' Slowly he stretched out a hand as though to draw her towards him.

Dawn barely flinched, but he'd noticed her reaction and withdrew his fingers with a wry smile. 'I thought you wanted to know if I could kiss properly.'

'Well, I don't any more . . .'

'Sure about that?'

'Positive,' Dawn whispered, hating him for bringing *that* up. 'Take me home.'

'Didn't have you down as a coward,' he taunted, relaxing back in his seat.

'Insults won't work, so save your breath,' Dawn scoffed. 'I won't rise to the bait.'

'Shame . . . on both counts . . .'

He started the engine and they drove to Bethnal Green in silence. Dawn's mind was in turmoil during the journey. She reckoned she could be in danger, and not just from spies and the like. A moment ago she'd wanted Glenn to pull her into his arms and kiss her, whatever she'd said to the contrary. She'd felt a pang of disappointment when he'd not. The car pulled to the kerb outside her door but he stopped her getting out by lightly clasping her arm.

'Your mum liked me, didn't she?'

Dawn glanced through the dusk at his angular face, half in shadow. Indeed her mother had liked him. The morning following Glenn Rafferty's visit Eliza had praised to the skies the handsome, charming pilot who'd had a cup of tea and a chat with her.

'You made sure she did, didn't you?' Dawn gave a sour laugh. 'I bet you were on your best behaviour. But wheedling your way into my mum's good books won't work either. Is there anything you won't stoop to, to get your own way?'

'Probably not, if there's a chance it's going to help win the war. I've got parents I'd like to see grow old and sisters I'd like to see grow up. You're not the only one with people relying on you.'

Dawn bit her lip, feeling chastened. She'd never before thought of Glenn Rafferty as a family member – just as Bill's friend, or Tina's lover.

'What problems have you got with your mum?'

'None of your business,' Dawn tightly replied.

'You really don't like me very much, do you?'

Dawn shook her head, rather than voice her answer.

'Why? Because I know girls like Tina? It's just work . . . she's useful.'

'I bet,' Dawn muttered.

'I consort with Tina, she consorts with Hooray Henrys and known Nazi sympathisers.'

Dawn had been sure there was nothing he could say that would overcome her desire to be away from him and safely inside her door. But she'd seen Tina with men who fitted that description at the 400 Club. Her hand hovered on the handle instead of gripping and turning it. And he'd noticed her hesitation.

'It started when I was approached to find out about an illegal still operating locally in Suffolk.' Glenn stretched his long legs out under the steering wheel as though settling in for a while. 'Hooch is readily available and the Air Ministry, along with every high command, I imagine, is aware it's being drunk by servicemen. A lethal batch of booze could ground a squadron, or worse. The consequences are unthinkable. I don't need to draw you a picture of what would happen if enough pilots drank stuff similar to the poison that sent that seaman off his rocker.'

Dawn knew exactly which incident Glenn was referring to as it had been widely reported at the time: a deranged sailor had jumped from a window in Waterloo Station, under the influence of hooch.

'Britain needs the RAF guarding the skies, and if hundreds of pilots weren't fit to fly, or worse, did fly then went nuts, it would be a total disaster.'

'Surely that would never happen,' Dawn said, aghast.

'There are people – our countrymen amongst them – who admire Hitler enough to hope it might happen.'

'You mean . . . like the Mitford sisters . . . those sorts?' Dawn had heard about members of the English aristocracy having a shameful closeness to Britain's enemy.

'Traitors come in all guises. You'd be surprised.' Glenn pulled his pack of cigarettes from his pocket.

When he offered one to her Dawn shook her head so he lit up alone. She waited for him to carry on but he seemed intent on frowning and blowing smoke into the darkness.

'Bill told me you were after the people operating illegal stills; I got the impression he thought you were a bit of a nark for doing it,' Dawn said honestly. 'Bill saw hooch as a good thing, amusing even, and considered it a shame when the fellow in Ipswich was arrested and the cheap spirits dried up.'

'That was Bill: never saw the bigger picture and prepared to take stupid risks.' Glenn looked at her. 'He took a stupid risk with you because he reckoned he'd get away with seeing Tina without you finding out.'

'But he knew he was home and dry where Ipswich

Valerie was concerned, didn't he?' Dawn blurted out bitterly.

'He'd have had to tell you at some time. Valerie wanted a ring on her finger as soon as she knew she was pregnant.'

'I don't blame her!' Following her forceful declaration Dawn regretted showing such passion. She was determined to eventually be indifferent to any mention of Bill. She was managing to push him a bit further into the background every day. She knew she must. He had fathered a child with another woman and Valerie was the one who could lay claim to Bill Sweetman's memory. Valerie would tell their child about its daddy and the infant would no doubt grow up to be proud of the flying officer father who had sadly perished before they could all become a family. Dawn hoped that her boyfriend would have done the decent thing and married the woman he'd got pregnant. But for an air raid on the evening they'd visited the Kitkat Club she would have spent the night with Bill and then perhaps he might have been the deceased father of two bastards.

Dawn felt she'd suffered enough where Bill was concerned, and recrimination was as pointless as torturing herself over who he would have chosen to marry had she got in the family way as well. Dawn thought of Sal Fiske who never would have a child – bastard or otherwise – and she felt a rush of sadness. She'd no right to feel sorry for herself, or Valerie. At least they were alive and still had futures waiting for them.

'Sorry . . . I shouldn't have brought up about Bill and Tina.' Glenn very gently and tentatively stroked the backs of his fingers on Dawn's cheek. He had taken her long

201

silence and glistening eyes as being his fault for having mentioned the couple.

'It's alright; I was thinking about something . . . someone else. I don't care about Bill and I don't care about you hunting down moonshine. That stuff might be a risk to people's health, but so is getting a damned great bomb land on your house. We might all be dead tomorrow if this bloody war isn't brought to an end. Wouldn't you be better off concentrating your efforts on tracking down the traitors?'

'Of course.' Glenn looked at her, a mixture of affection and encouragement in his smile. 'Don't look so terrified, sweetheart. Nothing will go wrong if you help me; I'll look after you.'

'Thanks; I'm reassured to know it.' Dawn's tone held such irony that Glenn burst out laughing.

'And don't call me sweetheart!' Dawn said crossly but she couldn't prevent a warm feeling enveloping her. Glenn Rafferty had an appealing way about him . . . sometimes . . .

'But don't underestimate the importance of rooting out rotgut. There's good money to be made from the stuff. Stills could be operating in every part of London soon.'

Dawn nibbled her lower lip, thinking that if all he wanted her to do was keep an eye and ear open for gossip about moonshine, that wouldn't be so bad; in fact she'd volunteer. What Glenn had just said about illegal distilleries springing up all over London had touched a nerve. The idea of her mother getting hold of some spirits from a bad batch was terrifying.

'I'll let you know if I hear anything that might be useful,' Dawn said. 'I expect dodgy booze ends up being sold down Loot Alley.'

Dawn imagined if anybody knew about under-the-counter hooch it would be Gertie's husband. It wouldn't surprise her to discover that Rufus had a finger in lots of criminal pies. But she kept her thoughts to herself. Gertie didn't deserve to have her life made even more difficult and Dawn had no proof of anything.

'Lorna Danvers is a colleague of yours, isn't she?'

'Why do you ask?' Dawn replied, surprised.

'Edward Danvers is her father and a known fascist. He and Mosley are pals. Mosley and Hitler are thick as thieves.'

Dawn was stunned by what Glenn was implying. Quickly she cast her mind back to when she and Lorna had talked at the 400 Club. Under the influence of a few brandies her fellow dancer had let on a bit about her background, and the one thing that had definitely stuck in Dawn's memory was that Lorna appeared to despise her father, and also be estranged from him. She quickly told Glenn about that because she liked Lorna and was ready to champion her.

'I'm not pointing the finger at anybody,' Glenn protested mildly. 'You've read the posters; keep mum – you can't trust anybody.'

Their eyes tangled for a moment; there was an unspoken question circling Dawn's mind and she abruptly blurted it out. 'Can I trust you?'

'Yes, you can; and I trust you.'

'Why?' Dawn gave an exasperated gesture. 'I still don't understand why you've told me any of this. You don't know me, not really. We've only been in each other's company a couple of times . . .'

'Sometimes that's all it takes . . .' Glenn interrupted.

'Yeah, I suppose so when the other person is as useful

as I am,' Dawn snapped. 'You're not interested in me; the flirting, the sympathy over Bill and his parents, it's all tripe. You want to recruit me to spy on Lorna for you. You think I'm a patsy like Tina, there to be used for the greater glory of Glenn Rafferty . . .'

'If I thought you were like Tina, we'd be done talking by now.' Glenn turned his head, gazing steadily at her, his eyes narrowed to sultry slits.

'I'm done talking,' Dawn said in a trembling voice. She was out of the car before he could stop her and by her gate when he gripped her wrist.

'If you're not going to help then forget everything I've told you tonight. Don't mention any of it.'

Dawn felt alarmed rather than reassured by the blazing concern in his face.

'Tell me you'll do that, Dawn,' he insisted, his fingers tightening on her in emphasis.

Suddenly a siren started to wail, making them both turn their eyes heavenwards.

Glenn shook her arm, wordlessly demanding an answer from her.

Dawn gave a single nod.

'I said asking you for help was only part of the reason for coming to see you in the first place. Do you want to know the main reason?' Glenn's eyes challenged her to answer him.

'No need to spell it out . . . I can guess,' Dawn said, wrenching herself free of him. Seconds later she was inside her door, leaning against the panels with a racing heart. Before she heard the car pull off she was regretting acting petulant and cowardly, as though a man telling her he fancied taking her to bed sent her into a fit of the vapours. But whenever she was with Glenn she felt thrown off balance . . . like a girl waiting to be kissed for the first time.

'You bastard,' she breathed. 'Why couldn't you have stayed away . . .'

The sound of her mother and brother moving about upstairs brought Dawn to her senses. They were no doubt hastily wrapping themselves up against a chilly night in the Anderson shelter. Dawn sniffed, rubbing her lashes clear of angry tears just as George hurtled down the stairs in his dressing gown with Eliza, grumbling and clinging to the banister, close behind him.

It wasn't until Dawn was following them down the back steps into the garden that she realised she ought to have offered shelter to Glenn rather than let him drive off with bombers overhead. And despite the friction that still seemed to exist between them, she felt mean that she hadn't asked him if he'd like to safely wait out the raid with them.

CHAPTER NINETEEN

Midge had been trying to waylay Rufus for a few days with no success. He had a feeling that his brother-in-law was avoiding him and Midge reckoned he knew why: Popeye's gang was now out of bounds to a deserter with a gammy hand.

A few minutes ago Midge had seen Gertie going into their house with a pram and two of the kids dragging either side of her. He'd been on the point of breaking cover to find out where Rufus was but had decided against it. Midge knew he looked and smelled like a pile of shit. His sister wouldn't mince her words in telling him so – before ordering him away from her and her kids, never to return.

Midge was desperate for some money so needed some work in the gang because he knew Gertie wouldn't come across with another penny. And getting anything out of Rufus – apart from a bit of snout – had always been a lost cause. Midge knew he wasn't up to going robbing on his own since he'd been maimed. He'd been deliberately hanging around in the haunts Rufus and Lenny knew about so they could contact him. But nothing doing; they were all trying to deal him out because he'd become an embarrassment and a liability.

An air-raid warning sounded but Midge barely stirred. He wasn't bothered about diving undercover; he'd stay where he was and gladly have a bomb put an end to his miserable life. Sometimes he had a chuckle at himself: he'd jumped ship to stay alive; now the idea of being blown to bits seemed quite appealing.

His morbid thoughts were interrupted as the Grimes's front door opened and Rufus came out with Joey. Gertie and the other kids followed. Rufus turned in one direction and his missus hurried in the other, no doubt towards the underground shelter.

For some reason Midge didn't whistle to draw Rufus's attention. He drew back into the shadows and then, at a distance, decided to follow. It was early May and the dusk was not fully descended but Midge had a feeling that Rufus was off on a job, and the brat was getting to go too.

When Lenny emerged from a side road pushing a cart and joined father and son Midge knew he'd hit the nail on the head. The bastards were off looting without him and Joey had been roped in to fill his role. Because of his size and agility Midge had always been the one squeezing through small spaces and darting to and fro. The other two were too clumsy and slow on their feet for a quick getaway. Now Midge knew he was being kicked into touch as though he was useless. Not only that, Popeye, Rufus and Lenny would share the slice of the profit that should rightfully be his. Joey wouldn't be getting a cut. He'd be lucky to get a bag of sweets for his night's work. A huge explosion curtailed Midge's brooding, instinctively making him crouch down.

Slowly he got to his feet, so incensed at his rejection by the gang that he forgot to notice the constant tormenting throb in his right arm. Since Popeye had lanced his wound he'd felt a bit better. But he couldn't kid himself that his hand was ever going to be as it was. He lifted it, gazed at the soiled bandage and then at the trio speeding up in the direction of a blaze in the distance. Even if Midge had wanted to keep up and watch them at work he knew he couldn't. His health and fitness had gone. And in Midge's opinion, those three were to blame for it. And someone had to pay. He was going to make sure of it.

'That bloke's been back again.'

'What bloke?' Dawn lifted her eyes from the newsprint she'd been reading to frown at her brother.

'Rod's his name. I heard Mum call him that.'

Dawn closed the paper and sat back in her chair. She'd been constantly turning over in her mind what Glenn had told her about rotgut and Nazi sympathisers, and had given no more thought to George's father having turned up out of the blue. Her mother had not said another word about Rod since their chat weeks ago. 'Did Rod come in the house?' Dawn asked.

George shook his head. 'I opened the door to him. Mum sent me upstairs then they went for a walk up the road together.'

'So you've not been introduced, then?'

'Nah . . . don't want to be neither. He stares at me and gives me the creeps. Mum just gets her coat and goes out with him.'

'Rod's been here at other times?' Dawn guessed from George's answer.

'Only once or twice . . .'

George began fiddling with the knob on the wireless, making it produce a whining noise that grated on Dawn's nerves.

'You gonna ask Mum about him?' George called over the racket he was making.

Dawn imagined that their mother had put the wind up George by acting jittery when Rod came calling. If Rod had acted odd too, staring at her brother – no doubt because he knew George was his own flesh and blood and he was searching for a resemblance – the poor lad was sure to suspect something was going on.

'For God's sake let that settle on a station, George.' Dawn frowned as her brother continued twiddling the dials on the set. As a pleasant melody filled the parlour, she volunteered, 'I've already spoken to Mum about Rod; he's just somebody she was friends with years ago . . . before you were born.'

Dawn was glad to be able to be honest. She yearned to add that there was nothing for George to worry about, but she couldn't lie. She was conscious of the fact that her brother was embroiled in a secret he knew nothing about. And when he did find out, and he was sure to at some time, how would he react? Dawn feared he'd take it very badly.

'There must be more to it,' George persevered in a rather ratty tone. 'Why's Rod keeping coming here, then?'

Dawn shrugged and turned her attention back to the newspaper. There was a tension building in the room and she sensed that George wasn't going to leave the

209

matter alone. She glanced at the clock. 'Crikey, I didn't realise it was so late. It's time I got off to work.' As she climbed the stairs to collect her handbag she felt a coward. She didn't need to leave for Soho for another hour as she was doing a late performance.

'Have you got a new boyfriend?' George was waiting at the bottom of the stairs for her.

'What makes you say that?' Dawn unhooked her coat from the peg in the hall then shrugged into it, avoiding her brother's eye.

'I heard Mum talking to a man one night.' George jerked his head at the landing. 'I sat up there and got a gander at him between the banisters. He was in flying togs, and I heard Mum tell him that you was out with your friends.' George's lip curled. 'Over Bill already, are you?'

'That's none of your damned business.' Dawn knew she'd over-reacted so gestured an apology, but George had stormed off into the kitchen. Dawn tilted up her head, closing her eyes in guilt and remorse. If she'd one good memory of Bill Sweetman it was that he had treated George well, never as though her brother were a nuisance to be tolerated. And George – as he'd just proved – could be a difficult so and so at times. On the day after the bombing at the Café de Paris, when it had been confirmed that Bill had perished, George had cried along with Dawn and Eliza.

Dawn swung about and went to the kitchen, unable to quit the house while there was bad feeling between them. Her brother had sawn himself a doorstep of bread and was spreading jam on it. Automatically Dawn took the knife and carried on preparing the food, mainly so she could scrape some of the generous helping of black-berry jam back into the pot. They were low on groceries and she didn't get paid till Friday. They were down to one last pot of jam from the batch they'd made with fruit picked last autumn.

'I didn't mean to jump down your throat. It's just . . . I've got a lot on my mind.' Dawn tied the pot cover back in place.

'Mum likes him,' George said gruffly. 'She said his name's Glenn Rafferty.'

Dawn nodded. 'That's right.'

'Do you like him?'

Dawn frowned. 'I'm not really sure.' She held out George's plate of food. 'He was one of Bill's pals . . . that's why he came over . . . pay condolences and so on.'

'He's a higher rank than Bill was. A squadron leader, Mum said.' George took an enormous bite out of the bread and jam. 'Bet he gets to do some stuff,' he spluttered cheerfully.

'Yeah.' Dawn's tone was rueful. 'I think he does . . .'

Rosie cursed beneath her breath as she saw her father had a visitor. She ignored Lenny Purves although he'd swung about with a grin on hearing her come in.

'See your daughter's looking as lovely as ever, then, Mr Gardiner.'

'Beauty, ain't she, Lenny?' John beamed proudly at Rosie's sophisticated appearance. She'd been to the hairdressers yesterday and the silver waves framing her face were as crisp and shiny as a newly minted florin. Her smart blue costume jacket was nipped in at the waist and showed off her curvy figure while her slender legs shimmered beneath a new pair of seamed nylons. His Rosie was doing alright, working at the Windmill Theatre, John had to give the lass that. He'd not liked the idea of her appearing in her birthday suit in front of strangers, but the generous wages she earned had helped him overcome his misgivings.

'Want tea, Rosie?' John called. 'Just made a pot for me and Lenny.'

'No, thanks. Going up to my room.' Rosie turned on her heel and approached the stairs.

'Don't go on my account, darling.' Lenny sauntered out into the hallway, admiringly eyeing Rosie's rear end. He glanced back to make sure that John was occupied setting the cups before he grabbed Rosie's elbow.

'You look good enough to eat. I'll take you out to dinner tonight if you want. Somewhere classy . . . just like you . . .'

Rosie had always thought herself pretty and had taken care with her appearance from the moment she'd noticed boys looking at her. Since she'd joined the theatre she'd learned from her colleagues how to professionally apply cosmetics and style her hair. She'd got vainer still on realising that she could wind any fellow she wanted around her little finger. Even top brass in the military drooled and winked when she made eye contact with them while posing on stage.

So the idea that this spotty creep thought he might be in the running for taking her out made her want to laugh . . . and to throw up.

'No thanks . . . I've got a boyfriend,' Rosie lied, hoping to put him off ever asking her out again. She slapped his sweaty clutch off her arm. 'Anyhow, I don't want you coming round here again.'

'Well, s'long as I've got business with yer old man, I'll be back.' Lenny's shrug of indifference didn't disguise his anger at being rebuffed.

As Rosie quickly climbed the stairs to escape him she was aware of him cocking his head to one side to try and see up her skirt.

Lenny earned enough from his regular and illicit jobs to pay for prostitutes a couple of times a week. But he wasn't like Rufus and Midge, satisfied with cheap scrubbers for a quick fix. Lenny thought he was a cut above all that. He frequented a brothel where you got offered girls who looked as good as Rosie Gardiner. But conquering the Windmill girl was becoming an obsession and the more she knocked him back, the more he wanted the stuck-up cow. He could bide his time. As soon as he'd prised open his father's fist, he'd be running all the businesses. He'd be rich and driving his own car, and Rosie Gardiner would be putty in his hands.

In Lenny's opinion all women had their price, and if he could afford to, he'd pay it; but he was damned sure he'd get his money's worth.

'Why's he been round here again?' The moment Rosie heard Lenny leave she flew down the stairs to confront her father. He'd promised her that he'd dismantle the apparatus in the basement. He'd made excuses for not already having done so and Rosie had believed him when he said he never used it.

Now she knew that for a lie. Lenny had brought her father round some bottle labels, she was sure of it.

John Gardiner was poking around in the larder, ignoring his daughter's question and her furious stare.

'I said, why's he been round? You know I can't stand him. He gives me the creeps, always staring and touching . . .'

'Len's harmless enough, love. He's just a silly lanky sod.' John swung about, feeling guilty at having deceived his daughter into thinking he'd packed in distilling. But he was exasperated with her too. He was the parent and she was his kid and he didn't want her telling him what to do. Besides, he liked what he did, he was good at it and he didn't see why he shouldn't carry on earning himself a bit of cash.

Doris, the widow in the bakery, had given him an extra currant bun earlier in the week. John knew she was after him. He didn't see why he shouldn't oblige her, and himself. Nobody knew how long the war might drag on for, or if they'd still be around when it did end. Rosie's lucky escape had brought home to John how easily any one of them could be in the wrong place at the wrong time. So it was wise to get on with life in case it got snatched away.

'You going to answer me, Dad?' Rosie shouted.

'Don't keep nagging me all the time!' John snapped. He got a tin of corned beef out of the pantry and looked for an opener in a drawer. 'We'll have corned beef sandwiches for tea,' he announced.

'You promised me you wouldn't keep on making the stuff down there. After I got hurt you promised me faithfully . . .' she wailed.

'Well, I am!' John roared. ''Cos you're not the only one who wants to earn spending money, you know.' He fingered the fine wool of his daughter's lapel. 'Bet that cost a bob or two. You're splashing out while you've got the chance, aren't you, 'cos clothing coupons are coming.'

'I give up a lot of housekeeping money to you,' Rosie protested.

'Ain't saying you don't help out with the kitty. But you dress up and go out with your friends, and from now on, I'm gonna go out with mine.'

'Friends?' Rosie repeated, mystified. 'You don't mean Lenny and his dad, do you?' she scoffed. 'You don't need friends like that!'

'I've been pals with Frank Purves for most of me life,' John said. 'You don't need to get above yourself, miss, not with what you do for a living. You're no better than us, so less of your airs and graces.'

Rosie blinked and fell back a step as though her father had slapped her face. She'd never thought that she seemed above herself.

'Get the bread out of the larder, and put the kettle on,' John ordered. 'I'll make us a sandwich and a cup of tea.'

Automatically Rosie did as her father asked, then she said, 'I don't want any. I'm going out.'

When again in her bedroom Rosie pulled out the case that was stored under the bed. She began emptying clothes from her chest of drawers into it. Then she sat down on the side of the mattress. Opening her handbag she found the piece of paper that Marlene had given her. Her friend had written down an address on it when telling Rosie that she was welcome to her spare room at any time because she'd be glad of some company.

Once her suitcase was full Rosie carried it downstairs and left it in the hall. She didn't want to have a right royal bust-up with her dad. She hoped he'd understand that she was grown up now and needed to be independent. She wanted them to part on reasonable terms, then if she didn't settle at Marlene's she could come back home. Perhaps her father needed a shock and might change his ways if she showed him that she wasn't putting up with him breaking the law and risking getting them both in serious trouble.

Rosie found her father washing up his tea things at the sink. He had on his brown overall and Rosie knew what that meant; despite their argument he was intending to go down into the cellar again to make rotgut.

'Thought you were off out.' John looked over a shoulder at his daughter.

'Yeah, I am . . . just come to say goodbye,' Rosie said flatly. If she'd been in two minds before about what she was doing, she wasn't any longer. 'I'm staying with Marlene for a while – she's got a cheap room going spare and says she'd like some company. Think we need a bit of space between us, Dad.'

'Do you now? So that's what you're doing, is it?' John dried his hands on a towel. 'Off you go, then, and see if the grass is greener, but know this: once you take your case out of that door, you don't come back. You make your bed elsewhere, then you lie on it, miss.'

CHAPTER TWENTY

'You've got a face like a wet weekend.'

Surprised by Lorna's remark, Dawn stopped adjusting her suspender. Instead her fingers anchored behind her ear a curtain of honey-blonde hair so she could assess her profile in the mirror. She gave herself a frown; she did look rather miserable.

'I need to paint on a smile too.' Lorna took a final drag on her cigarette before stubbing it out in the ashtray. 'I've got a God-awful hangover,' she moaned, twisting up her scarlet lipstick. 'Mummy had a few friends over and they brought some brandy. Very good it was too . . . at the time. But I swear it wasn't quite the ticket, if you get my meaning.' She dropped Dawn an exaggerated wink. 'Moonshine.' Lorna's vivid Cupid's bow lips silently formed the word. 'We wouldn't need to drink that awful stuff if Daddy would pay up to keep us,' she moaned. 'He's buggered off with some floozy young enough to be my sister and is living the life of Riley enjoying champagne and lobster at top hotels. Meanwhile *we* have to make do with Spam and rotgut!

217

Mummy is so furious that sometimes I think she'll kill him . . .'

'Three minutes!'

The call from beyond the dressing-room door alerted the girls to being next on stage.

Rosie fell in step beside Dawn as they climbed the stairs. Although Rosie and Marlene would be nude when the curtain went up, but for an artfully draped length of stout rope, they wore colourful silk wraps to keep the goosepimples at bay while traipsing to and from the dressing room. Rosie tightened her belt, glancing at Dawn. 'Lorna's right. You do seem quiet.'

'Oh, I've just got a few things on my mind.' Dawn knew that was an understatement. She'd been engrossed with picking over what Glenn had told her about his undercover activities. She'd been feeling increasingly ashamed of her cowardly reaction to his request for help. Despite their frosty parting she admired his bravery and now that she'd calmed down she'd like to tell him so. And wish him good luck. Last night she'd found herself adding his name to her family members when whispering into the darkness a prayer for their safety.

She knew Glenn was in grave danger stalking traitors, and it was a very different sort of peril to that encountered in dogfights with Messerschmitts in the open skies. Enemy pilots were more honourable foe than skulking Judases who might lie in wait to stab an adversary in the back then melt away into shadows.

Dawn chased the alarming thought away and turned her mind to another conversation she'd been constantly mulling over. George had told her about Rod coming round to their house again but she'd not yet found the right opportunity to bring up the subject with her mother.

She knew she must, before George's inquisitiveness got the better of him and he confronted Eliza, putting their mother back on the bottle.

'Thinking of Bill, are you?' Rosie said sympathetically, noticing Dawn's preoccupation.

'I'm fine, honestly.' Dawn forced cheerfulness into her tone. 'If anyone's a daydreamer, it's you!' she added with a grin. 'I waved at you in Wardour Street the other day but you ignored me.'

'Sorry . . . didn't see you . . .'

'You were with a rather dapper fellow,' Dawn said. She'd wondered at the time about Rosie's companion: a stocky Mediterranean-looking character, garbed in a sharp suit.

'Oh, that's Marlene's boyfriend. Nikola's his name but everybody calls him Malt as he's Maltese. I bumped into him and he took me for a coffee.' Rosie chuckled. 'He's very smooth . . . and generous. It's good of him to let me stay with Marlene as the house belongs to his family. I am paying rent though.'

They'd reached the stage wings and stood idly watching the previous act taking a bow. Marvin the Marvel was collecting his box of doves in readiness to quit the stage once he'd milked his moment. The dancers were got up as cowgirls in short skirts and jerkins with straw Stetsons and calf-high boots. Dawn dropped on top of a box the fancy hat she'd been idly rotating, then drew Rosie to one side to have a private word. 'You're still staying at Marlene's, then?'

'Yeah, it's great.' Rosie patted her hair into place and started undoing her robe. 'I've got my own room and Marlene's introduced me to some of her friends.' She looked impressed. 'They're all very rackety. A Major

Trent is taking me to the Ritz for cocktails,' she whispered. 'I've always wanted to go there.' She giggled. 'He's about thirty and I've only met him once at Marlene's. He came round with some other people and we all drank Scotch and ginger ale. He's going to teach me how to play roulette at a casino.'

Dawn knew that it was none of her business what Rosie did, but she'd never shaken off a protective feeling towards the younger woman. Marlene boasted about the fact that she led a racy life, and Dawn knew that Rosie, for all her bravado, was an innocent. The young woman at her side might flirt and tease her admirers but Rosie would never go to bed with a man after he took her for dinner unless she was in love with him.

Dawn was certain that Rosie, rather like herself, was a hopeless romantic, waiting for Mr Right to sweep her off her feet with promises of love and marriage before she took that final commitment to sleep with him. Dawn couldn't help suspecting that Major Trent might be annoyed if Rosie turned him down at the end of an expensive evening at the Ritz, especially if he believed her to be out of the same mould as Marlene. And she definitely wasn't.

'What does your dad think about you lodging with a housemate? Has he met Marlene?'

'She came over and had tea with us once and Dad liked her,' Rosie replied. 'You know Marlene, she's a saucy cow with the gift of the gab.' She smiled. 'He got out the biscuit tin for her, and he doesn't do that for everybody.'

'Will you go back home when the dust has settled?' Rosie had confided in Dawn that an argument at home

220

had prompted her to pack her case and take up Marlene's invitation to stay with her.

'Don't think the dust *will* settle. Dad told me I'd never be welcome back home.' Rosie grimaced. 'We had a really *bad* row. Dad's got dodgy friends, and I told him I don't like them. He made out it was *me* at fault . . . bloody cheek!' She omitted to mention that her father was as dodgy as his friends. She never told anybody about the still in the basement.

'He's probably calmed down now,' Dawn said encouragingly. She wanted Rosie to be safely back with her father.

'Dad's taken up with a woman since I left. I met a neighbour down the market and she told me he's seeing Doris from the bakery.' Rosie sounded huffy. 'Wouldn't be surprised if he's been rubbing me up the wrong way on purpose, just to get rid of me . . .' She broke off as music blared out. 'Oh, here we go, we're on.' She shrugged her gown from her shoulders and it slithered in a whisper of silk to the floor.

Rosie took up position, strategically draping the rope across a shoulder and around her hips. Finally she tilted her head to a proud angle and let a serene smile settle on her crimson lips as the curtain slowly drew up to a chorus of appreciative hoots and whistles.

Gertie heard the tapping on the wall and gave an answering bash with the broom handle. She propped the broom against the larder cupboard, wiping muck from her fingers onto her pinny.

'Just popping next door to see to Mrs Smith,' she told Joey. Her eldest boy was sitting at the table with a comic. The other two were eating toast seated opposite their big brother. Little Harry was in his vest balancing on a potty on the floor.

'I'm off out, seeing me pals.' Joey didn't even look up when replying to his mother.

Gertie swung back, irritated. 'You'll have to wait a bit, Joey, and go out later. You watch the kids for me for an hour and I'll get chips in dinner time.' She followed up the bribe with a smile.

'Can get me own chips . . . and I'm off out now.' Joey stood up, rolling up his Marvel comic and stuffing it into a pocket. With no more ado he let himself out into the street, ignoring his mother's demands that he come back.

Having ordered Adam to keep an eye on the two younger ones Gertie rushed after him. She'd had enough of her eldest son's disobedience. Joey could buy his own chips because he was getting paid for the work he did for the looting gang. Gertie knew he wasn't earning a lot – Rufus wouldn't give him much more than a couple of tanners out of his cut – but the wages were enough for their son to feel cocky and confident. Gertie feared that Joey was heading for a crash if he didn't watch it.

Catching up with her son she jerked him round by the elbow. 'You get back indoors now, you little sod!' She felt puffed out following her sprint. 'You're not too big for a clip round the ear, y'know.' Gertie raised a flat hand in warning.

Joey wriggled his arm free and sauntered off with an insolent smile.

Again Gertie gripped his arm but Joey shoved her in the chest, sending his mother stumbling backwards to land on her posterior on the pavement. At coming up to ten he was already showing signs of his father's stocky build and his strength had winded Gertie. Joey made a move as though to help her up, his face whitening because he knew he'd overstepped the mark. But instead of apologising, or returning home, he suddenly ran across the street and disappeared around the corner.

Gertie glanced about, hoping nobody had seen her own son knock her down. Quickly she scrambled to her feet. She knew Joey hadn't meant to do it and she didn't want nosy parkers gossiping about her family. She understood that her eldest boy was of an age where he wanted a bit of freedom and time to himself to play with pals; he wasn't a daughter to be kept close and taught homemaking.

But not long ago Joey had been a very different lad. He'd cheerfully supervised his brothers while Gertie nipped next door to help old Lou Smith with housework and cooking. Her neighbour was sixty-five and Gertie expected nothing in return from the woman other than Lou minded her kids while Gertie did her daytime shifts. Gertie regularly made Lou's breakfast of tea and toast and went in later to get the woman's tea ready. When she noticed Lou's rations were running out she'd try and supplement them with a bit of her own. Now Joey and Adam were getting regular school dinners they were less likely to come in after lessons and raid the larder behind her back.

But whenever Gertie asked Joey to mind the kids for her lately he was rude to her, or worse, he just ignored her – in the way Rufus did when he thought she wasn't worth the bother of an argument. A couple of times Joey had slammed out of the house, with Gertie shouting after him that he could wait till his father got home. It was a threat that Joey made clear he now found amusing. As well he might: her husband had brought about the change in Joey by taking him along on jobs and treating their eldest boy like an adult when he was still only a kid.

'How d'you know where to find me?' Rufus shoved Midge in the shoulder to propel him behind a brick pillar. Rufus wasn't bothered about concealing his brother-in-law for Midge's own good; he was more concerned about being seen with the little tramp. A moment ago Midge had sidled up out of the darkness, frightening the life out of Rufus just as he was about to do a bit of business.

'I always know where to find you at this time of night.' Midge's wheezing laugh turned to a cough. He glanced about at the gloomy courtyard; a few yards away an empty washing line was swaying in a stiff breeze. Suddenly a prick of light broke the solid blackness to one side of them. Neither Midge nor Rufus blinked an eye; they knew it was a prostitute shining a torch up at her face so a passing punter had an idea of what he was buying. The man walked on, shuffling out of sight. Midge would have liked to oblige her but he'd not got a pot to piss in. He'd come here in the hope of bumping into Rufus and demanding money before the big man emptied his pockets for a tart.

'Got five bob for us?'

'I'm brassic, mate; barely got enough to get me own end away.' Rufus sighed.

'Not had any work, then?' Midge asked slyly, suppressing another cough.

'Just me regular . . . not a sniff off Pop . . .'

'You fuckin' liar!' Midge hissed and used his good hand to grab Rufus's lapel. 'I saw you and Lenny out with that kid of your'n, doing a job just the other night.'

Rufus swiped away Midge's clinging fist. 'So what if we was? You ain't up to it any more, that's why you ain't invited along,' he growled.

'I was up to it before that brat of yours come on a job.' Midge raised his stinking limb. 'You owe me. You all fuckin' owe me.'

Rufus ignored Midge's complaint although he knew the little man had a fair grievance. But Rufus had a point of his own to make. 'Joey's needed now and plays a good part. The coppers are getting wise to the bomb-chasing. They've stopped me before; I thought I was for it seeing as I was pushing a cart loaded with loot.' Rufus poked his brother-in-law in the shoulder in emphasis. 'Then they saw my Joey lying there, looking for all the world like he's a poor lad been bombed out with his daddy. Pop and Lenny have come round to my way of thinking. They can see the sense as well in Joey tagging along.'

'Yeah . . . and I bet you're all happy sharing out my slice of the profit. Well, you can hand over something off that last job. I deserve a cut . . .'

'Piss off,' Rufus said contemptuously.

In desperation Midge tried to ram a hand into Rufus's pocket to snatch some coins.

Having a man – and one that was particularly revolting – scrabbling about by his groin was too much for Rufus, especially when his wedding tackle was rock hard. As Midge was five inches shorter Rufus nutted him on the crown rather than the forehead. The blow had the desired effect and Midge went down like a sack of spuds, shrieking in pain as he instinctively used his bad hand to cushion his fall.

'You should have turned yourself in and taken a

chance on it going your way,' Rufus bawled, feeling frustrated at having had to hurt his brother-in-law when he could understand the bloke's bitterness over such a run of back luck.

Drawn by the noise of men's voices, the tart sauntered closer, the torchlight dancing on her face. 'Anything I can do for you gents?'

'Nah . . . sling yer 'ook.' Rufus hadn't lost the urge but he knew it would be rubbing salt into Midge's wound to go off with her. And he wasn't a vindictive man. He left his brother-in-law moaning on the ground and strode off up the street, hoping that Gertie was in the mood for a bit of how's yer father.

'You're back early.'

Gertie upended the hot iron on the table and folded two pillowcases. She hadn't expected to hear her husband's key in the lock for hours yet. She'd not even got Joey to move his backside up the stairs to bed. Every time she'd asked him to get himself washed and into his pyjamas he'd grunted, 'In a minute.' But she'd had no more insolence off him, in fact he'd come home earlier looking very sheepish.

Joey was sitting by the fender playing solitaire on the threadbare rug. He gave his parents a sideways look, while laying down cards.

'Get yourself up to bed now, Joey, school in the morning,' Gertie said. She knew she couldn't hang out any longer telling Rufus about the baby. Her belly seemed to be growing every day and she could hardly do up the buttons over her swollen bosom. As he'd come back unexpectedly and didn't seem too grumpy it seemed the right time to break the news.

'Ain't tired yet.' Joey carried on placing the queen of spades. He knew that more often than not, his father sided with him against his mother's rules.

'You heard what was said!' Rufus grabbed hold of Joey by the arm and hauled him to his feet. 'Get yourself to bed and don't let me hear you give your mother lip, or you'll be for it.'

Leaving the cards scattered on the rug, Joey slouched off upstairs, having sent his mother a blameful glower.

'He's getting above himself since you started taking him on jobs.'

Gertie had meant to keep things placid between her and her husband due to the likelihood of him hitting the roof when he heard there'd soon be another mouth to feed. But, as Rufus had just backed her to the hilt against his favourite son, she'd take a chance and confront him over something else too: she was at the end of her tether with Joey constantly misbehaving. It had been the final straw when he'd pushed her over.

Hands on hips, Gertie recounted all of it to Rufus, then waited to hear what he was going to do about disciplining Joey.

'I'll have a word with him,' Rufus said gruffly. 'Not now though, love. Let's have an early night. Come home specially to see you, ain't I . . .' He gave her a wink.

Gertie gave her husband a faint smile, feeling disappointed in him, as normal. But she knew she still had the upper hand and had better take advantage of it before going upstairs with him. Once he'd had what he wanted he'd be back to his usual moods.

'Joey should stop with me when you go off on a job in future. He should come down the shelter during a bombing raid, not be off gallivanting with you. It's too dangerous; I ain't risking me sons for nothing or nobody.'

'Joey's coming with us 'cos he's useful.' Rufus softened his snapped response with an apologetic grin. He too wanted to keep things on an even keel between them till he'd soothed the itch in his trousers. 'Bedtime for us 'n' all. Ready to go up, gel?'

Gertie turned away and started folding a sheet. She might have known he'd only shown up early because he was feeling horny and either hadn't the cash or the inclination for a tart tonight. But she decided not to harp on about Joey. She'd leave that for another time. There was something more important to do.

'I'm in the family way again, Rufus,' Gertie stated, chin up. 'Don't know how it's happened when we're as careful as we are, but it has.'

Rufus hadn't been expecting that from her . . . not right now, anyhow. Of course, he knew that his wife would have to tell him at some time. Tonight, while brooding on his meeting with Midge and his lost chance of a five-bob alley shag, he'd forgotten all about his wife's condition.

He'd been keeping an eye on Gertie's comings and goings for a good few weeks, anticipating catching her out with a fancy man. But Gertie had met nobody so Rufus had given up tailing her. All she ever did was take the kids to school or go shopping or to her jobs. So he'd come to the conclusion, as she seemed to have done, that considering they rarely did it these days, she'd been unlucky getting knocked up.

'Ain't the best news I've had recently,' Rufus said gamely. 'But then it ain't the worst neither. At least we can have a cuddle in bed for a few months without worrying you'll get pregnant.' He chuckled dirtily, putting out his arms. 'Come here then, gel . . . we'll get by . . . always do, don't we?'

Gertie displayed her relief in a hiss of pent-up breath. She gladly went to her husband and gave him a hug. She'd never imagined it could be so easy.

'I've given in me notice to Pickering, Rufus. And I'll have to do the same at the Windmill, though I want to hang on there long as I can. We'll be short in the kitty till after the baby's born.'

'Not to worry, love; now Midge's out of the equation we've got a bit more to divvy up after a job. And as we've got Joey out working it won't hurt him to give up a few coppers, neither.'

Rufus nuzzled his wife's bosom through her old blouse in a way that put Gertie uneasily in mind of her baby's father.

'What did old Pickering say about you jacking in yer job? Miserable old sod'll miss you when you're gone.'

'I reckon he'll have someone else seeing to him straight away.' Gertie gave a sour chuckle and turned off the parlour light.

CHAPTER TWENTY-ONE

'We all go to the Palm House this evening. Bottle party night so lots of nobs and top brass about.'

Marlene liked her boyfriend's heavily accented English. But she didn't like what he'd just said. She put aside the *Woman's Own* she'd been reading. 'No . . . not yet, Malt; I don't think Rosie's ready for that.' Marlene could tell that Nikola was not happy with that answer. He had his back to her and she noticed the thick sinew below his nape flex so she rose from the settee to slide her arms about him, trying to soften him up.

The Maltese was dressed in flannels with just a vest covering his hairy chest. He undulated his beefy shoulders to escape her clinging arms. Moodily he stared out of the window, dragging hard on his roll-up.

'She been here long while,' Malt said. 'You tell her she here to do work or I do it. You think I won't?' He sounded belligerent and swung about to jerk a thumb over his tanned shoulder. 'She out of here . . . you see; don't you try cross my family, be worse for you.'

'I wouldn't, Malt, honestly,' Marlene whined. 'It's

just . . . Rosie's not as clued-up as I reckoned she was.'
And that was the truth, she thought. The girl might
flirt her heart out but she was green as grass where
men were concerned.

At first Marlene had been as keen as Malt to draw Rosie
into their prostitution ring and start creaming off her.
They'd introduced her to Jeremy Trent at a party at the
flat; he was smooth and polite and less intimidating for a
girl new to the profession. The trouble was, Rosie had no
idea she was getting roped into a new profession.

Just after war had been declared a previous boyfriend
of Marlene's had taken her to the Palm House where
she'd met Nikola, and his uncle Valentin Barbaro. She'd
been quite naïve back then and thought the basement
dive off Greek Street was just a bottle party club. In
reality the place made most of its money from operating
as a brothel and an illegal gaming house. When her
boyfriend joined up Marlene had got together with Malt.
He'd told her that his uncle's club was a gold mine.
Within a short while Marlene had realised it was no idle
boast.

Marlene now worked from time to time as a hostess
at the Palm House. She'd learned that punters were
willing to pay handsomely for a beer and a cocktail
for a girl who kept them company. And the more a
hostess got a punter to pay for his watered-down
drinks, the more commission she'd get from the
management. Then if she liked him enough to sleep
with him, she got to keep fifty per cent of the fee that
Malt negotiated for her.

Malt's uncle also owned the house they were in: a
modest building near Covent Garden. The ground floor
was rented to cousins of Malt's; Marlene and Malt paid

rent on the first-floor rooms, one of which Rosie now occupied. Rosie paid a fair rent to them, but Malt wanted more because he knew he could get more from a girl who entertained clients in her bedroom.

With all the people coming and going at the flat, Marlene had expected Rosie to twig what was going on, without needing to have it spelled out. But no dice; Rosie, in her innocence, just thought her flatmates had loads of rackety friends and it was all jolly good fun.

But it wasn't fun, it was business. The gentlemen were punters and their female companions were paid tarts, not girlfriends.

Marlene was hoping to eventually win Rosie round because the girl was already showing signs of being intoxicated by the sophistication of hobnobbing with rich, powerful men who paid for expensive drinks and dinners and occasionally turned up with nice gifts. In Marlene's opinion no girl in her right mind would turn down such a life.

On hearing her boyfriend's exasperated sigh Marlene piped up, 'Just leave Rosie to me a while longer; I'll work on her and put her in the picture.' She added brightly, 'She's said she'll go to the Ritz with Major Trent . . .'

'No, we don't leave her no longer,' Malt snarled in his thick tone. He suddenly turned on the charm. 'We have wedding or not?' He shrugged. 'Costs money to buy ring and dress.' He rubbed together a thumb and fingers, fleshy lips turned down.

Again Marlene put her arms around him, laying her head on his musky shoulder. 'I could try and find someone else . . . a girl just as pretty as Rosie . . .'

Malt angrily shoved Marlene away and she gasped, bouncing onto the settee.

'You stupid! Don't want no one else!' He flicked a hand. 'Trent want be first with Rosie and he already paid for her. You want me to give him back money?'

Marlene suddenly felt cold; she hadn't realised that her boyfriend had already done a deal for Rosie's virginity. Stupidly she'd told Malt that Rosie had admitted to never having slept with a man.

Marlene had cosied up to Rosie because she fitted the bill as a new recruit in Malt's harem but she knew she was kidding herself thinking Rosie would embrace a life of prostitution. Rosie was sampling grown-up ways, but had fanciful ideas. And she was a girl missing her dad although she was too stubborn to admit it.

Marlene picked herself up off the settee where her boyfriend had knocked her sprawling. She got a bottle of whisky out of the cupboard in the kitchen and poured a shot. The pinpricks of conscience she'd previously quashed for Malt's sake were allowed free rein. She thought of Rosie as a friend as well as a colleague. It was time to try to persuade Rosie to go back home, before it was too late . . .

'Come . . . we make up,' Malt drawled, fondling Marlene's neck. 'Trent pay good price for your friend. You wait till Rosie find out she got ten pounds coming from the nice Jeremy.' He growled a laugh. 'She be wanting more . . . you see . . . easy money . . . better than standing freezing tits off on stage at Windmill . . . eh? You tell her, swit'eart . . . good life coming . . .'

'I know what you want to say.'

'Oh . . . what's that then, Mum?' Dawn had waited till George had gone out to the shop then offered to help Eliza peel potatoes for tea. She knew if the two of them were alone, working side by side in the confined space of the small kitchen, her mother might open up to her about Rod. But it seemed Eliza had guessed Dawn had an ulterior motive in donning a pinafore.

'George told you that Rod came round again, didn't he? And you want to know why.' Eliza dropped a potato in the pot.

'Yes . . .' Dawn gave her mother a startled glance; Eliza was obviously not a bit surprised that she knew Rod was again on the scene.

'I know you've been trailing me about for a day or two, trying to pluck up the courage to find out what's going on.'

Eliza put down the peeling knife and looked at her daughter. 'Ain't only been you trying to find the guts to speak up, I have as well. I know you'll think me a fool but me and Rod are back together. I don't want you to hate me, Dawn.'

'I couldn't ever hate you, Mum.' Dawn licked her lips. 'But, *back together* . . . as in . . . *being engaged*, you mean?' she queried in a hoarse voice.

'Well, not that just yet.' Eliza smiled wryly. 'I know things about him that I didn't before, things that explain a lot about why he behaved the way he did.' She picked up the knife again and a potato, watching a spiral of peel lengthen as she explained, 'He's not the selfish git I thought him. He's quite an honourable man, and I know what he's told me's the truth 'cos he's showed me letters and things to back it all up.'

'What letters?' Dawn croaked, automatically peeling spuds.

'Medical reports from doctors and hospitals. His wife . . . well, if you can call the poor love that . . . she was in an institution. She had some sort of brain disease for years that sent her mad and put her away. So, though they was married they wasn't man and wife, if you see what I mean.' Eliza halted her rattling report to blink and sniff. 'Rod stuck by her though. He said he knew he was doing wrong being with me and lying to me about being a widower when his wife was still alive. But he couldn't help himself 'cos he loved me.' Eliza rubbed soil off a potato then started peeling it, carrying on more slowly, 'He thought we could just go on as we were, being an engaged couple till his wife passed away. After she got the illness the doctors told him she'd probably linger a few years; but it ended up being nine.' Eliza shook her head. 'That's how long the poor cow lasted, not knowing who she was . . . who he was.' She dropped halved potatoes into the water. 'Then when I fell pregnant with George, Rod knew he had a decision to make. He chose to stick by his wife.' Eliza looked up with tears glistening in her eyes. 'And I feel proud of him for that.'

'And what about George?' Dawn said. She felt in shock, unable to take in every implication surrounding her mother's news. 'How proud's George gonna feel when he finds out . . .'

'Finds out what?'

Mother and daughter turned round to see that George had opened the front door. Closing it he walked down the hall, swinging a bag of shopping.

While watching the colour drain from her mother's face Dawn thanked the Lord that her brother had interrupted her when he had. She'd been about to add that George would find out Rod was his father.

'Nothing for you to worry about, Georgie,' Eliza burbled. 'We was just talking about this and that . . .'

She dried her hands on her apron. 'You finish up the potatoes, Dawn,' she added cheerfully. 'I'm gonna get the copper alight and get those sheets in the wash before tea.' Eliza opened the back door and disappeared into the yard.

Dawn had to give it to her mother for pulling that one off; moments before George appeared she'd thought that Eliza was about to break down. Dawn put the pot on the gas stove and lit it. She knew George was itching to question her and was dreading the moment. She didn't want to lie to her brother yet she couldn't tell him what she'd been about to say. That information was for his mother to tell him . . . perhaps his father too . . .

'So what's going on and what am I gonna find out?' George dumped down the shopping.

'Get the lid for that saucepan out of the cupboard, will you, George, while I get the door.' Dawn had never felt more relieved to hear the knocker being used. 'And don't let the pot boil over!' she shouted over her shoulder, hurrying down the hallway with a sigh of relief.

'Sorry, is it a bad time?'

Dawn gazed at Glenn, feeling a burst of mingling euphoria and alarm.

'Umm . . . no . . .' Dawn glanced back to see that George was observing the scene from a few yards away. 'Come in, if you like . . .'

Glenn smiled an acceptance, wiping his shoes on the doormat before stepping over the threshold.

'This is my brother, George.' Dawn led Glenn to the kitchen doorway.

Glenn extended a hand to George. 'Pleased to meet you.' He glanced at the boiling pot, its lid rattling noisily. 'You're about to eat . . .'

'We'll not sit down for an hour yet,' Dawn reassured him. She turned off the gas under the potatoes, then realising she still wore an apron she untied it and stuffed it on a shelf in the larder. 'I'll put the kettle on, and let Mum know you're here. You'll stay for a cup of tea, won't you?'

'Are you Bill's friend, the squadron leader who came here before?' George asked.

'Yes.'

'You're in civvies,' George said.

'Got leave,' Glenn briefly explained.

'Oh . . . hello again.' Eliza had entered the kitchen having heard mingling voices coming from inside the house. She glanced from Glenn to her daughter. 'Make Mr Rafferty some tea, Dawn. There's some fruit cake left in the tin.' She gave Glenn a wink.

'I don't want to put you out,' Glenn said with a smile. 'Anyhow, I can't really stop now. I just came by to see if you'd like to go out later, if you're not working. We didn't get to finish our conversation and we still have a lot to talk about . . . don't we?'

Dawn noticed a glimmer of amusement far back in his eyes and was certain he relished putting her on the spot. During the expectant quiet that followed she felt her mother's and George's eyes on her as they waited for her answer. And how could she turn down such a polite offer from such a charming man?

'Thanks, that'd be nice,' she said with an exaggerated sweetness that deepened his smile.

'Good. I'll be back later – seven o'clock,' Glenn said.

CHAPTER TWENTY-TWO

'Where do you fancy going?' Glenn asked when he called for Dawn as arranged.

He looked smart so Dawn supposed he'd been expecting to go somewhere swish. She, on the other hand, had chosen a pretty rather than a sophisticated outfit. Her summery skirt and blouse were topped off with a fitted jacket to ward off any chill later in the evening. In her hand she had a small paper bag filled with crusts of stale bread.

'Do you fancy feeding the ducks with me?' Dawn shook the paper bag while eyeing his expensive suit and tie with mock sympathy.

He shrugged. 'Don't mind . . .'

She thought he probably did mind, but he didn't frown, as Bill no doubt would have done before insisting they go for a drink.

They settled into a stroll with Dawn struggling to ignore her mother and brother peeping at them from behind different sets of curtains.

Dawn was curious about many things where Squadron

Leader Glenn Rafferty was concerned. So far, she'd had few opportunities to ask him personal questions. They always seemed to end up having a row and she'd thought there was little point in showing an interest in a man she might never see again. Yet Glenn Rafferty had kept coming back, and Dawn was coming to realise that she was glad about that. She *did* want to see him, and she certainly wanted to know more about him.

Going *down to the water*, as her family always called feeding the ducks in the local park, was something Dawn made time for. She liked to stand and stare at the island of dense foliage at the centre of the lake where all manner of creatures sought refuge. Even when the park was filled with children playing the stillness of the lake offered a sense of peace and quiet to Dawn. She'd sit on a bench close by and watch the gliding waterfowl and reflect on many things; she'd often thought of her father and how much she missed him. She'd only been young when he died but she could quite clearly remember a fair-haired man with smiling tawny eyes bringing her here to play ball. More recently she'd come to the little oasis to sit and think about Bill. She'd never badgered him to come with her to the park, knowing something so tame would bore him.

'Sorry that I was a dreadful baby over the business of your undercover duties,' Dawn blurted quietly as they turned in the park gates. 'I know it's a job that somebody has to do, and I think you're brave to volunteer.'

'Wasn't quite like that,' Glenn said self-mockingly. 'I sort of got railroaded into it.'

'I still admire you, and I think you're being modest.'

Dawn sensed his eyes on her blushing profile and turned to him, anticipating a thank you.

239

'Sorry . . . just thought you might be taking the piss,' he said, having read her bashful expression.

'And I thought pilots were nice middle-class boys,' Dawn sighed out sarcastically. 'Seems I was wrong.'

'And I thought all Windmill girls were part-time tarts . . . seems we're both wrong.'

Dawn felt a surge of indignation but kept her voice level on replying, 'Perhaps I am a part-time tart.'

'I seriously doubt that.' Glenn shoved his hands into his pockets.

'Is that some sort of backhanded compliment?' Dawn asked.

'It's a compliment.'

Dawn mulled over what he'd said and concluded that his comment had been specifically about her rather than showgirls in general. 'Have you heard rumours about me?' she asked with a twinge of alarm.

'Forget it. I need to learn to keep my big mouth shut.' He pulled a new pack of cigarettes out of his pocket and began opening it.

Following some seconds of frantic concentration Dawn blurted, 'Did Bill talk about me?'

Glenn gave a non-committal shrug, staring over parkland to where some youths were playing football. 'Shall we go and have a kick about with them?'

At any other time such a bizarre suggestion might have won her over, making her laugh. But not now. 'Did Bill talk about me?' Dawn insisted on knowing.

'Let's not talk about Bill, eh?'

'I want to.' Dawn tapped away the pack of Players he'd offered to her. She wanted a better peace offering than that! She wanted the truth from him.

'Did Bill tell you personal things about me . . . us?'

Glenn stuck a cigarette in his mouth instead of answering.

'He told you he had no luck getting me into bed, didn't he?' The idea that she'd been gossiped over in some officer's mess was mortifying, but Dawn had to know.

'He said you were frigid and gave him no choice but to see other women. Satisfied?' Glenn cupped a match then drew on the cigarette till the tip blazed.

Dawn marched ahead of him to the bench and sat down. Through misty eyes she stared at zigzagging moorhens. Bill had betrayed her in so many ways, some of which she might have come to understand and overlook. But to have shown her so little respect was unbearable and unforgivable.

When Glenn planted a foot on the bench by her thigh and leaned towards her she shifted away. She knew he'd been about to offer sympathy and an apology. But she was too hurt to want either.

'I suppose you pitied him when he told you I wouldn't sleep with him,' Dawn said in a strangled voice. 'Whereas he envied everything about you.'

Glenn sat down on the bench, hands clasped together between his knees. 'I pitied him, but not for the reason you think. And I envied him . . . I just made sure he never knew it.'

'Why?'

'Arrogance, I suppose.'

'Why did you envy him?' Dawn snapped, aware he'd deliberately misunderstood her.

'You know why.' Clamping the cigarette in his mouth he reached out his right hand.

Dawn tried several times to throw him off but he

tightened his grip till she allowed him to keep his fingers on her wrist.

'I told you before Bill wasn't worthy of you.'

'And you are?' Dawn mocked.

He smiled, displaying nice white teeth in his dark complexion. 'Well, I think so . . . but I know convincing you of it might not be easy.'

Despite herself Dawn's lips twitched and he let go of her hand to trail the backs of his fingers on her cheek.

'We'll do alright, you and me.' He settled against the wooden slats extending an arm across the back of the bench.

Dawn could feel his warmth and closeness but he didn't touch her again, just sat smoking quietly at her side.

'You going to feed those ducks, then?' He took the bag from her and peered inside. ''Cos if not I might have to tuck in. I didn't eat much earlier as I thought we'd have a late supper somewhere.'

Dawn giggled, snatching back her bag of stale crusts. 'I thought you wanted a game of football.' She got up and approached the water's edge. Having torn the bread into smaller pieces, she began lobbing it.

Glenn joined her and also took a handful of crusts from the bag. 'You won't tell anybody about this, will you?' he said dryly as he joined her in throwing morsels. 'I have an image of suave sophistication to protect. Feeding the ducks with a girl instead of taking her on the razzle in the West End . . . really Rafferty, poor show . . .' He mimicked the voice of a toff to perfection.

Dawn burst out laughing.

Glenn threw the last crust in a bowling overarm then

watched Dawn traipsing to and fro to pick the right spot in the water to aim for.

'Just chuck it in; they'll sort it out,' Glenn advised, watching the ducks darting and spinning to fight for their food.

Dawn shook her head. 'Can't do that or the big one takes it all. The little brown one at the back hasn't had a look-in yet.'

'That's life, Dawn. Survival of the fittest. You might as well let the bully have his share or he'll peck the others to death later.'

Dawn's smile faded for there was a depressing truth in what he'd said.

'Do your parents or sisters know what you're doing?' There was no need to explain what she meant by her question; she'd sensed that the subject of his investigations was heavy on both their minds.

'No.'

'They'd be alarmed, wouldn't they?' Dawn emptied the residue of breadcrumbs onto the grass so the sparrows could have them.

'I expect so – Mum especially. How's your mum doing?' When Dawn shot him a sharp glance, Glenn explained, 'You told me you had a few problems with her.'

Dawn squashed the empty paper bag in her fist. 'She sometimes drinks too much, but she's fine at the moment.' She hoped that were true. It took very little emotional upset to make Eliza reach for the gin. Now that her mother and George's father were a couple again, there were bound to be many anxious moments for one and all until George finally learned – and Dawn prayed accepted – the news of his parentage.

'You said you had sisters,' she blurted, putting the focus back on Glenn. 'How old are they?'

'Lily's eleven and Penny's thirteen.'

'Oh, so much younger than you then,' Dawn exclaimed interestedly. 'I bet for a while you thought you'd be a spoiled only child.'

'I did, and so did my folks. My mum thought she'd never have kids of her own so they adopted me. Then she had Penny and Lily and proved herself wrong.' He gazed at the lads tearing to and fro with their football. 'Not that Mum and Dad ever put me fully in the picture about it. My uncle told me one Christmas when he'd had too much rum. I must have been about sixteen then.'

The casually imparted information shocked Dawn and for a moment she didn't know what to say. 'You found out that you were adopted from your uncle?' she breathed.

'No . . . my parents told me that part of my history on the day I left school; I suppose they thought it time to treat me as an adult as I was expected to earn my keep. My uncle told me my mum was supposed to be barren but he reckoned my father was firing blanks.'

Dawn blushed at his turn of phrase, wondering how he could seem so unaffected, even amused, about it all. She quashed an instinct to say that she was sorry; she knew he wouldn't want her pity, and neither did he seem to need it.

'It must have come as a great surprise.'

'I suppose it was, although I sensed something was different about us as a family, I just didn't know what it was. I've wondered since if my uncle was hinting that Mum had been unfaithful to Dad; probably he was just being a drunken prat.' He smiled at Dawn, playfully chucking her under the chin. 'It wasn't an awful upbringing, quite the reverse. My parents did spoil me and I've always been treated as their own flesh and blood. We're a happy family, and all that.' He sounded proud despite his self-mockery. 'I dote on my sisters although they drive me up the wall.'

'I adore my brother . . . he drives me up the wall,' Dawn said softly. She glanced at him. 'Are you curious about your real mum . . . sorry . . . I mean the woman who gave birth to you,' she spluttered. 'At the time I was more curious about my father. When they told me I'd been adopted I asked for some details and got a sketchy account of what had happened.'

Dawn gazed at him with wide green eyes, waiting expectantly.

'Nothing very original, I'm afraid,' he grunted with a rueful laugh. 'Just a clichéd tale of a rich man ruining a young girl.' He shrugged. 'My father was apparently a minor aristocrat; my mother a neighbour's daughter he took a fancy to.'

Dawn's jaw sagged.

'I'm not making it up,' Glenn said and offered her a cigarette.

This time Dawn took one and waited impatiently for him to light it. He lit his too and before the match had been snuffed out Dawn was flicking a length of ash onto the ground.

'Apparently the girl wanted to keep me but wasn't allowed to.' Unprompted Glenn had continued with his story. 'So I was sent far away from Mayfair to a children's home in East London so nobody would be embarrassed by me. I was there for nine months apparently.'

Dawn swallowed a lump in her throat. Glenn Rafferty, playboy squadron leader, was sensitive to his abandonment even now, and little wonder. In her mind's eye she pictured a baby, his dark curly head on sterile white cotton, and nobody heeding his cries. 'Then Mr and Mrs Rafferty came along and wanted you as the first of their children.' Her voice sounded very husky and she almost hugged him in comfort.

Glenn laughed. 'Yeah . . . and now I'm a Walthamstow barrow boy's kid.'

'Are you sorry about that?' Dawn was gazing up at him through their mingling exhaled smoke.

'Grammar school scholarship, university place at Cambridge . . .' He interrupted himself to interject, 'I turned that down to start my own business in importing and exporting, when I was eighteen. The company was making a good profit before Fritz threw a spanner in the works. Anyway, I reckon I've done alright as a Rafferty.'

'Me too,' Dawn said with sweet encouragement. 'D'you want to know something funny?'

'Depends,' he said with feigned suspicion.

'I reckoned you looked like a gypsy and it turns out you're posh . . .'

Glenn stared down at her through close black lashes. 'A sort of romantic hero like Heathcliff, you mean,' he suggested drolly.

'Not really.' Dawn assumed an expression of regret.

'I see. A pikey – that's nice.' He playfully grabbed her wrist keeping her arm rigidly, yet painlessly, at bay so her cigarette couldn't burn him as he drew her closer. 'An insult deserves a forfeit, I reckon . . .' He kissed her with teasing leisure then let her go and stuck the cigarette back in his mouth.

'Verdict?'

Dawn knew what he meant. 'Not bad . . . could do better . . .'

'Fancy going somewhere so I can practise on you?' he asked with an undercurrent of seriousness.

'Don't push your luck,' Dawn said and turned away. Her lips still pulsed from the pressure of his mouth, and of course he could kiss very well, as she was sure he knew.

'Right, let's challenge Stanley Matthews and his mate to a match.' Glenn nodded at the lads haring about. They were using spaced jumpers as improvised goalposts. 'Dad's a West Ham supporter, I'm more of a rugby man myself.'

'That's your breeding showing,' Dawn mocked, then she was the one apologising for having a big mouth. But he laughed.

'Bet your dad supports West Ham too, being as you're East Enders.'

'My mum's a widow. And my dad supported Tottenham Hotspur.'

'Sorry, didn't realise about your dad . . . Bill never said.' Glenn frowned, regretting bringing the name up.

But Dawn's thoughts slipped straight over her late boyfriend. Quite naturally she put a hand through Glenn's arm as they strolled, and he immediately enclosed it with his warm dark fingers.

'My dad was a North Londoner.' It seemed the most natural thing in the world to tell him about her family. 'He caught Spanish flu but could never properly shake it off. Mum reckons that's what led to the pneumonia that killed him years later.'

'Very sorry to hear it,' Glenn said with husky sincerity.

'Have you ever considered seeking out your father?'

Glenn shook his head. 'I'm not interested in knocking on a door in Mayfair and giving some poor bloke a heart attack. I'm Greg and Ruth Rafferty's kid. That's who I am. And I'm glad about it.'

'So am I . . .' Dawn said spontaneously then turned bashful. She was pleased Glenn Rafferty – despite his astonishing parentage – came from a similar background to her own. Had he not been sent away from Mayfair, they would never have moved in the same circles.

'I suppose you might have half-brothers or sisters,' Dawn said.

'That's a thought,' Glenn answered with a frown.

Dawn suddenly realised that what she'd said might be true for her own brother. Her mum had told her that Rod's wife had been ill for years but it was quite possible they'd had children early on in their marriage. Astonishingly, it had never occurred to Dawn that that might be the case and yet the matter seemed to be always on her mind.

'My brother . . .' Dawn came to an abrupt halt.

'What were you going to say?'

Dawn took a deep breath. 'My brother doesn't know who his father is either.'

Glenn looked surprised but didn't display the sort of curiosity that she had felt on hearing his news. He waited patiently for her to explain, without prompting her to start. Dawn recounted it all, including the fact that Rod was now back and hoping to win her mother over for a second time.

'Your brother might need a stiff drink the day they sit him down,' Glenn said succinctly.

'Oh, I know,' Dawn wailed. She pushed her fingers

through her thick blonde hair, holding it back from her forehead. 'I'm hoping for it all to pass off smoothly, but I'm kidding myself, aren't I?'

Glenn pulled her round to face him, holding her firmly by the shoulders. 'Listen, your brother might take it all in his stride, so don't get yourself in a lather too soon.' He gave her a little encouraging shake. 'George seems a bright kid; he knows if he were a few years older he'd be worried about handling a rifle rather than the fact that his dad's finally free to marry his mum. That's the thing about wartime; it helps you see what's important, and what's just life fouling up once in a while.'

CHAPTER TWENTY-THREE

'Fancy a match, lads?' Glenn called to the two boys as they drew closer to them.

The tallest boy stared at them. 'You sure you're up to it, mate?' He gave Glenn's suit a quizzical look. His eyes travelled over Dawn and he blushed then hung his head, shooting a sideways glance at his friend.

'Could give 'em a goal start. Evens it up a bit,' the boy with sandy hair and freckles said.

'Sounds fair to me.' Dawn smiled agreement.

She took off her jacket and began rolling up her blouse sleeves. She felt relieved rather than sorry to have unburdened herself to Glenn about her family crisis. He had a plain view of things that was strangely calming and helpful. She was sure he could be trusted to keep their family secret to himself, just as he trusted her to keep quiet about the work he was doing. 'I've played a bit of football with my brother in the past,' Dawn said, hoping the boys accepted her credentials. They looked unenthusiastic at the idea of having a knockabout with a girl and a bloke in a smart suit.

Glenn suddenly loped towards the ball and whacked it through the space between the two jerseys. 'One nil,' he announced smugly.

'That's an own goal. We're shooting that way,' the tall boy said, quick as a flash.

'Like that, is it?' Glenn retrieved the ball. 'Right. No holds barred.' He immediately passed the ball to Dawn and somehow or other she managed to receive it and start dribbling with it towards the other jumpers, her blonde hair streaming back from her laughing face. She got a shot at the goal and although it went wide she noticed that the boys appeared less mocking.

Twenty minutes later Dawn was sitting on the grass holding the stitch in her side. No amount of geeing up from her team mate could give her some extra puff, so the boys declared themselves the winners at seven to four – the three goals had been scored by Glenn – and the boys generously allowed them the one goal head start so it didn't seem too much of a whitewash. While the lads were collecting their jumpers Glenn scooped up his discarded jacket then sat down on the grass beside Dawn. He lounged back onto the turf, a forearm resting over his eyes to shield them from the setting sun.

Dawn gazed out over the water in the distance, feeling the happiest she had in a long while. The soft summery air, scented with mown grass, and the childish antics had brought back such vivid memories of long ago. But she knew such serenity couldn't last as much as she yearned that it might.

The wide blue sky drew her eyes. They wouldn't appear yet; if they were coming on this glorious day in May it would be more than likely after sunset. But it was easy to imagine German bombers, looking and sounding like a swarm of bluebottles, darkening the horizon with malevolent intent.

Glenn turned his head slightly, watching her frowning concentration. 'I'm going back to East Anglia next week.'

Dawn nodded. She knew they had things to talk about. He'd asked for her help in finding traitors in their midst, and if he asked her again she'd agree. Until they all did their utmost to win this war there would be few salad days for this generation of children to remember . . .

Glenn raised himself on an elbow. 'If I ask you about your colleagues, are you going to accuse me of using you and trying to grill you for information?'

Dawn shook her head.

'It's you I'm really interested in, not them or girls like Tina. I'm not callously using you and I won't disappear as soon as I've got what I want. Do you believe me, Dawn, and understand what I'm saying?'

There was no banter in his tone or his eyes now; nevertheless she paused before answering. 'Yes . . . I do . . . I understand it all.' He was talking about wanting to make love to her as well as securing her as a partner in crime. 'I'm not sure though that your superiors would like you talking to me about espionage.'

'My superiors are happy enough for me to enlist the help of others. They're putting trust in me to know who I can trust.'

Dawn gave a slow nod of acceptance.

He stretched out a few fingers, outlined her mouth with just one. 'I know I've not known you long, and I'm sure you hear this all the time from men . . . but I'm going to say it anyway: you're beautiful and I think I could quite easily fall in love with you.'

Dawn had heard something similar from Bill just

weeks before she found out he'd been sleeping around. But she didn't care; she turned her face into Glenn's touch, revelling in his skilful caress.

'But I've a job to do,' Glenn added huskily, 'and I need to ask you some questions about your friends and colleagues at the theatre.'

'Ask away.'

'Intelligence has come through from some of our people and the Windmill Theatre got a mention.' Glenn stared at the boys as they walked away bouncing the ball between them. 'A group of sympathisers has been under surveillance; they hold meetings in halls and clubs under the guise of social gatherings. When one meeting broke up a woman was followed to the Windmill Theatre.'

'Perhaps she was going to watch a show,' Dawn said.

'Don't think so . . . she didn't join the queue but went straight in as though she was an employee.'

'Can you describe her?'

'Unfortunately she was tracked on a day when it was pelting down. She had on a rain mac and a scarf and was using an umbrella. So the description we have is: taller than average and thin with a fair complexion and no glasses. Not a lot to go on, I know.'

Dawn knew that Lorna fitted that description. She was a tall, slender woman and she always protected her hair with a scarf if it rained. But then so did lots of women . . . Dawn included. Suddenly her mind darted to the day Lorna had had a hangover and moaned about some brandy, believing it to be moonshine donated by her mother's friends because they couldn't afford to buy proper spirits. Lorna had said her mother could cheerfully kill her father for keeping them short while he lived the life of Riley . . .

253

'Lorna Danvers had some rotgut, but she drunk it herself.' Dawn didn't believe that her colleague might be a Nazi sympathiser. Edward Danvers might be a fascist but it didn't mean that his estranged wife and daughter were too.

Glenn pulled a blade of grass and slid it between his teeth. He chewed slowly, eyes lowered to the turf.

Dawn felt a tremor of trepidation touch her spine just as she had when first told about his undercover work. 'You're getting closer to the traitors, aren't you?' she whispered. 'And you seriously suspect there might be one working at the Windmill Theatre?' She sounded as though torn between being affronted and shocked to the core.

'Nazi sympathisers have infiltrated everywhere, Dawn, even Whitehall.' He gazed steadily at her. 'And we need to catch the treacherous bastards before they put whatever plans they're hatching into action.'

'I promise I'll keep my eyes and ears open.' Dawn frowned; she hated the idea of spying on colleagues, some of whom she classed as friends. But she understood that saboteurs deserved no such tolerance or sentiment.

'Lorna Danvers lives with her mother, doesn't she?'

Dawn nodded, sensing Glenn was about to voice further suspicions about Lorna's family and their loyalty to the crown.

'Mrs Danvers went to school with Mosley's wife. They keep in touch and have been seen together recently having tea at the Ritz.'

'Lorna says that they're poor because her father is too selfish to help them financially, and that's why they're reduced to drinking moonshine. So I don't know how her mother affords luxurious teas at the Ritz . . .'

'Perhaps her friend pays for them in return for favours,' Glenn suggested. 'It's not just ideology that makes a turncoat. Sometimes they do it for hard cash.'

'Tea at the Ritz might not be cheap, but it's not *that* expensive either!' Dawn scoffed.

'I agree, but taking everything into account: the family's connections, Edward Danvers' politics and so on . . .' Glenn shrugged. 'Just because Danvers has gone off with a younger woman it doesn't mean the family don't still share similar views. Lorna would have been brought up listening to rabid nonsense and perhaps got brainwashed.' He shot her a glance. 'Mosley would have visited the Danvers family at home . . . talk round the dinner table . . . impressionable young mind . . . and so on . . .'

'You've certainly done your homework,' Dawn said quietly.

'Not me. The desk Johnnies do all that.' Glenn smiled, pushed himself off his elbow to sit with his forearms resting on his bent knees. 'We'll just have to keep watching and waiting I suppose, and in the meantime do our damnedest to beat the hell out of the Krauts.'

'We all want the war over with,' Dawn sighed. She eyed the grass he was chewing. He had a mouth that was not too thin or too wide . . . it was nicely moulded and just the right size, she thought. 'Still hungry?' she teased, determined to lighten the conversation.

'Starving,' Glenn said with a glint in his eye, slowly removing the grass held in his teeth. He snaked out a hand to catch her to him but Dawn rolled away, laughing, and scrambled onto her knees. 'If you think I'll let you kiss me again out in the open and scandalise those mums . . .' She jerked a nod at two women out for a late stroll, pushing prams. 'Probably trying to get the little mites off to sleep,' she murmured, and was put in mind suddenly of Gertie Grimes and little Harry. She'd not thought about seeing the looters at work for ages; the incident seemed unimportant to her now.

Dawn cast it all from her mind and jumped to her feet. She put out a hand to Glenn. 'Come on, then. You promised me supper earlier on, and I'm ready for it now.'

With a furious scowl Gertie let Midge into the house and put a finger against her lips. Seconds ago her brother had appeared at her kitchen window. Before he could get over the threshold Gertie had tried to shut the door in his face. But Midge wasn't having any of it and had kept bumping his shoulder against the panels. To keep him quiet Gertie had let him in, but her face was crimson with rage. She pointed then moved silently to close the parlour door standing ajar. 'Rufus is asleep on the sofa . . . don't wake him, and start him off, fer Gawd's sake! You've got five minutes, that's all.'

Midge made a small movement with his head, agreeing to terms. He leaned against the wall, just inside the back door, closing his eyes and allowing himself to relax. But he could tell from his sister's agitation that something bad had happened. He reckoned it was more than just the fear of Rufus waking up and going spare at the sight of him that was making her boil up.

'You've got to stop coming here, Michael!' Gertie hissed. 'It ain't safe. Police have been round after you 'cos they've had a report someone's seen you.' She moved her net curtain an inch. 'Ain't even properly dark yet. Don't know if the house is being watched . . .'

Suddenly Gertie broke off to wrinkle her nose. 'You need a bath! You stink to high heaven.'

'Won't be stopping long,' Midge mumbled. His sister's news should have frightened the life out of him, but it hadn't. He wasn't even going to ask her if the police had let on who'd grassed him up.

Midge was sure that Rufus had done it – probably anonymously – because after their run-in his brother-in-law had had a think about things and realised he was in danger.

Midge knew if he got caught he'd get found guilty of murdering Jack Chivers, which was fair enough as he had done it. So if he got arrested he'd swing; he might as well get hung for a sheep as a lamb. Next time he got Rufus alone he'd stripe him; he'd stripe all of them 'cos he was feeling murderous in the way he had when he'd knifed Chivers in a fit of rage for calling him a short-arsed little runt. But he hadn't meant to kill his fellow seaman, just shut him up.

'Good God.' Gertie had been giving her tramp-like brother the once-over and had got a glimpse of Midge's rotting flesh, partially concealed by a bandage stiff with muck.

'You gotta help me, Gert. Give us some cash so's I can find a sawbones what won't ask questions when he cuts off me hand before it poisons me to death. That's all I'm here for. Do that for me and I'll get out of your hair once and for all. Won't be back, promise.'

Gertie was gawking at Michael as though he'd garbled out double Dutch. 'You've got to get yourself to hospital,' she croaked. She knew he wasn't exaggerating the state of his health. She could see and smell how putrid his flesh was.

'Ain't seeing no kosher doc, not while I'm still alive, anyhow. If I get taken in by the police, I'm a dead man.'

'You killed that seaman, didn't you?'

Midge didn't answer his sister but his resigned shrug told Gertie all she needed to know.

Midge went to the drawer and snatched out a knife. 'I'd do it meself but reckon I'd pass out halfway through and bleed to death. So give us some money, I'm begging you.'

Gertie could tell that her brother was serious about having part of himself amputated. She studied him; his brown hair had grown long and was in rats' tails around his death mask of a face. The cocky, boisterous brother she'd known had transformed into an ugly stranger. She pitied Midge but she hated him too.

'Who's that? Who you talkin' to, Gert?' Rufus bawled in a drunken slur. He always went out Sunday dinner time and came back three sheets to the wind then fell asleep on the sofa till opening time sobered him up.

'Get going, Midge!' Gertie opened her purse and emptied the silver and copper into his healthy palm. 'All I've got . . . that's it . . . good luck,' she added as an afterthought, bundling her brother out of the door.

'Won't get nuthin' done with that,' Midge moaned but he set off at a limping trot towards the back fence.

CHAPTER TWENTY-FOUR

'You like my whisky sour, Rosie? Bottoms up, then. Plenty more in here.' Malt swayed the silver cocktail shaker between a thick thumb and finger.

The Maltese had poured the drink into a tumbler, slipped in a lemon slice then urged Rosie to down it by tipping up her elbow in a way that seemed playful.

The fiery spirit hit the back of Rosie's throat, making her giggle. Since she'd lived with Marlene she'd grown accustomed to drinking Scotch but this seemed unusually strong. She thumped her chest and croaked, 'Phew! You foreigners know how to mix a stiff drink!'

'I know how to show a girl a good time.' Malt lowered a heavy eyelid in a wink. 'You like my uncle's club?'

Rosie glanced about the interior of the Palm House; she was seated at a long bar set against a flank wall. Though the interior was dark and smoky Rosie could see men playing cards at a circular table near the back of the vast basement room. Young women were hanging about behind their chairs, watching the state of play and ferrying drinks to and fro. A tiny dance floor was midway between the gaming table and the bar; it was crowded with couples swaying to the soulful music provided by a jazz trio. Two doorways were situated on the opposite wall to the bar; Rosie imagined they led to a powder room and a kitchen. A waiter had edged out of one with a tray loaded with sandwiches, and headed towards the gamblers.

Marlene and Malt had often talked about this place and Rosie had looked forward to being invited along. They'd arrived about an hour ago and she hadn't yet decided if she liked the club enough to want to come again. But certainly there was a louche atmosphere that she found rather exhilarating.

'It's a very lively place,' she finally said in response to Malt's question.

Marlene was talking to some people but she gave Rosie a smile and raised her glass in salute. A moment later her friend had joined her at the bar and was offering Rosie a cigarette.

'There's a good crowd in here tonight,' Marlene said, dipping her head to Malt's lighter.

'Ah . . . here come Jeremy Trent.' Malt nudged Rosie's arm. 'That fellow like you . . . you lucky girl, catch the eye of important man.' Malt dropped Rosie another wink.

'Hey! Hey!' Malt suddenly remonstrated. 'You watch out for the lady! Outside you wanna fight.'

Two scuffling army officers had bumped into Rosie's bar stool, almost unseating her.

'It gets a bit rackety in here,' Rosie said with a nervous giggle, wiping splashes of her drink from her bare arm.

'Rosie, how nice to see you . . .'

Jeremy Trent lifted Rosie's fingers to his lips like a

true gent. He affably accepted Malt's offer of a whisky and soda. 'Would you like to dance, my dear?' Jeremy's fingers trailed Rosie's shoulder, straying close to her cleavage.

'Yes . . . you two dance . . . go on,' Malt urged. 'I get the drinks.'

As Rosie and Jeremy walked away arm in arm Malt turned to Marlene with a triumphant smile. 'See, I told you. Rosie not stupid. That girl know the score.'

Marlene grimaced uncertainly at her boyfriend. She hoped he was right and Rosie had been hamming up the part of a demure damsel because Major Trent was expecting a return on his money tonight. And who could blame him? She'd found out that the fellow had parted with fifty pounds for the pleasure of Rosie's company, although Malt only intended giving Rosie a tenner out of it.

There were so many couples surrounding them it was only possible to shuffle and sway to the music. Now Rosie was on her feet she was feeling the effects of the half a dozen cocktails she'd got through. But the major seemed not to mind her clinging to his shoulders to prevent herself stumbling. Dreamily she thought she wouldn't mind if he kissed her, although he was a bit older than she would have liked in a boyfriend. Rosie put her cheek against his, liking that he smelled nicely of lemons. 'Have you been here before, Major Trent?' she sighed out.

'Call me Jeremy,' Trent said. 'I've been here once or twice . . . but never with a young lady as lovely as you.' He nuzzled her ear. 'I know of better places. I said I'd take you to the Ritz, didn't I, sweetie. And I will, if you're good . . .'

'It must be close to midnight. I expect we'll be heading home soon.' Rosie giggled. 'Malt's been mixing me different cocktails. He's very good at it but enough's enough. I'm at work tomorrow and I don't want a sore head.'

'I don't want you sozzled either, sweetie.' Jeremy gave a subtle laugh.

'Is that the powder room?' Rosie nodded to a door. She knew she needed to use it before leaving.

'Shall we take a look?' Trent smiled in satisfaction. The Maltese had obviously put Rosie in the picture and she was delicately indicating she was ready now to get down to business. And so was he . . .

Malt gleefully rubbed his hands together, having watched the major lead Rosie through the door that led towards the bedrooms. There were four of them, gaudily done out in red light bulbs and cheap satin. But nobody complained, least of all the men who paid to use one with the women of their choice.

A pinkish light in the corridor made Rosie squint to see clearly. But Jeremy seemed to know where to head. He'd opened a door and entered a room. Rosie stood on the threshold peering in. If it were the powder room she'd go in alone. She didn't need his help for that!

'Crikey . . . looks like we're trespassing,' Rosie said, having noticed the bed.

'No, we're not, sweetie, I think you know that.' Impatiently, Trent pulled Rosie towards him and.closed the door. He'd had enough of girly games and was ready to take what he'd paid for.

At first Rosie thought he was messing about. She shoved him away, tutting, but he dragged her back and started fiddling with the buttons at the back of her dress.

When she struggled he impatiently used both hands to tear open the fastenings.

'Come on, you little tease.' Jeremy's breath felt hot against Rosie's ear. 'It's time to play the game my way now . . .'

Rosie stamped her heel down on his foot; she'd had enough of being manhandled, *and* he'd just ruined her best dress. 'I think you've had more to drink than I have,' she cried. ''Cos I'm not that sort of girl, and I don't know why you think I am. I only asked you where the lavvie was!' She knew that booze made people do and say stupid things so was still willing to give the major the benefit of the doubt; he'd always been nice to her before.

Jeremy Trent winced in pain, hopped once following her assault on his instep, then swung out with a fist, knocking Rosie back onto the bed. But instead of following her down onto it he dragged her up by an arm and propelled her, gasping in agony, towards the door.

'Go on, get out, you deceitful whore. And you can tell the foreigner he won't get away with this.' Jeremy Trent threw Rosie into the corridor with such force that she hit the opposite wall before fleeing.

In her blind haste Rosie ran the wrong way and ended up turning a corner into a dead end. She swung about and tried the nearest door handle. Inside the room a naked woman was rocking astride a man on the bed, her dark hair swaying about her shoulders. Suddenly she looked over her shoulder.

Rosie gawped at Tina. Despite the soft haze shed by the coloured light bulb she'd recognised the brunette at once. Tina hadn't forgotten either their altercation in the 400 Club and she gave a sly smile.

'Knew you was no better than me, Windmill girl,' she

hissed. 'Find your own room, or wait your turn.' She flung herself around on her punter, bouncing up and down with renewed vigour.

Rosie hurried back the way she'd come and met Jeremy Trent in the corridor. She halted, ready to fight him off if necessary, but there was no need. The light might have been dim but she could see a look of contempt on his face. He ignored her, striding ahead to the door that led back to the club. Rosie followed him and watched at a distance as the major marched up to Malt and Marlene, still at the bar. There was no need to have been any closer to them for Rosie to know what was being said. Jeremy Trent's furious expression and Malt's expressive Mediterranean shrug let Rosie know she'd been a naïve fool. Malt had promised the major that she was an easy lay.

Malt was trying to calm Trent down by offering him his whisky and soda but having accepted the glass Jeremy launched the drink at Malt's face before storming off.

Marlene spied Rosie but instead of looking ashamed at what she'd embroiled the girl in, she started weaving through the crowded room in her friend's direction.

'You stupid little cow!' Marlene snarled as soon as she was within Rosie's earshot. 'D'you know the trouble you've caused?'

'He thought I was a tart! And he punched me and tore my dress,' Rosie exploded. Her jaw was aching badly from the blow and she just wanted to go home.

Marlene snorted a harsh laugh. 'You're fuckin' lucky that's all he did then, aren't you.' Contemptuously she raked Rosie from head to foot. 'What are you saving it for anyhow? You've left home and it ain't as if you're sweet sixteen.'

Malt stalked over to them, his black eyes flinty, his cheek glistening with the drink he'd had thrown at him. 'You out of my house and never back there,' he spat at Rosie, dragging a handkerchief from his pocket and dabbing whisky off his olive skin.

'What d'you mean?' Rosie was feeling apprehensive now as well as hurt and betrayed by two people she'd thought liked her for herself. It was slowly sinking in that they'd never returned her friendship. She'd just been a pawn in a game to them. 'My stuff's round at yours and I want it. If you don't give it to me I'll call the police.'

'Don't think you will do that,' Malt said in a sinister voice. 'My girls cross me, threaten me with Old Bill, they don't look so pretty no more.'

In desperation Rosie looked at Marlene but the woman avoided her eyes. 'I finally get it,' she said slowly and gave a bitter laugh. 'You're right, Marlene, I am a stupid cow.' She swung a glance between the couple. 'I know what he is . . . and I know what you are. Well, *you* might be one of *his girls*, but I ain't, and I never will be.'

Rosie pushed past them both and, head high despite the throb in her chin, walked up to the bar. Her whisky sour was there waiting for her and she picked it up, intending to knock it back before leaving. Marlene rushed up behind and grabbed the glass, thumping it down. 'Get going, Rosie. You don't know what he's like when he's feeling mean.'

'I want my stuff back.' Rosie could tell that Marlene was starting to feel bad about what she'd done. The older woman seemed on the verge of an apology.

'I'll pack your case and put it out in the front garden

for you tomorrow,' Marlene promised hoarsely, trying to shove the girl on her way. She tensed as she looked over Rosie's shoulder and saw her boyfriend approaching them.

'You still here, little girl?' Malt ridiculed her viciously. 'Ah, I know, you hanging around to pay me for all those cocktails you had, eh?'

'Well . . . you can have this one back if you like.' Rosie threw the drink in his newly wiped face then darted for the exit.

Having scrambled up the steps to the street Rosie grabbed a railing and held on, drawing in a lungful of breath. She'd felt a burst of exhilaration on racing for the club's exit but the cool evening air had hit her like a brick wall. Despite the muzz in her head from the drinks she'd knocked back she knew she was in a dreadful mess . . . and she didn't know how to unravel it.

She started walking, head lowered and one hand hitching her torn dress into place. At intervals she glanced back, primed to spot Malt bounding up behind her to get his revenge. She glanced about for suitable alleys to dart into at the first glimpse of his beefy body hurtling in her direction. Rosie quickened her pace, picking her way round the people thronging the pavement. A fellow in a sharp suit deliberately walked into her path. When Rosie tried to avoid him he walked backwards in front of her, leering with his head cocked to one side. Seemingly impressed by what he saw he wordlessly pulled a banknote from a pocket to show her. He then folded it carefully and stuck it in his top pocket before trying to hustle her into an alleyway with him.

Rosie kicked his shin and hurried on, leaving him

swearing after her. She knew she must get to a place where she could slow down and concentrate on finding a place to stay the night. Going home to her father, smelling of booze and with a bruise on her face and her dress torn, was out of the question. She wasn't sure of what reception she'd get if she turned up all spick and span. If her dad saw her in this state he'd have a fit – and she couldn't blame him. What a fool she'd been . . .

With an inspiriting sniff she forced herself to buck up. There was no use in wallowing in self-pity. No real harm had been done, she told herself, and at least she'd learned a lesson about Marlene Brown! She'd let them all know at the Windmill just what a horrible cow the woman was. And serve her right too if she got the sack when it came out she was a no-good brass . . .

'So . . . what might you be doing round here then, Rosie?'

The voice wasn't Malt's but it was familiar so Rosie spun about and saw Lenny Purves standing by the kerb with his arms crossed over his chest. He had his head cocked to one side, a knowing look on his face.

Rosie cursed beneath her breath at the sight of him, wondering if he'd seen her being accosted a moment ago. She must have just passed Lenny without realising it. If there were one person she'd rather not have run into, it was him. He was a prime reason she'd argued with her father. If she hadn't stormed out she'd never have moved in with a prostitute and her pimp then ended up with no home to go to. Having projected all the blame for her predicament onto Lenny she gave him a scowl and her back view as she marched on.

Lenny was not to be put off. He swaggered after her, circling her and eyeing her dishevelled appearance.

Jeremy Trent had ripped off the top few buttons of Rosie's dress and where it sagged at the neckline, she was having a job keeping the drooping crepe from sliding off her shoulders.

'So . . . you been doing what yer shouldn't, have you?' Lenny suggested craftily.

'Might ask you the same thing, if I was interested enough in knowing why you're in Soho.'

'Me? I like a bit of nightlife with pretty girls . . .' Lenny settled down to walk just behind her. 'You a regular in that dive, then?' He jerked his head back towards the entrance to the Palm House. He'd watched her come out of it a few minutes ago and had crossed the road, stationing himself in a place where he knew she'd walk past. He'd seen her push a punter away and wondered how much the fellow had offered her.

He'd never seen Rosie working as a hostess in that brothel, and he'd found it hard to believe it *was* her till he got up close. But now he'd had his suspicions confirmed and Lenny was thinking his luck might finally be in tonight. If there were one girl he *really* did fancy, it was the one he was with.

'D'you hear what I said?' Lenny barked over the noise of a group of scuffling servicemen who'd fallen into the road. 'You go in the Palm House a lot, then?'

'That place ain't classy enough for me,' Rosie snapped over a shoulder, wishing he'd take the hint and piss off.

'Nah, not classy enough for me neither.' Lenny fell into step beside her now the pavement was clear. From beneath his lashes he took a good look at Rosie. He could see a graze on her chin and that her dress's buttons were missing. Lenny knew what happened when a tart gave lip to a punter. He'd dished out a few right-handers in his time to hookers who'd tried to take liberties. He knew the bloke who'd tried to drag her into an alley a moment ago hadn't clumped her and was curious to know who had.

'Oi, Len . . .'

Lenny spun about on hearing his name called. He muttered beneath his breath and stepped away from Rosie. 'Just speak to me pal then I'll be back.'

'Don't bother,' Rosie muttered beneath her breath as Lenny dashed off. She'd been about to cross the road to escape him when she suddenly spied the pal he had gone to talk to. Her pace faltered.

Lenny's friend had propped himself against a gas lamp giving Rosie a chance to study them together. She stood transfixed then noticed that the stocky fellow with gingery hair was staring back at her. It might have been many months since Roof had looted a shop then chased her and Dawn down an alley but Rosie remembered him – and judging from his expression he remembered her too.

Rosie transferred her attention to Lenny; she'd never got a good look at the third man who'd pushed away the cart loaded with clothes. It'd been dark and he'd had his back to her all the time, but he had been tall and thin . . . and just like Lenny . . .

Roof appeared to be putting Lenny in the picture about where he'd seen Rosie before. She could see their heads close together and suddenly Lenny shot a glance her way.

Rosie took a deep breath, then hurtled over the busy road, dodging people and vehicles as she headed towards Tottenham Court Road tube station. She'd no money with her other than a few shillings in a pocket. Everything she owned, even her small pot of savings, was back at Malt's place. She knew she'd never see the cash again. She'd be lucky if she saw her suitcase of clothes.

Suddenly Rosie was feeling quite sober, and dreadfully depressed as she trotted along, shivering.

''Ere, wait up . . . what you running off for.' Lenny came loping up behind her and grabbed her arm.

'Get lost; I'm off home . . .'

'Where's that, then?' Lenny jeered, dragging her roughly to a halt. 'I know your old man threw you out . . . he told me. I reckon he had good cause to now I know where you've been tonight.'

Rosie had had enough of him manhandling her and refusing to leave her in peace. Besides she was sure Lenny knew she'd witnessed him looting, and she didn't want him questioning her over that. As far as she was concerned it was all in the past and forgotten. Rosie shoved him away and broke into a run.

'Now that's rude, ain't it,' Lenny snarled. He'd caught up with Rosie in a few long strides. Grabbing her by the nape he frogmarched her rapidly into an alley with him.

He stood blocking her escape route then began advancing on her. 'Me pal reckons you're trouble. He reckons you was spying on us a while back when we was doing a job. That right?'

'Dunno know what you're talking about. Never seen him before. Now get out of the way.' Rosie could feel her heart racing. She'd always thought Lenny a bit of a pest but not a serious menace. Suddenly she was feeling very differently about that.

'I told him I could set things straight with you, 'cos we go way back, don't we.' Lenny stopped just inches in front of Rosie and straddled his legs either side of her.

Lazily he started fondling her breasts through her dress. 'You be nice to me and I'll make sure nothing happens to you . . .'

Rosie slapped his hands away but he continued touching her roughly with one hand and shoving her backwards by the shoulder with the other.

'I said get off me or I'll scream,' Rosie threatened hoarsely when he'd got her pinned against a brick wall.

'Go on then. Whore making a racket down an alley?' He grunted a laugh. 'Who d'you think's gonna take notice of that?' He gave the neck of her dress a tug and, already damaged, the bodice fell to her waist, exposing her dainty underwear. 'That's what you are, Miss High and Mighty, ain't it? I guessed it from the moment you started stripping off at the Windmill. When I saw you coming out of the Palm House I knew for certain you was on the game.' He pinched her bruised chin, making her wince. 'Who gave you a whack, then? Bet you tried to short-change some poor bastard, didn't you?' Lenny slammed his mouth against Rosie's and started battering at her lips with his tongue. 'You ain't gonna short-change me, gel,' he said between nipping her lips with his teeth.

Rosie frantically tried to knee him in the groin but he thrust her away, a savage hand around her windpipe holding her at arm's length. With his free hand, Lenny started unbuttoning his flies.

'What you gonna do?' Rosie choked, trying to squirm her neck from his grip.

'What d'you fuckin' think, you scrubber? I'm gonna show you what you've been missing and what you'll get if you even think of grassing me or me pals up to the coppers.'

With a savage swipe of his foot Lenny took Rosie's

legs from under her then leapt astride her, curbing her shouts and struggles by slapping her repeatedly across the face.

Tearing at her knickers he began pumping into her with all the force he could muster, his pinching fingers stifling her screams.

'You ain't on stage now, you're on yer other job . . .' he taunted close to Rosie's ear. 'Move for me . . . go on . . . I don't want no statue lying under me.' He grabbed Rosie's buttocks, forcing her up against him and grinding her hips back and forth.

Then when he'd finished and she lay still and quiet he rolled off and stood up, buttoning his trousers. He pulled a handful of coins out of his pocket and tossed them onto the floor close to Rosie's deathly pale cheek.

'Waste of time, you was. Five bob, that's all yer worth . . .'

CHAPTER TWENTY-FIVE

'What on earth . . .?'

Dawn pushed open the gate and rushed into her front garden to gawp at Rosie huddled on her front step.

'What's happened? What are you doing here?' Conscious of the lateness of the hour, Dawn kept her voice low so as not to disturb her family just inside the house.

Rosie remained hugging her knees with her face resting on them. 'Sorry . . . I didn't know where else to go . . .' she mumbled tearfully. 'I remembered you was working tonight so waited for you to come home.'

'You should have knocked on the door. Mum would have let you in to wait for me.'

Rosie remained rocking backwards and forwards on the step so Dawn crouched down in front of her, attempting to see her friend's features beneath the tangled platinum curls. She put a hand on Rosie's arm and realised that the girl was quaking. Tipping up Rosie's chin with a finger Dawn gasped. There was a dark crusting beneath Rosie's nostrils where they had bled, and bruise-like shadows on her cheeks and chin. 'Oh, Rosie . . .' Dawn whispered, pushing wisps of hair out of her friend's watering eyes. 'What on earth has happened to you?' Gently she drew Rosie to her feet and put an arm about her. 'Let's go inside.' Quietly, Dawn put her key in the lock.

'Don't want to cause trouble for you with your mum,' Rosie mumbled through chattering teeth.

'You don't need to worry about that . . .' Dawn knew that Eliza would be equally concerned to see the state of Rosie and wouldn't begrudge helping her.

Having settled Rosie in a chair in the parlour Dawn went to put the kettle on for tea. While waiting for it to boil she returned to try and prise some information from her friend. Dawn's gut feeling was that the calamity probably stemmed from Rosie's move to Marlene's flat.

Squatting down by Rosie's chair Dawn took hold of one of her friend's cold hands, chafing it between her palms. She was desperate to know what had gone on but kept quiet, sensing that Rosie would only open up in her own time.

'I've been raped.' Rosie squeezed shut her eyes to try and block out the memory of Lenny's sour smell and considerable strength as he pinned her down. Mostly she tried to forget all the painful and disgusting things he had done to her. After he'd flung money at her he'd disappeared, leaving her to pull herself to her feet and wipe the blood from her thighs with her underclothes.

A burst of rage consumed Dawn as it sunk in what her friend had endured; but anger wouldn't help Rosie any more than would sympathy. After a moment Dawn asked as calmly as she could, 'Who was he? Did you know him?'

Rosie nodded.

'I'll come with you to report it to the police tomorrow,' Dawn said firmly. 'He mustn't get away with it . . .'

'No, we can't do that!' Rosie snapped her tear-stained face towards Dawn.

'Why not?' The way her friend had said 'we' had put Dawn on alert; she sensed there might be more to it.

The kettle whistled and Dawn quickly went to cut off the shrill sound before it woke her sleeping family. She brought the teapot and cups and saucers into the parlour on a tray.

'What happened to you earlier . . . did it come about because you live with Marlene?' Dawn prompted her friend to continue talking although she realised it must be horrible for Rosie to relive the vile ordeal.

Rosie nodded. 'Can't ever go back there . . .' she whispered.

'You can stay here tonight.' Dawn poured their tea. 'You can bunk with me, Rosie. Mum won't mind at all.'

'Thanks,' Rosie croaked, raising her teacup to her lips with a shaking hand. She sipped then put down her cup. Sinking her head into her hands she started recounting to Dawn everything that had happened that evening. Her whispered story spanned from the moment she entered the Palm House to when she'd collapsed down onto Dawn's front step. In conclusion, Rosie stressed on a hiccup that the men they'd witnessed looting might have come back to haunt them and it was all her fault for being in the wrong place at the wrong time.

Having listened standing silently, Dawn pulled out a chair at the table and sat down in a daze. The looting gang had unexpectedly resurfaced but that wasn't the

275

cause of her despair; her impotent rage was directed at Lenny Purves – the third man – and also at Marlene Brown and her Maltese boyfriend.

Dawn wasn't a prude and in her line of work she heard a lot of sordid things. But she'd always thought Marlene too coarse and the woman's boast that she'd done everything and regretted none of it had disgusted rather than impressed her. Dawn would never have imagined though that the woman would be wicked enough to try and draw a teenage girl into a prostitution ring.

First thing tomorrow Dawn vowed she'd tell Marlene exactly what she thought of her. If Marlene refused to do the decent thing and hand in her notice, then Dawn would tell Phyllis just what Marlene Brown got up to in her spare time.

Dawn noticed Rosie fidgeting while wiping her face and hands with her handkerchief. After what she'd been through Dawn reckoned the poor thing was longing to have a bath. Dawn knew she couldn't run to arranging that at gone midnight but she'd do what she could to help Rosie feel better.

'I'll put the kettle on again and get some hot water in the bowl so you can have a good wash,' she offered.

'I don't want to be a trouble to you, Dawn.' Rosie's eyes welled up again. After having so many people be mean to her, her friend seemed unbearably kind.

'Well, you are a trouble to me, and you have been since that night I met you during the air raid,' Dawn teased, putting her arms about Rosie. 'But you stuck up for me at the 400 Club that evening when you whacked Tina. I suppose it's fair dos I carry on giving you a hand.'

'I forgot to tell you just now that Tina was at the Palm

House.' Rosie gave a mournful little giggle. 'I burst in on her with her *gentleman friend* when I was trying to find the exit.'

Dawn stopped herself asking for a description of the man. She trusted Glenn Rafferty was telling the truth when he'd said he'd only slept with Tina to pump the brunette for information about Nazi sympathisers.

'I think you should go and see your dad tomorrow, Rosie,' Dawn suggested gently.

'No . . . I can't . . .' Rosie covered her face with her hands, shaking her head. 'He'll hate me . . . think I'm disgusting. He'll say I brought it all on myself. I know he will,' she wailed.

'Of course he won't!' Dawn urged. 'You're his daughter and he'll naturally want to help you. I bet he'll insist on going to the police station with you so Purves gets locked up.'

Rosie concealed her anguished face with her hands, remaining quiet. If Dawn knew more about her father she'd realise that John Gardiner would never volunteer to get involved with the police, even to bring his daughter's rapist to justice. He'd be too bothered about the coppers finding out he ran an illegal still . . . and Lenny would grass him up . . .

Midge had been heading towards the railway embankment for a kip in his makeshift camp when he spotted his sister trundling along with the pram and decided to follow her. He was hoping for something from the chance encounter, although he wasn't exactly sure how he could persuade Gertie to help him, when she'd made it clear just days ago she wanted nothing more to do with him. Then Midge realised his sister was probably on her way to work, and as it was Friday, she'd probably have her wages on her later . . . So he reckoned it might be worth one last go to attempt to prise cash from the tight-fisted cow. He was hungry and thirsty and a pie and a pint would go down a treat. Of course, Midge knew a pub was out of the question; he'd not set foot in any of his old haunts in months. But he could get Gertie to get him some shopping.

His hunch paid off and Midge was soon very, *very* glad that he had made the decision to tag along behind his sister and see where she was off to.

Sneaking silently back along the corridor he let himself out into the night. Secreting himself behind a wall he waited, grinning to himself. His luck was suddenly on the up . . . and so buoyant did he feel that he forgot about the pain that was his constant companion.

'I shall miss you, Gertie, my dear, and must show you one last time how much you please me . . .'

The muffled mockery startled Gertie, making her suppress a shriek. She swung about, squinting into the shadows. Her instinct was to race on quickly pushing Harry's pram but she didn't. There'd been something familiar about the hoarse whispering tone and she reckoned that was because the man had tried to disguise his voice.

About twenty minutes ago Wilfred Pickering had come out with the very same line before bending her over his desk. Gertie had just done her final shift and collected her last pay packet, and had exited the office building feeling wistful that her exciting love affair was over.

'It's me, Gertie,' Midge said, emerging from the

shadows. He gave a lopsided smile that was brimming with triumph.

Gertie felt icy suspicion flood her insides and she moistened her lips.

'Now . . . what's Rufus going to say about his missus having it off with her boss?' Midge jerked his head at the office.

At that moment Pickering came out of the door and locked it. Gertie scuttled further into the shadows, closer to Midge. Oddly the idea of her lover seeing her with a tramp was as worrying as Midge knowing about her and Wilfred.

'Here he is . . . Romeo himself,' Midge purred sarcastically. 'Reckernised him too . . . not that I got a gander at much more than his bare arse. I come over all horny watching the two of yous at it, y'know. Don't reckon Rufus'll be that happy though when I tell him.'

'What d'you want?' Gertie croaked. 'You after money?'

'Well, if you've got some going spare, sis, I won't say no.'

'What then?' Gertie bounced the pram as the baby stirred but her staring eyes never left Midge.

'Fancy doing a job fer me, do you, gel? Then we'll call it quits.' He fingered the knife in his pocket. 'You help me out, I'll help you out by saying no more about me watching you sucking your boss's cock, and him sucking . . .'

'Alright!' Gertie gasped out. 'Alright . . . I'll do whatever it is . . . but make it quick 'cos I'm expected home,' she sobbed. It was slowly sinking into her mind just how awful was her predicament. She knew it was useless appealing to her brother's better nature. He didn't have one; he never had, even as a kid.

Midge showed his brown teeth in a smile. 'Come with me, I know just the place where we won't be disturbed.'

He looked back when his sister didn't immediately follow.

'You promise me faithfully that you won't say nuthin' to Rufus? If he finds out he'll . . .' Gertie couldn't finish the sentence because she didn't know how her husband would get revenge. But take it out on someone he most definitely would.

'Me lips are sealed on our bargain, just said so, ain't I. I'm a man of me word, Gertie . . . you should know that being as we're family.' He chuckled then stopped abruptly and cocked his head. 'You a woman of your word, Gertie?'

'You should know that being as we're family,' she sarcastically echoed.

Midge wasn't amused, or convinced. 'You swear on that baby's head you'll do all I ask you to?'

'Tell me what it is.' Gertie blinked rapidly, swallowed noisily.

'Told you over and over that I ain't well. You couldn't give a toss though, could you. Too wrapped up in yourself 'n' them brats to give your brother a minute of yer time.' He moved his useless hand. 'I need a bit of assistance . . . can't do nothing for meself. Can't hardly take a piss or wipe me own arse . . .'

'Ain't criminal, then?' Gertie whispered in relief. If he wanted a wash down she'd do it then scarper quick as she could. But she reckoned he'd demand she hand over the cash she had on her as well, the thieving git . . . she ground her teeth in impotent rage. Then she'd have to think up a tale as to why Pickering hadn't paid her. She knew her brother would take all her cash: her regular wages and the 'bonus' she got and kept for herself. She couldn't tell Rufus the truth, after all.

At a distance she followed him. They only stopped once. He demanded she go into an off licence to buy him a bottle of gin, snatching and swigging from it the moment she reappeared. Then they set off again in the direction of the railway line.

When they reached his camp Midge took a peek in at the sleeping infant in the pram. 'Dead to the world, the lucky blighter,' he said bitterly then set about lighting a fire.

'Come on . . . I've gotta get going,' Gertie said nervously as he collected timber. 'Rufus'll start getting suspicious if I'm late and he expects me wages handed straight over. They're already short now I bought that booze. You'll stir up big trouble . . .'

'You reckon you've got big trouble, do you?' Midge howled a nasty laugh. 'You selfish bitch; let me tell you, gel, it's me who's gonna suffer, not you or him.' He drew out the knife and stuck the blade in the flames. He turned to her, his face looking devilish with the firelight dancing on it. 'Now you just do what I tell you right down to the last letter. If I pass out from the pain, you carry on doing what I've told you to. Gotta deal?'

Gertie's eyes widened in shocked disbelief and she began shaking her head. But Midge, with surprising strength, dragged her closer and handed her the hilt of the burning knife to hold. 'Do it . . . or I tell Rufus every fucking detail of what I just saw . . .'

'What's up, love? Bellyache?' Rufus leaned over his wife as she lay shivering. Gertie had got up twice to be sick in the pot under the bed.

281

'I'm alright,' Gertie mumbled. She tried to turn away from her husband but Rufus put his arms about her.

'Don't worry, love, I ain't after a bit of slap and tickle,' Rufus said gently. 'I can see you're suffering, so ain't gonna bother you tonight. Baby's making you feel queasy, I expect . . .'

Gertie curled up, knees to chest, pulling the covers up over her ears in an attempt to deafen Midge's shrieks of pain echoing in her head. She'd tried to keep her eyes shut against the horror and the blood everywhere, but he'd writhed and screamed at her for being a useless cunt, so she'd had to watch as she'd used the knife on him under those railway arches. He'd seared the stump and incinerated the lump of flesh in the fire he'd got ready . . .

He hadn't passed out and had thrust his own handless limb into the flames, while she raced away with the pram with his screams ringing in her ears drowning out Harry's wailing.

Gertie leapt from the bed and vomited again.

Rufus got up, rubbing her back. 'Make you a cup of tea, shall I?' he asked in concern.

Gertie nodded and sat down on the sagging mattress, her eyes closed and her ashen face cupped in her trembling hands. 'I wish I'd stabbed you in the heart with that knife, you bastard,' she groaned.

'Here, drink that, love.' Rufus had come back into the room and put a cup and saucer in her hand. When Gertie held it, rattling, he took it away again and put it on the bedside table. Rufus sat beside his wife and put his arms about her. 'I know you're sick with worry 'cos you think we're in Queer Street. Did your last shift for Pickering earlier, didn't yer? Late home too. Suppose the old sod wanted his money's worth out of you, didn't he.' Rufus stroked his wife's lank hair. 'I know you've done yer best for us all, gel. But I'll work till me arms drop off now to give you a bit of a rest.' He paused. 'I ain't been the best husband, but I do love you, y'know, Gert.' Rufus planted a kiss on his wife's cheek and eased her back into bed with him.

Gertie lay against his big sweaty body feeling frozen; for all his fine words she knew that if Rufus discovered she was carrying the old sod's child he'd kill her, not cuddle her.

'Shame about that, mate, but you can get a false one, y'know. I've seen some of 'em and they look pretty nifty.' Popeye studied Midge's bandaged stump. The little man was dirty and gaunt but that apart seemed depressingly healthy. The flush of fever that had burned in Williams's cheeks recently was absent and he even smelled slightly better than Popeye remembered.

'Got any booze?' Midge demanded. He had his foot against the bottom of the door just in case his *mate* tried to shut it in his face.

'Yeah . . . come in the parlour and I'll join you in a tot.' Popeye led the way down the hallway. Beneath his breath he was cursing that Midge wouldn't take the hint and piss off permanently. But Frank Purves didn't want to rile Midge because the little bloke knew too much about the looting operation and the location of the warehouse in Houndsditch where the stolen merchandise was stashed.

Popeye had hoped that Midge would come a cropper naturally from his wound, but that didn't seem on the cards any more. Popeye was starting to think that the man might need a helping hand to kick the bucket and leave them in peace . . .

'Ain't seen Rufus in a while . . . think he's avoiding me. You seen him lately, Pop?' Midge had been staring moodily into his glass of whisky when he suddenly barked out his question. Having received a neutral shrug in response, Midge said, 'Tell me brother-in-law I need to see him urgently.'

'Get your sister to do that, can't you?' Pop said, narked. He wasn't a messenger boy.

'Ain't speaking. Had a falling out with the maggot. Just tell Rufus it'd be to his advantage to turn up on Friday at the place where I saw him last. He'll know where that is, so no need to elaborate.'

'Yeah?' Popeye said expectantly. 'What's all that about, then?'

Midge tapped the side of his nose.

Frank Purves gave a careless grimace although he was miffed that Midge wouldn't spill. He liked a gossip. 'Might not see Rufus for ages; he's hardly about since his missus got up the spout again.'

'Expecting another nipper, is she?' Midge chortled, feeling exultant. He'd thought Gertie was looking fat but paid it no heed. 'In that case tell Rufus he'll definitely like to hear what I've got to say.'

Frank was very curious to know what Midge was on about and there was a sure-fire way to get Midge talking: dangle the opportunity to make a bit of money.

'Rufus'll need every penny he can lay his hands on with another kid on the way. We'll all have to get back to doing our regular larks.' Frank nodded at Midge's bandaged stump. 'When you get sorted out with a falsy,

284

mate, you can give us a hand . . .' He snorted at his unintentional joke. 'No offence.'

'None taken. You have a laugh on me,' Midge muttered through his teeth and knocked back the rest of his whisky. 'Gonna get off now, Pop. Don't forget: tell Rufus . . . Friday, same place as before.'

Frank scowled as Midge slouched out. He'd not heard any juicy gossip and neither had he had the satisfaction of being the one to end Midge's visit by telling him to sling his hook.

'Mr Gardiner?'

'Who wants to know?' John Gardiner clipped out. It was gone nine o'clock in the evening and getting dark; the last person he'd expected to see on his front step was a pretty young woman.

'I'm a friend of Rosie's . . .'

'Are you now?' John interrupted. 'Well, in that case, you probably know that Rosie and me had a falling out.'

'Yes, I do know about it, but I'd like to come in and speak to you for a minute, please.'

Dawn hoped that Rosie's father wouldn't refuse to let her in. She didn't fancy giving the reason for her visit while on his doorstep. She'd been on her way home from work at the theatre when on impulse she'd diverted to Shoreditch. Over the past few days, she'd attempted to cajole then had begged Rosie to visit her father and tell him she'd been attacked, all to no avail. Dawn didn't like going behind her friend's back but she knew she had to do something. Rosie had refused point blank to report the rapist to the authorities and Dawn would sooner tackle the girl's father than have the dilemma of whether or not to go to the police on the quiet.

Eliza had been very understanding about Rosie staying with them so far, but she'd made it clear the situation couldn't go on indefinitely. George had been acting up; he was at the age when pretty young women made him feel awkward, so when a shapely Jean Harlow lookalike had emerged from a bedroom wearing just a nightie borrowed from his sister he'd felt confused enough to sulk. Eliza had joked that given a year or two George would have thought he was in his element to have such a beauty living under the same roof. But Eliza was wary of upsetting her son at such a delicate time. Things were progressing well with her and Rod and he was visiting regularly. George had even barked out hello at his mother's boyfriend the other evening when Rod turned up to take Eliza for a stroll. Eliza had confided in Dawn that she hoped to tell George the truth quite soon.

Dawn was in two minds about the wisdom of it but had kept her thoughts to herself. She remembered Glenn's advice about keeping things in perspective: George might be shocked and upset to know that particular truth, but he was approaching manhood and he'd have to deal with unpleasant emotions sooner or later. Besides, Dawn had other problems vying for her attention and she was hoping that speaking to Rosie's father might solve at least one of them.

'Can't see we've got anything to say to one another,' John said testily when his visitor seemed determined to remain planted on his step. He was annoyed that a bang on the door had drawn him from the cellar where a few minutes ago he'd been busy decanting whisky into bottles. 'Best get yourself off home, love,' he told Dawn, starting to push the door to. 'With that new moon shining like a beacon you can bet your life Fritz is on his way . . .' His warning came a second before the siren heralding the approach of German bombers.

'Oh, no.' Dawn frowned up at the sky, wondering how long she'd got to seek cover.

'In you come then,' John sighed. 'I've got a cellar to shelter in.'

Dawn hurried over the threshold with a grateful smile.

'Just hang on in the hallway . . . I'll make some room down there.' Closing the door after him, John disappeared down the cellar stairs, with the intention of throwing a tarpaulin over the still to hide everything from view. He knew he could have saved himself the bother by shutting the door in the girl's face, but his conscience wouldn't allow him to turn his daughter's friend away, perhaps to perish in the street.

A sudden explosion from a neighbouring property made Dawn hunch her shoulders then push open the cellar door and hurtle down the stairs after Rosie's father.

John shook the tarpaulin and let it settle over his distillery although he knew that the damage had been done. Rosie's friend had seen the apparatus and after a second-long stare at it had turned away to pretend that she hadn't.

'So . . . sit yourself down then.' John indicated a battered chair, and perched on a stool himself.

'This is very handy,' Dawn blurted, examining her surroundings but avoiding looking in the direction of the oilcloth. It smelled of tar and the contraption beneath was poking weird shapes into it. 'We've not got a cellar at home but we do have an Anderson shelter,' she added chattily.

'I'm guessing you work with Rosie at the Windmill. What's my daughter been up to, then?' John asked bluntly. 'I know you wouldn't come here unless she asked you to. I suppose she wants to come home. Had enough, has she, paying top rent to her friend Marlene?'

'Rosie's not sent me; she'd be angry if she knew I'd come to see you,' Dawn admitted. 'But I had to do something because she's not going to be able to bunk with me for much longer.' As Rosie's father shot her a quizzical glance Dawn briefly explained, 'Marlene turned out to be no good.' She could see she'd whetted his interest. But she didn't want to get sidetracked into talking about Marlene and Malt's involvement. The couple were vile opportunists who deserved their come-uppance, but Rosie had escaped their clutches without suffering any lasting damage. And then run into Lenny Purves. *He* was the one Dawn wanted to see locked up.

John Gardiner leaned forward on his stool as though to prompt Dawn into saying more. She knew that there was no point in beating about the bush trying to find a good way to tell a father his daughter had been raped. So she blurted it out in few words then realised after-wards that she'd probably sounded rather callous.

John's face drained of blood and he surged to his feet then collapsed back onto the stool. 'Was it one of those servicemen at the theatre?' he finally demanded, his fists tightening on his knees. 'I knew she'd pay for flaunting herself like that in front of randy men . . .'

'No, it wasn't a customer,' Dawn quickly said. 'Rosie told me it was Lenny Purves, a man you know . . .'

'*Lenny*?' John croaked in astonishment. He licked his lips. He'd been about to snort that it couldn't have been because his daughter had grown up with the lanky sod;

but he remembered times when he'd seen Lenny standing very close to Rosie looking at her as though he wanted to devour her. He remembered too that his daughter had told him she didn't like Lenny, that he gave her the creeps . . . looking and touching. And in response John had told her not to be silly . . .

John dropped his head into his hands. 'Was Rosie living at Marlene's when it happened? Is that why you said the woman's no good?'

Dawn bit her lip trying to decide just how much to tell Rosie's father. She'd already betrayed her trust, although she'd done it from concern for her friend, to get the girl safely back under her dad's roof. When Eliza said it was time for Rosie to move out Dawn was worried that her friend might go back to Marlene's with her tail between her legs rather than end up homeless. Rosie would then have little choice but to be nice to the men the Maltese found for her.

'That Marlene seemed a bit too saucy,' John spat, conveniently forgetting that he'd lapped up the woman's smiles. 'I guessed she'd be a bad influence on Rosie.' He got to his feet and started pacing the basement. He wanted to blame everybody but himself for what had happened to his daughter because the knowledge that his dodgy deals with Popeye and Lenny might have had a bearing on her suffering was unendurable.

'Rosie only took a day off work afterwards. She covered her cuts and bruises with make-up . . .' A hiss of indrawn breath from John Gardiner made Dawn stop at that point. 'What I want to ask is, will you turn up at the theatre and tell Rosie she can come home? She really needs you, I know she does.'

'Beat her up too, did he, the bastard?'

'Yes,' Dawn murmured. 'Your Rosie's not one to take it lying down, Mr Gardiner. I expect you know that. She put up a fight. She looked a very poor soul when I found her on my doorstep that night.'

John was quiet for so long that Dawn started to fidget and wonder whether she ought to ask again whether he'd have Rosie back home.

'I'll do what I have to to put things right for my girl, don't you worry,' John vowed. He looked up. 'You didn't tell me your name, dear.'

'Dawn . . . Dawn Nightingale and pleased to meet you.' Dawn rose from her chair and stepping gingerly between storage boxes went to shake Mr Gardiner's hand.

John cradled Dawn's five fingers between ten of his. 'Thanks for coming. Rosie's lucky to have a friend like you.'

CHAPTER TWENTY-SIX

'Brought you another load of labels round, mate . . .'

'Right y'are . . . come in, Len.'

Lenny grinned and stepped over the threshold, expelling a silent sigh of relief. He'd hung back on delivering the printing order to Rosie's father, unsure of the reception he'd get. He imagined if Rosie had gone crying to her daddy about what had happened in that alley, he might have had a visit from John Gardiner, or the police, by now. But the way John had just greeted him – which was no different to how he usually did – had reassured Lenny that Rosie had kept her mouth shut. Lenny had been banking on her feeling too ashamed and guilty to grass him up to anyone – least of all her old man – and it looked like his hunch had paid off.

In Lenny's mind he had no reason to feel sorry for what he'd done. It was Rosie's own fault that he'd forced himself on her: if she hadn't been such a stuck-up bitch, looking down her nose at him, he wouldn't have had to teach her a lesson. He'd've just gone to bed with her like he did with any other tart he picked up in the Palm House.

Lenny regretted slapping Rosie into submission; it offended his masculine pride to have to beat a prossie into accepting him as a punter. If she'd not wailed like a banshee he'd not have got so rough with her.

'Seen anything of Rosie, John?' Lenny asked casually, following the older man towards the kitchen.

'Seen nuthin' of her, Len. Ain't a surprise, 'cos you know how it's been between me and that daughter of mine, don't you.'

'Yeah,' Lenny drawled in amusement. 'Where's she stopping, d'you know?'

'If I wanted to know, I'd've found out a long while ago.' John kept his face lowered to the drawer where he was counting out some cash. 'There we are; that's us squared up then.' He handed over the banknotes.

Lenny didn't feel ready to leave yet; there was another matter pricking at his mind. When his gang had robbed the outfitters he hadn't seen Rosie watching him at work and he knew she hadn't recognised him either in the dark. Lenny was fairly certain John would have said something if he'd had a version of events about that night from his daughter. But Lenny thought he'd just bring the subject up anyhow and see where the conversation went.

'Me dad saw Midge Williams the other day; you'll never guess – he's had his manky hand amputated. I told you he got wounded on a looting job, didn't I?'

'Yeah, I remember. Poor sod,' John said.

'Got to watch out for yourself on a job; don't get seen, don't get injured, that's my motto.'

'You've done alright for yourself so far, ain't you, Len.'

Lenny puffed out his chest at the mild praise. 'I know how to conduct meself so I stay on the right side of things.'

'Yeah, that's it; it's all about getting away with it, ain't it?' John said. 'Trouble is . . . never know when your luck might turn, do you. Anyhow, before you get off, Len, I've got a real nice drop of stuff.' John turned to the sideboard and lifted out a full bottle. 'Here . . . you can have that. I know you like a whisky so I thought of you when I mixed it up.' John dropped Lenny a wink. 'Don't go letting yer old man get his hands on it. He'll down it quick as yer like.'

Grinning, Lenny took the bottle and put it in an inside pocket. 'Thanks, mate. Appreciate it . . . I'll let you know how I find it . . .'

John opened the front door. 'Yeah, you do that, Len,' he said.

'Did you tell him?'

'I did, Rosie,' Dawn immediately admitted. 'And I'm sorry if you're angry, but I had to.'

Rosie turned away, covering her mortified expression with her hands.

Following the end of the second act of the evening's performance, the chattering troupe had descended the stairs to the dressing rooms to find Mr Gardiner waiting for his daughter in the corridor.

The other girls knew something bad had happened to Rosie and that she no longer bunked with Marlene because of a big bust-up. Neither Rosie nor Dawn had put them fully in the picture about the ins and outs of what had gone on. And neither had Marlene. Nobody had seen or heard from the woman. Phyllis had said that if she'd not received word from Marlene by the end of the week, she'd go ahead and sack her.

Dawn was pleased to know it although the loss of a

job at the Windmill was far less punishment than Marlene deserved, considering what she and her Maltese boyfriend had plotted for Rosie.

The other dancers, clad in foamy muslin, had filed into the dressing room, taking care not to squash their golden angel's wings on passing by Dawn and Rosie grouped with Mr Gardiner.

'I want you to come home, Rosie.' John was manfully trying to keep his voice level; even the abundance of naked female flesh on view hadn't dragged his eyes from his daughter's blanching face. 'I'm sorry we had a ding dong and God knows I'm sorry about . . . what Lenny did.' He cleared his throat on hearing his daughter stifling a sob. 'Don't want you to feel ashamed, dear. It's me who's ashamed. I should have listened to you about him. It's going to be different when you come back. Everything will be better, I promise.' John put out his arms and immediately Rosie went to him and they hugged one another.

'Have you finished work? Will you come home with me now on the bus?' John asked, stroking his daughter's silver hair.

Rosie nodded. 'My suitcase is at Dawn's house . . .'

'Call in on the way home, if you like,' Dawn suggested. 'Mum won't mind at all if you collect your things.'

'Been a pain, haven't I?' Rosie was wiping her wet eyes on the sleeve of her dressing gown, smearing a sooty trail of mascara on her cheek.

'No!' Dawn reassured her. 'It's been nice having you stay, honest it has, but you'll be better off at home.'

Rosie approached Dawn and put her arms about her. 'Thanks for everything. Don't know what I'd've done without you.'

Dawn placed a kiss on her friend's platinum head then briskly patted her back. 'Come on! That's enough now! Off you go home and make sure you're back here tomorrow on time. We've got rehearsals for the big event. The show must go on, you know, 'cos we never close!'

The two girls simultaneously stood to attention, saluting.

John got out his hanky and blew his nose. 'I'm much obliged to you, Miss . . .' he croakily addressed Dawn.

'Hurry along, Dawn, we've got the jazz number to do, you know. You'd better get changed on the quick.'

Lorna had poked her head out of the dressing-room door to make her crisp announcement. Dawn rolled her eyes expressively and with a farewell smile she went off to find her Wren's costume to change into. Rosie might have finished for the evening but Dawn had another energetic dance routine to get through – in which the showgirls were dressed as servicewomen – before she could head home. She wished she could have had the WAAF uniform but there hadn't been enough time to shorten it to her size so Lorna, being taller, had commandeered it with a smug smile.

Then tomorrow they would be going through their paces for the big opening night next week. Only the management and Phyllis so far knew who the important guests were to be; Dawn and the other showgirls guessed that the proprietor, Mrs Henderson, was going to invite some of her posh friends and treat them to a champagne reception.

'What you doing in here?'

Gertie had come into Phyllis's office to find Olive already in there, bending over the desk. Gertie put down her box of dusters and polishes and crossed her arms, staring challengingly.

'I'm waiting for Phyllis . . . I was just about to write her a note.' Olive mirrored Gertie's belligerent stance. 'What's it to you, anyway?'

'I'm here to speak to Phyllis and I don't want you standing around listening. You can come back later.'

'I'll do no such thing. I was here first . . .'

'What's going on, then?' Phyllis had entered, carrying a mug of tea, to find the two women staring each other out.

Olive announced, 'We've run out of matinee tickets in the kiosk and I'm running low on change in the till drawer.'

'Oh . . . I'll get some silver and copper when I go to the bank later, and . . .' Phyllis opened a drawer and rummaged to and fro. 'Crikey, only got a few tickets left.' She grinned. 'We must be doing better than we expected on the matinees. Pats on the back all round about that.' She handed over the handful of tickets she'd found.

'There's something else,' Olive blurted. Phyllis had continued looking expectantly at her when she didn't head towards the door. 'It's private.' Olive slanted Gertie a significant look.

The cleaner had taken out her dusters and was making a show of polishing the wooden panelling in the office while listening to proceedings.

'Wait outside just for a moment, Gertie,' Phyllis said with a hint of an impatient sigh.

Gertie stalked out and shut the door, then put her ear to the keyhole.

Five minutes later Olive came out looking smug and

was on the point of marching off along the corridor when Gertie stopped her.

'So, got a few days off to go to Brighton and see your boys, have you?' Gertie taunted. 'Not before time, is it. Poor little sods probably won't recognise you, it's been so long . . .'

Olive's face turned bright red. 'You were listening!'

'You were talking too loud,' Gertie countered.

'You nosy bitch!' Olive snapped. 'One day soon you're going to regret ever crossing me, Gertie Grimes.'

'Yeah, 'course I am.' Gertie elbowed past and went back into the office.

As she quietly closed the door she was relieved to see that Phyllis seemed preoccupied, searching in her desk drawer. It gave Gertie time to marshal her thoughts. She was about to give in her notice at the Windmill Theatre; nobody had said a word to her, but she knew that she no longer just looked fatter than she had, her pregnancy was becoming obvious. Sooner or later one of her colleagues would make a comment; probably Olive would come out with some snide remark.

Gertie knew she shouldn't have riled Olive on purpose. But something about the woman irritated her. She felt sorry now that she'd given Olive the time of day when she had so many more important things to concentrate on. She was feeling ill with anxiety over Midge. Not that she cared a hoot for how he was recovering; he could curl up under a bush and die for all she cared. Her brother was evil and although days had passed quietly, giving her some relief that he'd keep his word and not say anything to Rufus, Gertie knew she could never truly trust her brother. At any time of the day or night she was primed for him creeping round to the house to blackmail her. If he was on the mend, getting stronger, he'd eventually want more money, more favours to keep what he knew about her to himself.

'So what can I do for you, Gertie?' Phyllis was still pulling papers out of her drawer while talking. 'Can't be right that all those tickets have gone,' she muttered and straightened up, hands on hips. 'Olive must be mistaken. I'll swear I ordered six gross and we've not taken that amount on matinees.' She pushed shut the drawer and gave Gertie her full attention and a big smile. 'Come on, out with it . . .' She nodded at the bump Gertie had lately been attempting to conceal by letting her pinny hang like a flag in front of her.

Gertie grimaced. 'You guessed, then . . .' She tried not to sound too defeated.

'I've got four myself and five grandchildren,' Phyllis said.

Gertie was surprised to hear it. She'd not been at the Windmill long but in that time she'd never heard the middle-aged woman mention her family. She was work, work, work, was Phyllis, and usually maintained a distance between herself and the other staff. But she was a good boss.

'So, when's your last day going to be, Mrs Grimes?' Phyllis had returned to her usual efficient manner, opening her diary.

'Friday, I'm afraid, if that's alright with you,' Gertie replied.

'Yes . . . yes . . . now off you go, dear. Gordon said that the stalls need attention. There are cigarette packs galore under the seats. Why these men can't take their litter with them is beyond me. Now where have I put those matinee tickets . . .'

* * *

'You needn't go looking at me as though I'm something you stepped in. You dancers always think yourselves a cut above us nudes, anyhow. Well, you ain't nuthin' special.'

'I think myself a cut above you, that's for sure,' Dawn replied. She grabbed Marlene's arm and hauled her back as the woman would have dodged past again.

Dawn had spotted Marlene in the Petticoat Lane market. Marlene had tried to avoid her by ducking down her head and turning to inspect some crockery on a stall but Dawn wasn't having any of that and had tapped her on the shoulder. Dawn had promised herself that if an opportunity arose she'd have it out with Marlene over what she and her Maltese boyfriend had done to Rosie.

'I don't give a damn what you think about me,' Marlene spat.

'Well, I'm gonna tell you anyway so you might as well settle down and listen.'

Marlene shoved Dawn in the shoulder and got an equally hefty whack in return. She tottered back against the stall, sending some crockery flying.

''Ere, woss your game?' the stallholder bellowed, barging out to steady his display.

'Don't worry, she'll pay for the damage,' Dawn said. 'Won't you, Marlene? Money you and your boyfriend are raking in from pimping innocent girls. You can shell out for a few plates, can't you?'

Marlene dusted herself down, high spots of colour blooming on her face. 'I'll tell you what I've got,' she hissed. She pulled a wave of dark hair off her cheek exposing a mottled patch of skin covered in make-up. 'That's what I've got for doing your friend Rosie a favour and letting her bunk with me.'

'So the Maltese clumped you, did he?' Dawn said. 'What for? Because he lost face or lost money?' she scoffed. 'I heard he got showered in a couple of drinks. Don't suppose the big man liked people seeing that. So, he took it out on you to make himself feel better, didn't he?' Dawn moved her head contemptuously. 'You stupid cow!'

Marlene grew red under the powder caking her complexion. Dawn Nightingale didn't even know her boyfriend, yet she'd summed up Nikola Barbaro with no trouble.

'Rosie knew the score with us; she was putting on the Miss Innocent act. She just changed her mind at the last minute and you can't blame a punter for getting narked about that,' Marlene lied robustly, letting her hair fall back into place. She knew very well that Rosie had been genuinely shocked to be mistaken for a tart by Jeremy Trent.

'It's not an act, and you know it!' Dawn pointed a finger close to Marlene's nose. 'Rosie wants to be sophisticated, but she's still wet behind the ears. She foolishly thought you were out to help her and that you were her friend. She didn't know till it was too late that you were on the game.' Dawn didn't want to feel sorry for Marlene but already her temper was cooling. The woman was pathetic, as much a victim of a brutish man as Rosie had been.

'For God's sake leave him,' Dawn muttered, walking off. She looked back to see Marlene was still staring at the ground with her shoulders hunched to her ears. 'Oh . . . and don't bother coming back to the Windmill; Phyllis's sacked you,' was Dawn's parting shout.

'Pop gave you my message?'

'Yeah . . . what you after, then?' Rufus hadn't

forgotten that last time he'd seen Midge he'd knocked his brother-in-law down. When Pop had told him Midge was after him Rufus had guessed it was to get even in some way. He avoided looking at the place where Midge's right hand should have been. Pop had told him about that too. Rufus felt sorry for Midge but he wasn't about to let that stop him putting Midge on the deck for a second time, if need be.

'See this?' Midge raised his stump. 'Know who sawed that off for me, do you?'

Rufus gawped at him as though he'd gone nuts. 'Doctor at the hospital?' he ventured, deciding to humour the man for a few minutes, for old times' sake, before telling him to piss off.

'Nah, weren't that lucky, was I. Bleedin' amateur did it, and I thought I was gonna die just from the pain of it.'

'Yeah . . . can imagine,' Rufus said. 'Anyhow I've got to get off, so if it ain't anything important . . .'

'It's important, just let me finish.' Midge came closer to Rufus. 'You hurt me badly, Rufus; you, that kid of yours, Lenny . . . you all had a part in me ending up like this. I could've had a life in front of me; but not now. I want me own back on you, then I'll start on Lenny.'

'Fuck off.' Rufus started to stride off even though something in Midge's mildly spoken threat had curdled his guts.

'Gertie did this.' Midge held up his stump again, waving it to and fro. 'Now I know you don't believe me, so you're gonna have to ask her. And while you're at it, ask her if she reckons that pipsqueak of a boss of hers is a better fuck than you are.' Midge walked up to Rufus and laughed in his face. 'Watched 'em at it, didn't

301

I? He was humping her on his office desk fit to bust her wide open and she was loving it, mate . . . should've heard her squeal . . .'

With a roar Rufus enclosed Midge's scrawny neck in both his hands and started to throttle him. He felt the nick of a blade against his belly, but Midge didn't plunge the knife in, just sliced side to side so Rufus yelped and sprang back. Midge gasped in air as Rufus let him go and he fell back wheezing a giggle through his crushed windpipe. 'I ain't gonna stab you to death . . . gonna let you suffer. Go home, go on, I dare you, and ask your missus about me blackmailing her. She really didn't want you finding out about her fancy man, did she, to agree to do something as bad as that.' Again Midge moved what remained of his right arm. 'While you're at it, mate, I'd ask her about that kid she's carrying as well. P'raps it might come out looking a bit like that jug-eared accountant.' He grinned. 'Oh . . . and another thing. I know it was you grassed me up to the coppers. Ain't caught me though, have they.' He spread his arms, showman-like. 'Look, still here . . . you can't get rid of me that easily. I'm gonna be around like a bad smell, for a while yet.'

Without another word Midge turned on his heel and disappeared into the darkness, leaving Rufus rooted to the spot.

CHAPTER TWENTY-SEVEN

'How much?'

'Same as last time you asked.'

'Remember me then, do you?' Lenny asked cockily.

'Yeah . . .' Tina gave him a weary glance. She'd seen the creep hanging around before in the Palm House. On that occasion he'd gone off swearing under his breath when she'd told him her price. She hoped he was feeling similarly tight-fisted this evening; there was something about him she didn't like that had little to do with his gangly body and spotty complexion. Tina had been in the game long enough to appreciate that a gut instinct about punters was a working girl's best defence against a punch in the mouth. But she was in need of some cash to pay her rent and beggars couldn't be choosers. The high rollers seemed few and far between lately and even the military were thin on the ground that night. Besides she could see Malt was watching her like a hawk while polishing glasses. He'd be annoyed not to get his cut of ready business and Tina didn't want to end up like Marlene by getting on the wrong side of Nikola

Barbaro. All the hostesses in the Palm House had watched their step since Malt beat up his girlfriend.

Lenny dug in his pocket and pulled out a couple of ten-bob notes.

Tina gave the money a lazy glance. 'That'll get you half an hour in there.' She jerked her head at the door that led to the brothel.

'That's enough for me love, and all you'll be able to take.' Lenny arrogantly cupped his groin. 'I'm a big boy, if you know what I mean.'

Tina gave a sour smile and, stubbing out her cigarette in the ashtray on the bar, she hopped off the barstool. 'Gonna get us a drink, then, to take with us?'

'You get one if you want; you can take it out of one of them ten-bob notes.' Lenny sauntered off towards the door that led to the bedrooms.

'Right . . . done . . .' Tina said twenty minutes later, raising a knee to dislodge Lenny from where'd he'd flopped on top of her. He'd stopped panting and groaning so she guessed he'd recovered enough to get up and get going.

Lenny rolled off her and sat up, easing his shoulders. He wiped himself off on the sheet then pulled on his trousers. He squinted at his watch through the pink hazy light. By his calculation he'd got ten minutes of time left and he told the tart so.

'So what d'you want to do for ten minutes?' Tina asked sullenly.

Lenny didn't like her attitude, or the way she was pulling on her underwear before he said she could. He knew he didn't have another session in him yet, and so did she. He had no money left to spend when he left here. So before he headed home to his miserable old man, he'd have Tina's company till his time was up whether she liked it or not.

'Sit down. You can have a drink with me.'

That offer stopped Tina in her tracks. She perched on the edge of the mattress in her petticoat, thinking he was going to order from the bar, but he pulled out of his pocket the whisky that John Gardiner had given him.

'Got any glasses?'

'Fuck the glasses.' Tina was impatient to have a drink with the tight-fist then get rid of him. She snatched the bottle he was holding out, unscrewed the top and swigged from it. She wiped her mouth with the back of her hand. It wasn't bad Scotch, and it certainly took the foul taste of Lenny out of her mouth. After another gulp she handed it back and got her cigarettes out of her bag.

Lenny took a couple of deep draughts too and was pleased to see that Tina had stopped looking at her watch and had relaxed back on the bed, smoking. She was holding out her hand for the bottle again. He undid his flies and shoved her hand inside before letting go of the whisky.

'Boys all in bed, are they?'

'Yeah, Joey's just gone up.' Gertie heard her husband's coat forcefully hit the armchair a second after he came in the front door. Dropping the plates back into the washing-up bowl she began drying her hands on her apron. 'Cup of tea?' she offered cheerily. She was glad that she and Rufus seemed to be getting on better than ever just lately. They'd cuddled up in bed last night in the way they used to when first married.

'Saw Midge this evening . . .' A burst of fiery rage ignited inside Rufus's head. His wife's startled reaction to his remark proved that Midge had tortured him with the truth earlier. Gertie had immediately coloured up and avoided his eye.

While trudging home he had tried to convince himself that Midge was so eaten up with bitterness since he'd been crippled that he'd been raving. At one point Rufus had even managed a chuckle at how outlandish it all was. Gertie amputate her brother's hand for him? Never. Gertie have an affair with scrawny middle-aged Wilfred Pickering? Not likely.

But suddenly Gertie's nightmares, her crying bouts, and especially her fancy knickers, took on a new and ugly meaning. Rufus had believed his wife's distress was caused by worries over the family's future with another baby on the way; but now he realised she'd been feeling sickened by the bargain she'd made with Midge. But Midge had never had any intention of buttoning his lip about her affair, keeping his side of the deal. Rufus wondered what Gertie would have done if she'd suspected from the outset that her brother would cheat her. Perhaps she'd have turned to her lover for help . . . because Rufus knew she'd never have owned up to her husband that she'd been with another man. Midge's coarse description of what he'd seen in Pickering's office returned to torment Rufus and with a howl of anguish he smashed his fist into his wife's jaw, slamming her against the sink.

He stood over her, quivering, bawling at her to get up until the red mist lifted and he started to quietly cry. As soon as he heard her whimper and knew she was coming round he barged towards the door, only stopping to whip his coat from the armchair before slamming it shut.

Gertie felt somebody pulling at her arms and struggled to combat the blackness descending on her in waves. Instinctively she put up her hands to protect her face from another blow.

'Mum . . .' Joey sobbed, shaking Gertie by the arm. 'D'you want a drink of water?'

'Where's your father?' Gertie whispered, blinking to try and focus on her eldest boy's strained features.

'He's gone out,' Joey spluttered through his sobs. 'Do you want a drink of water? It'll make you better . . .'

Gertie could see now that her son was in his pyjamas on his knees in front of her, his cheeks wet with tears. 'Did I pass out?' she asked, struggling to sit up.

'Think so,' Joey gurgled. 'I come downstairs when I heard the commotion . . .'

'Just fell over,' Gertie mumbled. She might be slightly concussed but she knew very well that her husband had knocked her unconscious. And she knew why he'd done it, too.

'Dad hit you . . .' Joey wailed.

Gertie squeezed shut her eyes, stemming the flow of water with her pinafore. When she took the cotton away she saw that it was pink with blood and brine.

'Just had a row, that's all,' she murmured, trying to soothe her son. 'No need for you to get upset, Joey.' She stroked the boy's hair with an unsteady hand. 'The others still asleep?'

Joey nodded.

A sudden dreadful thought occurred to Gertie that made her drag herself, tottering, to her feet, holding onto the table edge for support. Rufus might have gone after Wilfred to have it out with him. The accountant wouldn't be at the office at this time of the night but at home. And Rufus knew where he lived . . .

Midge had been hanging about outside the Grimes's house hoping he might catch some of the action when Rufus had it out with his missus. He'd listened to some swearing and shouting that had made him chuckle then had dived under cover behind the hedge when Rufus stormed out of the house. He would have rubbed his hands together if he could've done so. Midge was still rational enough to know that he was a pathetic bastard with nothing to do any more but plot how to cause trouble for the people he'd once called family. But he didn't care because he knew Gertie and Rufus weren't his family any longer. Either one of them would turn him in now, and laugh at the thought of him swinging.

He was about to amble off and turn his attention to making Lenny's life a misery – although he'd not yet decided how to go about it – when the Grimes's front door opened and Gertie rushed out, a cloth pressed to her face. With nothing better to do Midge reckoned he might as well follow her. It looked as though Rufus had given his wife a clump, making Gertie's mouth bleed. If she was going after her husband to have her own back Midge realised they might provide some lively entertainment. He was in the process of getting up from crouching behind the shrubbery to trail his sister at a distance when Joey came out and set off after his mother. Midge was now really interested in seeing this through to the bitter end.

Gertie turned her head this way and that, scouring the darkness, but she couldn't spot Rufus in front of her.

She carried on heading in the direction of Wilfred Pickering's house, hoping to intercept her husband at some point. If he wasn't there hollering at the house for Pickering to show himself when she arrived, Gertie didn't know what she'd do; she could hardly knock up her old employer to warn him her husband was on the warpath over their affair.

'Rufus!' Gertie hurried across the road, having glimpsed through the moon-spotted blackout her husband's slouched figure on the opposite pavement. So she'd been right! He was on his way to Pickering's. She felt relief swamping her at having caught him in time.

'Get yourself back home, you whore!' Rufus snarled, and rushed to meet his wife in the middle of the road. He gave her a savage shove that sent Gertie onto her backside. 'I'm going to deal with your fancy man then I'll be back to deal with you.'

Gertie scrambled up as fast as she could, supporting her big belly with her forearm. She'd had time to think while marching along in Rufus's wake. She'd never have let Wilfred touch her but for him blackmailing her about Joey's theft. She'd never have let Midge blackmail her but for fretting about keeping her family together. And the horrible bastard had gone straight back on his word. He'd sworn to her that he'd not tell Rufus about seeing her and Pickering together. Gertie was sick to death of men using her for their own good.

'You listen to me, you stupid sod,' Gertie screamed. 'None of this would have come about but for you! It's all *your* fault. *You* was the one praised Joey for stealing from Pickering. You thought it funny. Well, you ain't laughing now, are you, 'cos I was the one had to put things right after that. Pickering was going to get the police on us if I didn't do what he wanted. How long d'you think it would have been before they found out you'd been looting? You'd've ended up in court.'

Rufus stood, fists balled, inches from his wife's rigid form. 'You should've told me,' he spat. 'I'd've sorted Pickering out with one hand tied behind me back.'

'Yeah, I know!' Gertie cried sarcastically. 'That's why I took it on meself to keep him sweet. You'd've ended up swinging for him and left me and the kids all on our own. You stupid sod!' She keened in despair. 'Now look at us!'

'Whose kid is it?' Rufus croaked, nodding at her belly.

'Sorry, Mum . . . sorry . . .' Joey had emerged from the blackness to sidle up to his parents, wiping his eyes with his knuckles. 'Didn't mean to cause trouble . . .'

The wailing of an air-raid siren drowned out Joey's distress as they all turned their contorted faces up to the black skies. In the distance shooting stars of anti-aircraft fire could be seen and heard. Even Midge, hidden in shadows, looked up, cursing that the little show put on by the Grimes family was about to end courtesy of the damned Luftwaffe. He started to slip away, making his way back to the relative safety of his camp under the railway arches. He didn't even bother to turn round when a loud explosion came from somewhere close by, sending flames skywards. Midge speeded up, not wanting to be spotted by Rufus as the darkness was brightened by fire.

But Rufus, Gertie and Joey were already running back the way they'd come.

With every breath she took Gertie prayed for their safety; the child growing in her belly got no thought at all even though she felt stabbing pains shooting from

310

her groin to her belly button as she ran faster than she ever had in her life trying to keep up with her husband and Joey. She offered God her life; she gave him Rufus's too, if he'd just spare them and send the bombs a different way.

But she didn't need to round the corner to know what she'd see; when Gertie did finally drag to a stop there was a terrible serenity about the scene in front of her. The roof had gone and one side of the house and she stood transfixed, hearing nothing, as dust-covered neighbours emerged from their wrecked homes, looking dazed. But Gertie could see that it was her house that had taken the hit. They'd taken the punishment.

It was Joey's hysterics that brought her to; he was on his knees in front of her, hanging onto her skirt, wailing in one long drawn-out shriek as though he never wanted to take another breath in his young life.

Gertie drew him up, held him in fierce comfort for no more than a second before dragging him towards what remained of their home. Rufus was already on top of the rubble, lobbing jagged masonry and mangled timbers backwards in his savage search for his children. A neighbour wordlessly handed him a shovel then dug with another beside him. Rufus didn't acknowledge the fellow in any way; he continued ramming shovel against stone, tears streaming down the taut sinews of his face and neck.

Silently Gertie crouched beside him and plunged her hands into her boys' brick tomb.

CHAPTER TWENTY-EIGHT

'How long are you back for?' Dawn burst out, beaming in surprise and delight.

'Only got a two-day pass,' Glenn replied. 'But it could be extended if I need time to investigate anything odd . . .'

They stared at one another and then on impulse Dawn threw her arms about his neck and hugged him, raking her slim fingers through his long black hair. She broke away, feeling self-conscious. Although he'd kissed her twice on their last date he'd never actually asked her to be his girlfriend, yet she'd just acted as though she thought she was. Bill's death had brought them together, and then Glenn's undercover duties had forced them to carry on from there. Yet . . . despite loss and intrigue forming the bond between them Dawn felt oddly happy with Glenn Rafferty.

'I reckon you missed me,' Glenn said, gently amused on noticing her blush. 'I was hoping you would.'

'All servicemen home on leave deserve a welcoming hug. Might be the last one they ever get.' Dawn's slender shoulders undulated in a casual shrug but she guessed from his deepening grin that he wasn't fooled by her blasé remark.

'In thanks for that big hug, I reckon you deserve a thorough . . . kissing,' Glenn laughed with a hint of self-mockery.

His lips touched hers teasingly at first but then with a passion that Dawn realised he was finding hard to control. He penned her back against the hallway wall, holding her face in his fingers so he could caress her cheek while moulding his mouth with increasing pressure to hers. By the time he lifted his head, Dawn felt breathless, and he looked dangerously attentive.

She suddenly became aware of a neighbour gawping up the garden path at her. Breaking free of Glenn's entrapment Dawn closed the front door. The woman would probably be gossiping over the garden fence about her later.

Facing Glenn in the dim hallway Dawn realised that she'd launched herself at him without appreciating his heartbreakingly handsome appearance. His high cheekbones and dark complexion, contrasting with the pale sheepskin of his leather flying jacket, gave him a distinctly foreign air.

'Have you missed me?' Dawn blurted out.

'I think you already know the answer to that,' Glenn said. 'But if you're in any doubt . . .' He reached for her again. 'I can try harder to convince you, Dawn.'

Giggling, she wriggled from his predatory clutch, shooting a look at the closed parlour door. Her mother and Rod were sitting in there listening to the wireless while waiting for their tea to cook.

'Have you got company? Shall we go out?' Glenn suggested, having noticed the direction of Dawn's frown.

'My mum's boyfriend's come round for tea.' Dawn raised her eyebrows in a speaking look.

'Does your brother know about any of it yet?' Glenn took care to keep his voice low.

'No,' Dawn answered hoarsely. 'But I think the time's getting near for a heart to heart between the three of them. George is out with his pals at the moment. A lot's gone on actually since I saw you last.' She gave a tiny sigh. 'I'll tell you later,' she answered at his unspoken request, signalled by a pair of velvety brown eyes, to know more.

'I've got a lot to tell you too. But we'll make time for ourselves before the night's out, won't we.' It was a husky statement made while his fingers caressed her arm then moved to stroke close to her mouth.

Dawn resisted the urge to catch the tickling finger between her teeth. She suspected Glenn Rafferty was a practised seducer, and starting his charm offensive early so that later when he suggested they spend the night together he'd already be halfway to victory. Yet, with a sense of wonderment, Dawn knew what answer she might give, if he did ask her to stay with him. When he'd brought her home on their previous date he'd not done more than give her a long goodnight kiss on the doorstep. He'd been the perfect gentleman in every way, which on reflection had piqued Dawn . . . as perhaps he'd hoped it might.

'Would you mind hanging around on the corner while I get ready?' Dawn whispered. 'Sorry to ask; I'm not being rude . . . it's just I'd rather not make introductions at the moment. If Mum knows you're here she's bound to insist you stay and have tea. Then we'll have to wait till later on for a private chat.'

'That's fine by me.' He opened the front door, adding dryly, 'Don't be too long though, sweetheart, or I might get accosted.'

Dawn gave him a gimlet-eyed look. 'I expect you'd like that, and not for the first time.'

'Maybe . . . a few months back, I would've,' he replied with quiet seriousness. 'But not now.' He made a move as though he might again take her in his arms but instead frowned. 'No ducks this evening unless we're eating them in a restaurant, right?'

Dawn burst out laughing then grimaced regret at having made enough noise to draw attention to them. Quickly she ushered Glenn outside.

'Who was that?' Eliza asked, cocking her head as she approached.

'Glenn . . . he can't stop now . . . lots of things to do.'

'Oh, that's a shame! I'd like Rod to meet your boyfriend,' Eliza said. 'Is he coming back? Shall I save him some corned beef bake? There'll be enough to go round if I peel a few extra spuds.'

'No, we're going out to eat; and we're not officially a couple, Mum. You won't call him my boyfriend when he's here, will you?' Dawn warned.

'I know my p's and q's,' Eliza said. 'But you'd like it if he was your boyfriend, I can see that, my girl.'

Dawn gave a wry smile.

'Is everything alright?' Rod was by the parlour door, looking hesitant, almost shy, as was customary when Dawn was about.

An awkward atmosphere existed between them because Dawn was aware he'd abandoned Eliza years ago. Dawn felt she didn't *dislike* Rod; she'd no idea if, as a child, she'd had a stronger opinion of him. She remembered enjoying a ride in his car, and having the sweets that he always gave her when they went on a picnic. When he'd handed over a paper bag of barley twists her mother would tell him not to spoil her and never to do it again. Then Rod would give his girlfriend's daughter a private wink, letting Dawn know he'd get her sweets next time.

Eliza spoke cheerily into the silence. 'Dawn's new boyfriend's made a flying visit,' she smirked. 'No pun intended . . . he's a squadron leader in the RAF, ain't that right, Dawn?'

Dawn answered with a nod. 'Don't put me any tea by, Mum. More for you two and George to polish off.' She gave Rod in particular a smile.

He returned it immediately, blinking from her to Eliza.

'Off you go, then, and enjoy yourself,' Eliza said. When Rod had returned to sit in the parlour, Eliza followed Dawn halfway up the stairs. 'Thanks, love.'

'What for?' Dawn said over a shoulder.

'Oh . . . you know . . . making Rod feel welcome.'

'I want you to be happy, Mum.' Dawn swivelled about on the stair to face her mother.

'I want you to be happy too, more than anything,' Eliza said. 'Things are changing for all of us . . .'

'Yes, they are,' Dawn quietly agreed.

'And changing for the better, I know it,' Eliza added forcefully. 'So we must win this damned war soon; I ain't having me grandkids speaking German to me. And that's final.' Eliza descended the stairs. 'Get the table laid, will you, Rod,' she called out as she headed towards the kitchen. 'That corned beef bake will be crisping up nicely.'

With a contented sigh Dawn carried on towards her

bedroom then, suddenly remembering she'd told Glenn she'd not keep him waiting long, she ran the last few steps.

A few minutes later Dawn turned up on the corner and found Glenn with his hands clasped behind his back, puffing on a cigarette while staring into a shop window.

'No egg deliveries till next week, then,' he said, the cigarette wagging between his lips. He tapped a finger on the grocer's notice stuck behind the glass.

'Probably won't turn up even then,' Dawn replied. 'A lot of delivery vans have been commandeered by the forces for one reason or another. I haven't seen a fresh egg for weeks.'

'D'you fancy going for an omelette?' he solemnly suggested.

Dawn punched his arm for that jibe.

Grinning, he steered Dawn towards his car parked at the kerb. 'Where then?'

'Lyons Corner House.'

'You're a cheap date . . .'

'I don't expect you to spend a lot on me.' Dawn settled into the leather upholstery.

'I know, but I reckon you're worth taking to a hotel for a steak dinner.' Glenn glanced at her quizzical expression and taking his hands from the steering wheel gestured defeat. 'Corner House it is then.'

'I like the atmosphere in these places,' Dawn said, glancing about at the customers in the restaurant they'd entered a few minutes back. As a child, Dawn could remember being brought to a Corner House as a treat. The custom of bribing sons and daughters to behave with the promise of a nice feed seemed alive and well.

Children with scrubbed faces and neat clothes were sitting at tables with their parents.

'Did you get taken out for a special tea every so often when you were a kid?' she asked Glenn as he drew out her chair and they sat down. They had chosen a secluded table in the café on the High Street so they could talk without being overheard.

'Nah . . . my treat was going to my nan's for tea. It was a good blow-out too. Always had trifle, and a jam sponge with icing sugar on top.'

'I went on a Sunday to my nan's.' Dawn smiled at the lovely memory. 'We had coffee cake with walnuts on top.'

Once the nippy had taken their order for tea and macaroni cheese Glenn leaned across the table towards Dawn. The glint of amusement had gone from his eyes. 'You said a lot's gone on in my absence . . .' He reminded her of her promise to tell him what was bothering her.

'It has.' Dawn mulled over whether to say her friend had been raped; she wasn't sure how Glenn would take knowing that Tina featured in the sordid tale of violence. So far they'd enjoyed a very nice reunion and she was reluctant to create an atmosphere by mentioning that woman's name.

'What is it?' Glenn prompted softly. 'Have Bill's parents written to you again?' he suddenly asked in a tone verging on annoyance.

'No . . . nothing like that,' Dawn reassured him. 'A friend of mine's had a bad time of it,' she blurted. Once their meals had arrived Dawn related what Rosie had told her about her awful ordeal, ending with Lenny Purves's assault, and omitting the part about Tina being seen by Rosie servicing a client midway through the drama.

'Will Rosie's dad get the police on Purves?' Glenn asked.

'Doubt it.' Dawn knew her blunt reply begged a question but Glenn took a forkful of macaroni waiting for her to explain in her own time.

After Dawn had seen the still in Mr Gardiner's basement it had become clear to her why Rosie had fallen out with her father: the girl hadn't liked him acting like a criminal and bringing them both into regular contact with vermin like Lenny Purves.

'If I tell you something will you promise to keep it to yourself? I don't want Rosie or her dad getting into trouble.'

''Course . . .'

'It's about hooch but I want your solemn word 'cos I'm certain the person involved is just out to make money, not to make trouble.'

Dawn started to eat slowly although the topic of their conversation had rather killed her appetite.

Glenn put down his cup and sat back, crossing his arms. 'Promise,' he said quietly.

'Rosie's dad has a still in his basement. She's never said anything to me about what her father's been up to. I expect she's ashamed of him. And I'm guessing neither of them wants the police involved in investigating her being attacked, for obvious reasons.'

Glenn frowned. 'Purves shouldn't get away with it.'

'Neither should Marlene and her boyfriend. Rosie wishes she'd never left home or set foot inside the Palm House that evening . . .'

'Palm House?' Glenn interrupted.

Inwardly Dawn cursed for having let that slip. 'Mmm
. . . apparently it's a club owned by Malt's family.' She
noticed Glenn's inscrutable expression. 'You've been
there,' she said flatly, putting down her knife and fork.

'Only in the line of business . . . Tina works as a
hostess there. Wouldn't visit the dive under normal
circumstances.'

'Rosie told me she'd seen Tina plying her trade in one
of the bedrooms before she made her escape. She didn't
see the man clearly,' Dawn added distantly.

'It wasn't me. I've not seen Tina for months,' Glenn
said mildly. 'Valentin Barbaro owns the Palm House.
Malt's just a small-time crook and pimp, living in his
uncle's shadow.'

Dawn realised there was no sense in feeling bitter and
jealous because Tina's name had cropped up. Glenn had
neatly side-stepped further discussion about the woman
by turning the conversation to the Barbaros. Dawn imagined he'd done all the explaining he was prepared to
about the women in his past. He rarely mentioned Bill
now so she supposed she should also leave the subject
of their former relationships alone.

'I take it there's a bad atmosphere at work between
Marlene and Rosie,' Glenn said.

'Marlene's not been at work since it happened. I
bumped into her in the market and told her what
I thought of her. In an odd way I felt sorry for her
because Malt had beaten her up. She had a huge bruise
on her face that she'd tried to cover with make-up.'

'Malt's the sort to lay into a woman when he's feeling
pissed off and needs to take it out on someone.' Glenn
gave a grim smile. 'So your friend Rosie chucked a drink
in his face, did she? He won't forget that in a hurry.'

On the morning after Rosie's attack Dawn had accompanied her friend to pick up her suitcase from Marlene's place where it had been dumped, as promised, in the front garden. Rosie's clothes had been in it but her money was missing. Dawn had wanted to continue bashing on the door and demand Marlene hand over Rosie's cash. But Rosie wouldn't let her. She'd said she owed Malt for the drinks she'd had in the Palm House, and would sooner pay up than feel beholden to a pimp. Dawn had been sure she saw the curtain upstairs twitch but nobody answered the knock on the door. At the time Dawn had thought Marlene was too cowardly to come out and face them, but perhaps she'd been too badly beaten to do so.

Glenn pushed their cups and plates away and imprisoned Dawn's hands in his. With his elbows planted on the table he leaned closer. Seconds later Dawn realised he wasn't about to issue a loving declaration but was making sure people thought them canoodling while he discussed secrets.

'We've had some more information about the Windmill Theatre,' he said quietly.

'Oh . . .?' Dawn stared at him intently, trying to guess what was coming next.

He stroked her cheek, leaned in for a tender kiss.

'Are you acting?' Dawn accused, faintly mocking.

'Are you?' he said and glanced at her thumb moving in sensual rhythm against his.

Once her attention was drawn to the unconscious caress she'd been administering Dawn kept still. 'Carry on,' she said briskly.

'I was about to say that.' Glenn stared significantly at their clasped fingers.

Dawn smiled self-consciously but resisted the urge to resume stroking his hand.

'Intelligence has come through about a plot to destroy the Windmill Theatre, probably in the same way as the Café de Paris was wrecked, but we can't be sure.' Glenn glanced at an adjacent table as a middle-aged couple sat down and started bickering.

Dawn was unable to think rationally for several shocked seconds, then her mind became cluttered with questions and consequences arising from Glenn's astonishing statement. 'Surely the Café de Paris was just hit by chance,' she eventually burst out in a whisper. 'Besides, the Windmill is virtually bomb-proof. The dressing rooms are as good as an air-raid shelter being underground; lots of the staff bunk down there overnight.'

Glenn shrugged. 'I was sceptical too when I heard about it. It could be another false trail. The Windmill attracts a lot of servicemen enjoying rest and recreation but if it's the Nazis' strategy to target military personnel they could direct their bombs elsewhere with better success.' He frowned. 'The Blitz has brought a lot of hardship to ordinary Londoners but not crushed their morale. German high command wants British citizens to feel they're hopelessly vulnerable and the Third Reich is invincible.' He tapped a cigarette out of the pack and lit it then turned it, offering it to Dawn. She accepted, drawing on it immediately and filling her lungs with smoke. When Glenn had pocketed the pack of Players he resumed their quiet conversation, his own cigarette wagging between his lips. 'I reckon the Luftwaffe would want a more prominent target – perhaps Buckingham Palace or Downing Street. If our politicians or royalty can't protect themselves against disaster it might be a turning point in how Joe Public see things . . .'

'The Windmill *is* seen as a special place. We like to think we'll see this war through, however long it lasts – and never let the Hun close us down.' Having given her passionate little speech Dawn knocked ash into the glass ashtray midway between them on the table. 'It's the small things that count to ordinary people . . . like us putting on a great show every single day till we get victory. That's what'll be remembered when this blasted war is over.'

Glenn put his hands up by his face in a gesture of surrender. 'Give up . . . take me prisoner,' he said with a wicked gleam in his eye.

'Sorry . . .' Dawn smiled shyly. 'I get a bit carried away about the place . . .'

'No need to apologise. Nice to know you're loyal.'

'There's something that I've forgotten to say, actually.' Dawn quickly ground out her stub in the ashtray. Glenn's talk of influential people being a target had jogged her mind to the spectacular opening night they were rehearsing for. She told him about it then added, 'The tickets have all been allocated, you see, and aren't for general sale. Mrs Henderson who owns the theatre has a lot of well-to-do friends . . . socialites and politicians and so on. The management have been keeping mum about the guest list. But there is a rumour that some military top brass might attend a champagne reception.'

Glenn's fingers tightened on Dawn's, his eyes drawing together under knitted brows. 'Slow down, sweetheart . . . let me get this straight . . . so, the Germans *would* have a prime target at the Windmill Theatre this Saturday.'

'I suppose so . . .' Dawn nibbled her lower lip.

'The Café de Paris's ballroom was below street level,' Glenn remarked, looking reflective.

'But that was a fluke of a hit. The bombs went down the ventilation shafts by chance . . .'

'True.' Glenn ventured a suggestion. 'But if the bombs were planted in the theatre itself by enemy agents . . .'

Dawn frantically mulled that over. 'But . . . nobody could do something like that without being spotted. The theatre is always filled with people . . . day and night . . .'

'The woman who was followed from the fascist meeting . . . did you manage to discover who she might be?'

Dawn shook her head. In fairness she'd not put much effort into doing so. It was hard to believe that any of her colleagues were traitors; and Rosie's rape and the triangle closing at home between Eliza and Rod and George had seemed worthier of her attention, in Dawn's eyes. Rather sheepishly she told Glenn so, then added, 'Most of the women have boyfriends or fathers serving in the forces, apart from Lorna and Rosie. Gertie and Olive have husbands and children to worry about. Olive is in Brighton at present visiting her boys . . . and Gertie's just jacked her cleaning job in as she's expecting another baby.' Dawn was sad that she'd not had a chance to say goodbye to Gertie. The cleaner had left quite suddenly before there'd been the opportunity for their shifts to collide.

'It all seems far-fetched, doesn't it?' Glenn speared his fingers through his ebony hair.

'When I heard we were at war again with Germany because of Poland, I thought that was far-fetched. Turns out it wasn't,' Dawn tartly remarked.

Glenn chuckled, grimaced rueful agreement. 'Let's leave it at that for now and enjoy ourselves for the rest of the evening, eh? I don't want you to think all I want to do is talk shop.' He gave her a roguish grin.

'I wish I could be of more help,' Dawn said, flicking his face away with a finger, as it closed on hers as though he would snatch a kiss.

'Finished?' Glenn nodded at her empty cup. 'Do you want more eats and drinks or shall we make tracks?'

'I'm ready to go . . .'

When they were driving away from the restaurant Glenn turned to Dawn. 'I've met your family; would you like to meet mine?'

'Now?' Dawn asked with a surprised smile.

'On Sunday . . . I've told Mum and Dad about you and they'd like you to come for tea.'

'That'd be lovely. *What* have you told them about me?' Dawn enquired interestedly. She wondered if he'd mentioned her as being his girlfriend.

'Oh . . . I just said that you're one of those sauce-pots who works at the Windmill Theatre.'

'They'll think I'm a nude statue,' Dawn protested.

Glenn laughed. 'Have you ever considered doing that?'

'No . . . I couldn't strip off . . .'

'Good . . .'

'You don't approve of the shows?'

Dawn remembered Bill had held hypocritical views about showgirls; she supposed most men did. They all loved to go out with pals ogling female flesh, so long as the woman in question was no lover or relative of theirs.

'I've never seen one of the revues; I suppose I should, now I've a personal interest,' Glenn answered.

'You can come along on Saturday, if you like.'

He shot her a glance. 'I thought the show was invitation only – no general public allowed.'

'All the showgirls are given one ticket each for a guest.'

'And you want to give yours to me?'

'Nobody else to ask, unfortunately,' Dawn sighed theatrically. 'Mum wouldn't want to go without Rod. I expect George would love to have it, but he's too young . . . it's quite risqué in parts . . .'

'You make sure you give the ticket to me,' Glenn said with mock threat. 'That way I'll be able to keep an eye on you . . . in more ways than one.'

CHAPTER TWENTY-NINE

Marlene had been treading on eggshells with Malt since the night Rosie ran out on Jeremy Trent. Now that she had lost her job at the Windmill Theatre she needed Malt more than ever. And he knew it. Without her boyfriend finding high rollers for her Marlene knew she'd be reduced to going out on the street to earn herself a living. And she didn't fancy that one bit.

Malt still blamed her for everything that had gone on and in punishment had banned her from his uncle's club. Major Trent had been a good regular punter and Malt resented losing his custom.

Nikola Barbaro was an arrogant man full of his own self-importance. Getting showered in whisky twice in one night, in front of everybody in the club, had really got Malt's goat and Marlene had taken the brunt of his anger when they'd arrived home. A fellow drinking at the bar had sniggered on seeing Malt wiping his face after Rosie's drenching. His amusement had landed him in hospital with a fractured jaw. Of course Malt had an alibi for the attack; the Barbaros always covered their tracks; but Marlene knew sooner or later their luck would run out. Until that day she needed Malt to provide for her, although she'd given up on the idea of wedding bells for them. In fact, Marlene no longer wanted to marry into the Barbaro family. She didn't need a crystal ball to know that the bruises healing on her face wouldn't be the only ones she'd get if she shackled herself to a violent thug. In the past her boyfriend had pushed her around a bit but he'd never laid into her.

Malt hadn't been home for a couple of days and Marlene had guessed he'd been sleeping at the Palm House, probably with one of the hostesses. When he turned up he'd enjoy rubbing her nose in that, to teach her a lesson. Marlene no longer cared about his roving eye; she was going to use him just as he used her. And she urgently needed some money from him; she was down to her last cigarette and had barely half a bottle of whisky left. Apart from that the larder was home to just a tin of Bird's custard powder.

Ten minutes later Marlene heard his key in the lock and breathed a sigh of relief. Jumping up from her place lounging on the sofa she sped to the mirror to press her dark waves into shape. A moment after she'd spun about to welcome him, the smile froze on her face.

Malt looked dirty and unshaven, and very unlike his usual slick self. He took off his Homburg and placed it carefully on the table, then gave Marlene a hard stare from beneath his drooping lids.

'Where have you been? What's happened?' Marlene moved closer to him but stayed just out of his reach, sensing his pent-up anger.

'Where have I been?' he mimicked nastily. 'I been in the police station.' He held up a pair of thick, blunt

fingers. 'Two nights I been in stinking police station. Me
. . . Nikola Barbaro . . . arrested . . . and I done nothing
wrong. My uncle too. He still there in cell.' Malt smashed
his fist against the door panel in frustration.

He pointed menacingly at Marlene. 'It all started with
you. You and your friend. You two Windmill girls bad
luck for us Barbaros. My uncle very angry with me
getting involved with likes of you. He say everything
fine before you come along. And he right.'

'What in heaven's name's happened?' Marlene inter-
jected when he stopped ranting to draw breath.

'Fire at the club . . .'

'The Palm House has burned down?' Marlene gasped.

'No, fire put out quickly,' he snapped. 'Trouble is two
dead people in bedroom. Tina and punter in bed drinking
and smoking . . . they dead. Police have taken away
whisky bottle for test. They say it rotgut that killed them
then cigarette set light to bed.'

Marlene gawped at him, licking her lips. 'But it's not
your fault . . .'

'They think we Barbaros sell bad whisky.' Malt tapped
double-handed at his beefy shoulders. 'I tell them, we
only sell good stuff,' he roared. 'No, they don't believe
. . . they've taken licence and closed us down while
investigate.'

'They can't do that!' Marlene protested. She'd been
hoping to talk Malt into letting her work a shift as a
hostess that evening. The idea that there was no club
and no work was infuriating.

'Ha . . . ha . . . ha . . .' Malt sneered at her. 'You go
tell police then, can't do it.' He shot a glance at Marlene
from under his heavy eyelashes. 'You stay away from
my uncle Valentin and his club. He don't like you . . .

he want you out this house. Pack stuff up . . . get going
. . .' He wagged his fingers, waving her a mocking
goodbye.

'What?' Marlene was distraught at the idea of being
out of cash and homeless too. She rushed at Malt to
give him a cuddle. 'You don't mean that,' she sighed
against his shoulder. 'We're good together. I'll find
another girl . . . lots of girls . . . better than Rosie. We'll
make lots of money . . . start up our own place . . . we
don't need your uncle Valentin . . .'

Malt elbowed himself free of her. He knew which side
his bread was buttered. He needed his wealthy uncle,
not a ten-a-penny good-time girl. In Malt's opinion Soho
was overflowing with Marlenes. And in broken English
he told her so, and to be quick about getting her case
packed.

Marlene watched him swagger away from her into
the kitchen. He found what remained of the whisky and
started emptying the bottle into his mouth, swallowing
in greedy gulps. For some reason it enraged Marlene
that he'd not even offered her a swig. Now the Scotch
was gone all she had to cheer her up was one cigarette
and a couple of sixpences in an otherwise empty purse.

'Ain't going nowhere till you give me some money.
I've lost my job at the Windmill 'cos you beat me up
and I couldn't stand on stage starkers, covered in bruises.
You owe me, so hand something over,' she demanded.

Malt ignored her, wiping the back of a hairy hand
over his wet lips.

'I said I ain't going till you give us something!' Marlene
squealed indignantly.

Malt turned and hit her in quite a smooth motion
considering his bulk and the confined space in the small

330

kitchen. He heard her crack her head on the sink as she fell but left her sprawled at his feet until he suddenly felt something wet seeping into his shoes. He glanced down, the whisky hovering by his mouth. Slowly he put down the bottle and crouched by Marlene. Her eyes were half-open and from beneath her head flowed a thick pool of blood.

Malt's lips were drawn back against his teeth as he roughly grabbed her shoulder to wobble her lifeless body to and fro. 'Stupid bitch . . . see . . . you always trouble . . . my uncle right about you.'

'We'll get one of those big black marble headstones . . . have it carved and the names done in gold letters . . .'

'Don't want a fuckin' 'eadstone . . . want me kids back,' Gertie screamed at her husband, fighting off his big pacifying hands till he left her alone and retreated. She banged her forehead repeatedly against the wall, her face a mess of bubbling snot and streaming brine.

'Want me kids . . . want me kids . . .' Gertie keened over and over again. 'Oh, please God give me back me boys . . .'

Rufus backed away and went to sit down on the sofa next to the only child he had left. Joey was crying quietly, his head hanging low, almost touching his lap.

Rufus and Gertie and Joey had dug with shovels and their bare hands, hardly able to see what they were doing for their tears and the dust and the darkness with just flame and torchlight to guide them deeper into the rubble. Even walking wounded neighbours had helped, working till the early hours of the morning. At about four o'clock they'd unearthed the three small bodies, one after the other.

Their little boys had looked almost perfect, but for dirt, as though sleeping. The two older ones had been in the same bed and timbers had crushed their chests, leaving their small features unscathed. Harry had been given some protection by his pram but had suffocated, so the doctor at the hospital had told them. That morning they'd had the funeral and now the other mourners had gone off in dribs and drabs to get on with their own lives, and left them alone in the shabby house that was their new home, courtesy of the council housing department.

Accommodation close by had been found quickly for them but the place was a dump with damp running on the walls. But neither Rufus nor Gertie cared where they stayed. Neither did they care about the Blitz seemingly petering out. There had been fewer raids since.

Rufus undid his black tie and took it off. 'Put the kettle on, shall I?' he asked. He moved a plate of sandwiches that was left over from the wake closer to the edge of the table where his wife stood, as though in a peace offering. The women in the street had all rallied round to donate foodstuff for a small spread.

Gertie didn't even acknowledge the offer of tea. She stood with her back to him, her face pressed to the mouldy wall, her body rocking from side to side in anguish.

'Said I'd never leave them alone and I wouldn't have, but for you,' she gurgled. 'You killed them. If I hadn't had to go out after you to make sure you didn't do nothing stupid I'd've been on me way to a shelter with them when the bomb dropped.' She pivoted about, teetering on her toes in rage. 'It's your fault,' she bawled.

Joey pressed his small hands to his ears to shut out his mother's distress. He'd heard the same accusations a hundred times or more since his brothers had been killed. And he knew that it was his fault, not his father's, that they'd all been away from home that evening. He'd started it all by stealing money and he deserved to be dead, not the little 'uns.

'If you hadn't been opening your legs for that fucking bookkeeper I wouldn't have had to go out after him to sort it out!' Rufus answered his wife with the same yelled argument he'd used yesterday, and the day before that. He shoved his fingers through his hair, knowing it was pointless to keep blaming each other. 'Get yourself upstairs, to bed, son,' he told Joey.

Joey swung a red-eyed look between his parents then wordlessly did as he was told.

'Ain't no use arguing and fighting, Gertie,' Rufus choked out, pulling a thumb across his watering eyes. 'What's done is done and we gotta carry on for Joey's sake.' He tentatively put out a hand to touch her. When she didn't throw him off he drew her, quivering and sobbing, closer. He put a hand on her round belly. 'Got this one to look forward to, ain't we.'

'Ain't yours, it's his,' Gertie answered, deliberately blunt and brittle.

'Don't matter . . . precious anyhow, ain't he.'

Gertie blinked her hot, weary eyes and looked up into Rufus's haggard face. She'd thought after being beaten by her husband, then running and digging in rubble till dead on her feet, she'd lose the baby in the following days. She wouldn't have cared if she had. 'You mean that, or just saying it?'

Rufus was silent for a moment, trying to control the wedge of breathtaking emotion rising in his throat. 'Mean it with all me heart,' he burst out, his bloodshot eyes spilling fresh tears. 'I want him and gonna raise him as me own and love him as me own.' His voice resonated with sincerity. 'And I'm avenging me dead nippers in the only way I can, so don't try and stop me. I'm joining up, Gertie. Now the boys are laid to rest, I'm going down the recruiting office in the morning.' He turned away from her before he started crying like a baby, heading into the hallway.

Rufus pushed open the bedroom door and looked in. Joey was lying on his back on a sagging mattress, staring at the ceiling. The boy barely flickered an eyelid when his father sat down on the edge of the bed.

'Ain't your fault, son.'

Joey turned with a howl as his father's gentle words released a terrible tension in him. He grabbed at Rufus's waist as sobs jolted him.

'Ain't your fault . . . and you've got to believe me on that, Joey. It's my fault for thinking it was clever to steal stuff and letting you think the same. Been punished now though for it, ain't I, in a dreadful way.' Rufus stroked his son's hair till the boy lay quiet and still. 'Very sorry I am . . .' He sniffed. 'Now I've come to tell you some important news. Tomorrow I'm off to join the army and soon after that I'll be sent to fight. So you've got to promise me you'll look after your mum as best you can when I'm gone.'

Joey rolled away from his father so he could look up into his face.

'You're taking my place, see, Joey, while I'm off paying back them Germans for what they did to us. But you listen to your mum and you do what she tells you. Your mum's always had more sense than me. So you be good and you do stuff she asks you to do to make things easier for her, 'cos soon you'll have a new brother . . . or might be a sister, I suppose,' he added, as though the possibility had just occurred to him. 'Right . . . we straight on all that?' Rufus took out his handkerchief and blew his nose.

Joey nodded solemnly. 'Ain't your fault either, Dad,' he said, in a sweet attempt to lift his father's spirits. 'The Germans did it to us, didn't they?'

'Yeah . . . that's it, son . . . they did it, and I'm on me way to do something about it.'

But as Rufus closed his son's bedroom door he knew there was another score to settle closer to home, with Midge.

CHAPTER THIRTY

Malt dodged back into the burned-out property as two ARP wardens hared past in the direction of the fire close to the junction. Ten minutes ago the engines had been stationed just yards away but now the brigade was directing its hoses at infernos raging on either corner. Malt was concealing himself in wreckage that merely hours ago had been a family home but was now a steaming shell, dripping water. A few smouldering timbers were intermittently being fanned into flame by a strengthening breeze but Malt could tolerate the hot, humid atmosphere.

Having done a recce, and feeling satisfied by it, Malt waited till the coast was clear then, half-crouching, he darted nimbly over the debris. While on the move he constantly glanced to right and left to spot an observer then on reaching his car, parked some yards away, he opened the boot. He roughly hoisted Marlene's curled body onto his powerful shoulder as though it were no more than a suit of clothes. Grabbing the petrol can with his other hand he trotted back the way he'd come, fighting to keep his balance now his weight was uneven. Soon he was back within the shelter of the bombed-out building that was to be Marlene's final resting place.

Once out of sight he relaxed, turning to and fro to locate a suitable spot to dump her. Having let her body slide to the ground, Malt began swiftly gathering up stuff to pile on top of her corpse. He knew he had to dispose of the body completely. If she were ever identified he'd be questioned along with his uncle. Charges against them had been dropped concerning the lethal moonshine, for lack of proof, but Malt and his uncle knew that it would take very little for those frustrated coppers to re-open the case. Marlene had been a regular hostess at the Palm House, and was known to have been Malt's girlfriend. His intention was that she would simply disappear, and if her family ever came looking for her he would shrug and say she'd left him and he'd no idea where she might be. When a woman's charred remains were eventually unearthed from this bombsite Malt hoped it would be assumed she'd perished in the air raid.

As the wind flapped his trousers around his ankles and sent grit into his eyes he cursed, looking up warily at the blackened and battered beams that once had been a roof.

Unscrewing the lid of the petrol can he anointed Marlene's body beneath the crisscrossing timbers then squatted down with a box of matches. He stared at his girlfriend's face then weaved his fingers through the pyre. But he couldn't close her stiff eyelids and he desperately wanted to stop her looking at him. Cursing, Malt let the match he'd struck burn out and yanked at her body, turning her onto her belly.

Straightening up he struck another match, but the stiff breeze extinguished it almost immediately. Malt bowed his head and, being a good Catholic boy, began mumbling a little prayer asking forgiveness for his sins, thinking that might do the trick. He was sorry for killing Marlene. He'd only wanted to shut her up and get rid of her, so it was her own fault for not going quietly when she'd had the chance. He used the matches again, this time cupping a hand about the flame. It began burning brightly and his scowl transformed into a smirk. He squatted to drop the match just as the rafter overhead stopped groaning and fell directly on his back.

The ARP wardens turned in unison as the sound of the small explosion drew their attention. One of them started to retrace his steps. The other one shrugged; he knew that the brigade had dealt with that property already and wouldn't return for a second time when there were shattered buildings yet to be checked for survivors. There was nothing to be done back there even if the fire had re-ignited, he told his colleague.

'There's someone I'd like you to meet, Rosie.' John Gardiner drew his companion forward. 'This is my friend Doris who works at the bakers.'

John had been startled to hear his daughter's key in the lock. He'd not been expecting Rosie back for another hour. But he knew that this was as good a time as any to get introductions out of the way. He'd invited Doris round for a cup of tea and a natter that afternoon because he'd not seen her for a while and knew it was only fair to put her in the picture now Rosie was back living at home. He didn't want the two women at odds over him. But he knew if they did take against one another, his daughter had first claim on his love and loyalty, and always would.

Rosie extended her hand with a smile. 'Pleased to meet you.'

Doris gave the younger woman's hand a shake. 'Likewise,' she said briskly. 'I'm broad-minded, so no need to feel awkward with me about what you do. John's told me all about your job at the Windmill.'

'Oh, right . . . I won't, then,' Rosie said lightly. Perhaps at one time she might have felt niggled by the woman's comment. But not now. She gave her dad a subtle smile to let him know she'd not taken offence.

'Right-oh, I'll let you two have a chat while I make a brew,' John said. He disappeared into the kitchen but in between rattling the cups and saucers onto the draining board, he darted to get a glimpse at what was happening in the back parlour. He breathed a sigh of relief on seeing that Rosie and Doris had seated themselves and seemed to be getting on together.

Twenty minutes later they'd had their tea and biscuits and John returned to the parlour, having seen Doris out.

'You're back early from work, love.'

'We've all been given a few hours off as we've been rehearsing non-stop for days for the big show on Saturday.'

'That's a bonus, then,' John said.

'Doris seems nice.' Rosie guessed that was what her father was waiting to hear. And it wasn't a lie. The woman seemed pleasant, if rather forthright. 'You'll tell me if I'm in the way, Dad, won't you? I'll make myself scarce when she's here and you don't want me around . . .'

'I do want you around. And you're not in the way,' John cut across her gruffly. He cleared his throat. 'Got

339

some news for you actually. Went round to tell Frank Purves that I've packed up me still and won't need no more labels off him. Lenny's been found dead, so you won't need to worry about that nasty piece of work ever again.'

Rosie gawped at her father. 'Dead?' She gasped in astonishment.

'He was found in a dive with a woman; burned themselves by setting light to the bed with a fag.' John knew he ought to give a full explanation as Rosie was bound to hear it all on the grapevine sooner or later. 'The drinking club ran a brothel too and the guvnor's been arrested for supplying moonshine. Seems Lenny and the tart drank some and fell unconscious. Good riddance to bad rubbish all round, I say.' John grabbed his daughter in a protective hug, glad that he'd told no lies in describing how Lenny had met his end; only *he* suspected there was more to it. 'I've not told anybody, not even Doris, about what the bastard did to you. We've no need to mention it again, even between ourselves, now he's gone.' John turned his daughter's face up to his. 'Didn't let the Café de Paris bombing bring you low for long, did you. And you won't go under 'cos of this. Tough little thing, ain't you.'

Rosie was still trying to digest what she'd been told. She reckoned Lenny had been found in the Palm House but, like her father, felt the details best left unsaid. She thought of the whisky cocktails she'd drunk there and the one she'd thrown at Malt. Perhaps she'd had a lucky escape . . . that final drink might have come from a bad bottle . . .

'What goes round comes round; it would have driven me mad knowing he'd got away with it.'

'I know, Rosie,' John said hoarsely.

'He deserved punishment,' Rosie said with a note of finality in her voice.

'He deserved it alright.' John gave her a gentle pat on the back. 'Let's treat ourselves to fish and chips for tea, shall we, dear?'

Rufus climbed the embankment then slithered down the other side, keeping his body hunched close to the ground to avoid being seen. It was almost midsummer when the night's atmosphere, even at close to ten o'clock, held a milky bloom of the day that had gone before. Rufus knew Midge wouldn't hang around if he saw somebody approaching his camp. His brother-in-law might have lost his hand but Rufus reckoned he was still light on his feet. If they'd ever needed to make a quick getaway when out looting Midge had been able to outrun the lot of them. He'd take off like a greyhound out of a trap if he spotted Rufus coming for him.

Rounding a bend in the track Rufus saw the brick arches silhouetted against the navy sky and speeded up to a trot. He wasn't sure what he was going to do to Midge. He'd promised Gertie that he'd not kill him. But he wasn't here to give him a talking to either. Once back home with his wife and son it would be over and he'd never return to that life or those people. Lenny, Popeye, Midge would be nothing to him . . .

The savage disappointment he felt on seeing the wasteland was vacant broke in his throat a sob of frustration. Walking doggedly on Rufus stared down at a patch of disturbed earth, scattered with charred kindling and an empty tobacco tin that had lost its lid. It was all that showed Midge had ever been there.

Rufus bent back at the waist, tilting his face up to howl obscenities at the heavens until he'd extinguished the fire in his rage. He knew it was pointless looking for Midge anywhere else tonight. He'd gone; the man had found out what had happened to his little nephews and had made a swift getaway, fearing Rufus's retribution. Midge would be lying low somewhere and Rufus knew he'd no chance of unearthing him before he left for France in a few days.

Rufus plunged his hands into his pockets, walking back the way he'd come. A moment later he struck up a one-sided conversation with his fugitive brother-in-law, just in case the little weasel had dug himself a hole somewhere and was listening.

'Ain't gonna do you no good, mate, trying to escape. I'd've sooner given you a pasting meself, but gotta accept that might not happen. Won't be around for a while to carry on searching for you, you see, Midge. Anyhow the coppers'll catch up with you in the end. Thing is I didn't grass you up before . . . guess you was just unlucky that time. But I've pointed the Old Bill in your direction now . . . anonymously, of course, otherwise I'll be doing a stretch inside for not coming clean sooner. They ain't gonna be as disappointed as me though, when they turn up and don't find you here. So where are you heading, you little bastard? Down by the docks somewhere, that it, is it? Got no work and no money, have you, so can't have got very far. Then there's that stump to give the game away. Ain't easy disguising yourself when you've only got one hand, is it, Midge? Coppers know all of that. So you've got a choice . . . me or them. But know this, I'm gonna get you back one way or another. That's a promise, made on me dead sons' heads.'

CHAPTER THIRTY-ONE

'What's up, love? Lost something?'

Gordon had stopped work to observe from the stage as Dawn crouched and peered under the seats in the auditorium. Straightening, she gave him a wave while rubbing an earlobe.

'I've lost an earring somewhere. I was sitting out here with some of the other girls earlier in the week, watching the rehearsals. I reckon it dropped off and rolled away.' Dawn had indeed sat with Rosie and Lorna listening to a Scottish baritone belt out a medley of ballads. But she'd not lost any jewellery.

'Want me to give you a hand looking?' Gordon offered. ''Course, it might have got swept up by now, y'know.'

Gordon had been nailing into position on the scenery a large crescent moon. It formed part of the backdrop to the artistic tableau depicting water nymphs at play. He put down his hammer and approached the edge of the stage.

'No . . . you carry on with what you're doing,' Dawn called quickly. 'I'm probably wasting my time; don't suppose I'll find it.' Inwardly she prayed she *was* wasting her time, and she wouldn't spot anything concealed beneath the seats that might be an explosive device. Everybody who worked at the theatre was aware of the Windmill steeplechase that took place, when men seated at the back vaulted over the chairs to get a spot closer to the nudes on stage. It was logical to assume that if an employee *were* a traitor they'd not sabotage equipment that was checked so often. Nevertheless, Dawn continued on her hands and knees along the row.

Twenty minutes later, after a fruitless search that nonetheless boosted her spirits, she was back in the dressing room with the other girls and gratefully accepted the cup of tea Rosie held out to her.

'Penny for them,' Rosie said.

'Oh, just . . . daydreaming,' Dawn replied.

'You're thinking about that gorgeous Glenn, aren't you?' Lorna said with a wink. The leggy brunette was lounging on a chair with her crossed ankles resting on the seat of another. 'Have you given your ticket to him so he can come along tonight?'

'I have,' Dawn said, taking a sip of tea.

'Goody! I hope he's bringing some top-notch chums.' Lorna carried on painting her nails in scarlet varnish. 'You can introduce me to all of them, Dawn. I know there's a handsome chap for me somewhere with a nice private income that Mummy will approve of.' She sighed. 'I've told her that beggars can't be choosers and a coalman will do so long as he pays the bills.' She wafted her wet fingernails to and fro. 'Which is more than Daddy ever did.'

'Coalman?' Rosie scoffed good-naturedly. 'Thought you'd want a jeweller, La-di-da . . .'

'Oh no . . . jewellers and pawnbrokers? Jews on the whole, aren't they.'

Lorna didn't object to Rosie using her nickname but the idea of marrying a Jew had made her wrinkle her nose and Dawn had noticed, and started thinking . . .

She applied lipstick then closed the tube, letting her eyes rove the lively scene behind reflected in the mirror; they settled on Lorna. Was there a traitor in their midst, or was she simply being over sensitive to throwaway remarks because Glenn's secrets occupied the back of her mind?

Lorna was chatting to Rosie as though she'd not a care in the world, gesticulating with her blood-red-tipped fingers. Lorna's family connections to the British Union of Fascists counted against her; Glenn's comment that a child might absorb radical views, having listened to them being spouted by a parent over many years, was worryingly plausible. Dawn knew it was wrong to jump quickly to conclusions. Yet . . . Lorna didn't like Jews, she'd made that clear a moment ago, just as she'd made it clear that her mother's approval was important to her. And Mrs Danvers was friendly with the wife of a notorious Hitler worshipper. But again that didn't make her daughter a Nazi sympathiser, Dawn inwardly argued. A woman who fitted Lorna's description *had* been followed from a right-wing rally to the theatre though. If the MI5 source was accurate, and a plot had been hatched to bomb the Windmill Theatre, there was no denying that this evening's performance would be a prime time to carry out such an attack. But by being in the show Lorna was in as much danger as everybody else . . . unless she stayed away this evening . . .

Dawn felt her nape prickling with cold sweat. Just

yesterday it had all seemed far enough in the future for there to be time to solve the riddle; but the hours and minutes were now ticking away, bringing closer the risk of something truly dreadful happening. She rubbed together her clammy palms and closed her eyes against a wave of rising panic.

Glenn had told Dawn to make sure she behaved normally to avoid arousing suspicion, or hysteria. It was imperative that the network of Fifth Columnists weren't alerted, he'd told her, or the ringleaders would withdraw into their shells of respectability then those lawyers and civil servants would strike elsewhere like some slithering medusan reptile. Even a high-ranking member of His Majesty's constabulary had been uncovered as a fan of the Gestapo, Glenn had told her.

'Anyhow, Glenn's pals won't be allowed in,' Rosie suddenly pointed out, breaking into Dawn's frantic reflection. 'I asked Phyllis for a spare ticket so Dad could bring his lady friend, but nothing doing.'

'The extra fellows can be stage-door Johnnies then,' Lorna said airily. 'So long as they can prove their credentials I'll be nice to them.'

'So your dad's coming along tonight,' Dawn joined in, determined to act normally.

Rosie nodded. 'I thought he might be a bit . . . you know . . . embarrassed about me being in the altogether. But he said he's seen me in me birthday suit before.' She grimaced. 'Not since I was in ankle socks though.'

Dawn was pleased and relieved that Rosie was recovering well from Lenny's attack. It would have been too cruel if the brute had destroyed her friend's confidence and trust in men. Rosie's wild flirting seemed to be a thing of the past but she still had her favourite admirers at the stage door. She'd chat and joke with them before letting them down lightly and heading home alone to her dad.

Rosie hadn't gloated when telling Dawn that Lenny was dead. She was simply glad fate had turned the final page for her, she'd said, so she could push the episode to the back of her mind and get on with her life.

'How about you, Lorna? Is your mum coming tonight?' Dawn asked.

'Oh, definitely! I gave her a ticket and she said she's just dying to see all the rich bitches parading in their finery.' Lorna sighed. 'She's just jealous. She used to have a wonderful mink coat and a diamond tiara.' She snorted a horsey giggle. 'If the pawnbroker hadn't got in first those would have been mine one day! Can you imagine me in a tiara? So regal, my dear . . .' she mocked herself.

Rosie stood up, guffawing, and picked up a gold-painted prop that had been discarded amongst the tea things. 'There you are, Duchess!' She plonked the cardboard crown on Lorna's dark head.

'Do you reckon you might fancy a nice pilot to take you out on the town, Rosie?' Dawn asked, smiling at her friend's antics. She longed to be able to relax and join in the carefree fun but was too highly strung to do so.

'Mmmm . . . not this week . . . maybe next . . .' Rosie exchanged a knowing look with Dawn.

'Maybe next week he might be shot down,' Lorna said pithily. 'Grab your man while you can is my motto.' She glanced, regretfully, at Dawn. 'Me and my big mouth; of course Glenn's bound to have a guardian angel.'

Dawn might have dreadful suspicions about Lorna but

she hadn't taken offence at that because she understood what her colleague meant. She was falling heavily for Glenn and, as if she didn't have enough to worry about, now fretted over the risk of his Spitfire being hit. If he was forced to bale out he might be taken prisoner . . . or worse. She'd heard terrible tales of injured pilots being machine-gunned while parachuting to earth.

'Might I have this chair?' One of the new recruits had tapped Lorna on the shoulder.

The dressing room was crowded with girls changing their costumes and touching up their hair and make-up. The entire cast was mid-way through a dress rehearsal for the spectacular that evening and everybody seemed to be excited, apart from Dawn and Lorna. But Lorna rarely dropped her languid air. Dawn wondered if inside Lorna was also wound as tight as a spring, fretting about how the evening's events would play out. Were they both dancers calmly acting a part, while aware that their colleagues, and the guest audience, were in mortal danger after curtain-up?

'Oh, go on then . . . have my footrest,' Lorna said with a martyred sigh. 'My toes are killing me,' she moaned, putting her feet gingerly to the ground. 'I'll be in agony tonight if wardrobe can't turn up a bigger size for me.' She eased her heel out of one of the black leather tap shoes she'd been wearing. 'I'll swear one of the new girls has "borrowed" my shoes. Nobody's owned up to it, of course.' She rubbed a bloodied spot on her heel. 'Well . . . sod it! I just won't be in the show. I'm not crippling myself!'

'We'll find your shoes,' Dawn said with an oddly threatening inflection that made both Lorna and Rosie look at her in surprise. Dawn smiled. 'We need every hoofer we can get . . . the show must go on,' she added casually. But she got up, turning away from her two colleagues with a knot forming in her guts.

'Fellow outside, asking to see you, Dawn.' Phyllis poked her head round the door.

Dawn slipped on a dressing gown over her camisole, tying it about her waist. Glenn had said he'd visit her during the day to update her with any fresh news. To a chorus of ribald remarks urging her to bring him in, so the girls could give him the once over, she went out of the dressing room. She ran up the stairs to street level and emerged into sunshine.

Glenn had propped himself against the brick wall by the café across the street, but on seeing Dawn he dropped the smoke-curling cigarette in his fingers and walked rapidly to meet her by the theatre entrance.

Dawn felt her spirits sinking. She could tell from his severe expression that her hopes were to be dashed of hearing that the plot was just a false lead from a double agent.

Taking her elbow Glenn steered her to a secluded spot a yard or so away. 'Anything to report? Found anything that looks suspicious?'

Dawn shook her head. 'Nothing under the seats . . . I went over the whole place . . .'

'What is it?' Glenn had picked up on a strange note in her voice and his warm grip tightened on her arm.

'I'm not sure about Lorna.' Dawn made a small, hopeless gesture. 'Oh, I don't know . . . perhaps I'm just reading too much into it. But . . . she made a comment about Jews that got me thinking and now she's complaining about her tap shoes and hinting she might cry off being in the show this evening.' Dawn gazed into

Glenn's dark, anxious eyes. 'It's not like her to say something like that; she's got a blister on her heel but even so . . .'

'I know what you're thinking: it'd be convenient for a saboteur to be absent if the place goes up.' He touched her face with a hand that shook slightly then raked back raven hair from his forehead. 'I'll come in and find out what she's up to,' he burst out.

'No! You can't do that! What if I'm wrong! You'll have to explain yourself to the management. Everything will be out in the open, perhaps for no more reason than I've stupidly over-reacted . . .' Dawn frantically pointed out.

'I think the show should be cancelled,' Glenn said in a quiet, intense way. 'It's not worth risking lives – especially yours.'

'What did your superiors say?' Dawn whispered, her heart beating so fast now she felt faint. She had thought all along that the theatre management should be told of the possibility of an attack. Of course she understood why British Intelligence wanted to wait till the last minute in order to catch the traitor red-handed but so many lives were at stake.

'MI5's playing things down; my contact's clammed up. He's told me nothing other than they're investigating the source of the information because it could be another decoy.' Glenn frowned. 'They know how it is between us and suspect I could go soft on them to protect you, and foul everything up. And they're right to be worried.'

'What did you tell them about us?'

'Nothing . . . but I know how they work. I expect I'm being followed.' Glenn glanced over a shoulder. 'They didn't expect me to fall for you, but from the start I knew I would.' He touched her jaw with a stroking finger. 'First casualty of war might be the truth, but a spook will sacrifice a lot more than that for the greater good.'

'Including a theatre full of people?'

Glenn nodded, mouth thrust grimly.

'*And* his own skin?'

'Most of the time they're in the privileged position of knowing when to bow out. Like Lorna perhaps . . .'

'I'd've liked a chance to do that.' Dawn made a noise that was half-laugh, half-sob.

'You've got it,' Glenn said quietly. He cupped her face between his palms. 'Don't go back inside. Go home. I'll not think badly of you, Dawn.' His voice was wooingly tender as he added, 'You've got your mum and brother to worry about. I'm sorry . . . *really* sorry that I got you involved in any of this. If I could turn the clock back I swear I wouldn't have done so . . .'

Dawn stopped the rest of Glenn's apology with a finger pressed to his mouth. 'Well, I *am* involved, and you *would* think badly of me if I ran off snivelling . . . though not as badly as I would think of myself.' She smiled wryly. 'The show must go on, you know; I can't abandon my post and I certainly can't abandon Rosie and all the others with no word of warning.' She gazed up into his warm brown eyes. 'I just had a wobble when I said I'd've liked to bow out. I'm fine now. So don't be sorry for trusting me with your secrets.' She paused. 'In a daft way it's a privilege to do something, anything that might make a difference and help us win this damned war. Bill and Sal have gone . . . I was fond of them both. So have lots of other people. I might lose you next,' she said with tears thickening her voice. 'Oh, don't try and

351

deny it to make me feel better. And don't make any jokes about nine lives and the devil's own luck and so on. Somewhere tonight at least one British pilot will be shot down or captured, won't he.' She took his broad hands in her small white fingers. 'You risk so much every day but don't think you're the only one courageous enough to put your neck on the line, Glenn Rafferty, 'cos you're not.'

'I stand corrected, Miss Nightingale,' Glenn said huskily, raising their entwined fists to press his lips to her knuckles. 'As you were then . . .' he teased her with military jargon, letting her go. Then he looked thoughtful. 'Is that woman back from Brighton yet?'

Dawn frowned. 'Olive? No, she's not. Why?'

Glenn took a packet of Players from his pocket. 'Word came through about a hotel in Hastings catering to a gathering of toffs. They've been overheard spouting subversive stuff and it seems they hightailed it out of Mayfair to avoid the bombing rather than build sand-castles. They've been holed up there since about September last year; funny how they knew just the right time to skedaddle to beat the Blitz . . .' He lit their cigarettes and for a moment they both took comfort from the smoke warming their throats.

'Olive's gone to see her kids in Brighton so I suppose she's on holiday.' Dawn settled her elbow on her opposite wrist, leaning a shoulder against the wall. 'The management aren't happy that she's late back. She knew before she went that it's all hands on deck for the show tonight; and she's got a ticket for a guest. There'll be murders if she doesn't use it because some of the girls are desperate to get hold of a spare.'

'Hastings is on the same stretch of coastline.' He looked

thoughtful. 'Would she fit the description of the woman who was followed from the fascist meeting?'

'She is taller than me and thin,' Dawn confirmed. 'But she's a do-gooder more interested in wearing a badge for the WVS than visiting her boys. Before Gertie packed in her job they were always at loggerheads over Olive neglecting her kids at their foster home.'

'If she's away visiting her sons, that puts her out of the equation, anyhow.' Glenn leaned in to kiss Dawn. 'I'll be back to watch the show.' He pulled together the lapels of the flimsy wrap covering her, noticing her shivering. 'Cold?'

Dawn shook her head. 'Just a bit terrified, that's all,' she said self-mockingly.

'Don't be,' Glenn whispered. 'Even if the bastards do drop a bomb on the roof tonight we'll be safer in there than we would be in our own beds with a Heinkel overhead.'

'I've got to go back inside . . . we're rehearsing like mad. I'll be vigilant, promise. See you later on.' Dawn dropped her cigarette and put a toe on it then coiled her arms about Glenn's neck. She gave him a fierce kiss on the mouth then on the cheek before hurrying inside the theatre, savouring the taste of him on her smoky lips.

Midge watched from his crouching position behind a wall as limousines drew up at the kerb and women in furs and sparkling jewels stepped out, escorted by dinner-jacketed gentlemen with fringed scarves slung around their shoulders. He took a swig from the bottle of gin in his hand and then slumped onto his bony posterior behind the concealing brick. The contrast between himself and those fragrant folk going into the Windmill

Theatre made him chuckle. He knew he stank and his clothes were stiff with sweat and dirt. He swung the bottleneck between thumb and forefinger, and again had a giggle to himself as he recalled how he'd come by it, and the other bits that kept him alive and cheerful enough to stop him from diving under a bus.

In the hope of cadging a few fags or a bottle of beer off a customer he'd taken to loitering outside a few offies, looking pathetic. He'd been taken by surprise at how willingly people gave him stuff, and a pat on the back. Outside the baker's, an old dear had handed over her bag of currant buns, praised his bravery, then gone back inside to buy herself some more.

It had taken Midge a moment to realise she thought him a war cripple. He'd cottoned on quickly then he could make a bit of capital out of his stump. Of course, if those generous folk had realised how he'd really lost his hand they'd soon have back their fags and booze and buns.

But he never hung about in the same place twice – just in case the cops were there waiting to ambush him next time.

Midge knew he had only one chance now of beating the noose, and for that he wanted cash . . . not half-bottles of gin or bags of buns. He needed to get abroad. Ireland might do; he'd like to make Switzerland but he knew that was a wish too far. But if he didn't put distance between himself and these shores, he'd get sentenced to death. He couldn't even join up under a false name and take his chances on a battlefield. His mangled hand had put paid to that. But Midge could feel it in his bones that his days as a free man were numbered and it was make or break for him.

He'd slipped back to the railway arches just yesterday, and observed from a safe distance as the coppers began picking over the ground where he'd had his camp. It was the second time he'd seen them there, crawling about like flies. Midge knew who'd grassed him up; and he knew too that the coppers would have a recent description of him . . . one hand and all.

Midge hated Rufus and Gertie for turning on him.

He knew they blamed him for the nippers getting killed; but they'd no right to, in Midge's opinion. He might have stirred the pot but he'd not put the hemlock in it. Rufus and Gertie only had themselves to blame for the way things turned out. If Gertie hadn't been seeing her boss on the side Midge wouldn't ever have had a stick to beat them both with. He knew they'd have been straight down the air-raid shelter the moment the sirens went off if they hadn't been too busy tearing strips off one another that evening.

Hearing some shrill laughter Midge poked his head above the parapet and watched a woman with a huge diamond nestling against her throat entering the theatre. Midge had liked the Windmill's girly revues. He'd only been in there a half a dozen times when on leave, but he'd got the steeplechase down to a fine art, winning it every time.

He rolled back his sleeve to look at his stump with disgust. He'd not win a kid's egg and spoon race now. That was another reason why he hated his brother-in-law. Rufus had introduced him to Popeye and Lenny; and the looting lark had been his downfall, not murder or desertion.

After a while Midge realised the area had quietened down. He again turned and took a gander over the broken brick wall. The limousine was pulling off and there were no more vehicles waiting in line to disgorge their posh passengers onto the pavement. He stood up, five feet three in his boots, keeping in the shadows cast by an unkempt privet bush. Midge was in the process of ramming the small gin bottle in an inside pocket when something winked, catching his eye, and he remained stock still. A car passed; it was almost dusk and its headlights picked out the thing that interested Midge, making it glitter.

His heart was in his mouth as he scrambled over the low brickwork and raced across the road with a speed he thought he no longer possessed. He swooped, collecting the cold metal in his fingers, then dived around the corner of the building to examine his booty while gasping in air.

The disappointment was hard to stomach. Midge gazed at the gewgaw on his flat palm. It had probably been dropped by a dancer, not one of the guests. It was some sort of cheap hairslide, big on spangles and low on value, Midge reckoned. He heard a noise and automatically shrank back then glanced up.

Above him people were milling on a roof and he could hear the pop of champagne corks and glasses chinking, and a muffled hum of genteel voices. Midge cast his eyes to the ground, his expression foxy. He recalled Gertie having once mentioned that the Windmill Theatre had such a terrace where important guests were entertained in reception parties. Midge's eyes darted to the fire escape that led up there. Soon those Hooray Henrys and Henriettas would be trooping inside to watch the show.

Midge gave a gleeful snort: he reckoned it'd be worth climbing that iron staircase to have a gander when the coast was clear. With any luck, one of them might have glugged a bit too much champers and dropped something better than the tat in his hand . . .

Midge had a longer wait than he'd reckoned on but as soon as the night air remained still and unbroken for several minutes he ventured to the stairs and nipped up them. He slowed down towards the top, peeping, but was glad to see that the terrace was vacant and the doors leading inside closed. All that remained of the party were empty glasses and some bits of food. On the tables candle stumps were still burning, illuminating some tiny delicacies presented on a tray. He grabbed them in his hand, shoved them all together into his mouth then swallowed almost without chewing. The dregs in nearby champagne bottles were similarly swiftly despatched. Then, candle in hand, Midge set to work beetling back and forth searching the concrete ground for a sign of something valuable, all the while darting glances at the French doors. He knew staff would be coming to clear up.

He darted to the wall and flattened his back against it as he heard a noise by the doors that led inside. Cursing that he'd not heard somebody approaching, his eyes swivelled to and fro for an escape route. But there wasn't one close enough . . . just the top of the stairs taunting him, ten yards away.

He heard the key in the lock and silently grabbed an empty bottle, holding it ready to strike. He knew he had nothing to lose so was game for a bit of assault and battery . . .

After a moment, when nobody appeared on the terrace, Midge crept forward and took a furtive glance through the glass. He just glimpsed a woman's back view as she disappeared from sight. He frowned, tried the handle and the door opened. He froze wondering what to do next; then with a smirk realised fate had handed him an invitation too good to turn down. Why the woman had unlocked the door then gone off, he'd no idea. It seemed a daft thing to do.

But he wasn't going to look a gift horse in the mouth. He might not have stumbled across a diamond ring, but he'd had champagne and canapés. Theatres had takings, and the way his luck was going, he just might stumble across them.

CHAPTER THIRTY-TWO

'I wish Dad wouldn't keep waving at me,' Rosie giggled. 'He's making me laugh and I'm not supposed to jiggle.' She glanced down indicatively at her bosom now covered by the silk wrap she'd put on.

'He's proud of you,' Dawn panted; she'd just finished an energetic Charleston routine then had joined Rosie waiting off stage. In the wings the smell of greasepaint and mingling perspiration was heavy in the air as the dancers congregated, hands on heaving hips as they puffed to get their breath back. Dawn was now daring to hope that the evening would pass off without incident. They were close to the intermission and nothing untoward had happened.

'So far so good; the show's going down a storm, isn't it?' Rosie beamed.

Past the glaring footlights they could glimpse the packed auditorium as the weighty fringed curtain slowly drew up on the tenor posing, arms spread, in anticipation of his welcoming applause.

As the show had progressed Dawn had relaxed, despite

having spotted Glenn seated in the sixth row. He'd winked at her, blown her a discreet kiss, almost putting her off her stride in the opening tap dance when the troupe had marched on stage in their servicewomen uniforms – Lorna included in the line-up.

Gazing up at the boxes, Dawn could see Mrs Henderson seated with the Lord Chancellor and an admiral, loaded down with fancy brocade and medals adorning his chest. The stalls and circle were populated with a mixture of employees' relations, members of the voluntary services and upper-crust types with jewellery flashing in the lights. Dawn – now finding something suspicious in everything – wondered if fewer politicians than expected had attended because the spooks, as Glenn called his Whitehall spymasters, had warned off their own.

'We'd better get changed for the next routine.' Lorna had left the gaggle of showgirls taking a breather and hobbled over in her tight tap shoes. She pulled one off to reveal a red weal that started dripping blood. 'Olive should've had a proper search for a larger pair for me,' she wailed. 'That woman! I swear she thought it too much trouble to go in the dressing cupboard . . .'

'Olive?' Dawn swung about. 'I didn't think she was back.'

'Her train was late in, so she said. She's supposed to be giving everybody a hand as the kiosk is closed but she seems more interested in helping Gordon with the scenery.' Lorna flung down her shoe. 'Well, I'm off home if there's no bloody shoes to fit me. I'm in agony!'

'No . . . you're not leaving! You can't do that.' Dawn gripped at her fellow dancer's arm.

'Lorna's foot *is* a mess, Dawn.' Rosie grimaced at the sight of the blood slowly staining the floor.

'I'll come with you to look for some different shoes,' Dawn blurted; the relief she'd been feeling a moment ago had been whipped away in an instant. Olive was in the building and Lorna was ready to leave it! Dawn's mind was in chaos as adrenaline streaked through her veins, putting her on high alert. Olive had been to see her kids in Brighton and had arrived back late, that's all there was to it, Dawn told herself, trying to think logically. Yet she couldn't put from her mind the seed of doubt that Glenn had planted there earlier.

'Don't see why I should go back on,' Lorna huffed, snatching her arm from Dawn's fingers. 'There's nobody out there watching me.'

'I thought your mum had a ticket. Didn't she come after all?' Dawn demanded.

'Went off to a bloody meeting instead and I might as well join her. I'm getting changed. And I don't care if I do get the sack!' Lorna started hobbling, barefoot, towards the dressing rooms.

Dawn sprinted after her, the beads on her red Charleston dress swinging about her hips. 'What meeting? Fascist gathering, is it?' It was out and Dawn licked her heavily rouged lips, waiting with bated breath for Lorna to answer . . . or look guilty.

'Yes, since you ask.' Lorna shifted on the spot, colour rising in her cheeks. 'How did you know?'

Dawn fell back a step as though she'd been punched.

'Mummy knows it's the only place to find him lately. And she said he'd better hand over something or our electricity will be cut orf.' Lorna advanced on Dawn.

'My disgusting father's a fascist . . . so what? It's not a secret. What's this all about?'

'Have you been to one of those meetings before?' Dawn garbled.

'Yes, I have, and we didn't manage to get a bean out of the tight-fist . . . but I don't see that it's any of your business . . .'

'Let's find you those bloody shoes. Quickly, come on . . .' Dawn grabbed at Lorna's hand and yanked her along behind her. 'We need you in the line-up, you can't let us down,' she rattled off.

Dawn and Lorna exchanged a combatant look but they speeded up towards the dressing rooms, Rosie trotting behind and looking puzzled.

Olive wasn't in their dressing room so Dawn, taking a chance on Lorna staying right where she was, left Rosie searching for tap shoes and Lorna dabbing her heel with cotton wool, while she went in search of the woman. Dawn's mouth felt dry and her palms clammy, yet at the same time she felt guilty for even suspecting Olive of having returned on this particular opening night with a wicked ulterior motive. The woman had a husband serving in the army, two young sons, and was a member of the WVS. She swung about as she heard the dressing-room door open and Lorna emerged.

She retraced a step. 'You're not going home!' Dawn pointed a quivering finger at Lorna. 'Stay right where you are!'

'I'm looking for some TCP, that's all.' Lorna gave a snarling sigh. 'What in damnation is up with you? Why on earth are you picking on me?'

Dawn raked both hands into her hair, in dismayed confusion, dislodging her sequined headband in the

362

process. She left it on the floor and hurried on, wishing she could get a message to Glenn to come and help her. But she'd no time . . . she just needed to reassure herself that Olive was helping Gordon shift scenery, she told herself as her heart continued to drum a rapid tattoo beneath her ribs. Olive had helped Gordon before when they were short of stagehands; she was a big, strong woman. Dawn calmed herself with the thought that soon she'd be satisfied that all was well and she could concentrate on finishing the show . . .

Dawn had been hurrying past the maintenance cupboard when she heard a noise. Retracing her steps she opened the door to peer in. 'Olive,' she called.

Olive appeared from the back of the box room, looking harassed.

'What are you doing?' Dawn asked, relieved when the woman waved at her.

'Oh, Gordon sent me to find some paint. He needs to quickly touch up a panel. Stupid man shouldn't have left it so late . . .'

'I'll give you a hand,' Dawn immediately blurted, wanting to get closer to Olive so she could clearly see her expression. Then if the older woman seemed her normal bossy self, Dawn would have to race back to find where Lorna was . . .

The cupboard was lit with just one small electric bulb, and it held a pungent smell of turpentine.

'Don't be daft!' Olive snapped. 'You're in costume and due on stage. Why d'you want to poke about in here with me?' Her eyes narrowed on Dawn and her hand lifted to rest on a shelf close by where tools were kept.

Dawn had noticed Olive's crafty movement and felt

icy moisture dampen her spine. All thought of racing away to find Lorna dissolved.

'Oh, there you are, Dawn. Have you found bloody Olive?' A barefoot Lorna came barging in behind Dawn, knocking over Olive's shopping bag, left close to the wall. 'Have you had a look for my damned shoes or not?' Lorna demanded, displaying her damaged heel. She glanced down. 'And what the devil are you doing stealing the props, Olive? There won't be enough of these if you snaffle one for your kids to play with.' Lorna swooped on a small pistol that had skidded out of Olive's bag. After the intermission the dance troupe were to go on as cowgirls; they had all been allocated a toy gun in a holster.

'Give me that!' Olive hissed, lunging at Lorna and grabbing the gun.

From sheer instinct Dawn sprang forward to wrestle the pistol from Olive, their entwined arms rotating crazily as they fought for possession of the weapon. The ensuing retort made all three women freeze, ears ringing but otherwise unhurt, as the bullet hit the ceiling. Dawn twisted and yanked, winning the gun but Olive leapt at her, shoving Lorna over in the process. Dawn managed to swing up the revolver at the last moment and level it at Olive's chest, halting her a yard away.

'I'm guessing there's more than one bullet in here, or you wouldn't have wanted it so badly.' Dawn's calm, steely voice sounded foreign to her own ears. She tightened her grip on the pistol to stop the weapon shaking.

Lorna was struggling to her feet, massaging her sore head and looking stupefied. 'What's happened . . .?'

'Go and get Glenn, Lorna. Quickly, do it now!' Dawn's eyes never left Olive as she gave her order.

'But . . . what . . .'

'Olive's a traitor, aren't you, Olive. And as we just found out, this isn't a toy, it's a real gun. She wants to destroy the theatre and kill everybody in it.'

Lorna's jaw dropped but she seemed rooted to the spot, gawping at Olive as though she were vermin. Then she sent Dawn an affronted look. 'You didn't think it was me, did you? That's not fair! Just because Daddy's a right-winger . . .'

'Go and get Rosie to help you, Lorna. One or other of you must get a message to Glenn now! But for Christ's sake do it discreetly or there'll be pandemonium.' Dawn yelled the order so forcefully that Lorna stopped being peeved and skittered out of the cupboard into the corridor.

'What were you going to do? Burn the place down?' Dawn asked in a horrified whisper. Now her eyes had adjusted to the dimness of the cupboard's interior she could see that behind Olive was a pile of rags together with tins of paint and turpentine. She guessed that everything the woman had collected together at the back of the cupboard was highly flammable. Olive edged towards the hammer on the shelf, but Dawn shook the gun.

'Stay where you are and be quite still . . . or I'll shoot you.' Dawn was quivering from top to toe. 'I've proved I know how to use the thing, and I'll pull the trigger again if I have to.'

'You haven't got the guts for it.' Olive took a sly step forward. 'Whereas I have no compunction in killing any enemy of the Fatherland.' She jerked her head. 'Take a look and you'll see I'm not making an idle boast.'

Dawn knew it might be a trick to get her into a position where Olive could overpower her, but she was plagued by a terrible suspicion. She tilted to one side to see past Olive, and glimpsed a body crumpled on the floor.

'Gordon interrupted me at a very inconvenient time. I dealt with him and I'll deal with you too for my Führer.' Olive beckoned slyly. 'Give the gun to me quickly, and I'll let you get out of here alive.'

Olive was a lot bigger than Dawn was and she knew a hand-to-hand fight with her would be hard to win. The hairs on her nape stood to attention at the thought of it. 'If you'd've managed to set that lot alight you might've gone up along with the rest of us, you know.'

Olive snickered. 'Don't be stupid. Once I had the fire well under way, I had my escape route planned.' She pulled some keys from her pocket. 'I would have locked it after me, of course. I intended I'd be the only one using the fire escape.'

'You wicked bitch! Were you going to stand outside gloating too, watching the place burn?'

'It's not personal. It's war. A war Germany will win.'

Dawn felt sick to her stomach but knew she must conquer all feeling and be as calculating and ruthless as her opponent or Olive would outwit her. If Olive managed to get possession of the gun, Dawn knew the woman would shoot her without a second's thought.

'You can join us if you like, Dawn; the cause needs brave women like you. I can get you away to a safe house in Hastings.' Olive sidled closer, a fake smile pinned to her lips.

'So you *have* been to Hastings rather than Brighton! And you've crept in here late on purpose, haven't you,' Dawn spat. 'You wanted the rest of us fully occupied with the show so you could go gaily about your murderous business.' Her fiery anger had started to melt away her fear. 'You treacherous bitch! If you think I'll join your band of lunatics you must be insane.'

Succumbing to a wave of panic Dawn suddenly shouted Glenn's name in case he was hurtling along the corridor, unsure of which door to take to find her. It seemed ages since Lorna had rushed off to get help yet Dawn realised it was probably less than five minutes. It wouldn't be easy alerting Glenn to the peril afoot without interrupting the show. Dawn was starting to wish she'd not insisted Lorna be discreet. At the moment she didn't care if the entire cast and audience came to her rescue . . .

'You won't think me mad when the beach at Hastings is stormed by German troops, will you?' Olive sneered. 'And I shall be there to greet them.'

'What's happened to you, Olive?' Dawn whispered shakily. The woman seemed repulsively alien, not a colleague of almost a year's standing. 'What about your boys? And your husband's fighting in France; he'll kill you when he finds out you're a traitor.'

Olive tilted up her head to bark a laugh. Dawn had always thought the woman quite masculine, and arrogant, but those traits seemed now vilely magnified.

'My husband's proud of me. I'm a Nazi and so is he. He *is* fighting in France, in the Wehrmacht, and his name is Friedrich, not Fred. As for my sons . . . I have no sons. I dedicate my life to serving my country, not tending brats. My Friedrich was one of the first recruits to Hitler's Jugendbund and was singled out for praise by the Führer himself. Now he trains the youngsters joining up. They are *our* children.'

'But you're English, not German,' Dawn protested. Olive had no hint of a foreign accent. 'Why aren't you in Germany if you want to help the enemy's cause?' She realised she must keep Olive talking and buy time for help to arrive.

'I might have been born here but I'm German now and have been living in Köln with my husband. Why did I come back?' Olive had anticipated Dawn's next question. 'Why do you think, you fool!' she crowed. 'I've passed on invaluable information while working in this theatre. Do you know how often I've overheard officers boasting about their missions and so on while queuing for tickets?' Olive snorted a contemptuous laugh. 'Working for the WVS I've picked up intelligence while bandaging their heads when really I just wanted to slide a knife between their ribs.' She came a step closer. 'But I understand they must do their duty for Britain as I must do mine for Germany. Now I've said enough; I know your cavalry is coming. But know this . . . you will never win!' As though spurred on by her fervent proclamation, Olive charged at Dawn with the hammer swinging wildly in one hand.

Dawn managed to duck and avoid the worst of the blow but the tool made cracking contact with her shoulder, knocking her to the ground.

Despite the agonising pain in her arm Dawn grappled with Olive, thrashing to and fro on the floor. Pots of paint tipped over as they bashed into them, smearing slimy oils onto their legs and feet. Feeling the gun against one hand, but unable to turn her numb fingers to grab it, Dawn whacked the weapon as far away as possible with the side of her fist. Olive grunted in frustration as her scrabbling hand closed on air, rather than the iron barrel that a moment ago had been at the tip of her fingernails.

Olive's lips drew back in a silent snarl and her broad, mannish hands plunged to Dawn's throat and began tightening. Dawn swung her head to and fro trying to dislodge Olive's grip but she could feel a gentle blackness descending on her, drawing her, floating, towards the ceiling.

She felt a shudder pass through her then the weight on top of her shifted and a rough hand was pulling her out from beneath Olive's still body.

'I heard some of that,' Midge Williams said, shoving aside Olive's torso with his foot. 'So reckon she's got what she deserved. Now I want what I deserve. And you're gonna help me get it, love. I just saved your life.'

Dawn fell back against the open door, wheezing, her hand massaging her bruised throat. Olive was spread-eagled on her front with blood leaking from her scalp. From the way the small man was wiping the gun butt on his trousers Dawn guessed he'd crowned Olive with it. Although he looked a shadow of his former self, Dawn, with a gasp of disbelief, suddenly recognised Gertie's brother. Had she not been shocked into insensibility she would have been astonished at the sight of his crippled arm; as it was, she simply grimaced at him while her chest heaved and she painfully filled her lungs with air.

It took Midge a moment longer to recognise her than it had taken Dawn to identify him. His immediate reaction was to swear then, quickly pocketing the gun, he started dragging Dawn along the corridor, his lips flat against his teeth. He didn't need another reminder of his time looting with Lenny and Rufus . . . not now. He was incensed at the way things had turned out. It was just his luck for fate to dangle him a carrot that was rotten.

He'd hoped to have a ferret about and turn up some petty cash at least. Instead he'd got caught up in a Nazi plot. He'd not intended getting involved, but Midge had known he'd have to put a stop to it because the place would be crawling with people at any second, the racket they were making. He didn't give a toss about traitors or the bloody war. All he'd wanted was the cost of his ferry passage to Ireland. But it seemed that was too much to ask.

He tightened his grip on the girl, snarling in her face as she fought him and screamed. She was getting her strength back but he'd bet his life she knew where the safe was even if she didn't have the key. Now he had a gun Midge was ready to have a go at shooting the fucker open or die trying . . .

He didn't hear an assailant approaching till it was too late; Midge half-turned but the punch on the side of his head knocked him flying. But he managed to drag his hostage with him to the floor.

Glenn aimed a vicious boot at his opponent's ribs, pulling Dawn to her feet, then turned swiftly back to follow up with another kick. He'd not been able to punch the bastard as hard as he needed to for fear of hurting Dawn.

'He's got a gun, Glenn!' Dawn cried, using both hands to drag her boyfriend back as he lunged forward again and drove a fist at Midge's face. She'd seen Midge's hand dive into his pocket as he ducked to evade blows. 'And he's not involved with Olive . . . he's not a traitor . . .' Dawn coughed and gulped. 'He's just a thief . . . and he saved me from being strangled . . .'

'Yeah, I'm just a thief, pal. And I saved her.' Midge coughed up blood. 'Might as well let me go, eh?' He winced in pain but the gun held at arm's length was steady enough, pointing straight at Glenn's chest. Midge knew all he had to do was get back up the stairs to the terrace and he'd be away; that's all he had to do . . .

'Where's Olive?' Glenn demanded.

'He knocked her out with the gun,' Dawn said through chattering teeth. She was feeling faint and her head was thumping fit to burst.

Glenn slowly extended a hand. 'Gun,' he demanded through gritting teeth.

'Fuck off.' Midge struggled onto his knees, using his stump as a lever.

'Go . . . make them stay back.' Glenn gently pushed Dawn in the direction of her two friends who'd hared around the corner to catch up with Glenn and find out what was going on.

'Where's Olive . . . what's happened . . . who's that . . .'

Dawn was deaf to her friends' breathless questions; her gaze was fixed on Glenn as he stalked Midge back along the corridor.

'Give us the gun and you can go,' Glenn said quietly. He knew he daren't turn away to sort out Olive because the little bastard might put a bullet in his back.

Dawn couldn't bear watching the pistol being aimed at Glenn's chest. She was sure that all Gertie's brother wanted to do now was escape empty-handed. And she wouldn't let the man she'd fallen in love with get shot for that.

About to rush to Glenn Dawn suddenly became aware of somebody tugging at her arm. When Dawn turned to look at Rosie her eyes immediately darted past to Olive, swaying in the cupboard doorway with a hammer in one hand and a burning rag in the other.

Without uttering a sound Olive raised the burning rag and turned to throw it into the cupboard, her smile evil and triumphant. Spontaneously Dawn launched herself at the woman and the two of them fell backwards into the spilled paint. A second later Rosie and Lorna piled in too while behind them the rag ignited a trail of turpentine.

As soon as the catfight broke out, distracting his attacker, Midge saw his chance and took it. With all his might he chucked the gun at Glenn's head, catching him a glancing blow on the shoulder as he ducked his face aside. Midge scampered up the stairs towards the roof terrace. He'd no stomach for a cold-blooded murder and besides he was confident the bloke was unlikely to come after him with all hell breaking loose in the theatre. Midge had smelled the paint and turps and knew the whole place could go up.

'Get the fire extinguisher,' Glenn bawled at Rosie. She was on top of the pile of fighting women and he pulled her to her feet and shoved her in the back, hoping she knew where the damned thing was kept. A small explosion from further back in the cupboard made Lorna slither backwards then hare off to help Rosie.

Olive and Dawn were rolling to and fro on the floor and Glenn yanked Olive up by the scruff of her neck and with a single straight jab knocked her out cold. He punched her harder than he had the one-armed thief; but he didn't care about hitting a woman. He'd have clumped her simply for being a traitor; when he saw the state of Dawn's bruised face, and that the woman he adored with every fibre of his being was slipping into unconsciousness, he would gladly have battered Olive Roberts to death.

CHAPTER THIRTY-THREE

'Well, you're a sight for sore eyes, I must say. We were told you'd been in the wars but you look good as new,' Lorna quipped. 'Can we smoke in here?'

She sat down in the chair next to Dawn's hospital bed, crossing her coltish legs. As there wasn't another free seat, Rosie perched on the edge of the mattress until a passing matron gave her a glare and a finger flick, making her shoot upright.

'Crikey . . . the Gestapo *have* invaded,' Lorna said, then gestured lazy apology as she received censorious frowns from her friends. In view of what had gone on last night the joke had fallen flat. 'Oh, you know what I mean.' Lorna dropped her cigarettes back in her bag.

Rosie, in a fit of uncontrollable affection, leaned forward and kissed Dawn's forehead before plumping the pillow behind her friend's head. Despite what Lorna had kindly said about Dawn's appearance, she *did* look the worse for wear. Vivid purple splotches on her jaw and neck marred her pale complexion and there was more bruising beneath her eyes.

'Brought you something in to cheer you up; I expect you're bored . . . and hungry.' Rosie took from her bag a rolled magazine, and a small bar of Fry's chocolate.

'Yum. We'll open that then, shall we?' Lorna broke off a piece of Turkish Delight, popping it into Dawn's mouth before helping herself to a piece. She handed the chocolate to Rosie who, with a shrug, finished it off.

'Did the performance run through to the end?' Dawn croaked, having swallowed her chocolate with a wince. She was still having difficulty eating and talking after being throttled by Olive.

'It went like a dream. The show must go on!' Rosie and Lorna chorused, then burst into fits of giggles.

Dawn needed the release too and she put her head back against the pillows and laughed hysterically even though it hurt.

Lorna wagged a finger at Rosie, while wiping mirthful tears from her eyes. 'This one was late on stage; she made a lame excuse about a fiendish woman trying to burn down the theatre.' Lorna gave Rosie a grin. 'You crept in behind the crescent moon and held on to it, didn't you, because you were quaking so much. We were all there for the finale, apart from you, Dawn. We took fifteen curtain calls. Rosie waved at her dad, didn't you?' she teased the girl. 'Nobody will dare sack her though . . . not now they know she helped catch a German spy.'

'And nobody in the audience suspected a thing at the time?' Dawn whispered with a smile.

'Completely oblivious,' Lorna answered smugly. 'Phyllis said she guessed something was up when Rosie and I crept into the auditorium to hiss and wave at Glenn. But being a true pro she carried on talking to

Mrs Henderson and the Lord Chancellor.' Lorna flicked her dark hair over a shoulder. 'Everybody has been a bit tearful since they found out all about it. Gordon's recovering from his concussion by the way.'

'Thank God the fire was put out in time.' Dawn blew a sigh through her swollen lips. The idea of Gordon being burned to death at the back of the cupboard was indeed horrible.

'We've been told to play the whole thing down to avoid bad publicity. We don't want to lose customers to rival theatres.' Rosie grimaced.

'Our servicemen would risk any peril to see you waving your arms and wobbling your . . . assets . . .' Lorna nodded at Rosie's chest.

Dawn chuckled, and pulled a face, easing her right shoulder. She was stiff and sore all over and her collar-bone had been fractured during Olive's final attack. But suddenly she hardly felt the discomfort. The wonderful knowledge that no serious harm had been done to anything or anyone was all the analgesia she needed. 'I expect the papers will get hold of the story in the end,' she said. 'Did an ambulance bring me to hospital and cause a stir? Did the police turn up for Olive?' She wished she'd not lost consciousness and missed the drama's conclusion.

'Some men in suits took *her* away in a black saloon.' Rosie's eyes widened at the memory of it. 'As for you, Glenn whizzed you off in his car immediately after he knocked out Olive and saved the day with the sand bucket and fire extinguisher . . .' Rosie's voice held a throb of admiration for the hero of the hour. 'It was very romantic the way he swept you up in his arms and carried you off. Have you seen him?'

'No,' Dawn said softly. 'He told Mum he's coming in later on this afternoon.'

Earlier, Dawn had been allowed her first visitor. Her mother, having learned from Glenn that she'd been hurt following a brouhaha at the theatre, had come in to see how she was. As soon as Eliza saw her daughter's injuries she'd burst into tears. Dawn had pacified her mother, but her prime concern had been finding out how it had all ended. Eliza had said she knew that the theatre was still standing and Olive had been arrested but no more than that because that's all Glenn had told her.

'You were so brave, Dawn,' Rosie said in a rather wobbly tone. 'All the girls want you to know that, but especially me.'

'And me,' Lorna echoed solemnly.

'Everybody wants to come in and see you.'

'Tell them no need, I'll soon be back on my feet,' Dawn said briskly.

'Phyllis said she should have suspected Olive was up to no good when she found her in her office looking through stuff. Seems Olive made out she needed matinee tickets and change for the till but it turned out there was plenty of both.' Rosie gave a significant nod. 'Phyllis thinks Olive was after the guest list to let the Germans know who'd be in the theatre that night.'

After a short pause, Dawn blurted, 'Sorry that I thought you might be involved in some way, Lorna.' She frowned; she felt very guilty about that.

Lorna shrugged. 'Given what my bloody father's like . . .' Her voice tailed off into a forgiving smile.

'Does it hurt?' Rosie gently touched Dawn's bandaged collarbone.

'Only a bit . . . they've dosed me up with something.'

'There's somebody else waiting outside to see you.' A young nurse had come up quietly to make her announcement. 'A gentleman in the RAF.' She gave a knowing wink. 'Very handsome too.'

'Wonder who that might be?' Lorna said archly.

'Come on, time we made a move.' Rosie grabbed Lorna's arm, dragging her to her feet.

Dawn struggled up into a seated position, gasping with the effort. 'Mum said he'd not be in till teatime,' she wailed. 'How do I look?' Her large green eyes, circled with purple speckles, begged for an honest answer. 'Has somebody got a mirror?' She brushed down the bodice of her hospital nightgown using the arm that hurt the least, then forked her fingers through her hair. 'It's full of tangles,' she mumbled.

Rosie set her bag on the bed and got out a comb. Gently she teased the snarls from Dawn's thick honey-coloured hair, patting waves into it as she worked. Lorna delved into her bag and found a couple of lipsticks. She offered one colour then the other in quick succession for Dawn to make a choice. Dawn pointed at the lighter shade of red and tilted her face up for Lorna to outline her lips before rubbing them together.

Next out of Lorna's handbag was a perfume bottle. She upended it and dabbed Jicky behind both of Dawn's ears then rubbed some on her wrists. About to put it away, she unstoppered it again and tipped a drop down Dawn's cleavage exposed by the regulation nightgown.

'Well, you never know . . . if you pull the curtain around you might get lucky.' Lorna winked suggestively.

The two young women stood back to admire the result of their ministrations.

'You'll do,' Lorna said.

'You look lovely,' Rosie said, and thought with a contented smile it wasn't a lie. There couldn't be many girls who suited bruises in the way Dawn Nightingale did. 'Good luck . . .'

'Here he comes,' Lorna squeaked.

Dawn looked up, her breath scratching painfully at her throat at the sight of him. She gave her friends a wave, watching as Glenn spoke to them as they passed him, knowing he would have come out with something politely witty, judging from their wide smiles.

Then he was by her side, standing just inches away. She looked up to see him staring at her with such loving intensity that she felt tears well in her eyes. She blinked them away hoping the whites weren't now bloodshot.

'If I'd known you were coming in so early I'd have saved you a bit of chocolate,' Dawn burst out, not knowing what else to say. 'Rosie brought in a bar of Fry's Turkish Delight.' She fiddled with the blunt ends of her hair. 'I had to have some cut off . . . the nurses did it . . . they couldn't get the paint out . . . or off my legs; I look a mess, don't I . . .'

'You look beautiful. You always look beautiful.'

'Liar,' Dawn said but smiled.

Suddenly Glenn turned, whipped the curtains closed about the bed and bent to kiss her. His mouth was hard and demanding but his hands hovered over her as though he were frightened of touching her bruised body. And then she felt the warm salt water between their faces and was unsure which of them was crying.

Dawn wiped the wet from his cheeks with her fingers then used the back of her hand to smear away her own tears.

'Told you we'd make a good team,' Glenn hoarsely teased, collapsing down onto the chair Lorna had vacated. He planted his elbows on his knees, hanging his head.

When she heard his long shuddering sigh Dawn moved her hand despite the twinge of pain, and turned his face towards her. 'You look tired.' The joy of his presence had made her overlook at first that he didn't seem as suave as usual. His brown eyes were heavy with shadows and his jaw beneath her fingers felt abrasive with stubble.

'I was up all night. I was here; but they wouldn't let me see you. I went home at six o'clock when they told me you were sleeping soundly. Visited your mum at eight o'clock . . .'

'She turned up earlier – thanks for not telling her too much. She's fine now she's seen me. I hope she is, anyway, or she'll open a bottle of gin to calm her nerves.'

'I could do with a drink,' Glenn said self-mockingly, swiping a hand over his chin. 'Bet you could too.'

Dawn grimaced to show she couldn't deny it.

'Did Gertie's brother get away?'

Glenn nodded. 'He chucked the gun at me and scarpered as soon as the fire started. At that point he wasn't important. It was you I was worried about.' Glenn's hand again massaged his face. 'Police'll catch up with him. Besides he did save you from Olive . . .'

'Only for his own good.' Dawn snorted a laugh. 'He wanted me to show him where the safe was so he could rob the theatre.'

'I know he was up to no good, but I'm grateful he poked his nose in. It bought me a bit more time to get to you.'

'And Olive?'

'I hope the bitch swings,' Glenn said harshly. 'More for what she did to you than anything else.'

'I'm fine, Glenn,' Dawn soothed him. 'But I hope she gets what's coming to her as well. It's still hard to believe she could be that wicked. She kept her true self well hidden from us all.'

'It's what they're trained to do. And to be fair, I expect our people over there are no different.'

After a brief silence Dawn felt ready to lighten the atmosphere. She'd done with dwelling on how close they'd all come to disaster. War was war and she knew there would be plenty more peril and sadness to cope with before peace was won.

'I'm really sorry to have missed our visit to your parents today.' Dawn sighed. She'd been looking forward to tea with the Raffertys.

'There'll be plenty of other times, when you're feeling up to it. They send their very best wishes to you.'

'You've not told them much, have you?' Dawn guessed.

Glenn shook his head, choked a laugh that needed no explanation. Mr and Mrs Rafferty had enough to contend with knowing that their courageous son risked his life as a fighter pilot without having the added anxiety of knowing his exploits as a British agent.

'The girls said the show went off without a hitch.'

'Good . . .'

'Gordon's recovering well from his crack on the head.'

'Good . . .' Glenn was frowning at his linked fingers.

'What is it?' Dawn asked, sensing he was building up to say something. 'Have the spooks given you a hard time? They should be praising you to the skies for what you did.'

'They are and you too. I've just filed my report with them before coming here. Apparently we're both in line for some sort of official commendation.'

'Really?' Dawn couldn't conceal that she was chuffed at that. 'A Windmill girl with a medal?' But her amusement faded when Glenn again studied his fingernails, brows drawn together. 'What is it?'

'Can you forgive me?' he asked hoarsely. He turned his head to look at her, a man tortured by his conscience. 'You might have been killed. I put you in dreadful danger drawing you into espionage. I wish you'd not had to confront that mad bitch like that, Dawn. It's my fault you did . . .'

'Oh, is that all?' Dawn held out her arms and he buried his face gently against her neck. She comforted him, stroking his nape. 'Actually, I had every faith in you arriving to save me, you know.' She realised, as she said it, that it was true. 'Although I can't say I enjoyed the experience, I found it very exciting. Well, *now* I do; of course, at the time I was terrified, but bloody angry too.' Dawn held him away from her to look into his deep brown eyes. 'You, Glenn Rafferty, have brought out of me something I didn't know existed. I've always thought myself too weak and weary to get my hands dirty in the business of fighting this war. But I'm not. I'm tougher than I think – you've shown me that. So . . . thanks . . .' she finished rather bashfully.

'You're grateful?'

Dawn nodded.

'How grateful?' he asked, desire burning at the backs of his eyes.

'*That* grateful . . .' Dawn whispered, and stretched up so she could touch her mouth to his. 'I don't know why

I feel like this with you when I didn't with Bill,' she started awkwardly. 'But I really do . . . I want you and I'd do anything for you, throw caution to the wind and wave it off, I don't know why . . .' she repeated softly.

'It's called falling in love,' Glenn told her. 'That's what it is, sweetheart, and I've felt that way about you from the first time I saw you with him. Love at first sight, *coupe de foudre*, call it what you like, sometimes a few moments is all it takes to know you've met the only person who can fill the hole inside. And I hated Bill because he was in the way. I felt guilty about that too after he was killed.'

'You can't get in here with me,' Dawn teased as he kissed her again with such passion that her head was forced back onto the pillow. 'But as soon as I'm home . . .'

'. . . We'll be married,' he finished for her. 'If you'll have me.' He took her hands in his and sat on the side of the bed, facing her. 'But you were right of course when you said I could be next to be shot down.' He gently used a thumb on her wet lashes. 'Don't cry, you're too brave for that.' He caressed her moist cheek with his lips. 'After the Battle of Britain there were only eight of us left out of a Squadron of twenty-four. That's the reality. And now we're being brutally honest I won't insult you by pretending otherwise. But if there's one thing that'll make me determined to get through this war and come home, it's having you as my wife, waiting for me. And we'll squeeze every drop of happiness out of the time we spend together. Then when we win, and it's all over, we'll settle down and have kids. And when they're old enough I'll tell them that their mum was a Windmill girl who nabbed a German spy.'

'I'll marry you, Glenn Rafferty,' Dawn choked,

drawing his head down to hers. 'But if you think I'll be waiting indoors with your pipe and slippers, you're wrong. I'm joining the WAAF and nothing you can say will stop me . . .'

EPILOGUE

October 1941

'Gertie!'

The woman pushing the pram halted and looked over a shoulder. She smiled on seeing who'd called her name and, turning the pram about, she went to meet Dawn.

'You've got your new arrival!' Dawn exclaimed, smiling and peeping in the pram at a lemon bonnet. It was all she could see of the Grimes's tiny baby. 'And how's little Harry? Toddling now and not so little either, I expect . . .' Dawn's voice tailed off as she noticed Gertie's strained expression.

'You wouldn't know . . . we lost Harry and Adam and Simon in a blast. Our house took a direct hit while me and Rufus was out. Joey was with us . . .' Gertie swallowed repeatedly while composing herself. She squeezed Dawn's arm as the younger woman clapped a hand to her mouth to cover her shock and dismay. 'Don't be sorry for speaking about Harry,' she whispered. 'I like to talk about my boys . . . keeps them alive for me, you see; that, and going to their resting place.' She sniffed, squinting at Dawn through mellow autumn sunshine. 'Joey and Rufus like to come too. It's a nice quiet spot by the little lake. So we go over there and talk to them . . . tell them how we all are . . .'

'I'm so sorry, Gertie.' Dawn's eyes were glistening as she hugged the woman. She remembered Gertie telling her she'd never leave the children alone and knew something must have happened to make her do so. But she'd never ask more about it. Neither was she going to mention Gertie's brother.

Midge was in the past as far as Dawn was concerned and she reckoned Gertie had the same attitude towards him. Wherever he was, whatever he'd done, he was no longer important when they'd the future to tackle.

'Look. I've got me daughter at last.' Gertie sounded quite bright as she pulled the cover away so Dawn could see a plump pink face and a mop of dark hair. 'Victoria's her name.'

'It's lovely,' Dawn croaked. '*She's* lovely . . . dark, like you . . .'

'Yeah, she's like me . . . pleased about that,' Gertie said gruffly.

Dawn stretched out a finger, skimming it just once over the sleeping baby's soft cheek.

'Read about you in the paper,' Gertie said. 'Knew it was you found that traitor in the Windmill Theatre soon as I saw the report. What a thing! I said to Rufus, that's my friend from the Windmill helped get that dreadful Olive locked up. I knew she was a wrong'un from the start. Just couldn't put me finger on what it was about her . . .'

'Yeah, you sussed her out before the rest of us had a clue, didn't you.' But Dawn couldn't put from her mind the terrible tragedy the Grimes family had suffered. 'I hope you and Rufus and Joey will find peace and happiness with little Victoria . . . it must be so hard for you all, Gertie.'

'It is.' Gertie choked on a sob. 'But it's hard for lots of people now with this damned war dragging on, ain't it?'

'Yes,' Dawn murmured, rubbing Gertie on the shoulder in comfort. 'And no end in sight yet.'

'We do peculiar things in wartime, don't we? Things we never imagined we would do. Suppose it's because you never know if your time's up tomorrow, and it makes you brave, or foolish.' Gertie knuckled water from her eyes. 'I'm no better; it's made me act odd . . .'

Dawn knew that Gertie was including her husband and brother in her homespun philosophy. And Dawn understood exactly what Gertie meant by it. 'I've done my fair share of brave or foolish things recently, as well.' She gave a wry smile. 'For a start, I've joined the WAAF and now I've finished training I'm off to France next month.' She raised her hand. 'And I've got married on the spur of the moment.'

Gertie brushed the residue of tears from her face and gave a wide-eyed grin. 'Well . . . congratulations on that!' She admired Dawn's lovely diamond engagement ring and wedding band. 'Things *have* changed for you, then.'

'I've got a new husband, a new stepfather, and a new job. My mum's got married again and I thought my brother might take things hard, with a new man about the place. But he likes his dad.'

The vital conversation had taken place between George and his father six weeks ago yet even now Dawn's satisfaction at the outcome was tinged with surprise. When she had tentatively asked her brother about *the talk* the following day, he'd shrugged and said Rod didn't seem a bad bloke and besides he'd never known the other fellow. In a single sentence George had made the worry and uncertainty that had dogged Dawn fizzle out like damp squibs on Bonfire Night.

'My Rufus is serving in the Royal Engineers now.'

'I bet you miss him, Gertie.'

'I do,' Gertie agreed with a soft smile. 'But I'm proud he's gone, so's Joey.' She paused. 'Do you think when it's all over we'll go back to being the people we were?' Gertie began gently rocking the pram and gazing at her daughter's face.

'Don't see how we can,' Dawn replied. 'Not sure I want to anyhow,' she added.

'You won't be going back on stage?' Gertie asked.

'No . . . I won't be a Windmill girl again. Oh, it was good fun while it lasted, but I'm a married woman now. I know he wouldn't like it.'

'They're funny creatures, men . . . different in some ways but all the bloody same in others.' Gertie seemed as if she might attempt an explanation but she simply shook her head as though it was beyond her.

'But we need them, don't we, especially now; we need every single brave soul of them to help us win this war.' Dawn added on a chuckle, 'Besides, I can't imagine a life now without Glenn in it.'

'I pray for Rufus to come back safe and sound so we can be a family again.'

They stood quietly for a moment, both lost in thoughts of their men and recent events.

'Better get on.' On impulse Gertie hugged Dawn and was given a squeeze in return. 'Good luck to you, Dawn.'

'Good luck to you, Gertie, from the bottom of my heart.' Dawn watched Gertie go then looked up as she heard a plane's engine droning overhead. She guessed, from its size, it was a bomber, perhaps a Wellington, and flying at a sedate pace.

But it might have been a Spitfire with a handsome gypsy-visaged pilot in the cockpit. She closed her eyes, raised her wedding ring to her lips to press it there until the pain of her forceful finger became too much. 'Good luck to you too, my darling . . . see you soon . . .' she whispered to the skies.

If you enjoyed

THE
WINDMILL
Girls

discover these other fantastic reads from Kay Brellend.

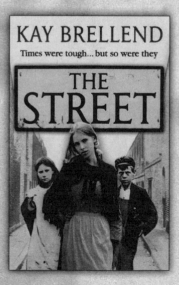

KAY BRELLEND

This is one street party they
will never forget...

CORONATION
DAY

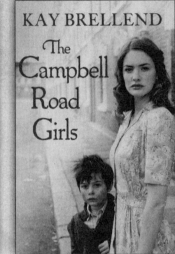

KAY BRELLEND

The
Campbell
Road
Girls

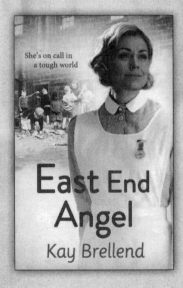

She's on call in
a tough world

East End
Angel

Kay Brellend

All available to buy now.

THE WINDMILL THEATRE

THEATRE

and the *Girls* behind the scenes